CAMBION'S RISE

ERIN FULMER

SOUNDTRACK

Demons – Hayley Kiyoko
Recessional – Vienna Teng
My Body Is a Cage – Sarah Lov
Haunted – Poe
Coals and Water – Angel Snow
In Your Room – Depeche Mode
Selke Song – Mason Daring
Trouble Is – Sierra Swan
Nobody's Daughter – Hole
Half Jack – The Dresden Dolls
Blood & Water – Mr Kamera & Frya
And You – Lennon
Invisible Man – Ashbury Heights
The Unforgiven II – Metallica
I am not a woman, I'm a god – Halsey
Anti-Hero – Taylor Swift
How Villains Are Made – Madalen Duke
Black Sea – Natasha Blume
Dead Enough For Life – Icon of Coil
What the Water Gave Me – Florence + the Machine
Darkangel – VNV Nation
Runs In the Family – Amanda Palmer
Both Hands – Ani DiFranco
To the Lighthouse – Patrick Wolf

Cailleach an Airgid – Niamh Ni Charra

Nemesis – VNV Nation

Lost Cause – Beck

Wait For It (Instrumental) – Lin-Manuel Miranda

Hurricane – MS MR

Monsters – Ruelle

It's No Good – Depeche Mode

Organs – Of Monsters and Men

The Promise – Tracy Chapman

If I Be Wrong – Trent Akins

Pure Morning – Placebo

Mercy In You – Depeche Mode

Devil You Know – KSHMR

Who Do You Think You Are – Kiana Lede & Cautious Clay

Northern Star – Hole

Last Dance – Covenant

You're Not a God – Jade LeMac

Falling – Edge of Dawn

Beloved – VNV Nation

Rise Up – Ben Barnes

Morning Sun – Carrellee

Gods & Monsters – Lana Del Rey

Author's Note

Cambion's Rise is a paranormal thriller flavored with hints of noir and featuring non-vanilla, non-monogamous, non-traditional central relationships. It explores themes related to coercive control, manipulation, chronic illness (of a sort), gendered violence, criminal justice, and intimate emotional abuse from a survivor's perspective.

There is on-the-page violence, including death, use of firearms, blades, blood, and beheading. Harm to animals is threatened but not carried out. It contains scenes with negotiated BDSM elements (impact, dominance and submission, and psychological power dynamics); negotiated nonmonogamy; opposite and same-gender pairings; and steamy open-door spice. The main character experiences bisexual attraction, with reference to past religious trauma, including conversion therapy and parental estrangement.

The author has endeavored to depict her most challenging themes with nuance, sensitivity, and respect for the complexity of trauma, while telling a fast-paced tale of romantic suspense that flirts with the darker side of desire.

Contents

1. Get Your Demon On — 1

2. Midlife Crisis Piano — 9

3. Sleeper Waves — 18

4. Storm Warnings — 27

5. Sins of the Father — 36

6. Against the Tide — 46

7. Thicker Than Water — 55

8. No Good Deed — 65

9. Person of Interest — 72

10. Birds of a Feather — 80

11. The Other Woman — 86

12. Unforgiven — 92

13. Missing Pieces — 98

14. Dealing With Demons — 105

15. Taking the Fall — 111

16. Watching Over You — 120

17. Blood and Bone — 130

18. Flight Patterns — 140

19. Into the Woods — 150

20.	The Sea Door	160
21.	Sanctuary	169
22.	Dark Mirror	180
23.	When the Devil Drives	190
24.	Between Sinners and Saints	197
25.	On My Own	205
26.	Home to Roost	211
27.	Leap of Faith	221
28.	Hostile Witness	229
29.	Collateral Damage	235
30.	Blood on the Keys	243
31.	Vigils	251
32.	Small Mercies	259
33.	Bolt from Heaven	267
34.	Fury Rising	274
35.	Sacraments	283
36.	Cinnamon and Maple	290
	Epilogue	294
	Acknowledgements	301
	About the Author	302

I

GET YOUR DEMON ON

The Black Cat Club pulsed with the sweet promise of human desire laid over a hard industrial bass line, its deep rhythm fueling an urge in me to get my demon on. I rolled my shoulders to settle the electric hunger curling up my spine and handed my best friend her drink. The demon inside could wait, for now.

"Are you sure you're OK with this?" I slid into the upper-level booth next to Danny, leaning in close so she could hear me over the throbbing music and general clamor.

Danny cut a sparkling sideways glance at me over a long sip of her margarita. "Please, Lily. I've been bugging you to let me tag along for months."

Her brilliant smile sought to reassure me, but a discordant spike in her personal energy signature—her desiderata—snagged my succubus senses. My friend had something on her mind, whether or not she wanted to admit it.

"I don't need to do this tonight. We can just hang out instead." In fact, I preferred to hunt for kether—the human life energy my demon side craved—alone and unobserved, but the friendship 911 code she'd sent me via text earlier in the day meant DEFCON 1: *this is not a test, do not ignore, do not decline requests for a night out on the town.*

Thanks to the demands of my latest case—defending a woman possessed by a murderous goddess—and the stress of planning what Danny called her Big Fat Lesbian Wedding, we hadn't spent much time together lately. So tonight I'd made an exception to my normal procedure and invited Danny along to act as my wing woman, even though I hardly needed one.

I had my own wings, after all.

"I'm not here to cramp your style," she said. "Let me live vicariously for one night. That's all I want."

"If you say so."

She groaned. "Don't look at me in that tone of voice."

"Then talk to me." I sipped my own drink, whiskey and ginger, savoring the way it blended with the smoky cinnamon of Danny's desiderata. "That's what a best ma'am is for, you know."

Danny looked away, her energy swirling with a burnt caramel tang on the verge of an unfamiliar bitterness. "I'd rather help you find your next one-night stand."

I frowned at the edge in her words and the sudden heat flaring around her in my second sight. "Gotta say, you seem less than thrilled."

Was Danny *jealous*? Maybe she missed single life. She'd played the field with gusto before Berry came along, but threw herself into commitment with equal enthusiasm and no sign of regret—until now.

"Quit reading me." Danny's jaw tightened, her restless gaze scanning the dance floor. "It's not fair."

"I literally can't help it," I said, stung. "And I told you how to stop it if you really wanted to." If she wore silver, like the ring I'd gifted to my lover, Sebastian, she could hide her energy from me. So far, though, she'd resisted my advice to invest in protective jewelry with surprising vehemence.

On the other hand, I'd miss her aura if I couldn't read it anymore. I missed Sebastian's too at times, though his new unreadability had a certain sexiness to it that left me craving more of him whenever we parted.

"I'm sorry." Danny's warm brown eyes, dark and pleading, finally met mine. "I want to have fun tonight. No serious stuff. Like old times."

I laughed despite the sudden crackle of tension in her gaze. "What, all our old times clubbing together? Dan, that never happened!"

"I know." She chuckled, the current in the air between us dissipating as fast as it had gathered. "We were too damn busy studying."

Danny and I met when she advertised for a roommate and got a demon instead. With her in med school and me in law school, our all-nighters together involved a lot more caffeine than booze. Back then, nightlife reminded me too much of where I came from, my old life in New York with my fallen mentor Ariel whispering in my ear, guiding me into ever more boundary-pushing exploits with the partners he selected for me.

But things were different now. Ariel was out of the picture, I'd gotten my wings, and with Sebastian's blessing I could seek casual liaisons to explore my half-demon need for the energy of human emotion and pleasure. I couldn't protect any partner from the soul bond that sprang from my touch, but if I kept my encounters short, sweet, and singular, I could safely stay the one who got away.

So far, so good. I hadn't killed anyone yet, and I called that a win.

Hadn't killed anyone *else*, at least.

"Well, here's to fun." I raised my drink.

"I'll drink to that." Danny clinked her margarita against my copper mug, careful not to brush her fingers against mine. "Go on, tell me. Who do you have your eye on tonight, Sugarbean?"

"I've hardly looked." Other than Danny's warm aura close beside me, no one's desiderata had captured my attention. Indulging her, I let my senses widen into the space.

"What about him?" She nudged my elbow, pointing down at the dance floor.

My long-sleeved blouse shielded her skin from mine, but I tensed anyway, on guard against stray touches. "Who?"

"That tall boy on the dance floor, with the corset and the eyeliner."

"I'm probably not his type."

"Oh, please. Don't tell me your bi-dar is that bad." She smirked. Intoxication had slowed the turmoil in her aura to a lazy, heated swell.

"He *is* pretty," I conceded. "Hm. Sweet and insubstantial, like meringue, but he'd do in a pinch."

"Picky, picky."

"I'm trying to eat healthy."

She snorted with laughter, which I counted as a win. "Don't be crass."

"Pot, this is kettle. You're the one in the gutter."

"It's fun here. Join me." Danny knocked back the rest of her drink, eyes alight. "You know, for a succubus, you're kind of a prude."

"Hey, give me some credit. I'm the one on the make here."

"I'll give you that. You've come a long way." Her energy rippled around us, her voice softening. "I'm proud of you, Sugarbean."

"Thanks, I think." Sweet cinnamon haunted my tongue. Mouth suddenly dry, I took another hasty sip of my Irish Mule.

Maybe I'd made a mistake, bringing Danny here and buying her tequila with my hunger on the rise. We had a history of near-misses and stray touches, including one ill-advised kiss long ago that left us soul-bound without knowing it. I'd released the bond in the process of saving her life, almost a year ago now, but tonight that history seemed more present than past.

"I mean it," Danny said. Then, with a wink, she added, "How about that one?"

This time, I knew who she meant immediately. The girl had taken to the dance floor as we talked, long dark braids swinging around her in time to her graceful, fluid movements. "Not bad," I admitted. "Much better, actually."

"I thought so." Danny pushed me out of the booth. "Go get her, tiger. I need another drink."

"Dan. Wait." I caught her upper arm, gloved hand over her jacket, but still she froze, eyes dark and wild as they met mine.

Her aura flared around us with the blue fire of ignited alcohol. "Yes, Lily?"

Damn, I made it worse. I dropped her arm as though the halo in my second sight had burned me. "Nothing. I wish you'd tell me what's going on with you."

"I'm sorry." The flame of her desiderata waned, ebbing to a faintly glowing ember. "I'm bringing the bad vibes. I should probably head home."

"No. Stay. Talk." I patted the seat. "And stop apologizing. I love your vibes, Danny Rios. Even when they're weird as hell."

"You're sweet, Sugarbean." She grimaced, then sighed. "Fine. But I really do need another drink for this."

"I've got you." I wasn't above using my supernatural powers to summon a bartender for a friend in need. I dragged her back to our table and re-supplied her before she could change her mind. "There. Now stop stalling and fess up. Is this about wedding stuff?"

Danny slumped into the corner of the booth, drawing one black jeans-clad knee up to her chest, the picture of resignation. "It's Berry's family again. They're having a fit over...well. It doesn't matter."

"Doesn't it?"

She made a face. "You're reading me again, aren't you?"

"It's who I am. What are they upset about this time?"

She swallowed a gulp of her fresh margarita, then gazed into its depths as if it offered a way out of the truth she didn't want to tell. "Her father is concerned about, um, the wedding party."

They'd decided to keep the party small, just me on Danny's side and Berry's sister on hers, with my teenage ward, Eve, handling the rings and flowers. "What, is he upset that you have a best ma'am and not a best man?"

"Something like that." Danny's tone turned fierce. "I told you, it doesn't matter. It's my goddamn wedding and I'm going to have you at my side."

"I could pull off a drag king look. Get Sebastian's tailor on it. Go all out—" I broke off at her expression, something between intrigue and panic. "Or not."

Her aura flickered brighter, then dimmed again. "Gender isn't the issue, Lily."

My gut twisted. "*Oh.* Shit. They saw the interview." The response to my public "coming out" as half-demon had surprised me—or rather, the non-response had. A few fundamentalist groups worked themselves into a righteous tizzy on the Internet, but the world at large talked it up for a day or so before giving a collective shrug. My earth-shaking revelation became a weird news item, and everyone else went on with life.

"Apparently her dad draws the line at having a demon *in* the wedding."

I hadn't expected to escape with no consequences at all, but I didn't think about how it might affect my friend's life. "When you put it that way, I can't exactly blame him."

"I can blame him plenty," Danny said, staunchly loyal but not entirely honest.

"I don't have to be in the wedding, Dan. I won't be offended."

"Well, I will," Danny said. "I don't care what else you are. You're my best friend, and I want you there."

"Then I'll do my best to wear him down with my preternatural charm." Ethically questionable, but I could justify using my powers in the name of familial harmony.

"That's..." Danny laughed. "Actually, not a bad idea. Maybe we can all have dinner together."

"I'll polish my halo for the occasion." I downed my drink. "There, that wasn't so hard, was it? Feeling better?"

"A little," Danny slurred. "Tipsy."

"You were tipsy before. Now you're tequila drunk." I slid out of the booth. "I'll get you some water. Stay here."

"Staying." Danny leaned her head back on the booth and shut her eyes. "Ooh. Spinnies."

Great. At this rate I would have to carry her home, which might end badly for both of us. Shaking my head, I headed for the bar, then halted mid-step. Prickles of ice crept along my spine and raised the small hairs on the back of my neck.

I scanned the dim, crowded recesses of the club's balcony, gripping the wood of the railing until it groaned and cracked. Alarmed, I let go and wiped my damp palms on the miniskirt barely covering my thighs. The railing didn't fall apart but looked somewhat the worse for wear.

Maybe I'd imagined it, but in my periphery, I could have sworn someone had leaned elbows on the railing across the open space that looked over the dance floor below, golden head turning to track me. I could have sworn that they had broad shoulders and a long coat that flared around them like dark wings, their absence of desiderata like a black hole in the club's shimmering human energy. And their face—I knew that face as well as I knew my own. It still haunted my dreams, the face of someone I'd loved and feared and murdered.

Someone impossible.

Water, I needed water for Danny and something stronger for myself. My pulse raced erratically in my ears, and I succubused my way to the front of the drink line, only half-aware of the humans who stepped aside to let me pass.

Clutching a neat whiskey and a water bottle icy as the adrenaline in my veins, I raced back to our booth. Danny was still there, slumped in the back corner with her eyes closed.

"Hey. You alive over there?" I scooted in. When she didn't answer immediately, I shook her shoulder hard in a sudden panic.

She jerked upright and relief bloomed in my chest. "I'm fine," she mumbled. "Just resting my eyes."

"Sure you are." I twisted open the water bottle, shoving it at her. "Drink this, or Berry will have my hide."

"Sweet Berry? Never." Danny swigged the water, then squinted at me. "What's wrong?"

"Nothing."

"Liar. You look spooked."

I swallowed half the contents of my glass. I couldn't get drunk so easily, but the whiskey burn blunted the chill rising within me. "I thought I saw someone I knew, that's all."

"You know people?" Danny guffawed, then hiccupped. "Damn it."

"That's what you get for being a jerk. Drink your water, lightweight."

"Lowered tolerance is a hazard of almost-married life. Would it be so bad, running into someone you know here?"

"It might be." Surreptitiously, I scanned the other balcony again, but no one stood watching me there. Probably no one had stood watching at all, except in my traitorous mind. "I'd rather avoid repeat customers. It keeps the soul-bonding to a minimum."

Danny set her half-finished water bottle on the table. "Lil, being bound by you isn't the huge burden you make it out to be." She paused. "Oops. Didn't mean to make that sound kinky."

Her aura blazed with notes of caramel and cinnamon that did more than the whiskey to distract me from my nightmarish imagination. I swallowed hard as she edged closer. "Danny, you're drunk."

"Yeah, I am. Super drunk." Her hand found mine, bare fingers with short-clipped nails interlacing with my gloved ones. "All I'm saying is, not everyone would mind it. Some might even—"

"Hush." Gently, I peeled her fingers from mine. "Come on. Let's get you home to your bed and your fiancée, shall we?"

"That's probably smart." She sank away from me into the corner of the bench, scrubbing her hands over her face. "I don't know what I—forgive me."

"There's nothing to forgive." I helped her out of the booth, steadying her with a hand on her upper arm. If she shivered at the touch, we both pretended to ignore it. "That's what friends are for."

"Hey, Lily," she said as I steered her toward the stairs. "Who did you think you saw back there?"

Between the whiskey, her eyes, and the sweet fire that had surged around us, I had almost managed to forget. "Nobody. It was nobody."

We made our slow way downstairs, Danny leaning heavily on me, but the unspoken truth hung leaden under my ribs.

Even now, after all I'd done to get away, some part of me still expected to see *him*. My mentor. The demon I'd killed. Some sick place in me still looked for that flash of gold, that preternatural grace, that cruel mouth in a beautiful face with its smirk sharp enough to shatter me. Something in me believed he would come back and come after me.

Something in me still waited for him to ruin me all over again.

2

MIDLIFE CRISIS PIANO

I climbed the stairs from Sebastian Ritter's cavernous garage, pulling off my gloves with slow, thoughtful movements. The underground carport lay strangely empty and echoing. I'd pulled Blue Betty, the roadster he insisted on lending me once I had a commute again, next to a single, unprepossessing Japanese hybrid.

The biometric keypad at the top of the staircase flashed green when I pressed my thumb to it. It didn't care that I wasn't entirely human, and neither did the man who half-rose from his seat at a warm-lit, dark-stained kitchen table strewn with stacks of files and paperwork.

"Lily! I wasn't expecting you." Sebastian blinked at me over an unfamiliar pair of reading glasses. He wore a gray collared shirt with the sleeves rolled above the elbow, his dark hair messy and sticking up as if he'd raked his hand through it repeatedly. "Wasn't tonight your night out?"

"I had a change of plans." I leaned against the door frame, frowning despite the effect his rumpled appearance had on me. "What happened to your cars?"

When I met the man, he had doted over his fleet of vehicles like so many pampered pets, collecting them the way some men collected stamps or Funko Pops. He had a car for every occasion, varied enough to match the colors of his pocket squares. They had names and a dedicated mechanic who visited at regular intervals to maintain their overpowered engines and polish their chrome to mirror-brightness.

"Liquidated. They're all assets in the settlement." His formal divorce from his long-separated wife, Helena, would finalize this week.

"You sold them *all*?" I studied him. Thanks to the ring he wore, I couldn't read his aura any more than I could his expression.

He'd already sold his company. He'd told me that he finally faced up to dissolving his dead marriage so he could become the man I deserved. Had he also sold the things he loved for *me*?

"It was easier that way. They're just things, Lily."

"Yes, but...they're beautiful things. And you love beautiful things."

"Things are replaceable. And people change." He quirked a bemused eyebrow at me. "Why, do you miss them?"

I shook my head, nonplussed. "You've got to be the only straight guy in modern history whose midlife crisis inspired him to sell all his fancy rides instead of buying a new one."

"It's not a midlife crisis," he said with a note of asperity. "It's practical."

"Of course it is." I rounded the table and bent to kiss him by way of apology. "But I don't think practicality is the standard reaction to divorce."

"Hm. Perhaps not." His lips lingered on mine. Then he pulled back with a flash of a grin. "If you want to see what a Ritter midlife crisis really looks like, take a peek in the living room."

"I thought you said it wasn't a midlife crisis."

He shrugged. "I prefer to call it a midlife re-evaluation."

"So, what is it? Bondage furniture?" Though we no longer exchanged energy as we had when our relationship began, we could still exchange power in non-supernatural ways, and surrendering to his sure dominance carried new weight now that I couldn't read his mind. I had to trust that he cared for me, read it in the way he touched me when I placed myself in his hands. It scared me a little, but I craved it almost as much as I craved the taste of his soul.

"I like where your mind goes first, but no, it's not." He wrapped an arm around my waist, drawing me close against his side, but the table with its stacks of documents had reclaimed his focus. "Much as I want to explore those thoughts further with you, I have to finish these up before tomorrow morning."

"Tomorrow...oh crap. Your court date." I released him and stepped back. "I'm so sorry. I forgot." After dropping Danny off at home and making sure she got inside safely, I'd driven to Sebastian's on impulse. I would have looked over my shoulder all night if I went back to the club, and I definitely didn't want to sleep alone.

Sebastian had told me to come over any time, but maybe I'd picked the wrong night to surprise him.

"Don't apologize." A note of sternness crept into his tone, and his gaze lingered over my curves, on display in my hunting outfit of laced corset top, pleated miniskirt, and over-the-knee stiletto boots. "You're a welcome sight for sore eyes that have stared at far too many financial disclosures. Give me a few minutes and then I'll happily show you just how welcome you are."

My cheeks heated as he lifted his eyes to mine. I could read *that* look well enough. "Take your time," I said, breathless. "I'll be in the other room checking out this midlife re-evaluation of yours."

"Let me know if it changes your assessment of my crisis state." He sounded amused, but a flicker of unidentifiable emotion passed over his face as he returned to his paperwork.

In the dim living room, my night vision revealed the graceful lines of the new addition filling the nearby corner. I approached it cautiously and lifted the corner of the protective canvas cover, peering beneath at the smooth, pale ivories of the baby grand piano beneath.

Sebastian had shown his musical side before. On Valentine's Day this year, he'd even sung to me—in public, no less—and though the spotlight on me made me want to sink into the floor, I couldn't deny the man had talent. Until now, though, he kept no instruments at home.

I slipped onto the bench and pressed a few keys with hesitant fingers. Quiet notes shivered out into the high-ceilinged space. They had an exquisite tone, even to my untrained ear.

"What do you think?" Sebastian spoke from behind me, husky and soft over the fading notes.

"It's beautiful." I depressed a lower key, its sound resonating with a timbre to match his voice. "I thought you had work to do."

"I work fast, given the right motivation." He dropped a light hand on my shoulder. "Move over."

He sat beside me and ran his fingers over the keys without striking them. I shivered as if the touch had skimmed my own skin. "Play something for me."

"I'm rusty. It's been years since I practiced." He plinked a key, listening with head tilted and expression abstracted.

"Please?" I ceded the bench to him. Folding myself into a seat on the floor at his feet, I leaned my head on his knee, the fine dark wool of his slacks whispering against my cheek.

He went still at that but for the quiet hitch of his breath. Then his right hand dropped from the keys to stroke my hair. I leaned in, the night's tension melting from my limbs. The feather-light sensation lit my nerve endings, sending tingling warmth down my spine.

When he lifted his hand, I stirred to protest, but the piano's voice stopped mine. If he was rusty as he claimed, I couldn't tell. The music swept over me like his caress, gentle but with the promise of power restrained. Its spell held me in his thrall as surely as I had once held him with my succubus wiles.

Finally, the last note echoed away into silence, and I drew a long, shuddering breath. "You're good."

"I'm passable." His fingers dropped from the keyboard to trace my jawline and down my neck to my exposed shoulder, drawing another shiver from me as he kneaded at the muscles there. "Hmm. You're all in knots tonight and you're not out hunting. Talk to me, Lily. Something's off."

"At the club, I saw…" I didn't want to talk about it, but I didn't want him to stop, either. "I couldn't have seen him…it. Maybe it was some kind of flashback."

He didn't take his hand away, but his leg tensed beneath my cheek. "You haven't had one of those in a while."

"I'm not sure flashback is the right word." I'd had a bad one before, at the peak of a mutual orgasm with him hard inside me. Full of the strength his life force granted me, I'd hurt him. I could have killed him. After that, I had given him the silver ring so I didn't get dangerous superpowers every time we touched. "My therapy sessions have stirred up some bad old memories lately, that's all."

Sebastian curved gentle fingers around my chin, drawing it up so I had to meet his gaze. His voice dropped, rough velvet over steel that undid me from the inside out. "Listen. You're safe here and now, with me. The past can't hurt you anymore. You know that, don't you?"

The knot of panic aching in my sternum eased, but I needed more than his words to release it. "I know. I'm sorry. I…"

"I mean it. Don't apologize for this." He tightened his grip when I tried to look away. "You don't deserve what happened to you. You survived. That's more than enough."

I swallowed hard against his palm and licked my dry lips. "Yes, Sebastian."

"Are you all right?" Sebastian spoke with shattering gentleness, and I nodded, his bright blue eyes anchoring me to this moment. *Here and now.*

"I am. But—" I needed his hands on me, erasing the cold dread under my skin. I needed the willing surrender he offered, so different from the subjugation Ariel had wrested from me with cajoling words and veiled threats. "Can we…can you…?"

"Can I what?" He wouldn't play this game without me asking for it in so many words, my explicit consent the price of my submission. Sometimes, like now, I wanted him to take me without asking, force me to yield, lift the weight of choice from me with a little cruelty when I couldn't bear his kindness. But that way led to flashbacks, like it had the time I hurt him.

This way kept us both safe. Wanting something didn't make it healthy for me. Besides, Sebastian couldn't actually force me to do anything. My demon strength meant he couldn't overpower me unless I let him.

"Please, Sebastian." I shuddered at the flex of his fingers on my throat. "Make me yours."

His face didn't change, but his eyes kindled. "You're mine already. Say it."

"I'm yours." My voice caught, mouth suddenly dry with wanting.

He rose from the bench, pulling me with him so I stood facing him. His firm grip under my jawline weakened my knees, though it didn't hinder my breath, which came short on its own. The intensity of his regard scalded me like hot water on a foggy evening.

Without the silver ring, we couldn't have done it like this, skin-to-skin contact with me letting down my guard completely. That small circle of metal had shifted the power between us, and I couldn't get enough.

"On the bench." He moved his grip to my hips and spun me, holding me close, and I gasped at the rigid press of his erection against the base of my spine.

I arched into him. "I need…"

"So eager." His mouth brushed the shell of my ear, setting off a wave of tingling pleasure that started at my nape and raced through me to pool between my legs. Behind the physical sensation, my succubus hunger beat like a drum, aching in the back of my throat. This touch without feeding confused my demon so much. It left her a weak and whimpering thing, calling back to the first time I'd wound up in Sebastian's bed, half-mad with desire and begging without shame.

I let that whimper rise in my throat, a low, needy sound, and Sebastian grasped the back of my neck, shoving me down onto the piano bench. I caught myself with my hands, but he tangled his fingers in my hair, pushing my cheek against the cool leather cushion. His other hand skimmed up my leg where my skirt had ridden high, dragging it higher to expose my bare ass in its lacy black thong.

"So this is how you dress for your adventures. I approve." He dipped his fingers further, slipping his hand past the scrap of fabric and then beneath me to cup my sex in his palm. "Oh, Lily. You're soaking wet for me already."

I bucked into his palm, desperate for more direct stimulation. "What are you going to do with me?"

The tip of one finger brushed my opening, just enough to make me moan before he drew back. "Stay there. I'll be right back."

"Where are you going?" I craned my head around to look at him. I could have wept for the loss of his touch.

"I said stay." He pushed my head back down, and I shuddered at the edge in his tone.

"Yes, Sebastian." I had tried to call him *sir* once, but he'd stopped me. *My name will do.*

His footsteps receded. I lay with my cheek on the bench, ass in the air, swimming in a daze of want. He expertly put me in this submissive state, his actions and commands calculated to leave my mind hazy as a summer afternoon, my thoughts slow and stuttering in a way I welcomed with a whole heart. The position he left me in didn't scream comfort—my knees bent and feet braced on the floor, the wood of the bench digging into my inner thighs—but I barely noticed.

He returned quickly, his steps pausing behind me. "That's a lovely sight," he murmured, and then a soft fall of supple leather brushed the sensitive skin of my bare thighs.

I quivered at the new sensation. "What is that?"

The leather tickled, traveling upward to caress my upturned ass. "You're so intent on flogging yourself for perceived misdeeds. But it's my turn now."

"Oh." The breath trembled out of me. He'd shown me his collection of handcrafted toys, urging me to handle each one and slap the ends against my palm to test the varying intensities, after I'd told him I wanted to try impact play sometime.

Apparently sometime was tonight. Another involuntary tremor shook me as he drew the tails up between my legs, the barest touch across the thin lace stretched over my tenderest parts.

I didn't like pain for its own sake, but that didn't mean I didn't enjoy it. For Sebastian's part, he didn't shy away from it as a tool of dominance, but he got little from pure sadism. We worked well together that way.

Pain play offered me something else nothing else could. My half-demon body responded to even minor bruises by using my energy reserves for fast healing, which meant I lost a little of my superhuman strength each time. When

I wanted him like this, over me and in me, I could shed my power and become, with every strike, more human, more equal, more his.

"You're awfully quiet down there." Sebastian bent over me, brushing my hair back from my face. "Tell me what you want, or I'll stop here."

I scrambled to assemble coherent speech from the haze of arousal fogging my brain. "I want it. Please."

He stroked my cheek, tracing the line of my jaw. "Be more specific."

I wanted his hands on me, his cock driving into me, his teeth grazing my neck. I wanted his control. I wanted him to lose control and take what he wanted. I wanted to drink from him like an alcoholic on a three-day bender.

Not that. Damn my demon and the way she never shut up.

I screwed my eyes closed, inescapably aware of his nearness and his heat, of the energy inside him, the kether I couldn't reach. "Hit me." The plea came as a ragged whisper. "Please, Sebastian."

"It would be my pleasure." He pressed a kiss to my temple and straightened, his warmth fading from my skin. The moment stretched as he stood over me, but his indrawn breath hitched audibly. I shook, waiting.

The flail came down across my thighs and wrung a startled yelp out of me. He struck me just hard enough to smart, then dragged the leather tails up over my dripping core, the light fall of sensation making me shiver more than the initial slap.

"Is that what you wanted?" He lifted the tails away.

I bit my lip and stole a glance at him. He'd shed his button-down, the thin undershirt beneath revealing the corded muscles in his arms and shoulders. "You could hit harder," I ventured, breathless.

A laugh startled out of him. "Oh, Lily. This is just one of the reasons I love you."

The unexpected words washed through me, punctuated by a sharp smack across my loins. "I love you too," I mumbled right before he struck again.

My skin warmed under his steady assault, kether reserves gathering to heal skin I'd asked him to bruise. I angled my ass up to expose myself further to him and hissed, then moaned, as the lash connected with my center.

He paused at that and pulled my soaked panties away, stripping them down my legs and throwing them aside. Now unimpeded, his fingers pressed between my slick folds with unerring precision, flicking over the nub of my clit as his other hand held me still with firm pressure at the back of my neck. I writhed, helpless against the cresting pleasure as he worked me to the desperate edge of orgasm—and stopped.

Thrashing under his hold, I let out a wordless, indignant cry, but he didn't relent.

"You wanted me to beat you," he said, rough-voiced. "Did you change your mind?"

"You can do whatever you want to me," I gasped, "as long as you fuck me afterwards."

He groaned at that, the sound shooting a bolt of arousal straight to my core. Suddenly he laid his body over mine and rocked his hips forward, the hard, hot length of his cock sliding against my dripping slit. I leaned backward, trying to slip onto him, but he didn't give me what I wanted.

"Not the most sustainable angle," he said. "Come here."

He yanked me up, holding me steady when my knees threatened to give way, and bent me face-first onto the keyboard with a discordant crash. I braced myself, hands splayed over the keys, whimpering as he spread my legs wide with a near-painful grasp.

Then he drove himself into me in a merciless rhythm, and I came apart, my own voice high and wild in my ears. In my peak, I forgot my demon, forgot the craving this coupling couldn't satisfy, forgot myself and the hunt I'd left behind.

In that moment of forgetting, I was his and his alone, and my surrender was the best gift he could give me.

3

SLEEPER WAVES

A brisk rush of air, moist as the early San Francisco morning outside, swept around me as I stepped inside the open-plan front room of the high-rise luxury condominium I shared with my ward and fellow succubus, Eve. The draft didn't chill my cold-resistant half-demon bones, but it did give me pause.

One of the French doors leading onto the sixty-fourth floor terrace swung to and fro on its hinges, banging with each gust of wind. Fog rolled by the rooftop patio like transparent tufts of some monstrous creature's gray-white fur.

"Damn it, Eve," I muttered. The succubus girl liked to sit on the terrace with her homework after school. Since I'd slept at Sebastian's overnight, she'd apparently forgotten to lock the back door.

Her frequent carelessness drove me to distraction, not least because she reminded me too much of my younger self. We didn't have to worry about burglars this high up, but we did have Delilah, my long-haired, fog-colored cream puff of an ex-street cat. I loved the little beast, but she consisted of ninety-five percent fluff and five percent attitude powered by a single brain cell.

Case in point, she had always liked Eve's father, my ex-mentor, the self-same incubus whose face haunted my nightmares and my overactive imagination in dark clubs.

Foreboding tightened my gut as I crossed to the French doors. Sure enough, there perched the goddamn cat on the terrace railing, prim as any princess, gazing over the precipice at the street five hundred feet below.

When that kid woke up, I'd—not kill her, but I mentally outlined an epic talking-to as I grabbed a pack of cat treats from the kitchen and slipped onto the patio, tiptoeing in my high-heeled club boots so as not to spook Delilah. The cat had a notorious tendency to bolt at the most inconvenient moments, and her tufted toes meant she could easily lose her footing.

At my first step onto the terrace, Delilah's ears twitched. She crouched, fixing me with an all-too-familiar wild-eyed look that warned she could go off at any moment in any direction, including off the side of the building.

I froze. Holding up the treat bag, I shook it lightly. "Here, kitty. Don't you want some crunchies?"

Delilah's tail swished, and I dumped a few morsels into my palm. She knew my trick for luring her from spots I didn't want her, though that usually meant the closet where I hung my best suits, not the edge of an urban cliff.

I had to drop a treat onto the tile before the cat stretched and jumped down, approaching with a soft trill of greeting. Payment in hand still worked, at least.

My relieved sigh came too soon. A door slammed inside, and Delilah flattened, sidling toward the edge again.

I dived after her, demon-quick, and captured her just before she slipped under the railing into oblivion. Landing in a half-crouch, I spun toward the apartment with the cat's tense, wriggling body cradled to my chest. Wind rustled in semi-corporeal feathers, my wings briefly manifesting to balance me.

Eve stood on the threshold in pajamas and a messy halo of long golden hair, rubbing her eyes. "What's going on? Why are your wings out?"

I pushed past her and slammed the door, flipping the latch with unnecessary force. "The damn cat got outside." Delilah, released, completed her bolt beneath the sofa. "You can't leave that door unlatched. It's not safe!"

Her forehead creased. "I didn't—"

"Don't," I snapped. "No lies, Eve."

"I'm not lying!" She paled at my tone but held her ground. "I thought I did latch it. Truly. I'm sorry, Lily."

In loco parentis, I owed Eve fairness and second chances, even when she challenged my limited patience. "We all make mistakes." I rubbed my temples, breathing deep and counting down like my new therapist had taught me until my adrenaline-fueled anger cooled to a mild seethe. *I'm safe. Delilah is safe. Nothing bad happened.* "Just double-check next time, OK?"

"I'll triple-check," she vowed, though I didn't place good odds on her follow-through. Bouncing into the kitchen, she rummaged until she came up with a Pop-Tart shoved in her mouth. Crumbs sprayed as she added accusingly, "You didn't come home from your hunt last night. That's new."

"Not that it's your business, but I stayed at Sebastian's." I peeled my boots off and padded toward the master bedroom, pursued by her delighted hoots.

Eve adored Sebastian, who visited often for weekend dinners and game nights. More than once, she'd not-so-subtly hinted that we should combine households. I couldn't deny he made a good substitute father figure for her. Goodness knew she needed one.

I clung to the independence granted by our current arrangement, stubborn and selfish as I might feel about it sometimes, but if I was honest, I didn't love the condo, either. Ariel had lived in it last year while swanning about the city, planting corpses for me to trip over. It belonged to Eve now, or it would once probate officially declared her father dead, but I considered it the least he owed me after all he'd put me through. Besides, given free rent in a building like this, in a city like this, with a view like this, I could afford not to think about it too hard.

"Get dressed," I called to Eve, flipping through hangers for a clean suit. "I'll drop you off at school on my way to the office."

"Ugh, *school.*" She grumbled, but after a minute, music blared from her room and muffled thumps heralded teenage preparations.

Half an hour later, in cut-off shorts, sandals, and a T-shirt that read "I heart New York," she flopped back in the passenger seat of Blue Betty with a long, gusty sigh.

"What's wrong, kiddo?" Focused on not stalling the roadster on the down-shift, I hadn't noticed her mood until we left our building's parking garage.

She sulked deeper into the bucket seat, arms crossed. "Just looking forward to another day of suck."

"I thought you said everything was fine with school." As her legal guardian, I had to ensure Eve received adequate education for her age. Unfortunately for her future and my blood pressure, Ariel had neither made her attend school in New York nor provided for her education himself, other than teaching her one or two particularly toxic tenets of his personal philosophy.

"I guess," she griped. "I hate it, though. You can't imagine how boring it is."

"You'd be surprised what boredom I can imagine." Three years of law school qualified me for that. "You've got this. You're smart. Just stick it out for another few months."

She made a face. "I still don't understand why I need a GED."

"You'll have to take that up with the dependency judge, I'm afraid." I swung the car up to the curb across from the school, a converted mission complete with an ornate dome that towered over the neighboring businesses and the nearby Dolores Park.

"Thanks for the ride, sis." Eve flung herself out of the roadster and shouldered her bag with another dramatic groan. "When do I get to drive myself? I'm a good driver, you know. Seb showed me how."

"You had *one* lesson," I said. "And we have one car. Which I don't own."

"I'm a better driver than you," she shot back. "You drive like somebody's grandma."

"We'll talk about it later." I reached over and pulled the passenger door shut. "For now, stay out of trouble...sis."

"Yeah, yeah," she said, rolling her eyes.

I pulled away, then checked my rear-view mirror. She stood at the curb, scowling, but when she caught me looking, she gave me a cursory wave and turned to trudge toward the campus.

I was doing the best I could with the daughter of my old enemy, my chance at redemption and her chance at a future better than my past. Maybe she was doing her best, too.

It remained to be seen if our best would do enough to beat the hand he'd dealt us both before he died.

My own woman at last, I made it to the office just before ten and shut the door, sinking gratefully into the brand-new, butter-smooth black leather chair Sebastian had insisted on gifting me to mark the opening of my solo practice.

Reflected light spilled in from the window to my right, where the San Francisco Bay sparkled in the early September sun. I pulled off my gloves and took a breath, taking it in. *Mine.* My law school diploma hung on the wall above my head, and the gold-lettered nameplate on the desk read *Lily Knight, Esq.*

A flower arrangement waited beside the nameplate, a dramatic explosion of huge, pale, fluted blooms with long, curving waxy white petals and deep red hearts. I spun it idly, checking among the slender leaves for a card, but found none.

Maybe Sebastian had sent them. He should have known better than to shower me with showy romantic gestures by now, but sometimes he couldn't help himself.

Heat bloomed at the base of my spine at the memory of the previous night's activities, and I shifted in the chair's embrace, recrossing my legs. I needed to focus on work, not sit here mooning about how my lover wielded control over me so skillfully with his clever hands.

In the lobby outside, a commotion arose. A woman's voice cracked with tension across the calm tones of the front desk secretary.

"I need to see her today. It's urgent!"

"I'm sorry, ma'am. Do you have an appointment?" The secretary remained unruffled. A veteran, she'd seen and heard it all, from angry opposing counsel to irrational clients, and everything in between.

"No, I don't. But it has to be today." The last word hitched on a sob. "Please, I don't have much time. Ms. Knight is the only one who can help me."

Wait, she wanted to see *me*? I cracked the door and peeked down the hallway to the lobby, wrapping a "don't notice me" Presence around myself so I could escape if necessary.

A petite, dark-skinned woman stood at the front desk, gripping a young child by the hand who looked like a smaller version of herself. She looked up then, and her large, deep brown eyes met mine, luminous with unshed tears.

I drew back, alarmed. She'd seen through my Presence. *How?* A sudden salt-tang clogged the back of my throat, a sleeper wave of grief cold and wide as the Pacific. I choked, and for a moment I drowned in it, as though a real current drew me down into the depths.

Was that sea-salt flooding her desiderata? If so, her aura had an unnerving, alien power I'd never sensed in a human before.

Still, her desperation tugged at me. I squared my shoulders, inhaled, and stepped into the hall. Sweet oxygen filled my lungs and the drowning sensation ebbed.

I became an attorney because I wanted to help people, and this woman needed my help.

"I'm Lily Knight." I opened the divider that closed off the lobby from the office space and waved off the secretary's apologies. "I have a little time to spare this morning. What can I do for you?"

She gave my hand a brief, trembling squeeze. "Oh...thank you. I know you're very busy..."

"Step into my office." I still couldn't believe I got to say that. "I can't promise I can help you, but I can offer a consultation."

Her expression turned cautious. "Is there—will it cost money?"

"The consultation is free." I could invite people to step into my office now, but not all of them wanted to pay me for my time. At least my first and only client had deep pockets. For now, I could afford a little pro bono practice.

I held the door, and the woman ushered the child ahead of her. The little girl gave me a long, solemn, silent look, then ran to the window. Pressing crocheted blue mittens against the glass, she stared out at the sparkling bay as if transfixed by the play of sun on water.

The woman sank into the chair that faced my desk. She tucked her long, flowing, blue-green dress around her feet and hid her hands in her lap. Waves of longing rolled from her aura, its rich and wild sea scent mingling with the heady fragrance of the flowers on my desk.

"What do you need to know?" Her gaze skated away from mine to linger on the little girl at the window..

I took my seat at the desk, pulling out a pad and pen. "We can start with your name."

With a little start, her attention snapped back to me. "Oh. Yes. Naia." She licked her lips, a quick sweep of pink tongue and a flash of small white teeth. "Uh...Williams."

Sure it was. I wrote it down anyway. "Tell me why you're here, Naia."

"There's a man."

I suppressed a sigh. Of course there was a man. Wasn't there always a man? I lowered my voice so the child tracing patterns on the window couldn't hear me. "I see. Are you in a relationship with him?"

"Jared. He's my husband." Naia hesitated, shook her head. "It's not what you think."

"If you're feeling unsafe at home, then I know people who can help you." Maybe I could refer her to Safe Haven, my client Rae McGuire's old clinic, now run in her absence by her office manager, Olivia. "They can give you a place to stay where he can't find you. Your daughter, too."

"No," she whispered. "I can't leave. Please, you have to help me."

"There's not much I can do as an attorney. I can file a restraining order for you, but a piece of paper can only do so much." It wouldn't stop a fist or a bullet if this man she clearly feared came after her. And even if he never did, it couldn't prevent the devastating emotional cost of trusting a monster with her body and heart.

For one breath, I stood on that precipice, in the silence of a desert night, scanning the inky black sky for the circling, hunting wingspan of my former mentor, lover, and tormentor. Then I pushed the memory away.

I'd survived my monster. Now I could help this woman do the same.

"You're not just an attorney," Naia said in low, fierce tones. "I saw you on TV. What you did, what you are. You're different." She swallowed. "Like me."

"Like you? But you're not a demon." At least, I didn't think so. Demons didn't have auras like hers. A full-blooded incubus or succubus like Ariel or Eve had no desiderata at all. Maybe Naia was a hybrid, another cambion, but she didn't feel like any cambions I'd ever met.

Granted, I only knew one, and he was a total jerk.

"Neither are you." Naia's smile quivered. "You're an angel. I know what I saw."

Sebastian had said something like that when I showed him my wings. It didn't fit then, and coming from this fragile woman with her saltwater-drenched aura, it fit even less. I didn't belong on that pedestal. I couldn't live up to it.

A hollow place nagged under my breastbone, a half-healed scar that resonated with Naia's despair. Pedestal or not, I didn't want to quench the hope in her eyes. "Tell me what you want me to do, and I'll tell you whether I can do it."

"He took them from us." Naia sat up straighter, steeling herself against her own story. "He'll burn them if I leave. We'll be lost, Keira and I." Her eyes flicked to the child daydreaming at the windowsill. "We have to get them back."

I leaned forward again, waiting for her to focus back on me. "I'm not following. What, or who, did this man take from you?"

"Our coats. We need them, or..." She shrugged, her desolation clear and yet incomprehensible.

"This is about clothing?"

"Not clothing," Naia said. "Ms. Knight, my husband took our skins."

She said it simply, expectantly, as if it were the most obvious thing in the world. As if I would *know*. As if it weren't several different kinds of horrible, besides the one I already understood, the betrayal of it.

At the window, Keira hummed tunelessly, lost in reverie, her yearning eyes fixed on the sea. The salt-tang thickened on the roof of my mouth. "Naia, what exactly are you?"

Her liquid brown eyes widened further, the whites nearly swallowed by the black ink of her pupils. "We're selkies, of course." She sounded surprised by my ignorance.

I groped for my limited knowledge of the legend she invoked. "You're a shapeshifter." Her oceanic aura made more sense now. "A seal shifter?"

"Sea lion. Without my skin, I can't shift. I can't go home to the pod." She leaned forward and opened her hands. Her fingers were ever so slightly webbed between the first and second knuckle. "Without our pod, we have nothing, my daughter and me. We're defenseless on land. Will you help us?"

For a long moment, I sat still. Nameless unease swirled in my chest. The tide of Naia's vulnerability and anguish tugged memories closer to the surface that I didn't care to relive.

I understood what she wanted now. It wasn't a lawyer's job, but maybe it was mine. Assuming her husband was only human, I could use my Presence to get the sealskins. If that didn't work, I had special powers of breaking and entering, of walking unseen into locked and secret places.

"Tell me exactly what happened between you and him," I said at last. "And tell me where you think he might have hidden your, er, coats."

I had vowed to uphold human laws when I became an attorney, but sometimes justice required me to make my own. Human law didn't mean much when it came to freeing a woman from a coercive relationship.

Ariel's betrayal had taught me that hard lesson, when the woman I had to free had been myself.

4

STORM WARNINGS

"I don't know why we're doing this," said the vessel of the ancient goddess, flatly.

A single, dingy overhead bulb lit the closet-sized room the city jail reserved for defense counsel and its clients. It washed out Rae McGuire's already pale complexion, throwing into sharp relief her harsh features and the sallow smudges of fatigue under her gray eyes. Her once-bright red hair had faded over the past six months to a dull, dark-rooted copper that hung limp around her shoulders and clashed with her orange prisoner's jumpsuit.

I set my pen down on my half-finished page of notes. "First off, you're not the bad guy here. Those guys deserved what they got."

The entity Rae called Morrighu—better known as the Morrigan of legend—had taken twelve men's lives while she possessed Rae. I had stopped her from taking the thirteenth, the sacrifice that would have unleashed a bloodthirsty goddess and brought her fully into our world.

Those men had also covered up decades of abuse by their San Francisco University fraternity while rising to prominent positions in society. Some of them had personally assaulted Rae during her student days, and that life-shattering trauma had eventually led her to barter her body to the Morrigan in exchange for the promise of justice.

To keep the Feds from pinning the murders on Eve, Rae had agreed to turn herself in, but only on the condition that I defend her against the charges. Now, though, with her trial date less than a week away and a confession on the books, my sole client seemed to have lost the last of her hope.

"Murder is murder." She spoke in fierce, cold tones, as if determined to condemn herself. "I may not have finished my degree, but I'm not ignorant, Lily. It doesn't matter that they were bad guys, too. I wanted them to die."

"There are extenuating circumstances. Your background, for instance."

"Yeah, right. Like being a survivor ever helped any woman in the court of public opinion. Why would it help me in a court of law?"

"You acted under duress." I kept my own voice even, speaking to the hollow fear and desperation echoing in her desiderata behind the flash of bright, aggressive steel. "When you agreed to become the Morrigan's vessel, you didn't ask her to kill them. You didn't know about the price she'd exact. You asked for justice."

She leaned back in the scarred plastic chair, arms crossed, mouth pressed in a tight line. "I did. And afterward, when she explained the sacrifice, I gave her their names."

"Yes. *After* the deal was struck." Once she made that deal and the goddess took control, Rae couldn't have stopped the Morrigan from taking what she demanded—the blood of the guilty. "Listen, Rae. You didn't have a choice. *She* made it for you. We call that an action by an intervening third party, and it's an affirmative defense to a charge that requires intent."

For my next trick, I would try to convince a jury of her peers to see it my way, despite the confession, the list of targets found tacked to her wall, the edged weapon she'd acquired in Ireland before the killings began, and her clear motive for wanting vengeance against the men who'd hurt her.

But first, I had to convince *her*.

"I disagree." She set her jaw, and for a moment her energy crackled like a storm, sharp-scented with ozone and lightning. "I chose my path. I made the deal. I picked the names. You can't take that from me."

"Ah." Now I understood. Accepting the argument that the goddess had chosen *for* her meant accepting she had no agency. Of course she resented that, given the nature of her trauma, even though her stubborn claims didn't serve her interests in this context. "Let me put it another way. Would you have killed them if you weren't bound by that deal?"

She fell silent. "I don't know," she said at last. "I wanted...consequences. They all went on with their lives like nothing happened. Like it didn't matter at all."

"It's a yes or no question," I said as gently as I could. We still hadn't decided if Rae would testify, but with answers like that, she probably shouldn't. The thought of her facing cross examination had me in a cold sweat whenever I thought about it too hard.

"I wanted them to suffer." Rae stared at me, steely-eyed. Then she drew a long, hitching breath. "But no. I never imagined it would be like that."

"Better," I said. "Now, your people have me on retainer and it's my job to fight for you. Let me fight."

Her lips twisted in a sardonic, mirthless smirk. "Do I have a choice?"

"Of course you have a choice." I pushed a folder across to her. "You can always plead out and skip the trial. It would take the death penalty off the table, but they'll still put you away for life."

The sudden shift in her aura startled me. The stormy flash subsided, and in its place lay something more, and less, than the absence of light. It had a weight of its own, a presence like the heavy darkness dwelling in a cavern's depths, cold and ancient, alien to sunlight.

"No," she said, shuddering, and the dark receded. It left her human, worn, resigned yet determined. "I don't fear the chair. Not so much as... No. We fight."

"All right." I opened my notes again. "The first day in court will likely be spent on jury selection. You have a right to be present for that, so let's talk about what to expect."

I walked her through the *voir dire* process, encouraging her to take notes on prospective jurors and pass me any questions she wanted me to ask. For all her fierce, wild energy, she had a good instinct for people and a scientist's eye for detail.

She had wanted to become a biologist, she'd told me once, but after what they'd done to her, she'd become a warrior instead. Even before she made herself a weapon in the Morrigan's hand, she acted as a shield for survivors like herself. She'd founded her nonprofit shelter, Safe Haven, to help people like Naia, who'd agreed to take her daughter to one of the organization's safe houses. I'd promised to get her sealskins back before her husband came home from his business trip.

We all had fight or flight in common, Rae and Naia and I, a sisterhood none of us had chosen. It meant that no matter the odds, I would give them every possible chance to win their freedom.

"I have a question for you." Finally, I closed the folder containing Rae's case discovery file and packed it away into my valise.

"Another one?" We'd gone through every nuance, every possibility, my client glancing over each page of the evidence that might damn her with an expression of bleak, unflinching resignation. Now she just sounded weary.

"*Not* case-related this time." I fumbled for words as with the clasp on the briefcase, her curiosity like a faint, cool draft in the poorly ventilated cubbyhole of a room. "Rae, do you know of any others who are like you? Like us? Or like...*her*?"

Her face changed. "You mean demons? Or goddesses?"

"I don't know if there's much of a difference," I said. "But I mean people who aren't quite human. People who can shift their shape at will. You turned into a raven, or a storm. I saw you."

"*She* did that. Not me."

"She told me there were others. 'More things in heaven and earth,' she said."

"Where she comes from, they have plenty of stories like that." The flicker of interest in Rae's expression had died away, drowned by fatigue. "Maybe she's right, but I wouldn't know. She doesn't tell me much of anything, lately. Not since..."

"She went dormant?"

"Right." Regret spread its bruise-purple penumbra through her energy field. "Sorry I don't have any better answers for you."

"Don't worry about it." I stood. "That's enough for today. Stay strong, rest up, and I'll see you soon. We're almost there."

"Thank you. I'm ready." With a grim nod, she stretched out her arms to let the guard fasten her wrist shackles for the walk back to her cell block. "It's the waiting that's the hard part."

She went out, queenly even in chains between two hard-faced women officers. The reinforced door buzzed, opened, and then shut her away. Another guard led me up and out of the jail's depths as if no terrible man's blood stained my own hands, but my steps weighed heavy with a conviction I couldn't shake.

Dormant or not, the momentary stir of darkness in Rae's energy had carried a warning. The goddess hadn't finished with her yet. She wanted something more.

Rae didn't deserve to serve time for the Morrigan's deeds, but if the goddess seized control again, I would have to find a way to stop her a second time, or more people would die. And then—

I didn't fully understand her end game, but I doubted it would end well for humanity. Most humans were guilty of *something*, after all, and this goddess didn't deal in mercy.

She would have her justice, even if she had to take it at the edge of a blade.

Unwilling to return to the condo and the joys of quasi-parenting a teenager, I lugged my files and misgivings from the city jail back to the office to finish up my trial prep. Unlike home, my office belonged to me alone. It had no ghosts of the past, no shadows to jump at, and plenty of other people's problems to solve.

Or so I thought, until I walked into the building lobby and the secretary flagged me down. "Ms. Knight! Good, you're finally back. Your client's been here quite a while."

"I don't have any more appointments today." I frowned at her, then at the empty lobby. "Damn. It's Ms. Williams again, isn't it? Where is she?" I told Naia to stay put while I took care of things, but clients in distress made bad decisions more often than not.

"No, no." Confusion flashed in her normally unflappable expression. "I told him you were out. He didn't seem to mind waiting in your office."

A sliver of ice slipped down my spine. "Him who?"

"I could have sworn I wrote it down." She glanced around her uncluttered desk with a disconcerted air.

"Never mind." I wished I could reassure myself as smoothly as I did her. Who the hell had come to see me? That would make two clients in one day who had tracked me down despite my lack of advertising.

Steeling myself, I counted out a long breath and pushed aside another wave of paranoia as I strode down the hall. Most new attorneys would probably welcome new clients. I had nothing to fear except a growing caseload. *I'm safe here. I'm safe now.*

The door to my office stood ajar. I lifted my hand to push it open, then froze. A whiff of spice and smoke teased my nostrils. My eyes watered, pulse thumping loud in my ears at the familiar scent of frankincense, the tell-tale smell of an incubus.

A tall figure turned, silhouetted at the window, and I flinched.

"Hello, Lillian."

For a moment, I couldn't speak. It wasn't who I thought it would be, of course. This demon had black hair, sleek and combed, not a riot of blond curls. He had dark eyes, not amber, and tanned, olive skin, not cherubic marble. His tone and accent were all wrong too, deep and grave as the roots of the earth given tongue, without a hint of mockery or jest.

Of course it wasn't Ariel. Ariel was dead. This was some other demon entirely.

"Who the hell are you?" I sputtered finally.

"I've looked forward to meeting you." He inclined his head in a slight bow, holding out a hand. "You may call me Samael."

"Is that supposed to mean something to me?" I didn't take his hand or cross to the desk. Maybe if I stayed by the door, he would take the hint and walk out of it.

"Perhaps I should apologize for arriving without warning." He seemed immune to the hint, waiting politely with his hand outstretched. "Given the circumstances, I chose haste over caution. Such meetings, I feel, are best conducted the old-fashioned way."

"Ah, yes," I muttered. "A good old-fashioned ambush."

"That was not my intent." A slight frown creased his smooth forehead. "Very much the opposite, in fact. I hoped to head one off." His features had the same ageless quality as other full-blooded demons I'd met, unmarked by time, toil, or trouble, all except the eyes. A demon's eyes looked human, at first, thanks to their—*our*—powers of illusion and glamour, until one met that fathomless, prehistoric, predatory gaze.

"Head what off? I have no idea what you're talking about."

"No, of course you don't," he murmured. "That's why I had to come."

"Stop." I pinched the bridge of my nose, an ineffective dam against the tension building in my temples. "Enough goddamn riddles. It's irritating, it's pretentious, and I don't have the patience. Not today." Not any day, truth be told.

"You are...not what I expected." The minuscule frown hadn't budged. His attention weighed on me with the calm, unhurried presence of a mountain on the horizon. "I would explain, if you will allow it."

"Great. Let's try some simple questions with simple answers." I ticked them off with my fingers. "Why are you here? What do you want from me? How did you know about me? And who the hell do you think you are?"

"Some of these questions are simpler than others." He cocked his head at a thoughtful angle. "I will start with the simplest. I learned of your existence when I saw you on the evening news."

"You saw my interview." I stalked around the desk on numb legs, not ready to sit yet but bolstered by the posturing, as if I had any control here. "That tracks, I guess. Maybe I should be more surprised that you're the first."

"I may be the first, but I will not be the last. That is why I came—to warn you." He said it with matter-of-fact earnestness, with the force of conviction. "Even now, you are in great danger."

I snorted. "What danger? I did that interview six months ago. Here's a news flash for you: no one cares. Humankind has a short attention span and a perennial talent for ignoring anything that doesn't fit into their frame of reference."

"Indeed," said Samael. "The danger is not from humans, but our own kind."

"We have met the enemy and he is us?" I scoffed again. "Way ahead of you there. I've been down that road before. Spoiler alert, I won. I should have gotten a T-shirt, but mostly I just got PTSD. Big whoop, we're killers. So am I."

"Perhaps so," he said. "But this is something new. One of us has turned and made a devil's bargain with humans who crave control and power, as of old. One of us has agreed to hunt our own."

I almost laughed because he was right. One of us *had* made a deal with the government to hunt other demons.

It was me. I did that. Hell, I'd half-expected the visitor in my office to be my government handler, Ira Delaney. I'd hoped as much, because I hadn't heard from Ira in some time. He'd gone off the grid after I captured Rae, and his radio silence worried me.

I probably shouldn't mention any of that to this guy. He seemed like the type who would take it the wrong way.

"You think they'll come after me because I'm visible," I said, playing along.

"I don't think," he said. "I know. This rogue cubine is hunting *you*."

That gave me pause. He sounded extremely sure of himself, but beyond the ominous words themselves, he sounded like he *cared*. It didn't make sense.

I didn't like it at all. "Thanks for the warning, but I'm still not sure why I should trust you. I don't even know you."

"Ah." Samael's frown deepened. "That is the question, isn't it. I fear I have no simple answers for you."

"Try." I crossed my arms.

"It is difficult." He spoke in a quiet rumble, as if to himself, but he met my challenging glare squarely, his eyes dark and undecipherable. "Very well. It is true you do not know me, but I hope that may yet change. I came to warn you because as soon as I saw your face, I knew you for what you are."

I didn't understand, and yet an unnamed, breathless sensation clawed its way up my throat, an answer to the emotion I couldn't read in his face. "And what is that?"

"Flesh of my flesh," he said. "Blood of my blood. A rarity, in this day and age. You are my daughter, Lillian."

5

SINS OF THE FATHER

My daughter. Samael's answer—so simple after all—struck the air from my lungs. For a moment, my heart stood still, cold and heavy as a stone.

"Maybe I misheard you." My voice didn't sound like my own. It belonged to a stranger, to a stranger's daughter. "Did you just say…" All the words that came to mind seemed wrong.

"I am your father." He said it too easily, as if it made all the sense in the world, but it made no sense at all. My face must have betrayed me, because he added, "Forgive me. Perhaps I should have started there."

"You think?" The room reeled around me, and I braced myself on the desk. "If you're really him, you should have started thirty years ago."

Head lowering a fraction, he took a half-step back. "I see. I should have anticipated—you are angry." He seemed to hesitate over the word, rolling it on his tongue as if comparing it with whatever he could doubtless taste in my aura.

Well, I hoped it stuck in his craw. "Great. You get me, Pops. That really warms my heart." Now that the initial shock had passed, in fact, red-hot rage boiled in the cage of my ribs.

Even before I knew my heritage, I daydreamed that a real father would come and find me, take me away from the man who, unbeknown to me at the time, had always recognized me as the changeling evidence of his wife's betrayal. How dare he waltz in here like this, this man I'd never met, this demon whose existence

I only knew as the necessary prerequisite for my cambion blood? Who was this tall, unsmiling person who looked nothing like the figure I'd once imagined as a child?

How dare he find me *now*, after all these years?

I didn't need this now. I didn't need this ever. I hadn't learned to survive without him for nothing.

"You must understand. Your mother...we thought it was better that way." His look pierced me. "I couldn't bear to watch from afar, so I stayed away. You seemed happy enough, and I had no choice but to respect your mother's wishes."

"Everyone has a choice."

"No. She and I had a covenant," he said. "We must honor the consent of those who bind with us. All those years—I came as soon as I knew, as soon as I could."

"Sure you did." Now, at last, I sank into my chair. My eyes burned, but I kept them trained on him. "I did that interview six months ago. You must have been living under a pretty big rock if it took you this long enough to dig yourself up."

"I suppose I feared you would not want to see me," he said slowly. "That fear was well-founded, it seems."

"A stunning insight, and yet here you are." I refused to let his admission get to me. So what if this was hard for him? If he'd shown up despite knowing that I might not welcome his sudden appearance, that almost made it worse.

His frown deepened. "I came only to warn you of the danger in which you placed yourself."

Fantastic. I had just met this alleged father of mine and he already found a reason to scold me. "Oh, so now I asked for it, is that it?"

"It is forbidden by our law for us to make ourselves known," he said. "And for good reason."

"You mean I'll be punished." A tendril of fear curled in my belly. Ariel had taught me the rule of secrecy, but he'd never made the penalty clear, and at this point I assumed that everything Ariel had told me was a lie unless proved otherwise.

"No. That is not our way." Samael looked pained. "Of course, you have not been taught the rule or the reason for it. It ensures our safety from ire, from envy, and from fear. I suppose it cannot be helped, but I had hoped—"

"I've been taught plenty," I said. "I just don't believe the lessons anymore."

"Then believe this. Exposure risks consequences. It makes you a target of those who do not understand, or those who would misuse our power, or those of our own kind who are simply afraid for their secrets and their survival. It has been so since the beginning."

"I appreciate the remedial catechism, but I'm not learning to live in fear again." I revealed myself to the world so I could stop hiding from everyone I loved and stop worrying that someone else would expose me first. For one glorious moment, as I spread my wings before God and everyone, I even believed that the truth would really make me free. "Besides, it's too late. The truth's already out there. The internet is forever, you know."

"Nothing is forever, Lillian. And it is very easy for our kind to vanish if we wish to. Subterfuge is part of who we are, and we all must learn how to start anew eventually."

I stared at him. "You think I should run away from this. Based on what—some rumor?"

"It is more than a rumor," he insisted. "I am quite certain. I would not have come otherwise."

"What makes you so sure?"

"There are those among us who have ways of seeing and knowing at a distance." A moment ago, he had stood across the room. Now, with a demon-quick movement, he loomed above my desk, leaning over me. "I only ask that you consider your own safety. If you choose to leave this place, I'll help you any way I can. If money is the issue—"

"What? No! This is ridiculous. I'm not going anywhere." I rose to face him. I couldn't match his height, but I would *not* let him think he could intimidate me. "And you couldn't pay me enough to go somewhere with *you*. Whether or not you really are my father, I still don't trust you."

For a long breath, he stared at me across the desk, jaw hard and set. "Is it so hard to believe that I would have my daughter's best interests at heart?"

"Frankly, yes." I glared, hands on hips. "Thanks to you, I have a less than stellar experience of paternal love, an attachment disorder, and a variety of other traumas. Not to mention a dim view of cubine family values. So what do you say, Pops? Should I send you my therapy bills?"

He rocked back a step, as if my cutting tone had finally pierced his defenses. "You truly are nothing like I thought you'd be," he murmured.

"I'm sorry I don't live up to your expectations." I tried to take solace in my victory, but it only left me hollow. I wanted more of a fight. It seemed he had disappointed me, too. "Go on, then. What do you think of me now?"

"You're sarcastic," he said. "Defiant. So guarded, as with spiked palisades. Yet you wear your wounded heart upon your sleeve as if it could protect you. And it does."

Thanks, I hate it. I didn't expect him to be so damn insightful, and I didn't even know what a palisade was. What gave him the right?

"Well, Sam. Can I call you Sam?" I ignored his frown of demurral. "I hope you said all you had to say, because we're done here. I have work to do for my real life here, in the real world, for people I care about. I'm not leaving any of that behind."

"I hoped we could talk more. You must have questions for me."

I did have questions, lots of them, but I couldn't take any more answers. "I don't think we have much to talk about."

A shadow of pain passed over his face. "You wish for me to leave?"

"Yeah, I do, Sam." I crossed to the office door. The smile I mustered went awry, so sharp it hurt my cheeks. "You should stick to what you're good at, anyway."

I said the last part *sotto voce*, but not quietly enough to evade his supernatural hearing. It hit home, palpable in his hitched step and the nearly imperceptible slump of his shoulders.

Maybe I'd wanted him to hear. I bit down on the guilt that writhed through me at his reaction and swallowed hard, acid and copper thick on my tongue.

In the doorway, he turned. "Here. In case you change your mind."

After a long pause, I took the card he offered. He bent his head in another of his odd little bows, an archaic gesture out of place and time, and swept away down the hall without looking back.

I shut the door, leaning against it. The square of card stock pressed its bladed corners into my palm, and I clenched my fist, crumpling it. My breath came in harsh gasps, but I wasn't sobbing, not with my eyes so dry and hot they ached like coals of fire.

No, crying didn't hurt like this, and I didn't owe him my tears.

Maybe I should have given Jared Williams the benefit of the doubt, but after the day I'd had, I wasn't in the mood for due process.

Instead, I leaned into my true nature and lay in wait for a good old-fashioned ambush.

According to Naia, her husband planned to return around five that afternoon. Based on their home address, he'd done well for himself in his real estate business, but his security system couldn't stop a determined demon who could walk through walls. I arrived at four with plenty of time to case the redwood shingle bungalow inside and out.

A thorough search of the closets didn't turn up any furs or skins. Too bad, but that would have made this too easy.

Nothing in the house betrayed its terrible secret. Nothing hinted at the oceanic sadness I'd sensed in Naia's energy. The walls displayed portraits of the three of them like any other family, smiling and happy together, Jared's arms spread wide to encompass his wife and daughter in a warm embrace. It didn't look like a possessive gesture, but that made it all the more dismal in a way. I shivered at how well appearances deceived, at the invisibility of Naia's private anguish within the four walls of her own home.

At the threshold of a girlish bedroom, replete with frills, toys, and stuffed animals, I lingered for a moment. Here, at least, some subtle clues surfaced, albeit ones any unsuspecting human would attribute to a child's interest in marine animals and mermaids. A white plush seal and blue whale occupied a place of honor beside the pillows on the bed's seashell-patterned coverlet. The small window looked out at the bungalow's closed courtyard, but a sizable poster tacked opposite it displayed a panorama of Monterey Bay, blue water and curving, rocky cliffs under a wide horizon.

Most people wouldn't say that the child who lived in this room experienced any form of neglect. It seemed that Keira had everything a human child could want.

Grimacing, I turned away. Stuffies and photographs couldn't substitute for the chance to embody one's true nature. Even at her young age, she had a right to choose a different life than the one assigned to her, and I had the power to give her that choice.

I hadn't gotten the same opportunity at her age. Samael had made the choice for me. He'd left me only half myself, learning to pretend I belonged as best I could, like a cuckoo's imposter egg hatched in a nest that didn't fit.

Back downstairs in the family room, I settled into a chair with a view of the door and wrapped a stealthy Presence around myself. I wanted my quarry off his guard and comfortable before I sprang.

The minutes stretched long in the quiet, empty house. Maybe I had given myself too much leeway, after all, because now I had time to think and nothing I cared to think about.

What if I wasn't the rogue demon he'd heard about, after all? I couldn't do much beyond always keeping an eye over my shoulder and insisting to my therapist that I wasn't hypervigilant, because someone really was out to get me. Samael had vague and ominous covered, but had neglected to share any useful specifics, another addition to his growing list of failures...if I believed his other, equally appalling claim.

It checked out, anyway. I almost wished I had more reason not to believe him, because I couldn't imagine calling that stranger my...*dad.* The word didn't suit him any better than the word "daughter" suited me.

I didn't regret venting my justified anger at him. If I'd paused to ask what I really wanted to know, maybe he would have told me, but it didn't matter. I didn't care why he'd left or whether he'd ever tried to find me before now.

With ruthless resolve, I squashed the small, traitorous part of me that whispered otherwise. No doubt he had his reasons, but they wouldn't change things for me. Nothing he could say would fill the void in my past.

I'd dragged myself into something resembling functional adulthood all on my own. I had found something close to family in Danny, Sebastian, and Eve. Samael couldn't offer me anything I hadn't already fought to get for myself.

The click of the lock rang out loud in the silence, and I stiffened, welcoming the sudden wash of adrenaline that refocused me on the task of the moment. I hardly needed unpleasant, expensive therapy when I could scare this jerk out of his own skin and the two he'd stolen for fun *and* for free.

Of course, the state bar association that had conditioned my license on continued counseling appointments wouldn't see it that way, but what they didn't know couldn't hurt me. Everyone got to have their unique self-care needs, and fucking this guy's day up qualified as mine.

I waited, poised and motionless, as the man I recognized from the family portraits stepped inside his house and closed the door. Dressed in a blue sport coat over khakis, he wore his thinning, sandy hair carefully styled to hide the sparseness at the crown, and his square, blunt features carried a dissatisfied, anxious expression. He had height and bulk on me, but nothing I couldn't handle with my supernatural strength.

Whatever Naia had seen in this man, it didn't show in this moment of unconscious vulnerability. His aura stank of insecurity, and he hadn't even met me yet. No wonder he had hidden his wife and daughter's skins from them, seeking to dominate with threats and coercion. He didn't have a chance against a woman with power, let alone a half-succubus in full command of her abilities.

Setting down his keys on the side table by the door, he frowned around as if looking for something—Naia, probably, who had feared the consequences of not meeting him when he came home.

I took the cue and flowed to my feet.

"Hello, Jared." My Presence shifted with me from 'unseen' to 'shock and awe', and a slow, malicious smile seized my lips as he started back from me, wide-eyed. "No, don't shout for help. Don't speak, in fact, unless I tell you to. And don't bother running, because I'll catch you on the first step."

Pungent fear crescendoed in his aura like a scream he didn't dare to voice. He froze in place, obedient to the command I layered into my words.

"Very good," I said, advancing on him. "Now you and I are going to have a little talk about taking things that don't belong to you."

He whimpered, eyes glazed and rolling, whites showing as he followed my stalking approach. It wasn't a good look.

"On second thought, why don't we skip the talk." I pitched my tone lower, aiming for a reasonable purr, though his reaction suggested I'd hit closer to a growl. "Tell me where you hid the seal skins, and we'll get this over with."

The sweat stood out in droplets on his brow, and he stammered something unintelligible.

"Yes, you can speak. Keep it down, please, and don't make any sudden movements."

"I don't know you, lady, but please don't hurt me," he gabbled. "Where's Naia? Where's my baby girl? What have you done with them?"

"They're safe," I said. "They're somewhere far away from you. The skins, Jared. Focus. Where are they?"

"What skins? I have no idea what you're talking about!"

"I think you do." I tilted my head, sampling his aura. It left a bad taste in my mouth, but the confusion there seemed honest enough. Maybe I should let him have a moment to catch up. "I don't know if you know this, but sea lions are an endangered species. You could go to jail for possessing their parts. Or you could give them back."

"I don't…I wouldn't…" Slowly, realization dawned. "You mean…Naia's furs. Oh. Oh, no. But they're not—"

"Oh no, indeed," I said. "Yes, I know what they are. Don't lie to me, Jared. It's bad for your health, and more to the point, it really pisses me off."

He cringed away from me. "Why do you care? Who are you?"

"I'm a friend of Naia's. She wants them back. That's all you need to know."

"Naia…" At that, he crumpled into a sob. "Oh, God. I can't. I love her. They're all I have. You don't understand."

"Don't I?" I smiled, cold enough to make him shudder. "You know what you did, and you know why you did it. You wanted control. I understand that all too well."

"But she'll leave me," he whined. "She'll take Keira! That's my little girl. She's only half… She's part human, too, not just some animal. She doesn't belong out there with them."

"She doesn't belong to you," I said through my teeth. "Neither of them do. Enough stalling. We could do this the hard way, if you'd prefer."

"All right! All right. Jesus." His aura took on a sickly sheen that brought my hackles up. He'd make a run for it if I let him. "I don't have them here. They're in storage. For…for safekeeping."

"Fine." I snatched up his keys from the table. "Let's go for a drive."

He raised his hands. "Take them. I'll give you the address, the locker number. Just leave me alone."

"No way." I grabbed him and shoved him toward the door. "I'm not letting you out of my sight. Not until I have what I came for."

For a moment, his energy blazed with desperation, and I tensed for a fight. I hadn't planned on resorting to violence, but when his desiderata shrank from me, dull and defeated, I entertained a twinge of disappointment.

Punching him would do me a world of good, but he'd probably bleed on my favorite shoes. I'd settle for his current state of utter demoralization.

Besides, he'd done far worse to himself long before I got involved. As soon as he set out to coerce Naia into staying, he destroyed any chance of real love between them.

Assuming, of course, that he had ever truly loved her at all.

6

AGAINST THE TIDE

The sun dropped halfway into the cresting marine layer, drenching the city in a diffuse twilight glow as I pulled Blue Betty up to the curb in front of Safe Haven.

I checked my rear-view mirror in case Jared Williams had made good on his shouted threats and called the cops, but the coast seemed clear. In the soft light of San Francisco's golden hour, the two silky, dark brown furs I'd laid on Betty's back seat shimmered like still water.

I'd left Jared behind in the bleak dust of his self-storage unit after loading the skins into the car, marveling at the weight of them, soft and curiously warm in my arms like living things. He'd tried to give chase, waving his arms and cursing, but the roadster made zero to sixty in two seconds flat.

He might still report me, but I put low odds on it, and significantly higher odds on my own ability to talk myself out of trouble. Besides, I'd forced him to leave his mobile phone at his house, which would buy me some time.

Either way, he'd find his way home, which was better than he deserved, but he would never see his family again except by their own choice.

Summoned by my text, Naia emerged onto the clinic porch, followed by Olivia, the shelter's director. The two exchanged a brief, tight embrace. The selkie woman clutched Keira's small mitten-sheathed hand, expression pinched with anxiety as she guided her daughter down the steps to my car. I lowered the passenger-side window and gave her an encouraging wave.

"Did you get them?" Naia asked, breathless.

I gestured behind me. "See for yourself."

Brown eyes huge and liquid, she pressed her hands to her mouth with a soft, wordless cry. Her salt-sea aura spilled over me in a shock of cold water and overwhelming emotion.

"Are you all right? Those are them, aren't they?"

Naia made a choking sound. Silent tears coursed down her cheeks, her struggle to compose herself written plainly on her face. "Yes. They are. Sorry. I just…"

"That's good," I said. "Are you ready to go home?"

She nodded and held the door for Keira, who slipped into the small back seat and buried her face in the pile of furs.

"They smell so nice." The girl's sweet, high, fluting voice surprised me. It was the first time I'd heard her speak. "Like happiness, Mama."

"I know, baby," Naia said. "Are you excited?"

Keira considered this, her small features solemn. "Ye-e-ss." She drew out the word. "But nervous too. What if the pod doesn't like me?"

"They'll like you, little one." Naia attempted a watery smile, reaching back to fasten Keira's seat belt. "They're our family. The sea will always welcome you home."

I pulled Blue Betty away from the curb and waved my thanks to Olivia. At first, I drove in silence, not wanting to intrude on their private moment, but my curiosity got the best of me as we headed downhill toward the sea. "Was Keira born on land?"

"Technically, all sea lions are born on the shore." Naia laughed at my flush of embarrassment. "It's all right. I know what you mean. Yes, she was born while I was in my human form."

It seemed rude to ask my most burning question, whether Keira had come out as a seal or a human child and if the former, how the doctors explained it away. "Why did you leave the ocean to begin with?"

Naia looked away and out the window at the city flying by. "I fell in love."

"Sorry." I cursed myself for bringing up yet another painful topic.

"No, don't be. I was very young and extremely foolish. And..." She cast a quick look over her shoulder. "I didn't know back then how much I'd have to lose."

"You couldn't have known it would turn out this way. That he would do this to you."

"Not true." She grimaced, a faint, wry, wincing smile. "It is an old story among our people. The elders warned me. But I didn't listen."

"It's not your fault." I turned down the road toward the Presidio, the Golden Gate glowing red orange to our left in the last rays of the sinking sun that streamed through a break in the fog. "I know what it's like, feeling drawn to something that will hurt you."

"Yes," Naia said softly. "There are always sharks in the ocean. But we'll be safer there than we ever were on land."

Following her directions, I drove us up to the western edge of the beach and parked in a mostly empty lot. The great bridge hulked across the horizon, a sentinel of steel and shadow over the old fortress beneath it. Cold salt air flowed in Betty's open window like the tide of Naia's joy, carrying the crash of waves against the rocky seawall and the faint roar of traffic from above.

Naia bundled Keira in the smaller fur coat and lifted her out of the back seat. She crouched in front of the girl, tucking the fur snugly around her, her low tone nearly lost beneath the sound of wind and water.

"Don't be afraid, my love. Remember, you were born to do this."

Keira nodded, and Naia hugged her close, then straightened, holding her daughter's hand as she turned to face me.

"Thank you," she said. "I wondered at first if I did right, coming to you. But I'm glad I did. You really are an angel."

"I'm really not. But I'm happy I could help."

"If there's any way for me to repay you, name it."

Well, damn. I could have asked her to write me a testimonial for the website I kept meaning to set up, but too late now. "If I'm ever in your neighborhood—" I inclined my head toward the sea— "I'll be sure to look you up."

Naia laughed. "Please do. Here, take this." She unhooked the necklace she wore on a simple cord, an iridescent shell pendant that shone green-blue like the sea at midday.

I ran a thumb over the glass-smooth surface, still sun-warm from her skin. "It's beautiful. What is it?"

"Abalone shell. A talisman of my people's friendship." Naia bent to smooth wild strands of black hair from Keira's hand. "Ready, baby?"

"Are we going swimming, Mama?"

"Yes," Naia said, laughing, and hand in hand, they ran into the surf.

The first big wave swamped them, and I winced. What if they weren't seals at all? What if Naia was delusional? My limited swimming skills didn't include water rescue at high tide. I would have to brute force my way through it with my demon strength and hope for the best. Sharpening my vision against the fading light, I searched the waves for any sign of them.

Far beyond the breakers, a dark head broke the water, followed by a second, smaller one. Their heads no longer human shaped, tapered and sleek, the two seals looked back at me with large dark eyes.

Then, moving as one, they dived beneath the surface and were gone.

With a sigh, I fastened Naia's token around my neck and tucked the pendant under my shirt against my skin, as she had worn it. A nameless pain twisted in my chest.

No, wait. I could name it. Maybe therapy had taught me something after all.

Our family. Those words opened a vein in me, spilling out yearning and resentment.

Naia had people waiting for her, but the people who raised me kicked me from the nest after they learned the truth about me. When I first escaped Ariel's influence all those years ago, I had nothing and no one to run to.

No familiar waters had welcomed me home back then. I had to learn the lessons of sink or swim on my own, while all that time, somewhere out there, an incubus named Samael had...existed.

Trudging alone up the beach with night coming on, I dashed at my wet cheeks and cursed the eye-watering wind. It had some nerve, sweeping into my life right when I finally started to get it together, mocking me with might-have-beens.

I'd gotten this far in life without a father. I had absolutely no reason not to go on the same way.

Meeting him, learning his name and his face, hearing his voice, none of that changed a goddamn thing.

Warm yellow light glowed from the big bay window above me, a beacon in the deepening twilight. On the sidewalk outside the house Danny shared with her fiancée, and had once shared with me, I slowed my stride to pull myself together.

If left to my own devices tonight, with no responsibilities, I wouldn't have come. I would have caught shade from Danny for missing our weekly game night, but I wouldn't have to face the woman who could read me better than anyone else—anyone human, at least.

I didn't have an option, though. Eve had come over here after school, and I had to pick her up either way. Besides, given the hour, Sebastian had probably beat me here. A last-minute no-show on my part would only raise more questions.

I would tell Danny about my new daddy issues eventually. Of course I would. At this moment, though, I didn't trust myself to talk about it without making the whole night about me and my demons. With the stress of the fast-approaching wedding on her plate, she needed my support, not the other way around. Our friendship had changed since the old days when she could set everything aside for her favorite hot mess at a moment's notice.

I had changed. I could do this. I would keep the mess on lock. Resolute, I climbed the stairs to the porch.

Before I could knock, the door swung wide. "You're late," Eve said, scowling on the threshold.

"Something came up at work," I mumbled, stepping around her.

She moved to block my path. "I didn't know you worked at the beach."

"What?" How did she know where I'd come from? "I never said—"

"Your shoes are covered in sand and your hair looks like a seagull tried to nest in it." Eve slouched back against the wall, smug to the brim. "No lies, huh? I'm not angry, I'm just disappointed."

I winced, glancing down at the soft, dark-brown suede of the low-heeled ankle boots I'd donned this morning as sensible footwear for a non-court day, now salt-stained and caked with wet sand. A real parent would probably reestablish their role as the adult in the room at this point, but I'd settle for keeping my cool. "It was a work thing. I wasn't lying."

"Really?" She squinted at me. "Because you're acting super weird."

"I am not," I said. So much for adulthood.

"Yeah, you are. You're all twisty inside."

I sighed. "Eve, you promised you wouldn't read me to pry into my business."

"Sooorry." Eve rolled her eyes with an exaggerated groan. "I didn't mean to, but you're loud as hell. How else did you think I knew it was you? You were standing outside for a while all like....*grr.*"

"'Grr?' Seriously?"

"Yeah, like a wheel grinding. I don't know. It made my teeth hurt."

I busied myself hanging up my coat. "Something happened today that I'm still processing. That's all. It's nothing to do with you."

"A toothache isn't nothing." She trailed me down the hall, relentless. "You're really upset. You're sad, but you're kicking yourself for being sad in the first place. And you're scared too, because you care and you don't want to."

I stopped so abruptly that she almost ran into me. "Eve..."

"What? Seriously, though, it's like a tornado in there."

"Never mind." I battened down my hatches against the roar inside of me. I refused to encourage Eve by validating her read. I couldn't let it upend everything.

"Sorry," she said again, still without a hint of repentance. "I thought it might help if you heard what it felt like out here."

I gritted my teeth. "I can feel my feelings just fine on my own, thank you."

"Yes, you're so emotionally open." Eve scoffed. "That's exactly how everyone who knows you at all would describe you."

"Oh, for the love of... Don't you have homework to do?"

"I finished it already," Eve said, full of blithe unconcern. "Hey, since you're so open and stuff, it's cool if I go to that big music festival next week, right?"

I frowned. "What festival?"

"Come on, we talked about this. It's the one downtown, where they take over a whole block. There's like five stages. It's not even expensive."

"I don't know, Eve. I don't think so."

"Ugh. Why do you hate freedom?"

I gritted my teeth. "I don't—because you're underage, first and foremost, and I have that big trial next week. I don't know when I'll be done, so I can't go with you."

"You never let me do anything fun." She heaved a dramatic sigh and flounced away into the kitchen, almost colliding with Danny in the doorway.

"Oh, hey Lily." With a curious look at the departing teenager, Danny wiped her hands on an apron emblazoned with the words *If you don't like dinner, eat me.* "I thought Eve was talking to someone who was emotionally open."

"Nope," I said, giving up. "Just me."

Danny squeezed my shoulder with a sympathetic grin. "Six months," she muttered. "Hang in there, Sugarbean."

I slumped. "Six months is long enough for her to be the death of me."

"Oh, come on. She's a pretty good kid these days. She even helped with dinner tonight." Danny pulled me toward the living room. "Here, take a load off. You look like you had a hell of a day."

"Thanks, I did." My sarcasm half-hearted, I flopped into my favorite spot, the worn-cushioned rattan bowl chair in the corner. It didn't fit with the rest of the decor in here, though she wouldn't admit she kept it for my sake. "Is my boyfriend here yet?"

She shook her head. "He texted earlier. His settlement meeting went late, but he'll drop by when he can."

"He texted you and not me?" I waggled an eyebrow at her. "Good thing I'm not a jealous woman."

"Pfft," Danny said. "We both know he's not my type. But he does have manners, unlike some people who don't bother to update their ETA."

"Don't you start." The pillow I lobbed fell short at her feet. Chagrined, I squirmed deeper into the chair, but comfort proved elusive. "Damn it.... You know, his ex didn't want anything to do with him for a decade. But now that he finally filed for dissolution, she's putting him through hell out of nothing but pure, unbridled spite."

"Divorce is always hell," Danny said. She picked up the cushion I'd tossed, scrutinizing its embroidery. "It's almost enough to make a gal think twice about marriage."

Arrested by her tone and the cold, uneasy energy behind it, I stilled my fretful movement and struggled upright from the chair's depths. "Hey, Dan. Anything we should talk about?"

"What? No, *nada*." She glanced over her shoulder, and down the hall, where the door from the kitchen stood open, Eve and Berry's lively voices chattering into the dining room. "It's... No. We're good."

"Could've fooled me." That *nada* sounded worse than the reservations of a recalcitrant patriarch. Maybe she'd held something more serious back from me the previous evening.

"But I can't, can I?" A pulse of bitterness laced her aura. "Not now, Lily. Later, maybe."

"I'll hold you to that. Best ma'am, remember?"

"Of course," she said softly. Her smile broke warm through the clouds for a moment, but it didn't dispel whatever doubt lurked beneath. "You make it hard to forget."

"Dinner's ready!" Eve called from the other room. "Aunt Danny, tell Lily to stop moping around and come try my fancy mac and cheese. It's not even from a box!"

"Whoa." I hauled myself to my feet. "This I gotta taste to believe."

Danny's wistful look had turned wry. "She's telling the truth. I watched her make it."

"You see?" I grumbled, following my best friend to the table. "She could be the death of me *tonight.*"

We all found our seats around the table, where Berry poured wine for me and Danny while Eve insisted on serving up her gooey, cheesy, breadcrumb topped creation onto every plate.

"It smells incredible," Berry said. "Is there gruyere in this?"

Eve beamed. "I used *so many* cheeses."

"We may have gone on a cheese spree at the fancy grocery store," Danny confessed. "All Eve's idea. I'm just the enabler here."

I scooped up a forkful, conscious of my ward's narrow gaze on me and ready to pretend I loved it, but I didn't have to. "Wow. That's actually...it's amazing."

"Don't sound so surprised," Eve huffed, but her face glowed with pride and an answering lightness bloomed in my chest. She didn't often like to show that she cared about my good opinion.

Maybe my substitute parenting had an impact after all. With that thought and another bite of cheesy goodness, warmed by the smiles of my little, found family, some of the day's tension began to slip away at last.

I was safe here. I was loved. I just had to keep repeating that mantra for the part of me, deep down, that warned me not to get used to it, as if someone or something would notice any undeserved shred of happiness and swoop in to steal it away right when I let down my guard.

7

THICKER THAN WATER

We had almost finished dinner when a sudden sharp rap rang out from the front of the house. I jumped and dropped my fork. Breaking off a discussion of the wedding tasting the brides-to-be had scheduled for the coming weekend, Danny, Berry, and Eve all gave me the exact same puzzled look.

"That'll be Sebastian," Danny said through a mouthful of mac and cheese.

"Oh. Right." Cheeks hot, I stood, nearly overturning my chair in the process. "I'll get it."

Eve squinted at me. "Jumpy much?"

Ignoring her, I headed for the hall. I couldn't have told her who else I expected, but I still checked the peephole just in case.

It *was* only Sebastian, of course. Anxiety transformed into a flutter of heat low in my belly as he stepped inside. Last night seemed like a long time ago with everything that had happened since, but my body remembered that less than twenty-four hours had passed since I'd had him inside of me, how good it felt, how simple everything became when I gave myself over to the sure touch of his hands.

Given the way he kissed me hello, he hadn't forgotten either. When he pulled away, though, his dark lashes fluttered closed and he leaned his forehead against mine for a moment. The shadow of strain under his eyes leaped out at me, worn deeper than the attractive air of dishabille I'd appreciated the night before.

"Tough day?" I smoothed light fingers over his temples, drawing a deep sigh from him.

He turned his cheek into my hand. "Just a lot of irrational drama."

"Helena?"

"She's dragging her feet on the agreement," he said. "I don't understand her at all. We're offering everything she asked for."

"It's her last chance to torture you." I slid his coat off his shoulders, palms lingering over the hard planes of his chest and triceps. "She won't give that up without a fight."

He tolerated my ministrations, but his jaw quivered with tension. "It's pointless. I don't know how you lawyers do this every day, honestly."

"I don't do divorce cases, that's how." I pulled him with me toward the dining room, the warmth of his bare hand in mine another pleasure I hadn't gotten used to yet. "Sit down and have some comfort food. More importantly, have some comfort wine."

"God, yes," he said fervently. "Yes to both, but especially the wine."

A chorus of greetings went up from around the table as we rejoined the party. Finding our first bottle of wine nearly empty, I grabbed another from the kitchen and poured a fresh glass for Sebastian.

"By the way," I said softly in his ear, "thank you for the flowers. They were beautiful."

He didn't react with the pleased flush I'd expected but hitched around in the chair with an odd expression. "What flowers, Lil?"

"The white lilies." My own face heated and a wave of queasiness dropped me into my seat. Maybe Eve's cheesy mac didn't agree with me after all. "I had a huge bouquet of them on my desk when I got to the office. I thought they must be from you."

"Sounds garish. Not to mention a bit too on the nose." His brow creased. "Is this your way of telling me you want flowers? If you do, I could—"

"No, no," I said hastily. "I just thought...never mind."

"Maybe you have a secret admirer," Eve said, her sly glance dancing between us.

"God, I hope not." I topped off my own wineglass, but my hand shook and the deep red liquid slopped over the tablecloth.

If I had a secret admirer, that probably meant one of my one-night stand kether partners. I shot Sebastian a quick look over the rim of my glass, but he didn't seem concerned or jealous. After all, he had suggested our current arrangement when I wanted to take the literal power exchange out of our relationship.

I rubbed at the wine I'd spilled. The scarlet stain spread and bloomed like blood, as indelible as the thought that none of my casual partners should have known my name, let alone my office address.

"Don't worry about the tablecloth." Berry, in her unfailing kindness, had misinterpreted my sudden silence as embarrassment. "A little bleach will get that right out."

"Thanks," I muttered and mustered a smile for her. *I'm safe here, remember?*

The self-soothing exercise didn't dull the edge of my creeping paranoia, no matter how many breaths I counted. Naia's story, the fear in her voice and aura, kept echoing beneath the grounding mantra.

My therapist, Dr. Harlow, would probably warn me about over-identifying with my client. Good thing I had my state bar-mandated appointment with her tomorrow. She could probably write a whole dissertation on the events of my last twenty-four hours.

Lost in thought, I barely noticed when Eve and Danny cleared the dinner dishes and the dirty tablecloth away. They left me alone for once, working around me while Berry and Sebastian engaged in a full type-A nerd debate about which board game we would play first.

They may have arrived at a conclusion on their own eventually. Well before any resolution, however, Danny came out of the kitchen, took one look at me, and said, "We're playing Scrabble."

Her tone brooked no argument. Behind her, Eve groaned, but the other two wasted no time in unfolding the board. I stirred in my seat, surprised. On a typical night, my favorite classic wouldn't have gotten more than one vote. Eve and Danny preferred co-op style tabletop games, while Berry and Sebastian preferred strategy epics, the longer and more complex the better.

"I see what you did there." I met Danny's steady gaze as Sebastian dealt out racks of letters with methodical efficiency.

She grinned and shrugged, though her worry still plucked at my energetic sense. "Anything to stop the brooding. I'm shameless that way."

Her transparent gambit to drag me out of my funk worked better than I wanted to admit. I took two in a row and suspected them of letting me win until Sebastian played "syzygy" on a triple-word space with a faint, triumphant smile, running away with the third game.

"I was feeling inspired," he said, packing the board away as I scowled at him. "Besides, I couldn't take another round of this."

The winner chose the next game, so I resigned myself to losing for the rest of the night and slipped out to the living room to grab my phone from my bag. The screen showed a series of missed calls from a local number I didn't recognize.

"What the hell...?" Whoever had dialed me six times in a row hadn't left any messages, and most of the people who had my number were laughing together in the other room. I frowned, slipping the device into my pocket.

A second later, it vibrated against my leg with yet another incoming call. It was probably a wrong number, but I couldn't risk missing a collect call from the jail. If Rae needed to get ahold of me at this hour, it didn't mean anything good.

"This is Lily Knight speaking."

"Lily Knight, huh? About time you picked up." The male voice on the other end sounded familiar, but I couldn't quite place it.

A cold seed sprouted beneath my breastbone, icy tendrils curling toward my heart. "Who is this?"

"Y'know, Lily, you left me standing there with nothing." His tone had an odd, indistinct quality, as if slurred by drink or strangled with emotion. "You took everything from me, so I started thinking."

"*Jared?*" Adrenaline shot through me, speeding the pulse in my ears. "How did you get this number?"

"That's not important." He went on like he hadn't heard me. "See, I've been thinking about sea lions. You must care a lot about those fat, lazy fucks that hang around the wharf. Seems like they matter more to you than a man's pride, his family, his *life*."

"Whoa, Jared." I switched the phone to my other ear, more out of the need to move than to hear him better. "Slow down, okay? I understand you're upset, but—"

"Damn right I'm upset! You did this to me. All because I happened to have some old pelts in storage."

"That's not it at all. You've got the wrong idea about me."

"Oh, I've got some idea." He spoke over me, fast and loud. "My wife put you up to this, didn't she? She told you some sob story and you decided to stick your nose into our family's business. Now she's gone and I have *nothing,* all because of you."

"That's not true," I said. "You did this to yourself. I was just the instrument. I wasn't there for the sea lions. I was there to take back the choice you took away from her."

"Yeah, maybe so. It doesn't matter, though. I don't know where she is, Lily. I don't know where she took my baby girl." The words came out on a broken sob. "But I do know where to find sea lions around here. Everybody knows that."

"Listen to me, Jared. I'm sorry you're hurting. But you're not thinking straight. Where are you?"

"I went and found them." Faint music tinkled behind his uneven voice, the saccharine, eerie tune of a carnival ride. "Maybe one of them is Naia, maybe it's not. They all kinda look the same to me."

*That music...*it wasn't from a carnival. It came from a carousel organ, a familiar one. "Pier 39." I inhaled sharply, swamped by a fresh wave of panic. The Fisherman's Wharf sea lions were a San Francisco institution, so much so that they had their own section of the pier roped off from the public, though they didn't have much respect for human boundaries. "What the hell are you doing out there?"

"This place is such a fucking tourist trap," he said. "I'm out here with these big dumb, smelly seals, and you know what's funny? They're not scared of me at all. I could just walk right up to one. Like shooting ducks in a barrel."

"Oh, *hell*." The cold in my chest had spread to my whole body. "Please tell me this isn't what I think it is. Please tell me you're not out there with a fucking gun."

"Okay, I won't," he said with dull satisfaction. "But if you really care about some stupid sea lions, you'll come stop me."

"Wait. You want *me* to...?" I closed my eyes. This was bad, and it kept getting worse. I had to talk him down. "Jared, whatever you're planning, that area is crawling with cops. They'll arrest you if you even make a move toward those animals. I wouldn't even have time to get over there. Besides, if you're really carrying, they'll probably just shoot you."

"I told you. It doesn't matter. My life is over. At least this way I'll get mine first." His voice steadied, hardening into a bleak, calculated brutality. "At least this way I'll go out like a man."

"Do you even hear yourself?" Desperate, I fumbled for a tack that would work. "Come on, buddy. We can talk about this. You're angry at me. Don't take it out on innocent lives."

"We can talk," he said. "But you better hurry. I don't have all night. Bye now, Lily."

"No, don't hang up," I gabbled. "Jared, wait—"

A soft beep cut me off, and the silence of the dead line rang loud in my ear. I lowered the phone and stared blankly at the screen. It shook in my hand. My whole body shook.

Why would Jared Williams want *me* to come talk him down from the ledge? It was obviously a ruse to lure me out there. He wanted revenge.

He didn't want to shoot those seals. He wanted to kill me.

If I didn't give him what he wanted, though, if I didn't get there in time, he would find another outlet for his injured rage. He would hurt innocent animals or innocent people, or both, and then he'd probably find a way to end himself, probably at the business end of a cop's automatic weapon.

I couldn't let any of that happen. I had to stop him.

I did have one advantage in this situation, at least. Normal bullets wouldn't kill me. They'd hurt like nobody's business, but unless Jared had somehow learned about my special vulnerabilities, he couldn't take me out with a gun the way he could every other unsuspecting human walking the marina tonight.

There were always people at Pier 39, too, even at this late hour on a weekday. Tourists and lovers and out-of-state business travelers would still be filtering out of the restaurants, probably drunk, taking in the view of the bay by night.

God, I had to get out there, and fast. I paced, doing the math in my head. Blue Betty would take me as fast as the streets would allow, twenty-five minutes from Danny's house to the Embarcadero with no traffic. With exceptional luck, parking would eat up at least ten more minutes. Then I would have to find the asshole, likely on the far end of the pier.

Call it forty minutes at best. So much could happen in that much time. When it came to an active shooter, it was basically forever.

Forty whole minutes, unless...

It would take no more than ten, as the demon flew.

Too bad I couldn't fly. Thanks to my visiting Sebastian the night before, instead of finding a kether donor as planned, I didn't have enough juice for more than a few flaps.

Well, no time to change that now, and that meant I had no time to waste.

"Hey, where are you going?" Eve called after me.

"I'll be back," I shouted over my shoulder, already on my way out the door. At least, I hoped I would. "Stay here, okay?"

"Um, okay."

I'd found a spot for Betty five blocks from Danny's. Damn SF and its narrow streets and no parking. I broke into a jog.

Behind me, a door slammed, and quick footsteps followed me. I expected Sebastian, but it was Danny's breathless voice calling my name.

"Lily, wait up!"

"I can't," I said, speed-walking. "I have to go."

"I saw your face when you went past the doorway." She didn't give up but hurried after me. "Something's wrong. What happened?"

"Work emergency. Go back to the house, Dan. I'll deal with it. It's fine."

"Sure it's fine," she said. "I've heard that one before, and I'm not buying it. You weren't fine when you came in tonight and you're really not fine now."

I paused mid-stride, then turned to let her catch up. Here at the heart of the city, ambient light from homes and storefronts diluted the night like a thousand moons and muddied my night vision into dusky monochrome. In the chiaroscuro of the city sidewalk, the soft, glowing beacon of her aura nearly obscured the way her gaze sought mine, her care and worry for me kindling a familiar ache just above my collarbone.

"Hey, Dan," I said before I could think better of it. "Did you mean what you said last night?"

Her energy rippled and she halted a little distance away. "What?"

"About the kether bond. That you wouldn't mind it—didn't mind it."

"I said that?" Despite her flustered stammer, her aura sparked like a stirred bonfire. "I don't... I was pretty drunk."

"Are you drunk now?" I moved toward her in the dark, a single step.

She inhaled sharply. "No."

"You know what it's like already." Damn it. I couldn't steady my voice for the life of me. "I think that's as close to informed consent as I can ask for at this point."

Frozen where she stood, she seemed to have stopped breathing altogether. "What are you saying?"

"There's a man with a gun. I have to stop him." I took another step. "To get there in time, I need to fly."

She said nothing, eyes shining wide and startled, but she didn't back away.

"I don't need too much," I said, already regretting my impulse. How could I ask this of her? Yet time pressed in on me, ticking away, every second marking another potential life I couldn't save. "I just need enough to take me a few miles, that's all. A touch will do it. We don't have to—"

"Yes."

"It doesn't have to be anything—" It took a moment for her whisper to sink in. "Huh?"

"I said yes." Now she stepped toward me. "Of course I'll do it, if that's what you need."

"Okay," I said, unsure of myself all of a sudden. "Um, all right. Give me your hand."

"Really? That's it?" She sounded almost disappointed.

I stripped off my glove. "Skin to skin. That's all it takes. We're pretty close, so..." I trailed off as her fingers twined with mine. "It should do for a short flight."

How could I have forgotten what it felt like—what *she* felt like, specifically? Our previous bond had come from a moment very like this, a single touch, albeit a less platonic one. I had released her from it when we almost died in the desert together, but now it snapped into place between us, as powerful as though it had never broken at all. The sweet warmth of her life energy flowed from her palm to mine, and we both drew a long breath together.

Emotional connection strengthened the intensity of my energy-drain abilities. Drenched in her aura, my limbs suddenly light and full at once, the rate of exchange took me by surprise. In mere seconds, Danny's eyelids fluttered closed, her lips parting. A richer well of kether thrummed right beneath her surface, easily within my reach if I just answered with my own desire.

No. I had to let her go before this went too far and turned into something we might both regret. With careful reluctance, I disentangled our linked hands, taking her shoulders to steady her. "Are you all right?"

"That was...whoa." Eyes still shut, she swayed in place. "Head rush."

"Sorry. I didn't mean to—that got a little intense."

"You can say that again." She blinked and shook herself. Her gaze sought mine with pupils blown wide, two dark and shining pools deep enough to drown in. "I'm good, Lil. Come on, don't look at me like that."

"Like what?" Her essence surged in me, the power of it itching to manifest, and belatedly I recalled my urgent purpose awaiting me, the threat of danger, fear, and death. I backed away, shadows of a nearby alley beckoning. "Never mind. Don't answer that."

"Wait. Lily—"

"I can't," I said, fully in darkness now. "I have to go."

Left standing in the dimly lighted street, she squinted after me. "Talk later, then?"

"Sure." With a rustle of half-substantial pinions, their sudden breeze stirring my hair, my demon wings unfolded. "Later."

Pulling a shroud of night around me, a subtle Presence to turn human sight aside, I launched upward, caught the wind, and soared. The short flight to the marina would give me little time to think about what I'd just done and what it meant, and I was grateful for that.

Still, if it did turn out that the wretched Jared had come to his big showdown prepared and armed with silver, at least this would make it a hell of a night for me to go out on.

8

No Good Deed

The San Francisco marina spread below me in long scalloped curves and traceries of light that stood out in sharp relief against the flat black surface of the bay. I followed its familiar contours to my destination, where the city's most famous pier marked the bright center of the tight-packed docks lining Fisherman's Wharf.

Trusting my Presence and the drifting fog to shield me from view of any humans who happened to look up, I dropped lower to glide above the rows of shops and restaurants that clung like barnacles at the water's edge.

Everything seemed eerily normal and quiet down there compared to the blood and chaos I expected. No one screamed or shouted. No gunshots split the night, no humans fled or cowered. The carousel sat silent under its ever-circling ring of lights, closed for the evening now, but people still wandered through the shuttered shops, unconcerned and unaware of the danger that must lurk somewhere nearby. A few couples meandered here and there, enjoying the romantic ambiance of the late evening on the waterfront, while a few sightseers and families took advantage of a less crowded time to visit the iconic spot.

I touched down on the boards of the upper level in a narrow passageway between two gift shops and a candy shop. The darkened shop windows reflected the silhouette of wings snapping closed, which faded into a glittering afterimage, then into nothingness, just as a pair of women passed by me with linked hands and without a second glance.

My palm tingled, somehow still warm with the memory of Danny's touch and the lasting imprint of the bond that had sprung up even at our brief moment of contact. I made a fist as if I could grip that thread to steady myself.

So Jared hadn't shot up the pier—yet. Maybe I had gotten here on time. Maybe I could still stop him. That would mean I hadn't imposed the bond on Danny for nothing based on the words of a madman.

First, though, I had to find the guy, easier said than done unless he made good on his threats and made a scene as promised.

The last of my don't-notice-me Presence dissolved as my boots thumped out a confident cadence on the walkway's boards, belying the doubt that shadowed me. The last thing I needed was to surprise the man with the gun. I wanted him to know I was here for him.

"Jared?" I paused at the railing overlooking the sea lion area to scan the level below. "Jared! Where the hell are you?"

Down the pier, a few people turned to look toward my voice. Stretching my energetic senses, I met curiosity, disinterest, and a touch of wariness that I had brought unwanted drama to a peaceful evening. The sparse human energies around me held little trace of the turmoil and rage I would expect from my quarry.

A series of hoarse, barking cries arose a little distance from the pier. I had roused one of the sea lions sleeping piled on the waterlogged pallets reserved for their use, and at the alert, several more took up the cause. Sleek dark heads lifted with an indignant air, like Delilah when I disturbed her nap. None of them seemed injured in any way, either.

Had I made a mistake, jumped to the wrong conclusion? It wouldn't be the first time for that, nor likely the last. Yet the carousel music over the phone line had been familiar, unmistakable. Given the late hour, it must have come from the last ride before it closed down for the night.

Why would Jared want me out here, if not to meet him? He was probably still here, somewhere. That didn't mean he hadn't lied, though. He might have never intended to shoot at anyone but me. Maybe he waited nearby, hoping to catch me unawares.

Nape prickling with a belated sense of danger, I backed away from the railing and gathered a less noticeable Presence around me once more. I cased the upper-level walkway with more stealth this time, keeping my back to the storefronts, every nerve alight and ready for an ambush.

No one leaped out at me. Though I spotted a few lone men along the pier, none of them posed any threat to me, and none of them looked a bit like Jared. A search of the lower level turned up no sign of him, either.

At last, hunt thoroughly frustrated, I stood at the far end of the pier and indulged myself in a soft, elaborate string of curses. Then, facing away from the dark water with the sea lion area to my right, I pulled out my phone and dialed the number that had last called me.

I had a truly inspired harangue of intimidation locked and loaded on the tip of my tongue as the ringer buzzed in my ear, but in no way did it prepare me for the sound of an answering ring tone shrilling somewhere behind me.

I spun. A few private docks jutted off from the end of the main pier, dark, deserted, and barricaded to the public at this hour. For all its glitz and amusement park style, even Pier 39 still operated as part of a working harbor. The faint sound of the ringing phone came from halfway down a row of fishing boats and small yachts, its tinny music nearly masked by the gentle slap of water against wood and the complaints of the sea lions.

There was no one out on that dock, though. Even my night vision revealed nothing out of the ordinary, no waiting figures or crouched attackers, only shapeless shadows filling the boats' interiors. The call continued to ring in my ear, each buzzing tone echoed by its counterpart floating across the water, a haunting, ethereal effect until I vaguely recognized the strains of a Nineties rock power ballad.

"Metallica, huh?" I muttered. "That's some *classic* man-pain."

No one answered my quip or the mournfully ringing phone, but I didn't really expect them to. The sea lions' barking calls faded to a single voice, which then fell silent as well.

When the call clicked over to a voice mailbox and Jared's voice said his name in my ear, I started, then hit the end button. Glancing over my shoulder to make sure I hadn't caught anyone else's attention, I stepped over the cordoned gate that blocked off the dock and approached the source of the ring tone.

My vision sharpened as I stepped beyond the reach of the pier's lights into truer darkness. The shadows shifted, took on depth and shape. In one of the boats, the shape it took didn't fit with the rest. It lay heavier, more solid, sprawled and untidier than the work of the most careless sailor. Its sprawl had limbs, an arm, a hand flung out, hanging limp over the side of the vessel in which it lay.

"Damn it." I sank to a crouch on the deck beside it. The shadows resolved themselves further and gave the shape a recognizable face.

Jared Williams lay in the bottom of the small, peeling dinghy, staring up empty-eyed at the foggy sky. He was obviously dead, and not by gunshot. There was no wound, no blood. His head twisted to the side at an unnatural, sickening angle, expression fixed forever in ludicrous surprise and indignation.

Someone, or something, had broken his neck.

I had just spoken to him less than half an hour ago, which meant he couldn't have been dead for long. Wrapping an arm around the nearest piling for stability, I leaned out and patted down his body, looking for the firearm he'd threatened to use against the occupants of the pier. If someone had attacked him, why hadn't he fought back? It must have happened fast, because he showed no sign of struggle, no defensive wounds on his hands, no torn clothing, no visible bruising on his face or wrists.

Why would someone else kill Jared?

Something splashed in the water a few feet from the boat, and I straightened, adrenaline jolting through me. A round, dark head with two shining eyes stared back at me from the smooth black water with frank curiosity. One of the pier's residents had come to investigate my strange behavior.

"Did you see what happened?" I asked it, just in case.

It didn't respond. I felt silly, but an idea struck me, and I fumbled for the abalone hanging on the chain around my neck. "Recognize this? Are you one of Naia's people?"

In a graceful, sinuous motion, the sea lion dived beneath the water, out of sight. I sighed. "I don't know what I expected."

Still, it wasn't an entirely crazy thought. In fact, it became more plausible the more I entertained it. Like Jared had said, regular sea lions and selkies looked pretty much the same, and I had no way of telling if any of the creatures hauled out by the pier could shift into human form.

What if one of Naia's people had taken revenge on Jared? What if they had heard his threats and struck before he could carry them out? Or what if Naia herself had emerged from the water to fight back? I could hardly blame them or her for that. I probably wouldn't have stopped them, if it came right down to it.

Even if I wanted to, I couldn't report my suspicions. No one would believe me, and besides, I had an obligation not to implicate my client, let alone on a mere theory unsupported by evidence.

So where did that leave me? It left me on a deserted private dock, standing over the very recently murdered body of a man who had threatened me a scant hour ago. It left me the last known person to have spoken to him before his death, a person who had threatened him and more or less kidnapped him earlier that day, right before his wife mysteriously left town.

It didn't just make me a person of interest. It made me a murder suspect.

That meant I had two choices. I could do the right thing, the responsible thing, the thing an innocent person would do, and call the cops to report that I'd found Jared's dead body. I could trust law enforcement to follow the clues, find all the evidence, and figure out the truth, rather than settle for the easy, obvious answer.

Or I could do the smart thing and fly the hell away from there as fast as my little demon wings could carry me. I could even run, if I had to—or better yet, walk calmly and coolly away like a good citizen out for a casual late-night stroll along the marina. I probably still had a little juice left, though, enough to get me off the wharf and out of sight of any other witnesses.

The cops might still try to pin it on me, given the victim's last phone call and my earlier indiscretions, but at least they wouldn't get me at the scene of the crime. Plus, given the body's location, no one would likely find him until dawn when the fishing boats went out.

It would buy me some time, maybe even enough to do a little investigating of my own.

I squared my shoulders, digging deep for the energy that would summon my wings. It didn't come easily. In the maelstrom of chaotic thoughts and barely controlled panic, I struggled to center myself. I didn't have much to work with. I'd stopped myself before I drew any more from Danny than I needed for a short flight. I would have to feed well or sleep for a good long while after this, to recharge.

My wings stirred within me. Energy became matter, and I mastered it. Pinions materialized, displacing the air around me, taking on form and mass, unfolding like a sigh.

At that moment, a beam of stark white light swept across the water and flooded the dock where I stood. I dropped the wings as the light touched them. Whatever came next, whoever had seen me, I preferred to meet it as a human. Let them think they'd seen a mirage, not a miracle.

Yeah, they would figure out the truth eventually, but in cases like this, first impressions mattered.

"Step away from the boat, ma'am," boomed out a male voice, amplified by a megaphone. "Turn around, please, and keep your hands where we can see them."

That didn't sound like routine harbor patrol procedure, but a girl could hope. I lifted my arms above my head and obeyed, a deliberate half-pirouette without a modicum of demon grace. The glare blinded me. I shielded my eyes with one hand, unable to make out anything beyond a host of black silhouettes at the end of the main pier.

"I'm not armed! Please, I was just trying to help."

"This is the SFPD. That dock is off-limits to the public. What are you doing out there?"

"There's a man in this boat." I shifted my Presence as I spoke, letting my panic tremble in my voice. I didn't pose any threat to them. I only wanted to help. "You should probably call an ambulance. Something's happened. I think...he might be dead."

When in doubt, tell the truth. I told the People's witnesses that a lot, back when I was still a DA. Well, *might be dead* was a stretch—he was indisputably a hundred percent dead—but the rest was true. Telling the truth made me a concerned citizen, not a killer or a demon or a flight risk or a person who had ever broken or considered breaking any law.

If they assumed the first of those characteristics precluded all of the latter, that was their problem, not mine. I could be more than one thing at once. I contained multitudes.

Most importantly, in this *particular* context, I was innocent.

I blinked, eyes streaming in the blaze of the floodlights—the fast transition from night vision to normal vision sucked, but the tears certainly didn't hurt my case—and waited patiently for them to figure that out.

Hopefully, my Presence would speed their deductive skills along, because multitudes notwithstanding, I didn't have anything close to the patience of a saint.

9

PERSON OF INTEREST

"Ms. Knight, are you even listening to me?" Detective Huang squinted at me across the dented table of the SFPD interview room. "Seems like you have something on your mind."

"I'm so sorry. Would you repeat the question, please?" I shot him my best prosecutor's smile. It said we played on the same team, that we held all the cards and the house always won.

The only problem was that it wasn't true anymore. Sitting at the other side of the table, on the defense after a sleepless night under official scrutiny, I was out of my element, and we both knew it.

Huang didn't have a demon's senses, but he was sharper than most of his peers. "You were the last known person to speak to Mr. Williams before his death." His energy tightened to a focused pinpoint as he pressed his advantage. "He called you seven times last night. The last time, you answered and spoke with him for several minutes. What did you talk about?"

I paused, considering my answer. As a lawyer, I would have advised myself not to answer any questions or volunteer information. I would tell my client that they had no obligation to make a statement. I'd agreed to this interview for a reason, though. If I played this right, I could learn what the cops suspected, what they knew, and whether they had any information I didn't have, without further incriminating myself. "Mr. Williams wanted me to divulge confidential information about one of my clients. Naturally, I declined to provide it."

"I see. And that client would be..."

I didn't say anything, letting his prompt hang in the air. Most witnesses would fill the silence by instinct, but I had used this ploy myself too many times to fall for it.

"You know as well as I do that client identity isn't privileged, Ms. Knight."

"And I know I have the right to remain silent. You're welcome to file a subpoena, of course."

He sighed. "That won't be necessary. We know you met with Mr. Williams' wife, Naia, earlier in the day. It stands to reason that Mr. Williams contacted you because of that meeting."

I said nothing, waiting for a real question while the detective's aura fizzed with frustration. He had a working theory, but two could play the silence game.

"We haven't been able to locate Mrs. Williams." He leaned back, arms crossed, dark eyes clocking my resistance. "She seems to have disappeared shortly after her meeting with you, along with her daughter. Do you know where she is?"

"Even if I did know her whereabouts, that information *is* privileged." Naia swam safely somewhere beneath the choppy water of the San Francisco Bay, or so I hoped.

He nodded, resignation dimming his aura, but then it flashed with sudden aggression. "You confronted Jared Williams in person at his residence mere hours before his death. Why did you go there? What did you want from him?"

They knew more than I expected. I smothered a spark of panic. "I visited Mr. Williams in my capacity as Naia Williams' attorney on a civil matter."

"Interesting." Huang paged through the folder on his desk. "We have a police report here from yesterday afternoon. Jared Williams alleged that you broke into his home, threatened him with bodily harm, and kidnapped him."

"Anyone can file a false report." I kept my cool, barely. Technically, I had done everything he alleged in his report, but I didn't have to admit it. Besides, that asshole had deserved it. "Do you have any familiarity with DARVO tactics, Detective Huang?"

His forehead creased, and momentary confusion disrupted his triumphant energy. "I can't say I do."

"If you've ever worked a domestic violence case, you should." I injected a subtle Presence into the stern tone, equalizing the power differential in the room a little. "It means deny, attack, and reverse victim and offender."

I had underestimated Jared's confidence that the justice system would protect him, a rookie mistake. Abusers like him didn't hesitate to enlist authority for their own ends. Of course, in hindsight, I had opened the door to his accusations. But I had done it to free Naia, and that was what mattered.

"How is that relevant here?" Huang favored me with a keen glance. He had a strong will and wouldn't bend to mine so easily.

His resistance brought a twinge of guilt. He was doing his job, and he believed he was doing the right thing. I couldn't let him continue down this path, and even though I knew the truth, I couldn't tell it without further jeopardizing myself and potentially Naia as well. "It's relevant because Mr. Williams was not a good man. For my client's sake, I can't say more than that."

"If you're saying he was a domestic abuser, there's no evidence of that. No record of 911 calls at his address."

I deepened my Presence. "Not all abuse leaves a record, Detective."

"We'll look into it, of course, if there's any evidence to look at. Good or not, the man is dead, and right now the evidence I have tells me you know more than you're saying."

"I know my rights." I had planted reasonable doubt in his mind, at least, the seed of an alternate theory. Time for a change of tactics. "I stand by the statement I made at the scene. When I found Jared Williams on the pier, he was already dead."

"Yet you never explained why you went there in the first place. You went to meet him, didn't you? Why?"

Maybe I could give him a crumb. "Based on his own statements and what I knew of his character, I had reason to believe that Mr. Williams' state of mind posed a threat to himself and others, including myself." I cleared my throat and took a breath. Was it worth the risk? "Mr. Williams told me he was armed and would perpetrate a mass shooting unless I met him last night. I had no choice."

That surprised him. His aura shifted, though the shade of skepticism didn't fully fade. "Why would he do that?"

"I wish I could say for sure." I poured my focus into a genuine Presence, making sure he could sense the truth of my words despite his suspicion. "He was irrational, enraged. I believe he had a grudge against me for helping Naia. Men like him pose the most danger for violence when a victim leaves them, you know. He couldn't hurt her, so he saw me as the next best target."

Huang took that in—really took it in, to my relief. "You shouldn't have gone there yourself. You should have reported it and let us take care of it."

"You're probably right," I said. "I wouldn't be in this position if I had, would I? But he made it clear that if I did try to call the cops, he would start shooting. I didn't want to put anyone else at risk, whether they be bystanders or your officers."

"Well, I appreciate it, but that's literally our job, ma'am."

I gave him an apologetic smile. "It was a stressful situation, and I didn't have much time to think it through, I'm afraid. I hoped I could talk him down, I suppose."

Huang shook his head. "Never be a hero, Ms. Knight. That's the first rule for civilians." He frowned down at his file and disquiet reentered his aura. "Let's say I believe your story, though. Would it surprise you to learn that Mr. Williams wasn't armed?"

Damn, and I'd just started to relax. On the other hand, that was the new information I'd wanted. "He lied, then."

"Maybe so." Detective Huang caught my attempt to read his notes upside down and closed the folder with a snap. "Still, you took a big risk, and I can't condone that."

"I did what I thought was right." I had probably pushed this as far as I could go. At least he seemed to believe me now. "Any other questions, or am I free to go?"

"You were always free to go." His dry tone called out the innocence of my question. "We're not filing charges—today. Don't go anywhere, though. It's safe to say you're still a person of interest in this investigation."

"Thorough of you," I said, equally dry. "I wouldn't expect any less from you men in blue."

"If you think of anything you've forgotten to share with us, please don't hesitate to call us."

"Of course." I stood. "I wish you the best of luck in your investigation. Maybe you could look into who else might have met Jared on that pier before I got there."

"We are pursuing all possible leads, Ms. Knight."

"I certainly hope so." I had the sinking feeling, however, that whoever had met Jared Williams out there on the dock had left no trace behind.

Had they descended from the foggy night, like me? Had they left the same way, silent and unseen, mere minutes before I arrived?

Or was my imagination simply getting the best of me again?

A few scant hours of sleep and a hasty shower later, I sat on the garden patio of a tiny yet expensive French bistro a few blocks from the courthouse, refolding my napkin on my lap for the twentieth or so time while I tried my hardest not to panic.

I didn't need another thing to worry about right now, yet my bad luck this week remained unabated. As of this moment, Sebastian was thirty-eight minutes late for our lunch date, and Sebastian was never late.

I checked my phone again, but he still hadn't called. What on earth was keeping him? He couldn't have forgotten—we'd planned it on the phone this morning as I blearily headed from my late night with the SFPD to the jail to meet with Rae and he got ready for his own day in court. He hadn't read my last text, either, and I'd sent it twenty-three minutes ago.

The server, a skinny young man with a beaked nose and slicked-back sandy hair, stopped at my table to give me a sympathetic smile. "Are you sure I can't get anything started for you, madam?"

I grimaced. "I'm fine—no, you know what? I could use a cocktail. Something strong, please. Preferably with whiskey."

"Perhaps you would like a Sabbatical, then. It's made with bourbon and cacao nib rum."

Sure, it was the middle of the workday, but my demon physiology would keep me from coming off like a bona fide day drunk. I could only hope the bourbon would at least take the edge off my rising sense of dread. "A Sabbatical sounds perfect." God, it really did. I needed a vacation. "I'm sure my lunch partner will be here soon," I added, more to reassure myself than anything else.

"Of course, ma'am." Oozing blandly discreet acquiescence, the server withdrew. He made it look convincing, but his desiderata gave away his skeptical pity. He thought I'd been stood up.

Maybe I had. I didn't think anything could top the week I'd already had, but getting ghosted without warning by the man I loved would certainly fit the bill.

It figured, didn't it? With all my trauma and my alleged addiction to drama, I couldn't blame him for bugging out. Mostly, it surprised me that it hadn't happened before now.

I hadn't even told him about the potential murder charges yet. Or the long-lost father lurking in the wings. Or the thing that happened last night with Danny.

The server dropped off my cocktail without a word, and I took a long sip that burned a bittersweet trail of fire down my throat.

Technically, taking Danny's hand like that didn't violate the terms of our relationships, but that energetic bond felt different than the casual encounters that had Sebastian's blessing. It meant more than any of them did, felt more intimate, and it had packed a real punch of a power-up.

I had acted impulsively. I hadn't thought about the consequences or who I might hurt. Maybe I deserved to be ghosted.

"Lily."

I choked on my drink and twisted around in my seat, airways aflame, unable to speak.

He looked like a ghost, the way he stood a few feet away from me in the doorway of the restaurant, his tone almost unrecognizable, eyes colorless and desolate as the winters I'd left behind with my childhood.

"What is it?" I found my voice. "Why didn't you call?"

He dropped his head, passing a hand over his face and sending the hair falling over his forehead into further disarray, a nervous tic. "I'm sorry. I meant to. I just…"

"I've been waiting for almost an hour." I bit back the rest of the recrimination I'd prepared. If any of the men in my life deserved the benefit of the doubt, Sebastian should get it first. It wasn't like him, forgetting to call ahead with an ETA. What could have thrown him this far off his game? "It's all right. Just tell me what happened. Is it Helena again?"

"Yes." He let me pull him toward the table, but the vortex around him around him didn't lessen. If anything, it intensified, blanking his aura in white-out conditions. "She's gone."

"I don't understand."

"She never showed up for court. Her attorney says he can't reach her. No one knows where she is. And I'm afraid—" He cut himself off and sank into the seat opposite me, his hand slipping from mine as he retreated inward, lost in the storm.

"You think something happened to her," I said softly. I wasn't the only one who went through something terrible around this time last year. Sebastian had watched an intimate partner die in gruesome circumstances. Though their relationship hadn't gone beyond a casual basis, the loss had still left a mark on him, as had the strain of facing charges for her murder.

"I don't know what to think." He shook his head, gaze still abstracted as if trying to parse a particularly difficult set of variables. "Things have been so strange with her lately."

"You still care about her, don't you?" I didn't mean it as an accusation, though when Helena first showed up in San Francisco, I had worried that their romantic bond would rekindle. I'd worked through my insecurities around that, for the most part. Besides, it would make me the worst kind of asshole if I acted possessive when he'd given me *carte blanche* for my extracurricular activities.

"Yeah. Yeah, I do. Not in the same way as I once did, of course." He gave me a shadow of a smile, reassuring me despite his obvious distress. "When you share your life with someone, that connection doesn't just go away."

"I know," I said. "It doesn't stop. It transmutes. Even if it turns to hatred, it's still part of you. They're still part of you." Maybe Ariel had taught me one true thing after all.

That made him look at me, really look at me this time, and he let out a breath. "You do understand. I wasn't sure... It's all so complicated."

"Please. Complicated is practically my middle name." I didn't get the laugh I wanted, but when I leaned forward and took his hand again, his fingers closed around mine and didn't fall away. Thoughts of my charged moment with Danny rose unbidden, but I pushed them aside for later. Now was not the time. "Tell me what I can do to help."

"I don't know what to do," he said. "My lawyer wants me to stay out of it. He thinks this is some kind of mind game and she'll turn up if we don't take the bait."

That didn't sound unlikely, but it wouldn't satisfy Sebastian, not in his current state. Intense didn't begin to cover it. "What do you want to do?"

"Someone should check on her." He stared down at our linked hands, then raised his eyes to mine. His plea shimmered in his energetic aura. "I know where she was staying. Will you go with me?"

I squeezed his hand as I knocked back the rest of my drink.

Sebastian's lawyer was right. This was a bad idea. But I wasn't his lawyer. I was his partner. His agitation blurred into my own, the familiar fear that the choices we made for ourselves had led to irreparable harm to someone else.

I wasn't about to tell him no and force him to face this by himself.

"Let's go, then." I set the empty glass on the table and stood. "I'll drive."

10

Birds of a Feather

Following Sebastian's terse directions, I sped south out of the city along the winding highway that traced the boundary between California and the Pacific Ocean. The afternoon had sent the fog retreating over the sea. Sun sparkled on the expanse of wind-stirred water to our right, though I couldn't afford to look for long, or I'd get preoccupied by the way the ragged cliffs plunged feet from the road into churning white surf far below.

In a classic film, the heroine would have made this drive with the convertible top down, a carefree smile on her face, and a stylish scarf tied over her perfectly coiffed hair as she glanced sidelong at her co-star. But this wasn't a movie, and my day hadn't given me much time for fashion choices beyond clipping my hair back in a twist that might come off as professional to an undiscerning eye. Eve had called it, with full teenage scorn, "basic cringe."

As a basic cringe non-starlet with too much on my mind, I tightened my jaw and focused on guiding Blue Betty safely through the twists and turns of Highway 1. Driving still made me nervous, especially on a single lane that veered too close to a steep drop-off. Heights didn't usually bother me, but the small car felt like a steel trap with no space to sprout my wings, no way to save us both if I made a mistake and sent us rolling over the edge.

"I didn't realize Helena was staying so far out of town," I said into the tense silence crackling between myself and my passenger, who had ceased to issue directions some time ago.

He sat still as a graven image beside me, staring straight ahead without sparing a glance at the sea or the dark pine forests that marched up the slopes on the other side of the road. Apparently, the scenic route was lost on both of us this afternoon.

"Sebastian?" I prompted him when he still didn't respond. "How much farther?"

"What?" He stirred, looking blank. "Oh. Just a few more miles, I think. It's right off the highway. You can't miss it."

"Are you all right?"

"No." His mouth twisted in a bitter smile. "But you knew that."

"Yeah. Sorry." His silver ring blocked my ability to taste his desiderata, but his wordless tension told me enough. He worried for this woman who had evicted him from their shared lives. She hadn't given him any reason to keep caring for her, but if she came to harm, he'd hold himself responsible, despite the possibility—probability?—that she had simply disappeared to leave him holding the bag yet again.

I loved him all the more for it, the kind of love that sent an unfamiliar sharp pang through my chest, but I didn't have to like it. He deserved better than this petty drama of hers.

I cast around for a better topic of conversation. I should probably tell him about my father's sudden appearance, but...*nope, not ready to talk about that, not now, maybe not ever.* My adventures on the wrong side of the law would definitely distract him, but it would also add to his worries.

Sebastian, perceptive even in crisis, beat me to the punch and changed the subject himself. "You never mentioned where you disappeared to last night."

I sent him a sidelong glance. "It was a work emergency, of sorts."

"Too bad. I was hoping you had a hot date."

"No way. You *were* my hot date." But I owed him more than banter in return for the tangible effort it took him to shift out of his dark mood. I owed him the truth, at least a little. "A client's husband called me and made some nasty threats. I had to take care of it before someone got hurt."

One eyebrow lifted, his attention caught. "That sounds serious. Dangerous, even."

"Not him. Not for me, at least." The import of that distinction left me abruptly somber. If things had gone differently, if sudden random death hadn't found Jared at just the right time—the few minutes between my conversation with him and my grisly discovery on the dock—innocent people might have died before I could stop him.

"Of course not," he said. "Still. You may be a superhero of sorts, Lily, but I wish you'd consider your own safety a little more."

"Safety? Please." I scoffed. "Have you even met me?"

"Yes, and anything at all is more than zero, so I feel more isn't too much to ask."

"He couldn't have harmed me." I had gotten lucky, perhaps. But luck didn't really cover it. If I didn't know better, I'd say someone—or something—had been looking out for me.

I suppressed a shiver. If I had a guardian angel, it struck swiftly and silently, with the strength to snap a man's neck before he could fight back.

"Every hero has their kryptonite." Sebastian sounded unconvinced.

"Sure they do, but he wasn't it." Or so I assumed. The police had refused to tell me if Jared had a weapon on him, and I'd decided not to ask about silver bullets. With a grimace, I added, "That guy wasn't a supervillain. He wasn't super anything. He was an entirely mediocre, boring, bog-standard asshole who decided to make it my problem."

"So you took care of it."

"Let's just say the problem solved itself." Jared's terrified, dead face floated on the surface of my mind, gleaming with the sickly light of a sodium lamp reflected in oily water. "He won't bother anyone else."

"You know, you scare me a little sometimes."

"That's the price you pay for dating a demon." I shot him a toothy grin, pushing back my morbid thoughts.

"Not at all. It's one of the things I like about you." A trace of affection warmed his tone, if only briefly. Like me, he was trying, and like me, he couldn't muster quite enough normalcy to lift the weight of the worries we carried.

I winced, haunted by a newly raised specter of guilt. "Sebastian, I—there's something I need to tell you."

A slight frown creased his forehead. "I don't like the sound of that."

"It's nothing big. Well, maybe it is. I don't know. I'm confused about it, to be honest." I just had to spit it out, the quicker the better. "Um, so last night, me and...Danny and I...we touched."

"You and Danny have always been close." He leaned toward me in his seat, his voice dropping to a soft, earnest rumble. "I have no problem with that. I never have. I thought you knew that."

"Not like this," I insisted. "I mean, really touched. Skin touched. Hands, at least. And...energy."

His frown deepened. "Lily—damn it! That's our turn—no, it's fine—oh, God."

This last he gritted out as I slammed on the brakes, bringing Blue Betty around in a tight half-skid with a shriek of protesting rubber. An extended honk from the semi-truck behind me left no illusions as to how narrowly I'd avoided a collision.

"Oops." Adopting somewhat more care and less alacrity, I eased the roadster down a gravel frontage road that brought us still closer to the cliffs, where a short row of elegant cottages declared their commitment to the ocean view. "Well, I didn't miss it, at least."

"We could have turned around at the next road." Sebastian released his white-knuckled grip on the door handle with obvious reluctance, probably regretting ever teaching me to drive. "Never mind. It's that blue house at the end."

"A vacation rental?"

"Not exactly." A muscle jumped in his jaw. "Our old beach house, once upon a time. I used to rent it out, after... Anyway, I told her she could stay here. It's hers once the settlement goes through, either way."

I turned to look at him, but he'd fixed his eyes on the little cottage and didn't meet my gaze. "Wait. She's planning on staying in the Bay Area?"

"Maybe." He shrugged, mouth tight. "It's her choice, not mine."

"I thought she lived in Europe."

His expression darkened. "She said she forgot how much she loved it out here."

"Of course she did. You think she's serious, or is she just fucking with you?"

Another shrug, and he twisted his lips, wry with self-deprecation. "You know, after all this time, I still can't tell."

"Ugh. Sounds familiar." I winced as Betty crunched to a halt on the loose shoulder outside the last house on the row. Sebastian's ex and mine had too much in common for comfort sometimes, adept at beautiful, cultured appearances that hid cold machinations and a sharp instinct for hurting those they claimed to love.

"Hm? Oh, yes. Birds of a feather." The beach house sat silent above us, a two-story cottage with a peaked roof and painted robin's egg blue. It didn't look very weathered, despite the location, but then, Sebastian wouldn't let a place he owned get run-down. It also didn't look particularly inhabited, with no lights on inside, but a covered vehicle with slender, sporty lines occupied the car park. It was still daytime, after all, but the brief sunshine we'd failed to enjoy on our drive had given way and the encroaching marine layer leached the colors from the afternoon, dimming the sea to rough, chilly gray.

"Well. We're here." In the tick of the cooling engine, I waited for him to move. "How do you want to play this? I can wait here if you prefer or knock on the door myself. I'm sure she'll be thrilled to see me." Helena and I had arrived at an uneasy détente of mutual unloving tolerance, though Sebastian rarely asked us to exercise it. The fact he'd wanted me with him for this said a lot about his state of mind.

Sebastian visibly steeled himself, seeming to come to a decision, and opened the passenger door. A stiff breeze washed into the small cabin, sharp with the cold, salt-laden breath of the Pacific. "I think we should go together."

I nodded and went around the car to meet him, slipping my hand into his as we climbed the steps to the dark-stained wood of the front door. He glanced up at the gesture, almost surprised, audibly exhaling, though he didn't smile as I'd hoped.

Yeah, neither of us had gotten used to casual contact yet. Maybe we never would.

"Ready when you are," I said.

He made a face and raised his hand to knock. Then he went rigid as the door swung away from his first touch. "Lily...it's open."

I dropped a hand on his shoulder. His tension vibrated under my palm, but he let me circle past him and push the unlocked door wide. Every sense on high alert, I stepped over the threshold to place my body between him and any danger within.

Inside, nothing stirred except the white curtains over the front window. The chilly wind wafting through the door behind me lifted them aside, revealing the cliff's edge and a gray expanse of the ocean stretching below.

"Hello?" I called. "Anyone home?"

II

THE OTHER WOMAN

"I don't like this," Sebastian muttered behind me.

"Me neither." Despite the eerie silence, the interior showed signs of recent habitation: a dark green and white plaid woolen blanket unfolded on the couch in front of the unlit fireplace, two plates and several wine glasses in the dish rack beside the sink of the small kitchen to my left, and a takeout box with a crab-shaped logo from a local seafood restaurant on the table in the breakfast nook near the cliff-side window.

"I think we should call the police," he insisted. "We shouldn't have come."

"Let's not get ahead of ourselves." I'd had more than enough of law enforcement involvement these last twenty-four hours, but now didn't seem like the time to explain that to him. "Stay here."

"Lily—"

"Give me a minute." I didn't have much to clear on the ground floor. The cottage had an open plan downstairs and a small footprint, so I turned my attention to the narrow staircase, climbing as quietly as I could manage in my high-heeled work shoes.

On the dim landing, lit only by the colorless light from the window downstairs, I paused to orient myself. A small bathroom on the right proved empty at first glance. My breath hitched in my throat, but when I pulled back the lace seashell-embroidered shower curtain, the bathtub held no horrors greater than obscenely expensive Italian shampoo.

Rolling my eyes—*Bvlgari? Really, Helena?*—I dropped the curtain and turned, passing several slatted linen closets to the closed door at the end of the short hall.

Dread dogged my stiletto heels, but I had come too far to turn back now. I rapped my knuckles lightly on the door and stood still, listening with my ears and my demon senses.

A whisper of energy tickled my awareness, too faint to get a read from, a mere ghost of an impression raising the small hairs on the back of my neck. No one otherwise answered my knock. My pulse quickened and I seized the knob, throwing the door open.

The bedroom was huge, taking up the rest of the top floor. Thick curtains shut out most of the daylight, but my dark vision picked up the details in the shadows, the items of clothing tossed on the floor as if discarded in a hurry and the shape curled motionless in a thoroughly unmade California king bed, blond hair tousled on the pillow. A scent lingered here too, the musk of sex and sweat mingled with a heavy sweet fragrance that made my nose itch and my blood curdle.

This was clearly a love nest. The unwelcome thought that Sebastian had once shared it with Helena barely registered, because that aroma unsettled me even more.

It smelled like frankincense. Like my worst nightmares. Like an incubus.

I wanted to back away. I wanted to run. I didn't want to know what I would find in that tangle of bedclothes. But the body there lay too still and silent, facing away from me, and I had to check. I had to make sure.

With unwilling steps, I circled the bed until I had a clear view of Helena Ritter's face, softer in repose than I had ever seen it. Just her, no strange bedfellows, and I thanked my lucky stars and killer guardian angels for that small blessing. Despite the hint of desiderata that lingered in the room, though, she lay too still. I leaned close, then closer, and my supernatural vision finally caught the oh-so-shallow rise and fall of her chest.

She wasn't dead. I backed away, a little too quickly. The flood of relief made me clumsy. I bumped into a long-necked floor lamp, knocking it against the wall with a thump and a clatter. Panicked, I held my breath, but Helena slept on—if her coma-like state could be described as sleep.

"Lily?" Sebastian's voice rang out from the hall. "Are you all right?"

Why didn't the man stay when I told him to stay? I took another sideways step, plotting my escape route to the door on the other side of the room.

Too late. Helena didn't lift her head or move, but her eyes snapped open and stared straight at me, wide and glassy. With her pupils blown, her face seemed strangely blank, almost doll-like. I froze like the final girl in a slasher flick, waiting for the jump scare.

"What is it?" Sebastian demanded from the doorway.

"Bazzy?" Helena's forehead crinkled, the thin trickle of her energy more pronounced, but clouded, weak, confused. Then recognition dawned as she focused on me. Her aura strengthened suddenly, laced with a dull malice, and I took an instinctive step back. "*You,*" she slurred, pushing herself half upright, though it seemed to require a lot of effort. "You shouldn't be here."

"I'm sorry," I said, glancing at Sebastian for help but getting nothing from his careful lack of expression. "We came to check on you. Sebastian was worried for your safety."

"How sweet of him." She bared her teeth, a smile that didn't reach still strangely wide and empty eyes before she twisted around toward him. "He always was a white knight, weren't you, Bazzy?"

"Bazzy?" I mouthed at him.

He shook his head in a fractional gesture, barely sparing me a glance. "Helena, you missed our meeting this morning. Of course I was concerned."

"No need. I'm fine." She stretched her arms over her head and rolled to face him with a languid gesture. The sheets fell away as she did, revealing her naked back, her spine a row of knobs, hips sharp as blades.

Sebastian flushed, averting his eyes as she propped herself up on her elbows, the sheet slipping lower. "Good God, woman." Grabbing a robe from the back of the door, he tossed it at her. "Put some clothes on, would you?"

"Don't act like it's anything you haven't seen before. Besides, you're the one who barged in on me unannounced and uninvited." She made no move to cover herself further, and her finger jabbed out at me. "You put him up to it, didn't you?"

I flinched from the startling venom in her tone. "What? No!"

What the hell was wrong with her? She didn't usually behave this way. Nasty sometimes, passive aggressive often, but this was different. Her aggression flashed out uninhibited and raw, as if some irrational, bizarre malevolence had possessed her.

"Liar," she sneered. "Of course you did. He never would have acted so rashly and foolishly before you came along. Selling the company, buying pianos...that's not the Sebastian Ritter I know. You're a bad influence on him."

I opened my mouth, then closed it again. Had my impulsive tendencies to leap before I looked and get myself into trouble rubbed off on Sebastian? Maybe Helena was right.

"Hel, stop it," Sebastian said. "It was my idea, not hers. I thought you might be dead."

"Dead!" She laughed, the sound brittle as old glass. "You wish, but not yet, darling. I overslept, that's all."

"Overslept? It's way past noon!"

"What can I say? I had a late night." She glanced between us, clocking our expressions. "Oh, come on. Don't tell me you thought my life ended after we did."

"Never for a moment." His voice wasn't just cold. It was glacial to an extent I hadn't seen from him—not for a long time, at least, since the first night we met, when I had done something he rightfully judged as shitty. "You made it clear to me years ago that you wanted no part of me. That's why I can't figure out why you're dragging your feet this late in the game."

"And that's where you're wrong." She leaned back into the pillows with a heavy sigh. "It was never merely a game to *me*."

"Everything is a game to you. But you play for keeps and you're a sore loser." Sebastian crossed his arms, planting himself in the doorway and incidentally blocking my exit. He seemed to have forgotten my presence entirely.

I cleared my throat, wanting nothing less in the world than to stand as witness and other woman to this old and bitter argument. "I should give you two a chance to hash this out. In private."

Neither of them paid me any attention. Helena trained her fevered gaze on Sebastian, her words swift as viper strikes. "Oh, honey, believe me. I'm not the loser here."

"I know it," Sebastian said through his teeth. "You left *me*. It's been over a decade. And the offer I've made is more than fair. So tell me what else you want. My signature in blood? My firstborn heir? My whole immortal soul?"

"Hey," I said, giving up. "No. You can't have that last part. His soul's all mine."

That snapped them out of it. They both turned to glare at me, and finally Sebastian seemed to remember himself. "Lily, I apologize. Can you give us a minute?"

"I thought you'd never ask." I softened my retort with a quick squeeze of his fingers as I slipped past him. "I'll be in the car."

"Thanks," he murmured and then went inside, closing the door behind him. Raised, muffled voices chased me down the stairs.

Hopefully they wouldn't kill each other when left to their own devices. I was already a witness—or potential suspect—in one too many active murder cases this week. I didn't need yet another capital case on my docket.

When Sebastian finally emerged from the beach house, head down and shoulders stiff, he got into the car without saying a word. After a few moments of sitting in silence, I started the engine. "Did she sign it?"

"No."

"That was weird as hell." I swung the car around, spared him a quick glance. "Do you want to talk about it?"

"No." He wouldn't look at me, his angular features hard and set.

It didn't get any clearer than that. Or did it? He probably wasn't angry with me at all, but I missed reading him so much it hurt, a hollow pang in my core. I pulled the roadster back onto the highway in a spray of gravel, earning more honks from motorists on both sides.

"I'm sorry I got you mixed up in this," he said at last. "It's not fair to you."

"It's not that. Something was going on with her. Didn't you smell it? She had an incubus in that room last night."

"Lily, I don't care who or what she sleeps with." He leaned back in the seat with a weary sigh. "I just want the damn paperwork signed."

He didn't want to talk about it, and I had to respect that. But I couldn't stop thinking about it.

I only knew two incubi, and one of them was dead. The other one claimed to be my father. The thought of either one of them carrying on an affair with Helena Ritter sent seven different chills down my spine.

12

UNFORGIVEN

"So that," I concluded, "is the story of my terrible, horrible, no good, very bad day. Otherwise known as the last forty-eight hours."

My therapist, Dr. Harlow, stared at me for a moment and then threw her head back and laughed. She had a good laugh, full-throated and generous. "Sorry! I don't mean to make light. It's just—" Her gesture encompassed a wide range—even perhaps, the kitchen sink of therapy problems—and she laughed again.

"No, you can laugh. It's funny, isn't it?" I'd played up the humor on purpose to get that laugh, but I couldn't tell for the life of me whether she actually found my delivery funny or if she simply didn't know how else to respond.

"Let me see if I've got this right." She wasn't telling, either. Her energy seemed genuine in its amusement, but she also had annoyingly good emotional control for a human. "Since yesterday morning, you thought you saw your dead ex, met your long-lost father, helped a woman leave her abusive marriage, discovered a body, just about got arrested for murder, and got threatened by your partner's ex-wife."

When she put it like that, how else could she respond besides laughing? By the time I finished telling the tale, the melodrama of it all seemed exhaustingly overblown to me, and I'd lived it.

I hadn't even told her the full story. I left out the part about casually soul-bonding with my best friend and the fact that I'd briefly kidnapped the murder victim a few hours before he turned up dead.

"Technically, they probably would have arrested me for trespassing," I explained helpfully. "Murder is harder, but they could easily show probable cause for the strict liability misdemeanor charge and then— You're laughing again."

"I've noticed you often use humor to deflect the topic from your feelings about things. Among other methods, like going into lawyer mode."

So the laughter was a ruse, which supported my theory that Dr. Harlow was either part-demon, had a silver alloy skeleton that made her impervious to my wiles, or was just a human who was very, very good at her job. I didn't like any of those options much.

Why did I pay this woman to constantly call me out when I already had Danny doing that to me for free? "*Anyway*, I wasn't arrested because the detective knows me from my old job, which is good for me but overall pretty screwed up."

She raised her eyebrows to let me know she recognized the statement as another deflection. "That sounds like a lot to process at once. How are you coping with it all?"

It was my turn to laugh. "I'm here, aren't I? You know, I almost didn't come today." If not for the conditions placed on my bar license, I would have canceled the appointment first thing in the morning.

The doctor leaned back, considering me in her calm, unnerving way. She waited me out, her desiderata no louder than a soft hum of detached interest. Whether I chose to talk or not, she got paid, and then she got to go home.

I scowled at the inspirational poster on the wall, which said in large, swooping black letters on a white background, *At the end of the day, the only thing you can control is yourself.*

What kind of crap was that? It wasn't even true. Not for me. "Out of everything that just happened," I said to the motivational quote, "the thing that bothers me the most is that moment in the club."

"Tell me more about that."

"I don't know what else there is to tell. He couldn't have been there. I just keep thinking, it's been almost a full year since—" I blinked, surprised by the sudden, fierce pressure that built behind my eyes as I spoke. "I shouldn't be jumping at shadows like I am. I should be over this by now."

I hadn't told Dr. Harlow everything, but she knew enough about my past with Ariel, and she'd watched my interview. She seemed to take it at face value that I wasn't entirely human. She just didn't know I had killed the man I kept choosing not to talk about.

Mandatory therapy or not, I drew the line at confessing to crimes, no matter how much my victim had it coming. Patient-doctor confidentiality was a thing, but so were court orders.

Not that I feared anyone would come after me for Ariel's death. It was the principle of the thing. Besides, she hadn't looked at me in fear for the first time, not yet, and though I dreaded our sessions, I didn't feel ready for that moment of truth.

"But..." she prompted.

"I survived. He's not coming back." I forced myself to meet her expectant gaze. "But it's like I'm always ready for something bad to happen."

"That sounds like hypervigilance."

"Does it? All I know is, the better things are going, the worse it feels." A wry grimace pulled at my mouth. "All that chaos yesterday almost felt easier. At least I know how to deal with things going sideways."

"Of course. That's what you're familiar with. Lily, what you're describing are common symptoms of post-traumatic stress. So are flashbacks, like the ones you've described to me."

"Trauma," I muttered. "I hate that word."

"You said everything happened about a year ago," she went on, ignoring this. "Anniversaries can tend to bring up more symptoms of past stressors. Even if you don't consciously remember the date of a traumatic event, your body will often remind you."

"Great. So even though he's dead and gone, he's still living rent-free in my head." I shivered. Just like I was living rent-free in his old apartment. "How do I evict him?"

"There's no easy answer, I'm afraid. From what you have told me, this was a lasting relationship, one that began when you were quite young, around the same age as that young woman you're fostering."

"I don't see what that has to do with it."

"It could have quite a lot. I mentioned anniversaries, but that's not the only possible trigger for you. When parents see their kids reach the age of their own trauma, it can open up old wounds from their past."

I shifted in my seat. "I'm not her parent."

"You are in a parental role. Your psyche doesn't know the difference."

"Well, it should. I'm in no way qualified to be her parent. She thinks she knows so much, she acts like she's invulnerable, and I just wish I could protect her. But I can't."

"That definitely sounds like feelings a parent would have."

"Shit." A laugh bubbled out of me, and I buried my face in my hands. "I didn't have good role models for this. What made me think I could parent Eve?"

"When we don't have good role models," the doctor said, "we have to learn to parent ourselves early."

"Yeah, well, I did a shitty job of it. Case in point, getting involved with Ariel in the first place."

"It seems to me like you did the best you could at the time. You were thrown out on your own. He gave you a way to survive." She tilted her head, expression thoughtful. "I do wonder, though. All this recent external chaos, as you called it, does make for a pretty good distraction, doesn't it?"

"What do you mean? I didn't ask for this case to fall into my lap. That client came to me out of the blue. It wasn't like I went looking for a reason to get involved!" The more I thought about her implications, the madder I got. "If you think I *wanted* to walk in and find my so-called father in my office with zero warning as a distraction from this trauma anniversary or whatever you want to call it—"

"I didn't say any of that, Lily." Her cool, quiet voice cut through my rising protests like a scalpel. "I merely asked a question, that's all. It seems it hit a nerve."

I hated how well she did that, asking questions and letting my reaction make her point for me. It would have made her an excellent trial attorney. "Fine." I spread my hands, giving up. "Therapize me. Fix me, Dr. Harlow. All I want to do is forget any of it ever happened and get him the hell out of my head."

"Which him are we talking about now? Your ex or your father?"

"Yes! Either. Both. All of it! I'm ready. I may as well get my money's worth for this therapy bullshit as long as the state bar is making me come here. Tell me how to start."

"Have you tried forgiveness?"

"What?" Taken aback, I gaped at her. "You think I should forgive them?"

"I think you should start with yourself. But yes, forgiveness is a good goal, or at least understanding. Right now, you're trying to forget without forgiving. The generally recommended route is to forgive, but not forget."

"You've got to be kidding me." Jumping up from the couch, I grabbed my purse from the floor. "I don't owe them forgiveness. I don't owe them *anything*."

"I never said you did," Dr. Harlow said. "You can sit down, Lily. Your time's not up."

"Yeah, yeah. You can put it on my tab." The doorknob rattled in my hand as I wrenched it open, wheeling around on the threshold. The doctor, rising, flinched and sat back down, the blood draining from her face.

"I will *never* forgive them for what they did to me," I spat. "Not my father, not the people he left me with, and certainly not Ariel. You know what he took from me. And that's not all he took."

He'd taken others' lives. He'd taken my sense of safety. He'd taken my trust in myself when my first bad flashback almost killed Sebastian. That moment taught me I couldn't risk a kether bond with him—maybe not with anyone I had that intimacy with, not like that, fueled by the full force of an emotional and sexual connection.

Even in death, Ariel had found a way to undermine my power.

Beneath her fear, interest sparked stronger in the doctor's aura. "There's a lot to unpack here. If you'd just sit down, we can—"

"Goodbye, Dr. Harlow." I spun on my heel and slammed the door behind me.

"See you next week," she called after me.

"Looking forward to it," I muttered.

So much for therapy. The shrink's tricks to make me talk about my trauma only made it worse. The dark and hollow ache I worked so hard to keep locked down beneath my sternum coiled up my spine as I stomped away down the hallway toward the elevators.

Forgive? No. I wouldn't even know where to begin. I certainly couldn't start with the person really at fault, the one who had let the demon do all that to her in the first place.

Because that was the worst part. Ariel did what he did because it was his nature. He was the scorpion, and I was the frog. I gave him the power to sting me, and of course I got stung.

I let him do it. And in that light, forgiveness didn't make an ounce of sense.

13

MISSING PIECES

My heels echoed in the parking garage outside Dr. Harlow's office building, beating out an angry, staccato rhythm. When my phone shrilled with the tone of an unfamiliar number, adrenaline shot through me.

"Who is this?" I snapped.

"I'm calling for Ms. Lily Knight, appointed guardian ad litem for Eve De Leon." The woman on the other end sounded taken aback at my tone.

"Huh?" My hand froze on the car's door latch. I had expected—who? Someone who spoke in a deeper register and called me daughter? Surely not. "Yes, this is she."

"I'm calling from Eve's school. Ms. Knight, I don't know if you're aware, but Eve had her third unexcused absence from class today."

"What?" I slumped against the roadster. "That makes no sense. No, I wasn't aware. I dropped her off this morning. I watched her walk onto campus."

"I see. Well, teenagers can be tricky that way." The woman didn't seem overly sympathetic. "I'm sorry to tell you this, Ms. Knight, but if this happens again, we'll have to report her as a truant. That could impact your guardianship, but moreover, it's Eve's future we're concerned about."

"You and me both." Chill fear licked at my spine, but the burn of rage overcame it. "Thanks for telling me. I'll talk to her."

"We'd like to meet with you both for a conference early next week, if you can make the time."

"Yes, of course." Damn it, I had Rae's trial all next week. "Let me call you back once I have a chance to look at my calendar."

She gave me the contact information and hung up without ceremony, doubtless to make several more such calls. Gritting my teeth, I sank into Blue Betty's seat and dialed Eve.

"Where the hell have you been?" I demanded.

"At school." She lied so easily, without a trace of worry or hesitation. "Where else would I be?"

I could have reached through the phone line and strangled her. "I just talked to the attendance officer. You're busted."

A short pause echoed down the line, then a small voice said, "Oh." No denial, no feigned shock, just *oh*. Like she was more surprised it had taken this long than anything else. "Are you coming to pick me up?"

"You better believe I am. And when I get there, you better be able to explain yourself." I stabbed the screen, hanging up before she could ply me with her excuses and before I said something I would regret later. Then I let out a stifled scream and banged my head against the steering wheel a few times.

It didn't help. It didn't even hurt much.

Well, now I had about twenty minutes to figure out how to deal with my teenage ward like an adult. That meant no yelling, swearing, crying, or sitting on my hands to keep from smacking her.

"Who am I kidding?" I moaned out loud. "I'm *definitely* not qualified for this."

But qualified or not, unresolved parenting issues of my own be damned, it was up to me. I had volunteered for this role—not just out of guilt for orphaning her, but because she reminded me all too much of myself at her age.

She had made a mistake, but that was what kids did. I'd made plenty in my time. It was my job to help her do better, to be the parent no one had been for me.

It was up to me now to break the cycle. That's what Dr. Harlow would say.

I couldn't let Ariel's daughter down. She needed me, and I wouldn't fail her the way he failed me.

Across the table from me, Eve slumped into the diner booth and swirled her straw in her milkshake. "I'm sorry, okay?" The brilliant green color of the mint cookie concoction matched the shade of her eyes, which assiduously avoided mine. "I didn't think anyone would notice."

"You know I'm legally required to make sure you get an education." My forced calm wouldn't fool anyone, but I did my best. "The school takes attendance for a reason."

"Whatever. Like they care about me? I'm just another juvie kid to them. A sob story. Everyone knows we never amount to anything."

"What? No one believes that, least of all me." The last of the anger drained out of me at her glum words. "Besides, what they think doesn't matter. In a few months, you'll be an adult, free to choose for yourself. This is about what kind of future *you* want."

Maybe I had finally gotten through to her. The pout faded to a frown, and she traced a restless pattern on the white and red checkered tablecloth. "I never thought about it like that."

"It's all right. It didn't occur to me at your age, either, but I didn't have anyone to remind me."

"Huh." She shot me a sly, wide-eyed look over the rim of her milkshake. "That explains a lot."

"You know, most people would say something nice like, *but Lily, you still turned out okay.*"

"I'm just being honest. You're *definitely* not okay. You're less okay than you were last night, if that's even possible."

I groaned. "Not this again. We didn't come here to talk about my problems."

"Maybe we should. I hear that helps." She grinned, obviously pleased with herself for using my adult wisdom against me. "Besides, your problems are really loud. It gives me a stomachache."

"Hate to break it to you, but I think that's the giant sandwich and two orders of fries you ate before you ordered that artificial nightmare of a milkshake."

"Nope. It's your *processing*. It's not going well, is it?"

"No," I admitted. "But I'll figure it out. It's not like I'm ever going to see him again, anyway."

"Aha!" Eve sat up straight, alert with interest. "Him who?"

"Just a man. He came to see me at my office. No, not a man, I guess." I swallowed a sudden thick, clogged feeling in my throat and pushed aside my own barely touched milkshake. The caramel chocolate brownie indulgence had seemed like a good idea when I ordered, but the intense sweetness overwhelmed me. "He said he was my father. My real one. My...demon sire."

"Holy...whoa." Eve sat back, mouth a perfect "O" of shock. "Lily, that's huge! No wonder you're a mess inside."

"Thanks."

"No, that's not—of course you're full of feelings about it. Fathers are important even if you don't like them. You don't have to pretend it doesn't mean anything."

"I wish it didn't." I took a small sip of milkshake, but it didn't wash the bitter taste from my mouth. "Ugh."

"You're really not going to talk to him again? Get to know him more?" A wistful tone crept into her voice.

I shook my head. "No. I don't...no."

"Oh." Her face fell, but then she jumped up from the table and grabbed my hand, pulling me to my feet. "You know what you need? A distraction. We should see a movie or something."

"I'm not sure a teenager who spent the week playing hooky deserves a movie." I had reservations about the burgers and milkshakes to begin with, but I hadn't wanted to cook either, so it didn't take too much of her sweet-talking to convince me.

"Aw." She hung her head but sneaked a peek at me under her long lashes. "But this isn't for me. It's for you."

"Sure it is," I grumbled. "And I'm sure the movie I deserve to see is that Batman reboot you've been talking about all month."

"Why not? That actor is *the* hotness." Eve sounded blithe as ever, but as we headed out of the restaurant, she startled me by slinging an arm around my shoulders. "It's all right, Lily. I get it, you know."

She would know, wouldn't she? Daddy issues, we had them. "Thanks." I hugged her back, only a little awkwardly. Physical affection didn't come easily to me after years of teaching myself to avoid touch, not like it did for her. "Really, Eve, you don't have to worry about me. You're a kid. It's not your job."

"I know I don't *have* to." Sounding almost offended, she released me. "It's like you said, though. We're a team. We gotta stick together."

Well, I couldn't say the kid didn't listen to me. Maybe I hadn't done such a bad job, after all. "Come on," I said, touched by her unexpected compassion. "We'll miss the previews if we don't hurry."

"Yes!" Exultant, Eve threw her arms around me again before dragging me down the street toward the theater entrance.

The movie ran longer than I expected, as Hollywood found it necessary to devote three full hours to a rich vigilante's man-pain. When we finally emerged, fatigue dogged my steps while Eve bounced ahead with the inhuman exuberance of youth.

Fortunately, our building waited only a short walk and a long elevator away. I yawned hugely as I unlocked the condo and let Eve push past me into the apartment to dump her heavy backpack on the floor beside the couch. Then I almost bumped into her as she stood stock still beside the terrarium, facing the patio.

"Eve, what is it?"

In answer, Eve gave a little gasp, her gaze fixed on the French doors. Beyond, shadows wreathed the back terrace. "There's someone out there," she said, a panicked whisper.

"What? Who?"

"Look. On the lounge chair." She pointed, and her finger trembled in the air.

The chair faced away from the doors, looking east where the distant lights of the bridge glowed like mirages through the fog. I could just make out what looked like the back of a person's head.

"One of the neighbors must have fallen asleep on the terrace." We shared our balcony with a few other well-to-do residents, though we rarely saw them out and about. Perhaps they recognized me from TV and chose to avoid us.

"I don't think so." Eve's voice shook. "I can't feel anything from them. Can you?"

She had a point. I shifted my shoulders against the prickle of tension gathering at the back of my neck. "That's strange."

Usually, even a sleeping human exuded a whisper of desiderata. It made living in a city interesting for us demons. I had learned to tune out the background noise of human desires for the most part, like white noise.

But no trace came from the figure on the lounge chair outside. That could mean the person wore silver against their skin to shield them from demon senses. It could also mean they weren't human at all.

Or it could mean they were dead.

A heavy weight settled in my chest as I moved to the back door and switched on the outside light. The figure on the lounge chair didn't move or turn.

"Stay here, Eve."

I tried to unlatch the door, but the latch didn't turn. A second later I realized why. Cold adrenaline washed over me, numbing my fingers as I reached for the handle.

"What is it?" Eve said, high and tremulous.

My voice sounded strained and flat in my own ears. "The door's unlocked again."

"You think I—I swear, it wasn't me. I haven't been home all day."

I still didn't know where she'd been. "We'll talk about it later," I said, and stepped out onto the thick, chilly air of the terrace.

At this hour, fog tucked itself around the city like a weighted blanket. Mist swirled through the low-wattage area lighting that lined the edge of the patio.

"Hello?" I took another step toward the lounge chair.

Nothing moved. The person on the chair lay back in a half-prone position, light hair gleaming faintly, their head lolling sideways against the canvas backing.

No human would choose to sleep out here unless they were very drunk or maybe high. Had one of our neighbors indulged in an ill-advised drug trip on the terrace? Maybe that would explain the absence of desiderata.

"Hey." I rounded the patio table. "Are you okay?"

They didn't answer. Stomach sinking, I edged forward, drawing even with the lounge chair. The person's neck twisted at an unnatural angle, a slight breeze stirring fine wisps of bleached-blond hair over a still, sharp-featured face.

"Oh, no," I whispered. "Oh, shit."

The person in the chair was not okay. The person in the chair was dead.

Worse, I recognized her.

14

DEALING WITH DEMONS

The body of Helena Ritter lay sprawled on the deck chair of my back patio, head tilted at an impossible angle, gaze fixed on the dark horizon. Tendrils of blond hair had come undone from her tight- coiled chignon and stuck in wet curls to her forehead. In contrast to her earlier state of undress, she wore a caramel-colored winter coat over a flowing silk pantsuit in a black and cream flowered pattern. The light fabric hung in damp, windblown folds around her lax limbs, lending a disheveled aspect to the otherwise stylish outfit.

No blood marred her pale skin, but her lolling head left the cause of death easy to guess and all too familiar. She had died the same way Jared Williams had, her neck broken with a swift attack, unresisted.

I leaned closer. Condensation beaded on her waxy skin like tears. The barest whiff of a faint, spicy aroma teased my nose, and I jerked back.

Maybe it clung in my nostrils from earlier, as strong scents sometimes did, or maybe I imagined it, but for a moment, I would have sworn I smelled frankincense again.

"Lily?" Eve called in wavering tones from behind me.

I whirled, glaring at her where she stood in the doorway. "I said stay there!"

"Why? What is it?"

"It's..." I swallowed. "Call the police, please. Tell them there's been a murder."

"*What?* Who?"

"Just do it. Now." I backed away from the corpse in the chair, my mind racing. A tingling numbness spread outward from the center of my chest, icy shock seeping into my veins in the wake of fading adrenaline.

With it came a sense of unreality, of disbelief. I had just seen Helena hours ago. She had been fine—weird, unpleasant, but very much alive. It made no sense to find her cold, lifeless, broken body here. Yet here she lay, undeniably a victim of a violent end.

Maybe she'd come here to see me and confront me about my "bad influence" on her ex-husband. I didn't think she even knew where I lived, but she must have tracked me down somehow. Then, while I sat in the darkened theater with Eve, half-watching a grown man do stunts in a bat costume, someone had snapped her neck and left her on the terrace for me to find.

I turned in a circle, clocking the neighbor's windows, but no one had their lights on. Most of them went to bed early, it seemed.

Still, one of them had to have seen something. From the condensation that had gathered on Helena's skin and clothing, her body must have lain there for quite some time while night fell and the fog rolled in.

Maybe I could ask them, knock on some doors, but not right now. I couldn't form the right questions in my head, my thoughts jumbled and mouth dry. Given the circumstances, it might behoove me to leave the routine investigation to the authorities anyway.

With halting steps, I turned and went inside. Eve sat on the couch with her mobile phone in hand, white-faced and owl eyed. She'd taken Lucifer, her green boa, out of his cage and had him wrapped around her shoulders like a scaled emerald scarf. He wasn't my idea of a comforting animal companion, but if she took solace in his presence, I wouldn't argue.

"I called 911," she said in a small voice. "They said they're on their way."

"Thanks, kiddo." Propelled by an aimless, restless energy, I busied myself with checking the apartment, flinging open every door with my heart thudding unevenly in my ears.

The unlocked patio entrance haunted me. The killer could have come inside, could have lain in wait here. My thorough search revealed nothing untoward, however, besides the horrifying state of Eve's closet and Delilah's eyes shining out at me from the farthest corner under my bed.

She might have witnessed the whole thing, but she couldn't tell me what she'd seen. I closed the door to the master bedroom so the cops wouldn't stress her out further and returned to pace the front room, my unease unabated.

"Will you sit down?" Eve scowled at me over the back of the couch. "You're freaking Luci out."

"Tell Luci I'm very sorry to offend his majesty's delicate sensibilities." With an effort, I directed my frantic motion to the kitchen and its sink full of dirty dishes.

"You're super freaked out too." The snake flowed with slow grace across Eve's upper arm, forked tongue flicking out to taste the air. "I can feel it. You're panicking."

"There's a dead woman on our back porch. I can't say I feel particularly calm about it." The sink overlooked the porch, and I couldn't stop my gaze from flicking to the still form on the chair.

"What do you think happened to her?" Eve's tone sharpened. "*Oh*. You knew her, didn't you?"

The scrubber shook in my hand, and I almost dropped a bowl. "Yes, I knew her. No, I don't know what happened. Please, Eve. Let's leave those questions to the cops."

"The cops suck at this," Eve said with the bluntness of a child who, at the tender age of seventeen, had already faced felony charges for the crime of showing her true face in the wrong place at the wrong time. "Why can't you investigate? You solved those murders this spring."

"Ira gave me jurisdiction for that. Plus, he paid me." I stacked plates into the dishwasher with unnecessary force, the clatter punctuating my words.

Ira Delaney, my government contact from an unnamed agency, had disappeared after Rae's arrest with some vague intimations about a dangerous mission ahead. I missed him. Though human, he knew more about the supernatural than I did, and though he hid his aura with silver, he gave an air of always having a plan.

I never had a plan, and I could really use one of Ira's right now.

A thunderous knock rang through the apartment, and I startled so hard that a coffee mug slipped out of my nerveless fingers and shattered on the tile. "Fucking hell!"

"That'll be the cops," Eve announced, unnecessarily.

My heels crunching through shards of ceramic, I trudged to the front door and wrenched it open. Then I stood frozen, my professional greeting dying in my throat.

"We meet again, Ms. Knight." The woman on the other side of the threshold looked me over with a coolly smug little smirk. A small army of SWAT officers crowded behind her in the hallway, expressions tense behind their face shields.

"What are you doing here?" I glanced back at Eve, who shrugged, eyes huge. "We called the police, not—whatever this is."

"Yes, and they called the FBI, as directed." Officer Meghan North strode inside the condo without waiting for an invitation. "When you're involved in a crime, it's our jurisdiction now. Fortunately, we'd already been notified of last night's incident and were prepared to move."

North wore tactical gear but no helmet, her ash blond hair pulled back in a no-nonsense ponytail. I couldn't sense her energy, not because she was a demon but because she wore silver bracelets under her uniform sleeves to ward off my abilities.

"Put that thing back in its cage," North snapped at Eve.

"It's a boa constrictor." Eve had leaped up from the couch, and the snake still draped over her shoulders had picked up on her agitation, moving his head from side to side as he followed North's movement with an audible hiss. "It doesn't bite."

"I won't ask again." North's hand went to her sidearm. "Put it away."

"Hold on a minute." The last time I'd crossed paths with this woman, she'd arrested Eve and put her in silver cuffs that almost killed her. Now I stepped between her and my charge, hands raised to show I posed no threat. "We did the right thing by reporting this. There's no active threat here. Why the strike team?"

"When you're dealing with demons, there's no such thing as disproportional force." North gestured to her team, which moved inside with choreographed precision, banging open each door with shouts of "Clear!"

I winced as they breached the master bedroom. Poor Delilah put up with so much. The high-strung feline had dealt with more than one armed entry in her time with me, but the noise would scare her out of her tiny, neurotic mind.

Eve edged toward the terrarium and slipped the snake back into his home with gentle but unsteady hands. I put an arm around her, drawing her close, and she released a shuddering breath as she huddled into my side.

"Listen, Officer North," I said. "We were out all day and came home late to find a corpse on our patio. There's no reason to treat us like criminals."

"You're a demon, Ms. Knight, known to the Bureau as a dangerous individual with unusual strength and a propensity for taking the law into your own hands." North's hard gaze and flushed cheeks burned with chilly fervor. "Surely you understand my position. I must take all necessary precautions and consider all possibilities."

"You haven't even started your investigation, but you've already concluded I'm a suspect." The words floated out with far more steadiness than I felt, my lawyer training taking over while the rest of me panicked itself into an out of body experience. "It seems I'm guilty until proved innocent. I'm telling you, I wasn't even here."

"*Can* you prove it?" North stood aside as more federal agents swarmed into the room, armed, wary, and carrying forensics equipment. "You're the first witness on the scene. Of course you're a suspect."

"Eve was with me all night. I have receipts from dinner, ticket stubs—"

"Lily didn't do this." Eve spoke up, quavering but fierce. "I'll vouch for her."

"A demon vouching for another demon? I'd be a fool to take that at face value." North scoffed, crossing her arms. "If you wish to give a statement, you'll have your chance. Sit tight, both of you."

Surrounded by tense officers in tactical gear, we didn't have much choice. We retreated to the kitchen, as far away from the rifles as we could get without leaving the common area. Eve hunched in a corner, as if making herself as small as possible. I couldn't blame her. I wanted to do the same, but I refused to let them see me flinch.

Instead, I swept up the shards of the broken mug while I fingered the phone in my pocket, wanting to text Danny or Sebastian or both—but what good would that do me? More to the point, it wouldn't do them any good to get them involved.

Sebastian had worried about his ex-wife's safety earlier. He deserved to know about her passing, but I didn't want to tell him in a text. Besides, this could blow back on him, too.

Come to think of it, maybe he had some reason to fear for her life. I hadn't even asked him, hadn't thought to ask, and now...

Now it was too late.

Outside the kitchen window, North broke away from the forensics specialists huddled around Helena's body and came striding back toward the house. The set line of her mouth held a warning, a threat of worse to come.

She stepped inside, steely eyes fixed on me. "Ms. Knight, if you would come with me for further questioning, we'll take your full statement at our field office."

I gulped, but did my best to keep my tone steady, deliberate, and authoritative. I couldn't use a Presence on North, not with those bracelets she wore. "Are you placing me under arrest, Officer North?"

"That depends." Smooth, dry amusement laced her voice. "Are you planning to make me?"

She moved her jacket aside as she spoke to show off the cuffs hanging on her belt, but I didn't have to look to know that they were made of silver.

15

TAKING THE FALL

"What is she saying?" Eve's voice shook. "Lily, you won't go with her, will you? You can't!"

"It's all right, Eve." I held up a warning hand. I didn't need my young charge playing hero. "Let's say I go quietly, Officer North. What happens to her?"

"I can take care of myself," Eve said. "Lily, don't do this."

"Your *ward* will be fine." North sneered. "My men will see that she stays out of trouble."

"Not good enough." I shook my head, staring North down. "I need assurances. Keep her out of this."

"You seem to think this is some kind of negotiation, Knight." Her smile flashed with malicious delight. "We can do things the hard way if you like."

"Sure. Put those cuffs on me if that's how you get your kicks." I smiled back, all mirth a distant memory. "But if you want to play it like that, you won't get any answers out of me until I have a lawyer present. Plus, those things will make me sick and useless to you if you make me wait too long."

"Don't assume I need you healthy." North scowled. "I have plenty of methods for getting the answers I need."

"So, you have ways of making me talk. Very on brand for you." I had to think fast and talk faster if I wanted to get out of this free and whole. "North, I know you want to do this the easy way. That means I come willingly and you don't have to read me my rights. I'll do it, but I'm not leaving Eve alone with a room full of your goons." If this worked, I could call Danny or Sebastian and have them come by to pick up Eve. It wouldn't hurt to let them know who had custody of me, either.

North seemed to hesitate. Then she shrugged, her expression hardening. "Suit yourself."

I let out my breath, a gusty sigh of relief. "Great. Now, if I can just—"

Before I could finish, North jerked her head, and the business ends of six assault rifles came up to point directly at my center of mass. Eve gasped.

North unhooked the cuffs from her belt with a soft click that rippled through the thick air of tension in the room. "Lillian Knight," she said, advancing on me. "You are under arrest for obstructing a federal officer in her duties. You have the right to remain silent. Anything you say or do can be used against you in a court of law."

What the hell happened? "Whoa, wait. I said I'd cooperate." How had I misread North this badly?

"This isn't a negotiation, Knight. Turn around and put your hands on the counter."

"You can't do this," Eve cried out. "She didn't do anything!"

"Hush, Eve." Heart pounding, I put my palms flat on the counter and my back to North, seeking and holding Eve's wild green eyes. "Listen. We've talked about this. Do you remember what to do if something happens to me?"

"Yes," she said, mulish, but she looked as if she would burst into tears. "But Lily—"

"No buts. Promise me."

"I promise," she whispered and dashed her hand across her face.

North frisked me with businesslike speed that spared me no dignity. Her hands brushed the bare skin at my nape, and I shuddered. Thank goodness she wore silver. She did it to protect herself from me, but it protected me too. I didn't want any of her malice seeping into me or the soul bond it would carry with it.

Finished with the search, she twisted my arms behind me with sudden, painful force and shoved my cheek down onto the counter. I didn't resist. Those rifles now aimed at the back of my skull almost certainly had silver bullets loaded in their chambers. With Eve a de facto hostage, I couldn't afford a twitch that would startle an itchy trigger finger.

The cuffs clinked again, and the metal rings closed around my bare wrists. A sharp hiss escaped my clenched teeth. I'd forgotten how much silver burns hurt. The metal scalded my skin with a bitter, searing cold that made my eyes water and my stomach churn.

"I told you, I'm happy to do this the hard way." North yanked me upward by my cuffed wrists. The pressure ratcheted up the pain to a screaming fire that seemed to chew toward my bone.

I refused to scream out loud but sweat prickled at my temples and my head swam. The silver worked with frightening speed, sapping my kether reserves. I was half-human, so the supernatural energy would slowly regenerate, but it would go to waste as my body uselessly tried to heal the burn. It would do nothing to stop the corrosive effect from eating into my skin.

At this rate, how long could I stay conscious? When they did this to Eve, she still had some lucidity a couple of hours later. After that, though, she faded fast, until I came back to find her close to death. Would my human blood keep me going longer, or would I lose my strength faster?

"This is bullshit, North," I grated, teeth bared against the pain.

"Shut up." She shoved me out into the hall and toward the elevator.

The sick, dizzy throb of the silver echoed through me, and I had to focus hard to keep from stumbling. "I didn't kill anyone. Why the hell would I call *you* if I did?"

"You didn't call me." She slammed the elevator call button with the heel of her palm and pushed me inside. "You called the SFPD. Maybe you would have fooled the locals with your tricks and charms, but you don't fool me. All demons are liars. You're no different than the rest of them."

The elevator's sudden drop left my stomach behind. I swayed, then grunted in pain as North yanked on my wrists to hold me upright.

If I had lied like she said, if I hadn't asked Eve to call the police, I wouldn't have silver eating into my wrists and a federal agent disparaging my character. "No good deed goes unpunished," I muttered.

North scoffed in my ear. "You have the right to silence, Knight. If only you were smart enough to use it."

I shut my mouth and my eyes. The elevator ride seemed to last forever, an endless fall from grace. My thoughts lagged in time with the sickening pulse of the silver and pulsing red floaters swirled on the inside of my eyelids.

Finally we jerked to a nauseating halt and North hustled me forward. The bright lights of the building's lobby stabbed into my ocular nerves with migraine intensity. When the relative darkness and chilly air of the night outside struck my face, I bit back a moan of relief.

North frog-walked me to a black SUV waiting by the curb and pushed me inside, slamming the door. I curled sideways in the seat, breathing through clenched teeth, holding as still as possible to avoid further friction of my wrists against the cuffs. Distantly, another slamming sound shook the vehicle. I squinted, vision smearing, but an opaque pane obscured the front seat. If North was driving, I couldn't see her.

The SUV accelerated and I lost my balance, falling heavily against the far door. She hadn't even had the decency to strap me in.

My throat tightened, ears pounding with an erratic rhythm. Ariel had warned me once about government black sites and terrible experiments. I'd fought and killed him in the ruins of one such site in the desolate Nevada desert.

I had taken a skeptical view of his horror stories, but I wouldn't put it past North to disappear me. I could end up in a holding cell in some undisclosed location. I might never see Danny or Sebastian or Eve ever again.

Dizzy, I struggled upright in my seat. I needed a plan. I couldn't let them take me like this. I had to get away before I lost my strength, my clarity, my will to fight.

Lassitude had already spread through my muscles like a drug, stealing my demon strength. But I still had one ace up my sleeve. My ability to phase through solid matter didn't spend kether.

It wasn't my strong suit. My human flesh didn't take kindly to this trick, for one thing. The departure from rational, normal physics disturbed all of me, for another.

It also wouldn't necessarily leave me better off. I still needed to get the cuffs off somehow, and I would have to pick my timing well or end up as a smear on the pavement.

It was a bad idea. It could kill me. It would definitely make me a federal fugitive. Still, I didn't have a lot of options available. I couldn't prove anything from a maximum security prison while dying from silver exposure.

If I could pull this off, maybe I could find out who was really behind these murders and clear my name. North might hate demons in general, and me in particular, but even she would have to let me go if I could prove my innocence beyond a shadow of a doubt.

Never mind that the burden of proof shouldn't have fallen on me. The normal presumptions and rights didn't matter here, because she didn't see me as human. The rules didn't work the same for me.

But that blade could cut both ways, couldn't it?

I pressed my nose up against the cold, tinted glass of the SUV's window. My night vision had drained away already with my kether reserves, leaving my view no sharper than that of any other human. Sodium-orange lights flashed by outside, illuminating glimpses of tall steel barriers like vertical bars with nothing but darkness beyond. The sound of the vehicle's wheels had shifted to a new rhythm, the thump-thump of sectioned roadway under the tires.

Then the shadows dropped away for a moment, revealing a rippling, reflective surface stretching toward a clouded horizon, dark and gleaming, the city lights glancing off the San Francisco Bay.

The bridge. I twisted around and could barely make out the dark slopes of Treasure Island behind us. Dread hollowed out my chest, my worst fears confirmed. My captors had headed east, out of town, not to the local field office at all—but where? The nearest Air Force base lay northeast of the bay, but for all I knew they had somewhere farther, more secret, better hidden in mind.

I had to act now. I might not get another chance.

Forehead against the window, I turned the mantra I'd learned over in my head. *I am the master of my matter.* If I got it right, if I willed it so, the glass should have given way like smoke and let me slip through the empty space between its atoms, out into the night.

Nothing happened.

"Crap," I whispered. Of course it didn't work. The silver grounded me, binding me to my mortal flesh and bones with the promise of their waiting death. Even if my succubus trick could get the rest of me out of the SUV's door, I couldn't affect the cuffs themselves. Good thing I was so bad at this, or I might have gotten myself stuck halfway.

I needed the damn things off me. Experimentally, I grasped one hand with the other behind me and squeezed. It hurt a lot. The effort left me breathless, but I squeezed harder, pressing the joint of my thumb beyond the range of its socket.

Something inside my hand cracked and sharp, hot agony shot up my forearm. I stifled a cry, but some sound must have carried, because the one-way divider lowered between me and the driver's cabin. North's face peered over the back of the seat.

I went still, doing my best to embody a demon who had philosophically accepted her fate and would never dream of attempting a daring escape. It didn't take much to cower with chastened suffering at least. My hand hurt like hell. Why did movies always make dislocating a thumb look so easy?

"All right back there, Knight?" North asked in dulcet tones, as if she cared. "We wouldn't want you to experience an unfortunate incident in custody."

"Where the hell are you taking me?" My voice rasped, breathy and broken, like I had gathered the last shards of my defiance and thrown them at her.

"You're in no position to ask questions. We have a secure facility for...*people like you.*"

"This can't be legal!"

"So sue me," she said. "You're a lawyer, aren't you? You must understand what it means when a federal agent says the words *national security interest.*"

It meant civil rights went out the window. "Come on, North." I leaned forward in my seat to take the pressure off my wrists. "You can't possibly have probable cause to hold me on this. What's your game plan here?"

"Sit tight." She smiled her cold smile, and with that the smoked glass screen rose, sealing me away.

I sprang into action, yanking the shackle down over my throbbing thumb. My palm burned where I grasped the metal, and the cuff scraped over the knuckle, taking skin with it. I swallowed a scream and fell back against the seat, but my hand popped free at last, the stultifying drain of the silver lessoning a fraction.

One thumb down, one to go. The SUV seemed to have slowed halfway across the bridge. For once, I had a reason to appreciate Bay Area gridlock. Even around midnight on a Friday night, traffic here could reach a standstill, clogged with city folks headed out of town or visiting club goers on their way home.

Still, I had no time to waste. After a moment of slow breathing, I set to work breaking my other hand. Having one arm loose would help, in theory, but in fact every nerve of it screamed with hot and cold running agony. Cursing under my breath, I gritted my teeth, grabbed my intact thumb with the working fingers of my free hand, and wrenched the joint sideways until bone snapped.

Tiny white lights twinkled in my field of vision like malevolent fireflies and sweat stood out on my forehead. *Fuck*, that hurt. Lightheaded, I pulled my sleeve down over my free palm and dragged the remaining shackle off, dropping the cuffs onto the seat.

Now, for my next trick, I would disappear from the back of an unmarked federal law enforcement vehicle without a trace.

I closed my eyes and smothered my fears. Pain strobed through me in bloody flashes, but I sank away from it into an expanded state of consciousness. This SUV and I were both made of the same stuff at our essence, shaped from dust and empty space, traveling at the same speed. But I could change my trajectory. I didn't have to follow the same rules.

I am the master of my matter.

Free of the silver, I owned myself again, and the knowledge clicked into place inside me. I could do this. I'd done it before. No time like the present.

With one last deep breath, I hurled myself sideways, diving *through* the door. For a moment, I shared space with the machine that carried me, a strange dual awareness of its cold metal skeleton and explosive power, the combustion that fueled it beating like a second heart beside my own.

Then I left it behind. Curling into a ball, I let go of my extended awareness and slammed into the reality of solid pavement. I didn't want to pass through the bridge itself, though *not* passing through it brought on even more exciting varieties of pain.

Brakes screeched around me, the glare of headlights nearly blinding me. I rolled, hip glancing off the bumper of an oncoming car that skidded to a stop a moment too late, then stumbled up and scrambled for the narrow walkway between the rightmost lane and the bridge railing. Almost there.

I couldn't fly my way out of this. I could only run. Maybe I could make it back to Treasure Island and hole up somewhere hidden while I regenerated my kether and figured out what came next.

That all depended on whether I could stay on my feet that long, however. Afterimages crawled across my vision, chased by ominous dark spots.

A shout echoed behind me, the words lost to honking horns and more screeching tires. Somewhere deep inside me, adrenaline sparked, clearing my mind for an instant.

I couldn't rest yet. My last strength would have to carry me through this part. I reached the walkway and hazarded a glance over my shoulder.

A few hundred feet down the span, the SUV had halted. Dark figures zig-zagged toward me through the bumper-to-bumper traffic. Harsh voices reached me, faint and distant. They wanted me to stop right there. They wanted me to lie on the pavement while they bound me in silver again. They would shoot me if I didn't comply.

I had nowhere to run, nowhere to go. I was injured, weak, ill. They would catch up.

Desperate instinct urged me to run anyway. Like an animal at bay, I turned, then hesitated. On the other side of the railing, dark waves and pale breakers shone like wrinkled aluminum foil under the stark lights of the bridge.

The top rung of the barrier fence bit into the burned flesh of my hand, but I gritted my teeth, gripping with just my fingers as I swung myself over the edge.

Now I perched upon the narrow ledge on the wrong side of the guardrail. Cold wind sliced my face, whipping loose strands of hair into my mouth. I spat it out, still hanging on despite the shattering pain shooting up both wrists. Far below me, the black water waited, less smooth than expected, foam churning around the base of the bridge's towers.

Of all the terrible ideas I'd come up with in my life, this one didn't rate among my best and brightest. But beggars and demons couldn't be choosers.

"Don't move!" One of the pursuing officers had reached the walkway.

I didn't have to move, not really. I only had to loosen my grip.

"Fuck. She's gonna jump!"

"Don't let her—"

Their sudden dismay almost made me smile. "Too late," I murmured.

My abused fingers uncurled, slipping from the railing. I let go, and the dark water of the bay rushed up to meet me.

16

WATCHING OVER YOU

The gnawing pain in my wrists dragged me from unconsciousness, while twin white-hot stars of agony pulsed in both thumbs. My bruises had bruises, my head throbbed, and grit scratched my throat. Cocooned in soft warmth, I couldn't stir, weakened muscles screaming in protest at the merest twitch.

A familiar spicy scent mingled with the salt-stench of drying seawater. Pulse racing, I squinted through eyelids gluey with sand, the yellow glow of lamplight still bright enough to blur my surroundings.

I had fallen for what seemed like a long time. I remembered that much. The waves had seemed closer when I clung to the bridge than when I let gravity have its way with me. I remembered inky blackness closing around me, the crushing weight of water, the sea filling my nose, mouth, and lungs, salt stinging my eyes and searing the welts on my wrists.

I should have drowned, but I hadn't. More memories rose from the depths, graceful shapes that swirled around me in the murky water. A rounded, warm bulk had borne me toward the faint light that shimmered, mirage-like, far above. When I surfaced, choking and coughing as I gasped for air, a whiskered face had turned to mine, eyes shining in the moonlight.

The bridge had loomed over me in the night in that instant, its towers like pillars of shadow. Its span blotted out the distant sky before the sea swallowed me again.

Time slid, stopped, and started again. I foundered and sank, but my rescuers lifted me up. Soft muzzles and smooth flippers nudged me forward. They herded me through the choppy swells with gentle insistence, until coarse sand scraped my knees and blistered palms as I washed up on a cold, muddy spit like so much flotsam.

Another skip in time, and then a tall figure stooped over me, a darker silhouette against scudding clouds that glowed faintly with the city's far-off light. A distant throbbing rhythm carried on the wind, the growl of engine rotors, and a spotlight skated over the waves near the bridge.

"It's all right, Lily." His voice held a deep resonance, not the one I expected, but one I recognized nonetheless with a sinking sensation that lived somewhere between relief and defeat. "Don't be afraid."

"Samael," I croaked, now, in the lamp-lit room. "Where...?" It looked like a hotel suite, and a fancy one at that.

"Ah, good. You're awake." He sat beside the wide bed in which I lay, hands folded on his crossed knees, expression grave as he bent toward me. "You're safe here. Do not try to move."

"I can't—" I didn't want to obey him, but the struggle proved too exhausting for the moment. "You *kidnapped* me?"

"I rescued you," he rumbled. "I would not leave you defenseless for your enemies to find."

"I would have been fine."

"You cannot truly believe that. If you do, you are more foolish than I realized."

"Everyone's a critic." I rolled my eyes. It hurt a lot, more than I wanted to admit. "It's a bit early in our relationship to start questioning my life choices, Pops."

"Leaping from that bridge was courageous, but foolhardy. What was your plan if I hadn't found you?"

Me, have a plan? For such a dour-looking guy, my prodigal father was hilarious. "Anything was better than being trapped by the Feds like an animal."

"Indeed," he said. "The silver drains our rational thought away and leaves us with our wild instincts. Like a trapped creature, you broke your own hands to win your freedom, but now they will hunt you more than ever."

"It seemed like a good idea at the time." I hated to agree with him. Of course I had made things worse for myself by escaping from the Feds. I'd made myself a fugitive. "I couldn't let them take me. They think I killed someone."

"Did you?"

"No. This officer, North, she has it out for me. She was going to lock me up and throw away the key. No one would even know where to find me."

"I would have known." He cleared his throat. "I was...watching over you."

Icy pinpricks crept along my skin. "I thought I told you to leave me alone."

He stirred in his seat, an expression of sorts stealing over his face and then fading back into impassiveness. Embarrassment, perhaps, or uncertainty. "You told me to *leave*. So I left. But I still wished to know more about you, so I continued to observe you and your young charge. From a discreet distance, of course."

"You were stalking me."

"You never would have known I was there had I not intervened to pluck you from that sandbar."

"So you followed the letter but not the spirit of the law. Typical." He might not be Ariel, but they seemed to operate from the same play book. Same shady behavior, same excuses, same lip service to consent, same insistence that he had done me a favor instead of violating my privacy.

"It was not my intention to offend you."

"Sure it wasn't." The heavy smell of frankincense that now hung around the bed had lingered around the body of Helena Ritter on my patio. Now this demon claimed to want my kinship. He admitted he had followed me today. He knew where I lived.

What else did he know? What else had he done?

"It was you." Panic tight in my throat, I kicked myself free from the nest of covers. "The frankincense—I smelled it on her. You did this." Under the comforter, my clothes were stiff with seawater, filthy with sand and seaweed. My feet were bare and sandy too. I must have lost my shoes in the bay.

At least he hadn't undressed me. That would have given me an extra special brand of daddy issues on top of the ones I already had.

His eyes widened. "What are you talking about? Calm yourself. Your body is still healing. You must rest."

I ignored him, scrambling away. "Why did you do it?" The effort of swinging my legs over the other side of the bed, combined with the pain in my hands, left me lightheaded and panting, but I had to get out of there. "Is this some sick plot to bring me closer? God, I should have known."

It seemed so obvious now. Instead of imagining ghosts and shadows, demons back from the dead, the answer had come to see me at my office yesterday.

Maybe I hadn't wanted to see it. I didn't want to believe that he, too, might be a killer just like Ariel had been.

Like I was.

"Lily, stop." In a flash, he had rounded the bed and stood before me. "You're in kether-drain. You'll only hurt yourself. You need time."

"Get away from me." On my feet, I swayed, vision swimming with dark spots.

"You must listen to me," he said. "I warned you of the danger you faced."

"You're lying." I struck out at him, but the weak punch cost me. Excruciating pain sliced up my arm and the movement overbalanced me. I would have fallen had he not grasped me by the shoulders.

"You jump to conclusions very quickly." Holding me upright, he guided me back toward the bed. "Perhaps you are not thinking clearly. If you would allow me to explain—"

"I don't need an explanation." My knees gave way, a controlled collapse onto the mattress. "What I need is for you to let me go."

"That would be unwise. You're still being hunted. If you run from this room now, in your current state of weakness and dishabille, they will catch you easily."

I hated him more every minute, especially since he was right. "So I'm your prisoner instead. Is that it?"

He sighed. "I know you are inclined to think of me as a villain, and perhaps I deserve that. No matter how difficult you may find believing it, however, I am only trying to protect you."

"I never asked you to do that," I said. "I never asked for you at all."

"That is a common complaint made by children about their parents," he said dryly. "Or so I hear. You are free to leave, of course. Is that what you wish?"

Did he just make a joke? "I...yes." It sank in suddenly that I had nothing—no money, no ID, no phone. North had confiscated it all at the condo. Then again, my phone wouldn't have survived a dip in the bay anyway.

"Is there someone I could call for you, perhaps?" Samael's deep voice took on a delicate, almost hesitant timbre. "You'll need a source to heal those hands of yours."

"A source...you mean a kether donor?" I spread my mangled hands in front of me, wincing at the shooting pain radiating down my forearm. "No. There's no one."

"No one at all?" His surprise was palpable. "What of that man you were seeing? Sebastian Ritter. Are you and he no longer..."

Sitting on the bed of my father's posh hotel while he interrogated me about my boyfriend, I almost laughed. "We don't do that anymore. I mean, we're still—no. He's not my source."

"I see," he said, in the tone of a person who was doing his best not to judge and absolutely failing. "Surely there must be someone you...depend on. A friend, perhaps."

"I mean, there's Danny," I said without thinking, then amended hastily, "but we don't do that either. She's getting married for Pete's sake. To someone else. Although I guess that never stopped *you*, did it?" *Judge not lest you be judged, Pops.*

"I've found that most humans' relationships are far more complex and unique than allowed for by this culture's monogamous customs." He sounded unruffled.

"I *could* call her, but..." Guilt flickered in my belly. I had made myself a fugitive. Anyone I tried to contact now would risk becoming an accomplice to a federal crime. "They're still hunting me, aren't they?"

Danny's number was pretty much the only one I knew by heart, and if Eve had followed my instructions and contacted her after North arrested me, she'd be worried sick. *Eve.* I'd left her in the hands of North's goons. I hadn't protected her like I'd promised.

"See for yourself." He clicked on the wide screen hotel TV and a late-night news bulletin blared through the room. An overhead helicopter shot showed the bridge as a long string of lights stretching across the dark bay, with flashing emergency strobes in blue and red lined up on the span below. A reporter's crisp voiceover accompanied it.

"A developing story here on the Bay Bridge tonight, where a fugitive leaped from a moving law enforcement vehicle and attempted to escape on foot through oncoming traffic. Searches continue by air and water as several eyewitnesses tell us they saw someone jump from the eastern section of the bridge into the bay over five hundred feet below. Authorities say the suspect is still at large and may have survived the jump. In fact, we're just getting word that the suspect has been identified as thirty-one-year-old San Francisco attorney Lillian Knight."

"*Damn* you, North." Of course she'd publicized this. She hadn't even officially charged me, and they'd done a whole damn press release, not caring just how much they'd damage my reputation.

Or maybe that was *why* North had done it. What the hell was her problem with me?

The reporter continued, her tone serious in that way journalists adopted when they knew whatever they said next would make a huge splash. "A shocking development in tonight's story, as Ms. Knight makes headlines a second time this year after she claimed to reveal her own demon heritage on live TV. For more on that, let's go to Jim in our news room with the latest."

"Well, Marnie, take a look at this footage from our archives. Ms. Knight briefly became a household name in the Bay Area this spring when she appeared on Tobias Kaine's talk show and unfurled what appeared to be large, feathered wings as evidence of supernatural beings living among us. In a year full of strange news stories, however, I think a lot of us dismissed her as a local kook with a knack for special effects, someone just looking for her fifteen minutes of fame—until tonight, when we've just learned that Ms. Knight may be an alleged killer as well."

"Yes, Jim. According to a source close to the case, shortly before Ms. Knight's dramatic escape tonight, she was placed in FBI custody in connection with an active murder investigation. No word yet on the details of any charges, but again, Ms. Knight is still at large, and according to the FBI, she should be assumed armed and dangerous."

I leaned my head against the wall and watched them play the footage of my little coming out interview over and over again. In the video, I had my dark hair artfully curled—Eve had done it for me—and wore an impeccable Serious Lawyer Suit, dark jacket over my signature indigo blouse, my face animated and defiant. I looked so confident I hardly recognized myself, my eyes sparkling with mischief right before they shone out their true gold, before I let my pupils contract against the light and opened my wings like two dark, glittering clouds behind me.

In that moment, I looked like I was having *fun*.

And now, here I sat, my power drained from me, facing the consequences. Seeing that footage juxtaposed against the words "murder charges" would bring all my demonic chickens home to roost. They would hunt me until they found me, or until they satisfied themselves that I was dead. I was a fugitive from the law and at the mercy of my alleged father who might also be a murderer himself.

"It takes great courage to tell the world the truth without fear," Samael said in a deep, soft voice. "Unwise, perhaps. But know this, I am proud of you, daughter."

The words cut deep into a place inside me I didn't know existed. Unwillingly, I raised my eyes to meet his. "Let's get one thing straight," I said. "I don't trust you, Samael."

"I understand." He dipped his head. "You have made that abundantly clear. But...?"

"*But*," I said, clenching my teeth around the word, "it seems I don't have much choice right now. Whether you're really my father or not, I need your help."

Admitting it almost hurt worse than my throbbing thumbs. Worse yet, though, was the feeling that welled up behind that pain, the way it felt to hear him say those words.

I am proud of you, daughter.

My younger self would have done almost anything to hear that from the man she believed to be her father. Apparently, all it took was breaking my taboos, my silence, and my thumbs to hear it from this one.

Too bad for me because I didn't want it anymore.

"Give me your hands," Samael said. He pulled his chair up to face me where I sat at the end of the bed.

I pulled my hands back, an instinctive movement cut short by the shock of pain that shot through them "Why?"

"You said you wished for my help." His tone bespoke patience, but the kind of patience that wanted you to know just how much patience it took. "You need strength to heal. Allow me to give you mine."

"You want to give me kether?" I edged away from him. "I'm not sure I'm comfortable with that. Isn't it weird for us to do that if we're...you know. Related?"

He sighed. "Only if you make it weird, as you put it."

"Oh, so it's my fault if I'm not okay with it?"

"I did *not* say that." He squeezed the bridge of his nose between his fingertips, looking down at me. It was a spectacular, aquiline nose, the type of profile to which Greek statues aspired. "You have a succubus child in your care, do you not?"

"You know about Eve?" I frowned. *Oh, right.* He'd followed us.

"Have you never provided her with a kether gift before?"

I shifted, not liking where this was going. "I have. But that's different. She knows me, trusts me..." She didn't always, though, not at first. I used my kether gift to bring her back from the brink of a toxic pull the first night we met.

"You must know, then, that the exchange of vital energy doesn't require sexuality. It only asks for connection."

"Of course I know that."

"The bond between lovers is only the most obvious form. Others will do as well. There is the bond of friendship. The bond of caregiving. And there is the bond of kin, of parent and child."

That wasn't the problem. What if I didn't want to have that kind of connection with him? Maybe we did share blood, but that was it. "I thought cubines sent their children away to live with humans because you *can't* feed them."

"That is what we call the changeling custom, yes. But it doesn't have to be that way." Crouching before me, he extended his hand once more. "You asked for my help. Let me give you this much, at least."

I studied his face, ageless as Ariel's, the lines of its habits more pronounced around the shape of a frown than a smirk. He waited, offering me a tangible taste of what I might have had if he'd chosen to stay instead of leave. *The bond of kin.*

I didn't want to know what I'd missed. I could heal on my own, in time, but I didn't have time. The throbbing pain in my wrists at every fractional movement reminded me of the stakes. I needed my strength now so I could stay one step ahead of Officer North and clear my name.

At the same time, I still couldn't swear that the man in front of me wasn't the culprit. If he wanted to drive me to his doorstep, give me no choice but to depend on him, he could hardly have come up with a better plan. And when I washed up on the beach, nearly depleted, wounded, in pain, and desperate, there he stood, ready to help.

I didn't trust him one bit. But if it did turn out that I needed to fight him, what better way than with the strength he gave me?

"Fine. Do it." Slowly, reluctantly, I held out my hands, palms down, shaking with the effort it took to hold them steady. "But no funny stuff."

"No funny stuff," he agreed, gravely, and folded his fingers around mine.

17

BLOOD AND BONE

I could say this for Samael, at least. He didn't push his energy on me like Ariel once had, in an overwhelming rush. Instead, it stole over me with a measured, gentle warmth. It sank into my joints, where the shattered metacarpals ground together, their jagged agony mingling with the nauseating discomfort of the still-oozing silver burns.

The pain began to ebb almost immediately. Then a subtle popping sensation vibrated along my thumbs. I gasped and pulled my hands away. "What was that?"

Samael felt behind him for the chair, dropping into it as if he too could no longer stand steadily. "Bones."

I turned my hands over. The deep purple bruising marring my palms and wrists had faded, the misshapen swelling around the thumbs draining away.

"Wow." I flexed my fingers and found that only a slight stiffness lingered, a faint ache. I was used to healing fast, but this... "You unbroke them." And not only that. The silver burns had closed, the skin across the burn marks pink and smooth, no longer pulsing with inflammation.

"Indeed." He leaned his head back, eyes closed. "The damage was...extensive." His face looked drawn suddenly, older than before, and he breathed deep through his nose.

"Are you all right?" I peered at him, an unwelcome twinge of guilt arising. "You gave me too much."

It was easy to do, of course. All of my kether gifts had led to me feeling like ass, or even passing out, especially when I didn't have much left to start with. At the same time, I would have expected that after untold centuries, Samael could control his power better than his half-human daughter.

"I gave what you needed." He didn't open his eyes. "I will be fine. I have my own sources here."

I didn't miss the subtle implication that I had neglected my self-care. "I have sources, too."

"But none that you can call on in your time of need." He looked at me then, his dark eyes glinting with a hint of gold behind half-open lids. "It is no sin to depend on others, you know...daughter."

"Maybe not." I looked away. "But that doesn't mean I have to like feeding on the people I love. I'd rather keep my sources separate."

"And yet interdependence is our way," he said, voice soft and slightly slurring. The gift really had taken it out of him.

"Yes. Because we're parasites."

"No. It is the way of all things. Separateness, independence, that is humanity's illusion. Our dependence on that connection is more powerful, yes. But we are not so different from any other form of mortal life. We all need each other, Lily, human or not."

"Except we aren't mortal." I grimaced, his words sparking a memory. Ariel had told me something similar. *Is a cat evil because it kills a mouse? No, because that is what is in its nature.*

"All things must die." His eyes had drifted closed again. "Even us."

"This danger you mentioned, your rogue demon." Cautiously, I rose from the bed. For the moment, my legs seemed inclined to hold me. "If you're right, why would they go after someone who wanted to hurt me? It doesn't make sense."

"She threatened you?" Breath coming hard as if he'd run a race, he swung around to look at me under lowered brows.

"Not her." Whoever had killed Helena had to have also taken care of Jared. The two humans had died the same way, neck cleanly broken before they could fight back. "She wasn't the first. There was a man, on the docks. Jared Williams. That's why I wondered—he meant me harm."

"You still think I did this to protect you." He sounded genuinely surprised at my continued suspicion, but who could really tell with a demon? "No, Lily. That isn't my way. Whatever else you might think of me, I'm not in the habit of murdering humans."

"Maybe not, but I don't know you." I shuffled toward the bathroom. "Besides, even habits have exceptions."

"I understand. I have not earned your trust." He sank back into the chair. "Believe what you will. I have done what I could."

"That's it?" His gift had knitted my shattered bones together, but after a lifetime of absence, it seemed like literally the least he could do. I winced at the reflection in the full-length mirror, a bedraggled woman, clothes stained with salt and mud, damp hair a snarled, seaweed-strewn horror.

He didn't lift his head. "You are free to go. Is that not what you wanted?"

"Well, I'm not staying, if that's what you're asking." At the same time, I needed a ride, at least, or I'd be walking home. Not that I could go home again, not with North almost certainly staking out my condo. "I don't mean to sound ungrateful, Pops, but I don't even have the juice to fly away from here."

"As I said, you need a source. A real one, not my second-hand gift."

"Then what? Leave town like you said, to go…where?" I had no phone, no money, and no good options. Besides, I couldn't just leave. People needed me here. Eve needed me. Rae needed me. Shit, I had a *trial* next week. What the hell was I going to do about that? "Just so you know, I'd rather face this rogue asshole in single combat than slink back East to the fam. We're not exactly on speaking terms these days."

"Ah." His tone seemed pained, but maybe that was the kether-drain talking. "No, I know a place…safe from those who hunt us. Closer, within a day's flight."

A safe house for demons? Trying for skepticism, I hit sarcastic. "Do tell."

"There's a lighthouse," he said. "Less than three hundred miles north, on an island off the coast. It's tall, old, decaying even, unreachable now except by flight. No one mans it anymore."

"Sounds charming." Sure, I needed a vacation, but on a tropical beach, not some rock in the Pacific. "Not exactly a long-term solution, Pops. I still need to eat."

"It is more than it appears." Samael took a long breath, almost labored, possibly a sigh I'd earned. "Go down from the light, through the sea-door. Tell her I sent you. She'll know what to do."

"Who's she?"

"*Cee*," he said. "That's what she goes by. Not as in the ocean, but the letter. It's not her true name, but close enough."

"She's a demon, then." Our people had a tradition of secret names, since most of us lived long enough to depend on aliases for camouflage and cover.

"Not exactly. Not like us. But a friend who knows our ways."

I waited for him to continue, but he offered nothing more. "Mind if I clean up a little?" I asked finally. "Then I promise I'll get out of your hair."

"You are not in my hair," he said, but didn't rouse further. His hair was, in fact, impeccably combed and pomaded, dark and sleek in a classic Cary Grant-like style. "You're my guest. You don't have to ask permission."

His generosity reminded me a little of Sebastian and made me ashamed of my suspicions. "Thanks," I mumbled and escaped to the bathroom.

I didn't have anything to change into beyond my filthy, stained clothing, but I craved a hot shower in the worst way. A fluffy hotel robe hung on the back of the door, so at least I could wrap up in that while I figured out my next step. I turned the water on as hot as I could make it.

The pounding spray eased the lingering aches a little. I combed conditioner through my hair, coaxing out the salt-caked snarls with miraculously pain-free fingers, and for a few minutes I almost forgot that I was technically a fugitive on the run from the law hiding out with my incubus father.

When I stepped cautiously out of the bathroom some thirty minutes later, Samael was gone.

Well, then. I shouldn't have expected anything different. Leaving was his specialty, after all, and I refused to feel any kind of way about that.

The bedside lamp still glowed, but pale light seeped in around the edges of the thick curtains on the suite's window. The clock beside the lamp said 6:30 a.m.—early, but not too early for an emergency call to my best friend.

Danny picked up on the first ring. "Hello?"

"Danny, it's me."

"*Lily.*" Her voice broke on my name. "I thought... You're alive. Thank God."

"You should know by now I don't die easy." I attempted a light tone without high hopes for success. "I take it you've seen the news. Is Eve with you?"

"Eve? No. I've been worried sick about you both. What the hell happened?"

I clutched the phone to my ear as if I could absorb the comfort of her through the telecom wires. "I didn't do what they think I did. I didn't kill anyone."

"I know you didn't, Sugarbean." She seemed almost offended that I would suggest otherwise. "But running from the Feds is a real bold choice, even for you."

"It wasn't a choice," I said. "Someone framed me for this, and the Feds bought it. If they catch me, I'll never see daylight again. She...they put silver cuffs on me, Dan."

"*Silver?* Geez. Are you OK?"

"Yeah. I'm fine, at least for now." *For certain values of fine.* "Listen, I could really use a change of clothes. Maybe some shoes. I'm sorry to ask, but—"

"Say no more. I got you. Operation Clothe the Lily is a go. I always wanted to be in a spy movie," Danny added. "The Spy Who Succubused Me... Catchy title, right?"

"We'll workshop it." I could have cried with relief, but I held it together, barely, as I rattled off the hotel name and number from the notepad by the phone. "Seriously, please be careful. This officer really has it out for me."

"Got it," she said. "No jokes, no playing. This time it's personal. T minus thirty, Rios out."

"You're a bad listener," I told her. "But you're still the MVP."

"Always have been."

Shaking my head, I replaced the handset. If there was one thing Danny took seriously, it was her one-woman campaign for Getting Lily Knight to Smile.

Today, though, the smile faded fast. Pulling the borrowed robe tighter around me, I paced the suite, all my senses on alert.

Maybe I should have dealt with this alone and left Danny out of it. I could have stolen some clothes and fled the city, staying on the run, like Samael had advised the other day in my office.

Instead, I'd made my best friend an accessory to my alleged crimes.

Even if I got my kether elsewhere, the fact remained I still needed people for other things. Support. Love. A change of clothes. A ride on the wrong side of the law.

We all need each other, Lily. Samael's words haunted my restless steps.

Therein lay the problem. No matter what I did, if I never took their life force again, I would still endanger the ones I loved.

The soft knock on the hotel suite's door made me jump, even though I was expecting it. I checked the peephole and breathed a sigh of relief before unlocking the door. Danny stood on the other side with a Giants cap pulled low over her eyes, a backpack in hand, and a worried expression on her face.

"Thanks for coming." I just about got the words out before she threw her arms around me.

"What else are friends for?" she mumbled into my robed shoulder, still hanging onto me. Her energy engulfed me, comforting as a warm blanket and hot chocolate with a trace of her signature cinnamon.

I allowed myself to hug her close for a few seconds. Then I extricated myself and took the bag she handed me, senses already sharpening at her proximity. After the heady taste of her the other night, the demon inside wouldn't let me forget it. "You took a big risk coming here. You weren't followed, were you?"

"I don't think so." She peered over my shoulder, taking in the room with a speculative expression. "Nice place."

"It's not what it looks like." I plunked the backpack on the bathroom counter. "But you wouldn't believe me if I told you."

"Try me."

"He *says* he's my father." I did my best to sound nonchalant.

"*What?!*"

"Yeah, exactly." The bag held neatly folded dark jeans, a sports bra, T-shirt, and a flannel button-down, along with ankle socks. Under it I found a pair of black sneakers, a second baseball hat, gloves, and shades. "This is perfect, Dan. You have real potential as a secret agent." Or a criminal, as the case might be.

"Wait. Stop. You mean your *real* dad?"

"Allegedly." Bless her, she had even remembered panties. I shut the bathroom door between us and stripped off the robe, throwing on the clean clothes. "He picked me up off the beach last night like so much driftwood."

"Wow. Where is he now?"

"Hell if I know. He left." Again.

"Oof. I'm sorry." Danny's voice floated to me from close by, soft with sympathy on the other side of the door. "Wish I could have met him. We would have had words, for one thing. What's he like?"

I frowned at my reflection, any resemblance to him eluding me. "Tall. Dark. Frowns a lot. Deep voice, like a tomb. Looks and talks like a Hollywood star circa 1950."

"And he just came out of nowhere to save your life? How very demon ex machina of him."

"Not exactly." Emerging from the bathroom, I looped my hair through the back of the baseball cap in a makeshift ponytail. "He came to my office the other day, but I yelled at him until he went away. Or so I thought. Turns out he was still following me, hence the convenient rescue."

Danny leaned against the wall opposite, arms folded, one eyebrow raised. "Seems sketch."

"Definitely sketch." The sneakers didn't fit quite right, but close enough. "Whose clothes am I wearing, by the way?"

"Mostly Berry's, if I'm honest. The shirt's mine though." Danny tilted her head, a frank assessment. "It's a good look, not gonna lie."

"And the panties?"

"Um, those are Berry's, too." A rosy flush darkened her cheeks under her tan. "Don't look at me like that. It's not my fault you two are the same size!"

"I'm not sure how I feel about wearing your fiancée's underwear. Or how she'll feel about it."

"It was an emergency." Danny's eyes skated away from mine. "Anyway, she won't miss them." An undercurrent of shadow stirred in her aura, a hollow misgiving she struggled to keep hidden.

I didn't have time to press for her secrets now, no more than I had the right to read them. Shouldering the bag, which now held my saltwater-stained outfit from the previous night, I donned the sunglasses she'd brought. "We should get moving."

"Right. Women on the run." She straightened from the wall and held the door for me. "Come on. Let's be gay, do crime, and pray that we don't do the time."

"Pithy." Pausing on the threshold, I took one last look around the room. A fleeting impulse urged me to leave a note for Samael, but I didn't know what to say. Besides, I didn't want to leave any clues in case the Feds somehow traced me here.

If my father cared to see me again, he would have to find me himself. He had no problem tracking me down the first time, anyway.

I trailed Danny down the hall, swathing myself in a don't-notice-me Presence. It wouldn't help me if the Feds all wore silver like North, but it would help me avoid notice by average citizens who might recognize me from the most-wanted list.

Ahead of us, the elevator bell dinged. The doors slid open and a strapping gentleman in a blue FBI jacket stepped out.

Quicker than human eyes could follow, I yanked Danny with me into a side corridor, holding a finger to my lips as panic spiked in her aura.

Low, sharp voices carried from the main hallway, another officer joining the first as they spread out to canvass the floor. At the end of our corridor, I pushed through a nondescript door into a back stairwell and eased it closed behind us.

Danny whispered, "What do we—?"

"Quiet." No footsteps echoed on the stairs, but we were six floors up and we couldn't stay on the landing. "We go down."

We didn't even make it to the next floor when the sound of booted feet and voices floated up from below.

"Shit," Danny muttered under her breath. "How did they find you so fast?"

"They probably had a tail on you. Come on." The voices on the stairs were several floors down, stomping their way up. I reached the next level and pushed through the access door. If we could just get to the elevators while they searched the floor above—

"Hey, you there!" A Fed turned the corner of the hallway at the other end, his hand on the grip of his pistol. When I backed up, he broke into a run.

If he was running, he wasn't shooting. I slammed back into the stairwell with Danny at my heels. Below us, someone shouted, and heavy footsteps sped up.

There was only one way to go from here and no time to think. We headed back upward at a half-run. I could go faster, but Danny didn't have my stamina and soon she was breathing hard. One flight, two flights, and now the officers below were banging through the door on the floor below.

"Stop! FBI!"

We had run out of stairs, but another door waited ahead of me. I grabbed the handle and swore when it didn't budge.

"Turn around and put your hands in the air! Do it now!"

Danny backed up into me, her body shielding mine. "Please, don't shoot!"

They wouldn't shoot a human bystander, would they? Maybe I could use that to keep her out of trouble for helping me and buy us another minute. I wrapped one arm around Danny, pulling her tight against me.

"I have a hostage. Don't come any closer." I took her chin in my gloved hand, squeezing gently and hoping she would play along. "I'll snap her neck. Don't think I won't do it."

Danny gasped, tensing in my arms. "Please, you're scaring me," she called out, her voice shaky and breathless. "Do what she says!"

Damn, she really was good at this. "You're amazing," I murmured in her ear, while mugging horribly for the benefit of the officers below.

She elbowed me in the ribs, but not very hard. I hissed and made a show of tightening my grip.

My ploy worked, at least for the moment. The officers lowered their weapons and huddled together, talking in low voices. One of them got on their radio, calling for backup.

This breathing room wouldn't last. Keeping Danny between me and the officer's line of sight, I reached behind me and plunged my hand through the reinforced wood and metal of the door.

The precious seconds of fumbling for the handle and unlatching it seemed to stretch interminably, the sensation of sharing space with another solid object itching at the back of my mind. I leaned my shoulder into the solid surface of the door to keep it a fraction ajar and retrieved my hand—just as Officer North stepped onto the landing below, weapon trained on us.

"It's over, Ms. Knight." She stepped up one stair. "I know you don't want to hurt your friend, and you've got nowhere to go."

"Wrong," I snarled, and slammed backwards through the unlatched door.

We plunged into the relative brightness of what passed for daylight this early on a San Francisco morning. I let the door close, the lock engaging with a satisfying click, and released Danny. She leaned over, hands on knees, breathing hard.

I turned, taking stock of my next move. Cold wind swirled around us, carrying the distant roar of traffic and occasional blaring horns.

North had it right, after all. Cornered on the hotel roof, we had nowhere else to go.

18

FLIGHT PATTERNS

A loud pounding echoed from the other side of the roof access door. It wouldn't hold for long. North could shoot the lock off or they'd break it down. Or, failing that, they could probably just call hotel maintenance and get the key.

North had called my bluff. I wouldn't hurt Danny to get away. I would have to surrender. They'd put me in silver cuffs again, and I would end up right back where I'd run from, with a few extra charges of resisting arrest, obstructing justice, and kidnapping to compound my hopeless situation.

Hell, they didn't even have to prove I did the murders at this point. They had plenty to work with already.

I slumped. I'd messed up when I ran in the first place, and now I'd put Danny's life in danger while making things worse for myself.

"What is it?" Danny said, and then caught her breath. "Oh, wow. We're really high up."

"I'm sorry, Dan." I bowed my head. "I never should have called. I shouldn't have gotten you mixed up in this."

"Don't say that." Another thump shook the door that stood between us and North, and she winced. "Well, come on, super spy. Fly us out of here already. You've got wings and a plan, right?"

"Not exactly." Why did everyone keep assuming I had plans for these things? Had they met me? "I can't fly. Not right now. I'd need a source for that." I had to admit I liked Samael's terminology, not as clinical as *donor* but without the baggage of *claim.*

"A source? You mean like—*oh.*"

"Yes. *Oh.*" I paced to the edge of the roof. It was a long way down, with no convenient ledges below us that I could feasibly leap down to. "We're screwed."

Yet another crash echoed from the access door. I turned to face my fate, and instead found myself face to face with Danny.

She stood mere inches away from me, her dark eyes wide, but not with fear, not now. Her aura flared around her like a halo, bright enough that colors bled into my visual spectrum, the gold and soft pink of sunrise.

"Not yet, we're not," she said.

"What do you mean?" That surge of energy pulled like a tide at the craving in my core. "Why are you looking at me like that?"

"You said you need a source." A tremor underlaid her voice, her energy heightening further. "Well, here I am."

"Danny, it's not— The other night, that was one thing. People could have died. This is different."

"If it's to save you, how is that different?" She held my gaze, challenging me. "I told you, Lily. *I'm* not afraid."

"It's not that," I protested, but I knew it was a lie. I was scared, but not of what she offered nor of the desire stirring along with my hunger for her kether. I was afraid of what I could lose if this went all wrong. "You're engaged. What about—?"

"It's fine." Danny raised her chin, the stubborn set of her jaw achingly familiar to me, the one that brooked no argument. "I talked to her. About you."

"You...wait, what—?" I broke off at the tearing sound of a door frame in distress. "Tell me you're sure."

"*Yes,* I'm sure," she said. "Now hurry the hell up and kiss me, Lily Knight."

The door splintered behind her words. With no time to waste, I swept her up against me.

Kissing her was very different than kissing Sebastian. Her lips were soft and full, gentle on my own, a slow opening, an exploration. She tasted as sweet as her aura, as sweet as I remembered her.

Her energy surged through me instantly, a euphoric rush that tingled at the base of my spine. Its bright wave suffused my body with weightlessness, as if we were already flying.

I deepened the kiss and Danny moaned, mouth opening to mine. The small sound sparked a rising conflagration in my core. Her hands dropped from my hair and roamed under my borrowed T-shirt, stroking up over my ribs and higher with an expert touch, thumbs skating across the sensitive flesh below the band of the sports bra that didn't quite fit.

I wanted her. The truth rang in me like a struck bell. This was my best friend, the one I'd loved for many years and held at arms' length for just as long because I didn't want to hurt her of all people.

I didn't want to use her. I didn't want this one pure thing in my life tainted by the demon inside me. But now, in her embrace, it didn't feel tainted at all. It felt right and needful and sweeter than I could bear.

It seemed to last forever, that kiss. I lost myself in it. Danny pulled back first, gasping slightly, eyes glazed and full of wonder. "Did we do that? They're *beautiful*."

My wings unfurled above us, feathers ruffled by the gusty breeze sweeping the city heights. Dark blue-black still, the pinions shimmered in the morning light with a subtle spectrum of rainbow iridescence. "Yeah," I said, breathless. "We did that."

Just in time, too, as the access door burst open with a splintering crash. "Hold it right there!" North charged through, but the other officers stopped short behind her, gaping and murmuring.

"Holy shit, what is that?"

"It's a fucking demon," North screamed. "Of course she has wings. Stop her!"

"That doesn't look like a demon. It looks like a—"

"Shut the fuck up. Knight, put her down, *now*."

I aimed a feral grin at North over Danny's shoulder. Then I scooped my friend up, one arm under her knees and the other around her waist. "Not a chance," I said. "Hang on."

Danny laced her hands behind my neck, and I sprang into the air with the speed of a hunting falcon. The Feds shrank rapidly into small ant-like figures on the roof below.

The small of my back itched, waiting for a bullet, but it never came. Maybe North didn't want me dead after all, or maybe she just didn't want to risk killing my human hostage.

Either way, I wouldn't stick around to find out. The moist, foggy air closed around us like a damp blanket as I circled higher into the marine layer that hung above the city.

Where could I go? The Feds had probably tracked Danny from her place, and I couldn't bring this trouble to Sebastian's doorstep, either. Meanwhile, my condo was a federal crime scene and the first place they'd expect me to flee.

Danny stirred in my arms. Condensation from the fog we flew through beaded on her eyelashes, and she shivered, lids at half-mast. "'S cold," she muttered, the words barely audible over the rush of air beneath my wings.

Right, I couldn't linger, nor could we fly too far, not in these conditions, not even with the fog hiding us from prying eyes. She didn't have my resistance to the wind chill, and the kiss we'd shared had packed a hell of a punch, strengthening me as it weakened her.

Emotional connection and passionate desire both heightened the power of my kether-pulling abilities, and our bond clearly carried both. The kiss hadn't rendered Danny unconscious, but she would feel the effects for a while. She would need to rest, and despite the power of the energy flowing through me in this moment, I didn't know how long I could fly on what I had.

An ominous sound penetrated the fog, the thud-thud-thud of a helicopter's rotors somewhere below and behind me. Of course they wouldn't let me go so easily, and flight wouldn't save me from a dedicated search by air with radar and silver-equipped lookouts, no matter how much effort I put into a Presence that would keep me hidden from human eyes.

As I circled, another noise echoed through the overcast sky, long, low, and loud. Familiar yet haunting, the foghorns of the Golden Gate beckoned me onward.

I scudded along the thin top layer of the fog bank and turned north, away from the unseen chopper. Soon the rust-orange towers of the bridge pierced the blanketing mist to my left like gigantic, silent sentinels, signal lights winking on their topmost girders. I used them as guideposts, flying on a parallel track toward the distant dark peaks of Mount Tamalpais.

If I could get us down somewhere remote and forested, we might earn ourselves a little breathing room. Danny could rest and I could come up with a real plan, something that would return her to safety and keep me out of reach of North's people.

Then what? I would have to disappear, like Samael had urged me the other day. I'd have to leave my life behind. Danny, Sebastian, Eve... North wouldn't hesitate to put pressure on the ones I cared about to flush me out.

Maybe I couldn't win, no matter what I did. If I ran, I would lose all I'd worked for, but for the moment, staying and fighting seemed like a losing proposition. I would have to prove my innocence and find who or what had really killed that poor woman on my terrace. Or, failing that, I would have to appeal for due process from the justice system within which I had worked so hard to make a place for myself.

Surrender would only lead to my dull and tarnished end, crumbling to the power of silver. What odds did I have of a fair trial in North's hands? Something I didn't understand drove her, obsessed her, convinced her of my guilt beyond reason.

I didn't have any option but flight, but my energy burst from Danny proved short-lived. I had only flown for about fifteen minutes when fatigue started to set in. My shoulders ached right between the blades, where my wings attached, and my speed flagged, my altitude dipping lower. The fog around us had thinned, too, dissolving under the morning sun. Between using my boosted strength to carry Danny and maintaining a concealing Presence, I couldn't keep up this pace for long.

Senses alert for the distant whirl of helicopters, the bridge sinking beneath the cresting fog behind me, I circled lower. The dark, scraggly spires of redwood crowns rose out of the fog, and I had to jerk my wings up and swerve to avoid getting knocked from the sky by a tree to the face. With a final burst of energy, I used a backbeat of my wings to slow my descent to a near-hover, desperately scanning for a place to touch down.

Finally, a small rocky outcropping beckoned me from a break in the trees. Half-sobbing in relief, I made for it.

I let us down as gently as possible on the uneven surface and exhaled, letting my wings fade. They dissolved like blowing fog and left me terrestrial, sore, and exhausted.

How far from civilization had I landed? The redwoods around us meant I had gotten us at least as far as the small grove of old growth giants nestled at the mountain's roots. Better than the city, yes, but it was hardly a trackless wilderness, luring day trippers and hikers out for a taste of the primordial Pacific rainforest.

I could probably count on the fact that few people we encountered here would wear silver, except by chance, but I also had Danny to worry about. She rested curled in my weary arms as if asleep, eyes closed, her breathing even, but her wet hair and damp clothes gave me cause for concern. Down here, the trees shielded us from the worst of the wind, but exposure and hypothermia would quickly become a problem for her if we had to stay out here too long.

As I set her carefully down, she shifted against me, blinking. "Where are we?"

"Safe, for now." I guided her to a sitting position where she could lean her back against the rocks and crouched in front of her. "How are you feeling?"

"Woozy." Her forehead crinkled, and she squinted at me, lifting a hand to touch her lips. "It was just one kiss. Is it always like that?"

"It depends." I found my gloves where I'd shoved them into my jeans pocket and pulled them on, my movements not quite steady. "Heightened emotion increases the effect of the energy drain. I can control it, but..." I hadn't controlled myself so well in the moment, with her body pressed to mine and danger bearing down on us. I had needed what she offered and taken what I could. "I'm sorry, Danny. I didn't want it to be this way."

Her head came up at that, indignation enlivening her and driving the dazed slackness from her face. "Don't apologize, you twit. I was there. I basically jumped you." Then her grin slipped. "Unless... Lily, if I misread you—"

"You didn't misread," I said, voice rough. "You saved us. You saved me. And I..." What else could I say? She was still my best friend, a friend engaged to another woman. The chemistry that had fueled that kiss didn't come out of nowhere—it had always lived in the unspoken space between us—but I still hadn't expected to find it roaring into the open like this, with the intensity of a summer wildfire. "I don't regret what we did, to be clear. I just don't want to be the one to hurt you. Or anyone else."

I had more than just the two of us to think about. Berry didn't deserve me swooping in on her fiancée like this, no matter what Danny said about life and death situations. And how would Sebastian react if I told him the truth about today?

Confusion and guilt clutched my heart. He didn't even know where I was right now. For all he knew, I could be dead at the bottom of the bay or back in custody being tortured by the Feds.

"I know," Danny said. "It's complicated."

It was more than complicated, but I would have to think of the full implications later. For now, I had our immediate survival to distract me. "We should get moving, find some shelter. Can you stand?"

"Only one way to find out." Danny set her jaw and pushed herself upright.

"Careful." I offered her my gloved hand and helped her to her feet. "Take it slow."

She stood for a moment, swaying, gripping my arm to steady herself. "I'm okay."

"No, you're not. Here, lean on me."

One arm around her shoulders, I guided us both down the uneven slope of the outcropping and under the trees. Beneath the canopy, the air held a little more warmth than in the open, but Danny still shivered occasionally, teeth chattering in the silence.

The forest floor sloped downward from our position, and navigating it proved almost as treacherous as the rocks, with fallen logs, boulders, and underbrush hampering our progress. The soft red loam beneath our feet absorbed sound, lending a preternaturally calm atmosphere to our surroundings, as though we walked through an ancient, abandoned cathedral.

A squirrel scolded us from the branches above, and distant birdsong cascaded in bubbling trills downslope, where the trees clustered thickly together. Somewhere nearby, running water trickled. At least we wouldn't go thirsty. I focused my senses, trying to determine the right direction to travel, but only Danny's energy shone beside me, muted from exhaustion but still cinnamon-sugary as always.

This area seemed hidden away from the trails and campgrounds of the state park. That meant less chance of discovery, but it also meant shelter and food might prove hard to come by. I made an executive decision and set off down the slope, keeping my pace slow to accommodate Danny's halting steps.

"I hope you know where you're going," she said after a few minutes. She sounded a little breathless, but when I tried to pause, she pressed on with grim-faced determination.

"Me too."

"Do you think I could get a signal out here? I have my phone." She had it in her hand, in fact, and waved it at me.

"Crap." I stopped short, panic stirring my adrenaline out of its fatigued state. "Give me that."

"What? Why?"

I snatched it from her. It claimed to have no signal, after all, but I powered it down as quickly as I could anyway. "GPS works both ways. They could be tracking us."

"Geez. Paranoid much?"

"It's not paranoia if the FBI really does have a manhunt on for you. They tracked you to the hotel, didn't they?"

"I still don't understand why this is happening," she grumbled. "You didn't do anything wrong."

"Maybe not before," I said, grim. "But I have now. Come on. We can't stay here."

We descended the slope with painful slowness and stopped to rest at a small stream that trickled down from a hidden spring somewhere above. Once again, I stretched out my demon senses.

This time, a whispered shred of desiderata reached me. I stiffened, but it was far off and fading quickly. A road, perhaps, or a trail, somewhere below us and to our right. I headed to the left, deeper into the woods, staying alert for more traces of human presence.

My senses gave no warning several hours later, however, when the trees finally thinned and a small structure came into view. Danny, stumbling beside me, gave a soft cry of triumph, but I pulled her back.

"Wait here." I found her a mossy boulder to rest on. She didn't look good, her face gray from strain. She leaned her elbows on her knees, resting her head in her hands.

I circled the little cabin cautiously until I found the dirt access road downslope. With no vehicles in sight, the track seemed poorly maintained and grown over with a season's worth of ground cover. The cabin itself had a worn appearance, its windows dusty and its porch littered with fallen branches and cones. Detecting no trace of human energy, I ventured up the rickety steps to the front door and peered inside the dirty glass.

It didn't look like much, a single room at most, but I couldn't have asked for better at the moment. It gave us a place to rest out of sight of any searchers and out of the elements. Danny could recover and I could regroup.

The door's rusted lock yielded easily to my strength. Relieved I didn't have to shove my hand through another solid object today, I returned to my friend.

She sat where I'd left her, leaning back against the tree trunk, her eyes closed, apparently asleep. Cold fear shot through me for a moment, but then her chest rose and fell with a sleeper's long breath, and I blinked back the prickling tears of relief that smeared my vision.

It seemed a shame to wake her after how hard I'd pushed her, after stealing her strength and kidnapping her on my wild run from the law. She'd given me everything, kept me safe and alive, risked federal charges to throw in her lot with me, and probably risked her relationship too. My chest tightened, an ache settling in my throat.

I loved this woman. I knew that much. I had loved her semi-platonically as a friend for over a decade. What had happened today didn't change that, even as it complicated everything else, confused my heart and mind, electrified my body.

With a sharp inhalation, I bent down to her, squeezing her shoulder gently. "Come on, Dan. Wake up."

"Hmm?" Then she started awake. "What is it? Are they coming?"

"No." Another pang roughened my voice at the naked fear in her wide brown eyes. "It's safe. We can rest here. Can you walk a little bit more?"

"I think so." She frowned in concentration, struggling to her feet, then swayed and almost fell. "Oops. Maybe not."

"It's all right," I said. "I've got you."

I didn't have much strength left either, but I had enough to lift her in my arms once again. Ignoring her faint protests, I strode up the porch stairs, kicked open the door, and carried her across the threshold.

19

INTO THE WOODS

An angled ray of diffused sunlight through the filthy window illuminated the single room. Bare of most furniture, it had a defunct looking stove in the corner and a naked mattress against the far wall.

I headed for it, and Danny started to laugh. The sound had a touch of hysterical fatigue behind it, but it welled up from somewhere deep inside her and shook us both.

Confused, I stopped short. "What is it?"

"Nothing." Danny wiped tears of mirth from her face, then dissolved into another round of giggles. "I can't...it's just...Lily, *there's only one bed.*"

"Huh? It's fine." I set her down on the mattress. "I can sleep on the floor."

"Oh, Sugarbean. You're such an ass." Her eyelids had already dropped halfway closed, her voice fading to a soft slur, and I had to lean down closer to catch the next words. "Don't you dare."

"But..." I trailed off, because Danny's desiderata smoothed out, fading to a whisper of warmth against my skin. She had fallen asleep.

Sitting at the end of the narrow mattress by her feet, I propped my back against the planks of the wall. I could come up with a plan to get us out of this while she recovered and I rested my eyes.

Any moment now, an idea would come to me. I was certain of it. The logic took shape in my mind, perfect and glistening, like a soap bubble blown by the wind, just out of my grasp.

The next thing I knew, I woke sprawled sideways on the old mattress, my back pressed into the wall and Danny's warm, soft curves melded against me.

She lay with her head pillowed on my arm, one leg hooked over mine. Her desiderata's scent of cinnamon and salted caramel blanketed me, much stronger than before. The room had grown dim, and outside the grimy window, shadows of trees seemed to gather close around the cabin in the deepening twilight.

I held perfectly still, keeping my breathing slow and regular despite the heat blooming in my belly and the panic gripping my throat.

Fatigue had gotten the best of me, obviously. I'd misjudged my own capacity, another bad call. Had we slept the day away like this? How much time had I lost?

Why the hell had I let Danny talk me out of taking the floor?

I swallowed hard, the memory of her kiss lingering on my tongue. With slow, stealthy movements, inch by inch, I extricated my arm. I needed breathing room. I needed to think.

I didn't get the chance. She stirred and rolled toward me, eyes wide and dark, the perfect depth to drown in.

"Hi, Sugarbean," she said after an endless moment, her voice breathy with sleep. "You're still here."

"Staying was the least I could do, after..." After she ran with me. After she kissed me. After she saved me by giving me another piece of her soul. "How do you feel?"

"Better. What do we do now?"

"*We* don't do anything." Chest painfully tight, pinned between her and the wall, I couldn't draw away. I had nowhere to go. "You've done more than enough for me. You should go home."

Her jaw hardened, mouth pressed into that familiar, stubborn line. "I'm not leaving you to be hunted down."

"I can stay ahead of them. I'm good at keeping out of sight."

"That's not a plan. It's suicide."

"Danny…"

"Don't you Danny me. Listen. I'm not letting you go on the run like this, alone."

"Great." I stared up at the ceiling, avoiding her gaze. "If you have a better plan, I'm all ears."

"If you stop being morose and sarcastic at me for just one minute, I'll tell you. I can help you, but you have to let me."

"You already have."

"Not as much as I could." She brushed light fingertips across my cheek, the brief shock of her energy tingling along every nerve. "If you're really doing this, you need your strength. You need your wings."

She shone like a beacon in the twilight, illuminated by my night vision and the soft pulse of her aura. What she offered me sang in her voice, in the beat of her desire, in the way her hips settled against mine.

The heat smoldering in my belly sparked into flame. "I shouldn't." I licked my lips and tried not to think of the way her mouth had felt upon them, like water in the desert. "We… No. You can't. It's too much. That kiss was one thing, but this…"

"Maybe," she said. "I don't think I care. That says something, doesn't it? God, Lily, if only you knew—" She broke off, staring at me.

"What?"

"You do know." Her voice dropped, surprise and a taint of hurt lacing her aura with soft shadows. "You must. You could read me all this time, and you never… Wow. I can't believe I didn't see it before."

She drew away as she spoke, giving me the space I thought I wanted, and suddenly I couldn't bear it. I reached for her before I could stop myself, and we both went still.

"I'm sorry," I whispered. "I always thought—no, it doesn't matter. Maybe it was easier to pretend you'd put it aside, that I had, that it didn't mean anything."

It was the wrong thing to say. "That's fucked up." The words bled through her like an open wound. "Lily, it's *us*. How could it not mean something?"

"God, no. That's not—" I covered my face with my hands. "All right, this absolutely makes me sound like an asshole, but most people have certain...reactions around me. It comes with the territory."

The breath huffed out of her in a laugh, or a half-sob. "You don't sound like an asshole."

"You're giving me way too much credit."

"No, I'm not. You *are* an asshole." A smile quirked the side of her mouth, a salve I didn't deserve. "That's never been in doubt."

"Right. I'm an asshole, and a demon, and you're my best friend. For a long time, you were my only friend." I turned on my side to face her, drew a long, shaky breath. "The truth is, I was scared, Dan. I'm scared now. I don't want to use you. I can't risk losing you."

"You won't lose me." Without warning, she pressed her forehead to mine. The warm pulse of her energy seeped into my skin, slow and sweet as lilac honey, strong as wine, overwhelming me. "No matter what. It's you and me, always. Oh, Lily. It's always been you."

"Danny, I—"

"Don't say anything else. Let us have this. One night, please." The renewed blaze of desire in her faltered. "Unless...you don't want to."

"Oh, I want to." It took everything I had to hold my demon back from taking all she had to give, drying my mouth and roughening my voice. "I've wanted you, too."

"So have me," she said, her lips brushing mine, and I drowned in her sweetness again.

Before I released my claim on Sebastian and gave him his silver ring, I'd started to learn a new trick, how to moderate the speed that I took power for pleasure. I used it with Danny now, drinking her in and then gently pushing energy back from my skin to hers. Unlike our rooftop kiss, we had time, and I wanted this to last.

I might not get another chance. I might never see her again. After this, she would go back to her life with Berry and become her wife. I would disappear, a fugitive, a demon in the wind. But right now, for this one night, in this shabby little cabin on the edge of the wilderness, we belonged to each other alone.

She trailed her mouth down my neck from ear to shoulder, and I shuddered. The rush of shared desire tested my control. I skimmed open palms up her spine under her thin T-shirt, every inch of her skin an electric revelation I couldn't get enough of.

I had been with women before, even lately since my forays into one-night stands, but touching Danny didn't feel the same. I knew every mood of hers, every smile and every tone, but not this. Not the eager heat with which she pressed against me, nor the way her breath caught under my hands, nor the sweetness of her kiss, strange and familiar at once in a way that dizzied my senses.

Suddenly, she sat up. Doubt yawned under my breastbone: would she reconsider, come to her senses, walk away?

Instead, she shrugged her shirt over her head and tossed it into the dark with a single, emphatic movement. Her gaze met mine with a challenge clear as day in the half-light, energy burning brighter than ever as she reached around to unhook her bra.

My heart stuttered in my chest at the sight, her full breasts and lovely curves, and I reached to draw her back toward me. "You're beautiful."

She slapped my hand away. "No. Your turn."

I stripped hastily, shimmying out of my jeans with more enthusiasm than grace. When I reached for the band of the panties she'd brought for me, my gaze returning her challenge, she grabbed my wrist, stilling me.

"Let me," she said, husky-toned, and pushed me down on the mattress with surprising force.

"Want to top me, do you?"

"You like it." A wicked smile bowed her lips at the catch in my voice. She knelt over me, tracing light, lazy fingers over the cage of my ribs with agonizing slowness.

I arched into her touch. "Never said I didn't."

"You didn't have to." She ran the pad of her thumb along the waistband of the panties. "You're the most bottomy bottom imaginable."

"I didn't realize it was that obvious," I said, breathless.

"Well, it's probably not to everyone. But I know you very, *very* well." On the last *very*, with her eyes fixed on mine, she closed her lips over my nipple, circling it expertly with her tongue.

Lost in the rush of pleasure and sweet kether, I arched into her mouth, then gasped at the graze of teeth over the sensitive flesh. It took all my wherewithal to push some of the energy back to her so she could stay alert—and so she wouldn't have to stop. I really didn't want her to stop. "That's not...fair."

She released my nipple with a slight suction that left me breathless, and watched it harden with an air of satisfaction. "I don't think you're in much of a position to argue." Turning her attention to my other breast, she added, "It's all in the vibe, you know. All buttoned up and protesting too much, and full of *this* underneath."

"Full of what, exactly?" Every skin-on-skin contact made me quiver as she slipped a hand lower between us to roll the fabric of the panties past my hips, kissing her way down my body between my breasts and over my belly.

Pausing under my navel, she grinned up at me. "Full of shit." She bent and pressed another scalding kiss below my pubic bone as she laid me bare. "You can't pretend you don't want me to do this. Not anymore."

"I'm not pretending anything," I said, trembling, exposed, and if I had any other words, I lost them when she dipped her fingers in the aching core of me.

She held me still while I whimpered and thrashed, spread me open with both hands and tongued me until I fell apart under her ruthless mouth. My wordless cries echoed in the small, bare room. Her essence crested over me in waves, pooling in lazy eddies between us as I fed it back across our charged skin.

When she finally raised her head, the glazed arousal in her eyes warned me I hadn't given enough back, not yet.

"My turn," I whispered and pushed her down, rolling over her but leaving a bare inch of space between us. We both would benefit from breaking the energy pull for a moment, even if neither of us wanted to.

"Lily," she said, and the breathless way she said my name nearly undid me all over again.

I couldn't let it, not yet. I had to give her something in return for all she offered me, all the pleasure in my power, a night to remember us by.

The salt-tang of her tasted sweeter than the sea, her scent intoxicating me. Her hands tangled in my hair as I plied her with slow, deliberate flicks of my tongue.

"Stop...teasing." She ground her hips up into my face. "You've done this before." Her breath hitched, tone hovering between accusation and admiration.

"Once or twice," I admitted when she let me come up for air, and slid questing fingers lower, finding her slick as rainwater. "May I?"

"Fuck, yes."

I curved my fingers up inside her and she dropped her head back, arching into my willing mouth as she came for me again and again.

Her energy spilled over me in torrents, more than I needed, almost more than I could hold. When her orgasmic tremors plateaued, I pushed some of that rich kether back to her and raised my head.

"Whatever you just did," she said, half-groaning, "it feels amazing."

"Just a little succubus magic." I grinned up at her.

"And I'm still awake after all that? You've been holding out on me, Sugar-bean. You always act like you could kill me with a touch."

"Yeah, well, I've learned some things. Turns out it's not that simple." I moved up to lie beside her, propping myself on one elbow. "The claim though—that's still true."

In a way, my claim could keep her safe. No other demon could seduce or feed from a human already bound to a cubine partner. If a rogue demon really did have me in their sights, Danny could face danger too, just as she had with Ariel.

My claim had protected her from his charms then. Maybe it would protect her now.

"You're brooding again," Danny said, turning to face me.

"I'm not." I found a smile for her. "Just thinking."

"Yes, you are. You think you can fool me because I can't see, but you got all tense and stopped breathing." She molded her body to mine, and the renewed flow of her kether pulled me back to the present. "I hope you're not too tired. I could go all night at this rate."

Full dark had fallen outside, leaving the interior of the cabin in almostfull darkness. Only my demon sight let me see her expression, though my other senses gave me more to work with, the quickening pulse of her desire. My energy gift had worked similarly with Sebastian, who'd reported a reduced refractory period and a heightened desire for a second round.

"I have no intention of stopping," I said into the soft curve of her neck.

She shoved me away gently. "Doesn't that defeat the purpose, if you keep giving it back?"

"I'll take what I need. I promise."

"*God,*" she groaned. "That's a hell of a promise. You better not be lying to me, Sugarbean."

"No more lying." I stroked my fingers down the back of her neck, where she kept her bright-dyed hair shaved close to her nape in a punky undercut. How many times had I idly wondered how it would feel to touch her like this and never let myself admit it? "If we only have one night, we have to make it count."

If we never did this again, I had to memorize every inch of her. And I fully intended to take my time about it.

A deep, velvet night unmarred by city lights pressed against the windows of the little cabin when I finally kissed my friend and lover into the exhausted oblivion of pleasure I had promised her. With gentle movements, I unwound her arms from around me and slipped out of the narrow bed we'd shared. Her essence hummed in my veins, sweet and hot as her mouth on mine, and my wings stirred and whispered, scraping the beams of the ceiling until I willed them back under my skin.

I pulled on my jeans and T-shirt, then donned my gloves. Danny lay in an untroubled sleep, her chest rising and falling in a slow, even rhythm, her lips curving upward in a smile. Confident I wouldn't need more insulation for a good long while with the warmth she'd gifted me, I laid over her the flannel shirt she'd brought me earlier, then covered her legs with her jacket. The air in the small room had heated somewhat with our exertions, and morning would come soon enough. Hopefully she wouldn't get too chilled before her body replenished her vital energy and she awoke.

By then, if I followed the plan we'd made together in the space between kisses, I would be long gone. She could turn on her phone without fear of leading anyone to me and call for help that way.

Would she call Berry to drive over the bridge and pick her up? What would she tell her fiancée?

She had made a big deal about staying honest with Berry earlier in the year, when they asked me to move out of the house they shared. Still, honesty about your friend's secret demon side was one thing. Honesty about sharing earthshaking orgasms with said demon friend in the woods while on the run from federal agents was a whole other proposition.

I winced and paused, staring down at Danny's sleeping form. Had we made the right choices tonight? Almost certainly not. We had more likely blown up her life, as if the advanced state of combustion my own existence somehow sustained wasn't enough.

The ache in my chest didn't come from regret, at least not regret for the right reasons. I didn't want to leave her like this, even though I'd promised, even though that was ostensibly the point of what we'd done.

That was part of the deal, unspoken but understood. What had happened between us in the woods would stay in the woods. I would go north, find Samael's contact. Failing that, the wild Pacific coast had plenty of remote wild places where I could hide until the trail went cold.

After that, I would have to keep moving. Demons like me didn't belong in the wilderness. We needed humans and the anonymity of cities, the bigger and busier the better.

As for Danny...well, she certainly loved me, but what I'd told her still held true. Most humans couldn't help wanting a succubus, and she had something special with Berry, an ease and safety I couldn't offer her.

No, I couldn't take that from her, lure her further from her hard-won happiness.

It wasn't right. I'd done enough damage already. I had to let her go and disappear before dawn, like the monster I always had been deep down.

Child of night, Ariel had called me once, luring me into his world.

Maybe I belonged there now. Ariel's death meant I could choose it for myself, and it seemed like the only good choice left to me.

Whoever had come after me had killed to corner me like this, and I had no doubt they'd kill again. I'd tried my best to live in the human world, but I couldn't do that anymore. I'd chosen a different path when I revealed myself in public. I couldn't take back the truth, but the truth I told had put the ones I loved at risk again.

I bent to kiss Danny's forehead, a bare brush of lips on skin, which could draw nothing from her while she lay unconscious. Then I pushed my feet into my borrowed sneakers, threw the backpack Danny had brought me over my shoulder, and stepped out into the night.

The damp, cool air of the forest filled my nostrils, fragrant with petrichor, rich loam, and sharp notes of evergreen. The soft click of the latch seemed to ring out loudly in the silent clearing.

No birds sang yet, and stars still glimmered where the fog thinned, though my enhanced night vision told me that the sky had begun to lighten ever so faintly in the east. My footsteps crunched on dead-fall twigs and echoed hollow on the old planks of the three stairs that led down from the porch.

Rolling my shoulder blades, I let my wings unfurl to their full span and sprang into the air to fly north in darkness, a desperate race against the dawn, alone.

20

THE SEA DOOR

I flew fast, but I couldn't beat the sun. As the sky grew lighter, I skirted farther out from the wild, rocky coastline, soaring over gray water with birds whose wingspan almost matched mine. A casual observer would take me for an albatross. As for any perceptive fishermen out with the early tide, I would have already left them behind before they could look twice.

The fog wrapped closer to the shore as I arrowed northward. I passed more than one lighthouse, but none matched Samael's description, rising from high mainland promontories too close to human settlements. As time wore on and my energy waned, the miles blended into each other. Anxiety seeped into me with the colorless morning light. One tree-lined rocky shore looked a lot like another and nothing like any map of California I'd never bothered to commit to memory. Samael's riddle-like instructions made me wish for the certainty of GPS.

In the end, I almost missed it. As I scanned the coast to my right with weary, wind-torn eyes, a fleeting light swept past me from the left, far out to sea.

Dodging fresh memories of helicopter searchlights over the waves of the bay, I swerved away. I would have kept moving, faster than ever, but then the fog blew aside and revealed the tower.

Silent and solitary, pale stone stained by salt and time, it rose out of the mists just as Samael had described it, except one thing. He'd mentioned no one manned the light anymore. I circled closer, and the windows at its apex remained dark, quiescent, glass long-shattered. Yet I would have sworn the beacon had flashed in the corner of my vision, calling my attention to it.

I shuddered, spine prickling with cold foreboding. Lashed by waves that flung spray high enough to wet my face, the rocky outcropping to which the tower clung betrayed no sign of recent habitation. Nothing waited to greet me, only a decaying set of outbuildings crowded onto an eroded circular terrace built atop the natural rock formation. Quantities of smelly white guano caked every available surface, and seabirds rose around me in swirling drifts as I descended. Their high, keening protests mixed with the wind into an eerie music that did nothing for the state of my nerves.

My so-called father had sent me to a desolate, lonely place far from home, with no one here to greet me and no sign of the help he'd promised. Maybe it shouldn't have surprised me when I put it like that. Maybe I'd only trusted him because I wanted something that had never truly existed, not for me.

Go down from the light, he'd told me. *To the sea door.* What did that even mean?

I stalked the perimeter of the stony platform. Only a few hundred feet across and slippery with salt-spray, it didn't yield much in the way of shelter, direction, or sightseeing, not with the fog wreathing the isolated rock. The lighthouse itself could boast impressive height, but not much else to recommend it.

"Ugh." Disgusted and disconsolate, I scraped bird waste off my shoes on the lip of the terrace.

If I wanted to get the most out of my wings, I should probably move on soon. Danny's energy gift probably wouldn't get me all the way to Canada, but I could head that way eventually. The Feds couldn't get me there, probably, unless governments secretly extradited their wayward supernaturals. On second thought, that seemed likely, but they'd still have to find me first.

I gave up on dislodging the gunk from my borrowed sneakers and summoned my wings again, taking a beat into the air. Then I paused, hovering.

Close to the base of the lighthouse tower, a narrow set of steps led from the foundation toward the sea. They looked treacherous, carved into the stone and then the native rock without handhold or railing. I swooped lower, following them down. They curved around the platform, then turned inward through a natural opening in the rock.

I hesitated, still airborne. The waves boiled just below me, roaring and hissing like an angry, hungry living thing, ready to drag me down to the depths at the first provocation. The small cavern at the base of the stairs didn't seem safe or welcoming, and even a slight rise in the tide would quickly cut off the entrance.

An imaginative person might call that arch of rock a sea door. A cynical person would call it an obvious death trap.

On the other hand, I'd come too far to back out now. I alighted on the slick, seaweed-laced stone, letting my wings fade into the misty air. Beyond the arch, tide pools shone in dim recesses, bright clumps of corals glimmering under the surfaces.

"Damn you, Samael," I muttered and stepped across the threshold, into...somewhere else.

The silence hit me first, the abrupt cessation of the sea's crashing percussion. Off balance and reeling, I blinked, mind at a loss to make sense of what lay before me.

I stood in a forest of gigantic, towering redwoods, their crowns soaring almost out of sight above me. For a moment, I wondered if I'd somehow returned whence I'd fled and turned in place, expecting to find the cave's arch with rocks and ocean beyond. Instead, a tree's dark hollow yawned in a trunk as wide as a San Francisco street. Thick with impenetrable shadow, the interior led sharply downward, as if into the bowels of the earth. I stumbled backward, breath coming hard and fast.

Nothing I had ever encountered before and nothing Samael had told me had prepared me for this. Sure, I could manifest ethereal feathers and walk through solid matter if I managed to talk myself into it, but spatial relationships didn't change. This was entirely different, wholly unprecedented, and I didn't like it one bit.

The thought of walking *through a magic fucking portal* seemed ridiculous, unreal. Maybe I was dreaming all of this, head pillowed on Danny's breast as the FBI closed in around us. Maybe North had me in silver chains again and this was a fever dream, a hallucination on the edge of death. I should try to wake up now, before I ran out of time.

I squeezed my eyelids tight until colors flashed in the dark inside, but when I cracked them open, squinting, the forest remained, indifferent to my panic or its own impossibility. It stretched as far as I could see, trackless and apparently untouched by human development.

"Hello?" I called into the hush of the grove. "Is anyone there?"

From unseen heights, a bird's staccato, laughing cry startled me. Dark wings flashed across a gap in the canopy, large enough to blot out the light for a moment before it disappeared into branches far above.

"I don't mean any harm. I'm looking for Cee. I'm..." I took a breath and bit the inside of my cheek. "I'm Samael's daughter."

In the expanse of forest, underbrush rustled. A twig cracked. I froze, scanning the deep patterns of light and shadow. Thick, thorny brambles blocked my view and any path forward, and the odd ray of sunlight gleamed on ripe blackberries hanging among the thorns.

Then the brambles parted, and a huge black dog padded out.

No—not a dog. No dog would stand and look at me like that with wild, intelligent, yellow eyes, heavy paws as big as dinner plates, so tall that the raised, alert muzzle could have cleared my shoulder.

"Holy fuck," I whispered. Wolves didn't still live in California forests—did they? Maybe I wasn't in California anymore.

The wolf's ears pricked up at my words and he sniffed the air, tail high, entirely unafraid. I reached within for the energy to spread my wings, just in case, but he didn't seem inclined to make any aggressive moves. He waited at the edge of the blackberry thicket, almost expectant, watching me.

"Hello there," I said, feeling more than a little silly. "Wow. Um, do you know Cee?"

The wolf's mouth dropped open, a smile that displayed teeth like blades. I tensed, but the beast didn't spring. He shook his head, the long fur of his ruff rippling, and took off at a trot to the left, expertly navigating through the underbrush. Then he turned and looked at me.

"You want me to follow you?" I shook my head, sighed. "All right then. When in a fairy tale, I guess."

I set off after him at a healthy distance, not about to play the role of Red Riding Hood in this surreal dream of a day. The path I hadn't seen seemed to reveal itself as the wolf padded onward, winding through trees that by their size had seen a thousand years or more.

After half an hour or so, the trees began to thin around me, the undergrowth fading to reveal reddish earth and leafy ground cover with tiny yellow flowers that gave a sweet, citrus smell when my boots bruised them. Redwoods soon gave way to oaks, not as wide in the trunk but equally old-growth trees, with broad spreading branches and roots lined with golden, scallop-shaped mushrooms.

Beyond the oaks—

I stifled a laugh behind my hand. It might have been a sob. This was all too much. A wolf had led me through a mysterious forest to the door of a building so ornate and elaborate and out of place that it may as well have had walls of gingerbread.

It boasted Victorian buttresses, gables, and even a tower window that would have put San Francisco's famed Painted Ladies to shame. With siding black as the wolf's back and royal purple trim, it had the energy of a cartoon haunted house. No one human painted their home like that, of that and that alone I felt sure.

With confident nonchalance, the wolf trotted around the side of the place and out of sight. Apparently all this was normal for him. I decided to stay put, the better to contemplate whether I could turn and run back to the tree from which I had come. Of course, I had no way of knowing whether stepping into that deep hollow would take me to the cave, no guarantee I hadn't trapped myself in this strange dream of a place.

Before I could test the trap, a vision entranced me. A bent woman with a wide-brimmed straw hat jammed low over a messy mane of white hair stumped around the corner of the house, pursued and quickly outpaced by a small flock of exuberant black goats. The animals swarmed around me, one particularly bold one butting its horned head into my hand, a gentle but persistent demand.

"I welcome you to my home, Samael's daughter." The old woman brushed dirt off her gardening gloves, her eyes dark, sparkling chips of obsidian under the brim of her hat. "If you seek sanctuary here, you will have it. If you mean me and mine harm, you will have that instead."

"I mean no harm," I said hastily. "How did you— You heard me back there?"

"You might say that." She gripped a carved wooden cane as gnarled as her fingers. Under the other arm, she carried a woven basket brimming with small ruby-red tomatoes and green peas. "I have ways of knowing who passes through the sea door, child—shoo, you lot!" This last she directed at the goats, which had given up on me and returned to her side, stealing pea pods from her haul. "Away with you. Mind your manners, now. Don't let me catch you harassing our guest."

The goats scattered at the nudge of her cane, though not far, chewing defiantly and glancing sideways at me with their weird horizontal pupils. "You must be Cee." I relaxed slightly now that I no longer had to bear up under assault by livestock. "I'm Lily Knight. I take it you're a friend of my father."

"Don't take it too far, Lily Knight. I know him, all right, but I wouldn't call us friends. Old acquaintances, sure. Associates, maybe."

"Oh," I said. She didn't sound like a fan, but then again, neither was I. "Well, he sent me. I hope that's OK."

"Yes, yes. I know this story, love." She thumped her cane into the dust with obvious impatience. "Happens you're in some kind of trouble in the big wide world out there. Your father can't protect you because he's as scared as you, hiding among the human folk. Well, it's my specialty, taking in strays, but I'll warn you first. I've got no magic that can solve your problems for you, and staying here too long will cost you dearly. Did he tell you that part, now?"

I drew back, small hairs standing up as she leaned in closer than I had expected. Had she moved toward me while she spoke, and I somehow hadn't noticed? "He said I'd be safe here."

"Sure, and safety is as safety does, I always say." Her grin showed jagged teeth, unnervingly white and sharp. "It's an illusion, child, what some might call it a matter of perspective. Yes, you're safe enough here from everything out there. It's what's in here that will get you in the end."

"You mentioned a cost." I stepped backwards, away from the finger with its long, curving nail she jabbed at my chest. "I don't have any money on me."

"Pssh. I don't want your money." She looked downright offended. "I said you're welcome, and I meant it."

"Then what do you want from me? Some kind of favor?"

"A favor freely given in trade? I wouldn't say no to it." A wave of her cane gestured me nearer. "Come, you've traveled a long way. I'm sure you're hungry."

I didn't move. "Tell me the price first. What favor?"

"You mistake me, child." She clucked her tongue and turned, hobbling back toward the house. "There's no bargain to be struck here, and the price you speak of won't be paid to me. It's this place. It always takes its due."

"I don't understand. I don't know what this place is!" Uneasy, I glanced around at the vibrant forest, but no shadowy tendrils reached for me. Birdsong floated through the canopy, branches stirring in a wind that smelled sweet and sharp as wine.

She shook her head, muttering to herself as she climbed the stairs to the door. "Oh, dearie me. He didn't tell you."

"Didn't tell me what?" Alarmed, I followed her to the base of the steps, looking up.

"This is the Otherworld, love." She tapped the door with her cane and it opened, seemingly on its own. "The cost of it is what you leave behind you."

Her words left me cold. What had I left behind? Everyone I cared for. Danny. Sebastian. Eve. Rae, whose trial began next week, who trusted me to defend her in an impossible situation. "I should go."

"Nonsense. You've come this far." She stood on the threshold, welcoming me into the dim interior with her bright eyes and jagged smile. "One day won't hurt. You're tired and hungry, child, and you're a fright to see."

Self-consciously, I raised a hand to my hair, a windblown, sea-salt tangle all over again. The temptation of rest, a meal, and a chance to clean up almost overrode the fact that the offer came from a crone with too-sharp teeth who lived in an ostentatiously spooky house and had a giant wolf as a messenger.

"Maybe...do you have a phone I could use?" The question sounded silly as soon as I voiced it. If this was some other world, as she claimed, it wouldn't have telecommunications wiring. Still, her words reminded me that I needed to talk to my client, get a postponement, maybe get someone to stand in for me until I could figure out the rest. "I don't want to impose."

"Oh, you're not imposing, dearie. It's what I'm here for. As for a telephone, it's probably not what you're used to, but we'll see what we can do." Stumping into the house, door still flung wide, she said over her shoulder, "Stay a while. Eat with us."

"Who is 'us'?" I followed, wary. She couldn't mean the wolf, could she? When I glanced back, it seemed he had made himself scarce, which didn't make me less uneasy. I would rather have the apex predator in my line of sight than not, all else being equal.

"Why, the children, of course. He really didn't tell you much, did he?" Cee murmured something under her breath, and lamps flared in the foyer. Their greenish glow didn't make the place any less spooky. At the base of a winding staircase, the old woman thumped her cane and called, "Come, now, stop your skulking about. We have a guest."

Her words had an immediate and electric effect. Footsteps clattered above, and two small, pointed faces peered over the banister, one owl-eyed, the other squinting and suspicious. To my left, an androgynous teenager slipped sideways through a door left ajar, gripping a covered pan in oven-mitted hands, expression somewhere between curious and flustered.

"You're not a kid. Who're you?"

I spun at the clear, high voice behind me. Seeing no one, I addressed the air. "I'm just passing through. Visiting your, ah…"

"Grandmother?" the two children above chorused as one. The bolder one had edged a little further down, revealing herself as a brown, gangly pre-teen with short-cropped, jet-black hair. The other still hung back. They looked almost identical, except the shy one had a more pronounced Adam's apple and wore his dark hair long.

"Don't you fret," Cee reassured them, a new note of fondness in the tone. "This is Lily Knight. She may not look like much, but she's one of us. Or close enough."

"Thanks, I think," I muttered, still searching for the other person in the room, the one who had addressed me unseen. The presence of the children would have reassured me except for one thing.

I couldn't sense any of them.

21

SANCTUARY

"You're seeking sanctuary?" The teenager holding the pan frowned. "From who?"

"That's a very good question, Quinn," Cee said. "You never did tell me what you're running from, Lily dear."

"Everyone's running from something, out there," the clear, unseen voice chimed in. "That's what Grandmother says."

"Well..." I hesitated, mindful of the mixed ages among my audience—the disembodied voice couldn't belong to a child older than ten. On the other hand, people might mature at different rates here, but I erred on the side of cautious. "The police arrested me, but I escaped. They think that I...did a very bad thing. Unfortunately, running from them is a crime too—even if you're innocent."

Quinn shuddered. "Ugh. I don't miss that place."

"How bad of a thing?" The short-haired girl leaned over the banister with an expression of intense interest. "Did you kill someone? Was it *murder*?"

"I didn't kill them." So much for sensitive ears. I sighed. "I was framed, I think. I don't know what happened."

"A mystery!" exclaimed the staircase girl. She clapped her hands, eyes shining with delight. "I love mysteries. Are you a detective?"

"Sometimes. A little. Technically, I'm a lawyer."

The girl looked disappointed. "You should really just be a detective," she said in decisive terms. "That's way less boring."

"That's enough, Mara. Go help Quinn set the table. You too, Keiran." Her tone indulgent, Cee shooed the two of them down the stairs before she trained her piercing black eyes back on me. "Falsely accused, eh? You know, they used to say I ate children myself."

I tried not to shudder as Mara and Keiran trotted toward the kitchen at Quinn's heels, elbowing each other and whispering as they cast surreptitious glances over their shoulders. "Why would they say that?"

"Don't look so worried, dearie. It was only a tale to keep their sons and daughters away from me. But they still found their way to me, just the same."

"Some might call that kidnapping."

"Oh, they call it all kinds of things, but I never had to lift a finger for it, did I? The secret ways are always open for the queer ones, the different ones, the changeling kin who belong between the worlds. Sometimes the real monsters are the people back at home, you see."

"I can believe that." The lump in my throat made the words fall flat. I could have used a haven like this to run to when I was Quinn's age, but the ways had never opened for me. Instead of a creepy-but-loving witch grandmother, I got Ariel. It didn't seem fair. "Is that what these kids are—changelings?" Was that what I was, living between two worlds like she'd said?

"Some of us are," said the clear, unseen speaker. "Quinn's mostly human. We think. But they needed a safe place, just like we did."

Cee glared at a spot a few feet up the far wall. "Don't think I don't see you there, shirking your chores, young Neall. Go help with the table if you want to sit at it."

With a dramatic sigh, the kitchen door opened on its own, then closed, laughter pealing from within. Cee shook her head, turning back to me. "I know he takes getting used to, that boy. I've told him it's a bit rude to play his tricks around guests, but he's a bit of a shy one, and he seems to speak more often when he can't be seen."

"It doesn't bother me," I lied. "I'm curious, though. How do you know my father?" What if he had been one of her strays? I tried to picture a young version of the man who had scooped me from the bay—dark-headed, pale, and too serious for his own good—but mostly failed. Perhaps he never had been a child. I should have asked him more about our kind and where he came from when I had a chance.

"Most of us know each other, love. With precious few of us left in the world, we've got to stick together these days."

I couldn't help but notice that she hadn't answered my question. "It can't be that bad. There are selkies in San Francisco Bay." There were no portraits over the mantelpiece for me to investigate, only a dusty collection of odds and ends: carvings of animals with features that implied the artist had captured them in the act of transformation, here a fox with the tail of a snake, there a swan shedding carefully detailed feathers from a human arm.

"Remnants of a once-great people who ruled the seven seas. Oh, child, you're so caught up in your own story you can't see all the ways the world is broken."

"What do you mean, like climate change? That kind of broken?" I frowned, distracted by my examination of the mantelpiece. "With respect, some problems aren't mine to solve, Grandmother. And I haven't been a child for a long time." A small stone box no bigger than a thimble, with intricate, clockwork-style etchings across every surface, lay among a haphazard array of bulbous pieces of wood, the tumors of trees. On one end sat a glass jar with something fleshy and unmentionable sealed inside. A large, shimmering feather the slate gray color of a stormy sky at twilight leaned upright against the brick. *One of ours?*

Cee tutted, somehow just behind me, and I pulled my reaching hand back as if she'd slapped it. "Some things can't be seen until you're ready to see them," she said. "But we'll speak no more of that now, dear. It's easier to see what you can and do what you will on a full belly, no matter what you are and where you're going."

I let her herd me through the door where the small bevy of children had vanished. The table had been set, if in eclectic fashion, no single utensil matching another, some old and tarnished enough to make me leery of silver. After considering my options, I chose a place setting with a knife carved from a white substance that looked like bone and a plastic fork. I might have to eat with someone's trash Cee had picked up on the beach, but at least I wouldn't accidentally poison myself.

The children found their places according to a process only known to them, stealing glances at me, except Mara, who stared openly. Another boy had joined them, slightly built and pointed of face, with a mop of brown hair and green eyes that sparkled with mischief.

"You must be Neall," I said, smiling at him, and he ducked his head with a shy smile back at me.

Beaming with obvious pride, Quinn brought out dish after dish until they crowded the table. First came an array of tender greens, fresh and steamed with melted butter, their small clover-like leaves and lemony aroma reminding me of the ground cover in the sequoia grove. Bright gold mushrooms followed, their scent rich and earthy, sautéed in butter and herbs with soft cheese crumbled on top. "Chantarelles," Quinn proclaimed proudly. "I collected them myself."

Cee filled my glass with a light, fizzy cider. In due time, Quinn returned with the main course, a creamy, complexly spiced tomato curry with chunks of new potatoes and cubes of fried cheese over wild rice, accompanied by a dense, nutty-flavored flatbread.

"It's all vegetarian," I said, casting a surprised glance at Cee. I wouldn't have expected it of her, given her sharp teeth and the general vibe, which screamed *the better to eat you with, my dear.*

Quinn looked shocked, but Cee just laughed. "I told you, dear. I don't eat my friends. We do very well with the forest's gifts, the fruit of the garden, and milk from the goats."

"I'm surprised the goats are safe out there with that wolf around."

"Nowhere safer. Nothing in this realm would dare hunt anything under my protection. Just like the goats know not to eat the vegetables before the harvest. They are excellent at weeding, though."

That only raised more questions, like whether Cee could speak wolf or goat or both, and what she might do with those she did not consider friends. Deciding I might not want to know the answers, I concentrated on chewing my flatbread. The texture took getting used to, but it soaked up the curry well and filled my hollow belly.

I took a cautious sip of the effervescent liquid in my glass and found it crisp as winter apples, with a subtle sweetness and the barest hint of an alcoholic kick. The fatigue of my breakneck flight ebbed a fraction with each mouthful, and I let the voices around the little table wash over me like a balm.

As if to fill my silence, Mara launched into a rambling story of a morning spent roaming the woods, with a litany of observations—wind, weather, new oak saplings in the upper grove, the friends she'd met who seemed in fact to be different types of animals while Cee asked questions that seemed nonsensical. Who was the saplings' mother? What had the wind said? Had Mara checked the northwestern pixie rings?

Mara blithely took the queries in stride, answering in great detail that made even less sense. The saplings belonged to the Gnarl-root, the wind spoke of something stirring in the withered bog, and business was slow at the rings.

They left me to eat in silence for a while, and I half-tuned out Mara's fantastical narrative, already losing its tenuous plot. The girl reminded me a little of Eve, not in her appearance but in her exuberance and wild nature. Did Cee's "strays" ever get a chance to go to school, to live a normal life? Maybe they did better without it. Would Eve thrive more in an environment less bound by human rules?

Who was I kidding? Eve would probably be bored to tears in this place. I hadn't seen a single electronic device in these kids' hands, and I somehow doubt the gingerbread house got cable.

Besides, Eve wasn't a stray, not anymore. She had me.

"Well, then, Lily Knight," Cee said suddenly, making me jump. "You've had a wee bite to keep your body and soul together. Tell me what you seek, and whether you intend to stay."

"I don't know." I pushed the last of my buttery greens around on my plate, finding I had lost my appetite. "I wish I knew whether my people were all right. Or knew anything at all, really. Why this is happening now, why I'm being targeted like this...it makes no sense."

"Ah! Now that is something I can help with." Cee rose from her seat, leaning heavily on her cane. Mara leaped up to help her, but she waved her away with an irascible snort. "Follow me, daughter of Samael. You're as ready as you'll ever be for the answers you seek."

"Can I come too?" Keiran spoke up for the first time, his soft voice swiftly drowned out as the others chorused in agreement.

"No, no. You know that's not how this works. The glass gets misty when there are too many curious minds crowded about, and our guest needs answers, not riddles."

"That's what you always say," Keiran argued. "How will I learn if I can't watch you?"

"Patience, young one. Your time will come. Lily, this way, please."

Mystified, I trailed her into a smaller room off the main one, with a large bay window that overlooked the garden. On a small round table in the center of the room, something sat covered with a hand-woven gray cloth. Cee immediately snapped the blinds closed, leaving the room in dim shadow. She waved me to a seat and took one opposite from me, drawing the cloth away with the flourish of a street performer.

"What is this?" The cloth had revealed a dark, shining surface of black glass or translucent stone, all too reminiscent of the glinting onyx eyes in the face of the woman across from me. "Some kind of magic mirror? I don't put stock in parlor tricks, Cee."

"Neither do I." She smiled, toothily. "This glass will show the truth of whatever you ask, my child, but only if you are ready to see it."

"That's all I want—the truth." Was she for real? Nothing but my own reflection peered back at me from the glass. The surface seemed to swallow the light around it, but it couldn't hide my skeptical frown. "Show me what you got. I'm ready."

"If you say so. But you don't have to tell me. We'll see exactly what you're ready for, soon enough." Her grin widened as I hesitated. "No more tarrying. Ask your questions. Neither the glass nor I can abide a seeker who stalls at the gate."

"Fine," I said, playing along more in desperation than in hope. "Did Danny make it home safe? Is she OK?"

Cee's bushy, unkempt eyebrows arched, but she bent to the glass, blowing on it until her breath misted it over. Then she passed her hands over it, once, twice, thrice.

I leaned over the reflective surface and flinched when Cee's worn, leathery hands closed over mine, guiding them to either side of the uneven circle. "You shouldn't touch—" But I broke off because no energy passed from her to me. I felt something, though, a strange resistance, like a magnet held near another magnet. "Never mind."

"You're no threat to the likes of me, if that's what you mean. Stop staring at me, child, and *look*."

I looked.

The darkness of the mirrored surface had a gravity of its own, drawing my gaze into it like a black hole swallowing starlight. It lay flat on the table, but its depths were fathomless. The lamplight guttering in the curtained room dimmed, and the walls leaned close around me, breathlessly close. My vision tunneled and shrank.

Then the darkness shifted, shards of light coalescing into—a different interior space, one I recognized immediately as Danny's front room.

She'd made it home, but the warm bloom of relief in my chest faded as soon as I took in the two women facing each other on the threshold. Hands on hips, eyes flashing, Berry looked angrier than I'd ever seen her. She carried a suitcase in her hand, and Danny stared at her with a flushed, panicked expression, brimming with the consciousness of guilt.

"Oh, no," I whispered.

"You're okay," Danny said. "Thank God."

"*I'm* okay?" Berry scoffed, incredulous. "It's been thirty-six hours, D!"

"I called as soon as I could. You didn't answer." Danny reached a pleading hand toward her, but Berry stepped back.

"Can you blame me?" Berry's lip trembled, and she spun away. "After what you said the other night, I assumed you just left."

"B, I'm so sorry. It's just—with everything we talked about and everything going on, I couldn't sleep. When Lily called, I didn't think—she needed me."

Berry stiffened, stumbled, as if my name was a bullet aimed between her shoulder blades. "Of course. I should have known." She put out a hand to the wall as if to steady herself, head bowed, facing away from my vantage point. "It's always Lily, isn't it?"

I winced, remembering Danny's breathless voice in the dark. *It's always been you.*

"I never meant to disappear on you," Danny said. "I thought I would just run a few things over to her and be back home before you woke up. I didn't plan on running from the Feds!"

"I don't want to hear it." Berry didn't raise her voice, but the quiet cold in her words sliced across Danny's explanation. "You got what you wanted, all right? The wedding's off."

I stiffened, pressing my nose closer to the glass. *What?* She hadn't mentioned anything about this to me. Was that the shadow I'd noticed beneath her surface? Why hadn't she told me?

"I know," Danny mumbled. "I fucked it all up with her. With both of you, big time. And sorry doesn't cut it, but—"

"You—no. You know what? This isn't about her." The words held a tremor, echoed by the shake in the other woman's shoulders. "This is about us, you and me. Or it *should* be, and it just isn't, is it? It never was."

"Babe. Honeybun." Danny cycled through pet names, but they didn't seem to make a dent in Berry's rage. "Gooseberry. Wait."

"I've been waiting," Berry tossed back, but she kept walking, disappearing through the kitchen. "I'm tired of waiting to be the one who comes first, D." The slam of the door leading to the garage punctuated her words.

Pain etched Danny's face, and she released a long, shuddering breath, loud in the now empty house. Back to the wall, she slid down to sit on the floor, and her lips moved, as if shaping a prayer, a word, a name.

"Lily," she whispered. "Where are you? I need you right now."

"Dan?" Instinctively, I reached for her, but she couldn't hear me. It was only a dream I had called into being. As soon as I stirred, the vision shattered, shrinking away. It folded itself into a single point of light and vanished, leaving me staring across the table, bereft, confused, and aching with guilt.

"Ah yes," the witch murmured. "The truth isn't easy. It never is."

"She spoke to me. Did she know I was there?"

"No, dear. It's not like one of your new devices." With a dry chuckle, Cee passed her hand over the mirror again, but in the opposite direction this time, counter-clockwise. "The glass doesn't lie, but it only goes one way. You can't gaze into the same moment twice."

"That's...probably for the best." I didn't need that kind of temptation. Seeing my more than best friend like that brought comfort, but with a voyeuristic edge.

Maybe she would be better off without me, as I'd almost convinced myself. She'd wanted me to leave. She'd urged me to flee while we lay naked together in that little cabin, drinking the sweetness of each other's skin.

Was that true? Or had I convinced myself of that because I feared facing what it meant?

The glass doesn't lie. Danny needed me, and I'd flown away like the world's biggest, most cowardly dirtbag after throwing a Molotov cocktail into the center of the life she'd built.

"Well, child?" Cee was watching me intently with those eyes like chips of the black stone mirror between us. "Is that all?"

"No." I had run from all of it, from everyone. Others besides Danny depended on me, too. "I want to check on Eve. My—" *Ward* didn't sound right to me suddenly. "She's my foster kid. I think she might be in some kind of trouble."

"Ah." Cee nodded, her tone knowing as she gestured above the dark surface. "Not all families are of blood. Look and see."

This time, the surface bloomed with muted daylight. A thin strip of lonely beach spread under a foggy sky, encroached upon by the incoming tide. A girl's slim form sat hunched on a wind-swept dune, one arm locked around her drawn-up knees, the other digging into the chilly looking sand as if holding on for dear life. A steep, rocky cliff loomed behind her, climbing out of my field of view.

"She's alive," I whispered. "Where is this?"

Eve had begged me to take her to the beach all summer long, despite her disgust with the often-gloomy weather. It should have eased my mind to see her out there, alive and free, no silver wounds marring her arms or legs.

It didn't. She looked lost out there, young and alone, too young for the weight implied in the slump of her shoulders. At least she hadn't strayed too far from home, though the rocky cliff face and the fog didn't narrow it down past somewhere on the Pacific coast.

The glass shimmered at my question, the image distorting with ripples like heat waves before it blurred and then bled away into darkness.

"Curious," Cee said.

"Unhelpful is more like it." I pushed my chair away from the table, ready to get up, but Cee's gnarled claw-like hand caught my wrist in a grip of unexpected steel.

"Sometimes the answers that don't come tell more than the ones that do, my child."

"Enough. These are parlor tricks." A harsh laugh tore my throat, and restlessness boiled behind it, the need to pace, to run, to fly—or just flee? "Literally. I'm just wasting my time."

"My tricks, as you call them, show what you ask for." Cee released my arm and sat back, apparently unruffled. "If you didn't see what you wanted, perhaps you should ask different questions."

"If I can't find something that I can use—" I licked dry lips. Just because I'd run didn't mean I had to run forever. If I could get a step ahead of North somehow, I could regroup, maybe turn things around. "This government agent who's after me did a sloppy job. She didn't bother with evidence or probable cause, and that's not like her. I just need to know why so I can prove it. Show me what I'm up against, Cee."

"Ah, now that is a real question." Cee repeated her hand motions over the glass, then closed her gnarled fingers over mine once more. "Look where the shadows lie deep in your wake, my lamb, if you would see the one who hunts you."

Her voice echoed strangely as the opaque surface of the mirror drew me in again. As if cued by her words, it opened not into a lighted room, but into the familiar restless kaleidoscope of a cityscape half-drenched in night.

22

DARK MIRROR

The scene in the mirror teemed with the familiar contrasts of San Francisco after dark. Shadowy trees hung overhead, and the bright facility lighting that illuminated the blocky angles of the building nearby only served to deepen the hidden corners where it couldn't reach.

"Is that Golden Gate Park?" The shadows fell in odd, distorted shapes across the grass, disorienting me. Try as I might, I couldn't shift my point of view within the vision, but I was pretty sure I recognized the building as one of the park's museums. A bulbous sculpture loomed in the foreground, a giant cast metal vase encrusted with cavorting figures of satyrs and cherubs out of some horny classicist's wine-infused nightmare.

In the distance beyond the statue, a circle of lights spun slowly against the sky—a Ferris wheel, incongruous to the point of surrealism. Distant screams floated on the wind from riders swinging in the cars at the top of the ride.

"Don't know what they were thinking when they put that thing in," I muttered, then caught my breath as Special Agent Meghan North stepped into my field of view.

She stopped in front of the bronze vase, her glance darting side to side in a furtive assessment of the surroundings. After a moment, she stiffened, attention caught and held by—what? Shadows on the other side of the statue shifted and thickened, but for the life of me I couldn't bring them into focus.

"Oh good, you're here," North said, curt and quiet. "We have a problem. Maybe more than one."

Who was she talking to? Why couldn't I see whether a figure stood there beside the statue where the shadows gathered? Wind gusted through the trees above, snatching away any response, but whatever North heard made her flush, mouth flattening to a tight, strained line.

"No, I haven't *lost* her! We—I have leads. I'll lean harder on the boyfriend. He knows more than he's telling, but he's no dummy. He'll lawyer up the moment I say boo."

"Good man, Sebastian," I whispered, but the spark of pride faded quickly, replaced by new worry. Of course she'd go after Sebastian, and even the best lawyer might not help him. I already knew how little respect she had for due process of law.

How much did she know about our beach house trip? It didn't look good for either of us that we had visited Helena a few hours before she turned up dead.

North kept talking. "When I find her, I'll tell you, but I have to be more careful. My superintendent wants me to drop this. Says it's radioactive. I get the feeling she's an asset or something. He threatened to reassign my team."

She listened again, grim-faced, and again a trick of the breeze made the shouts from the Ferris wheel swell, drowning out the other speaker. "I won't let you down," she said. "I'll find a way. I'm not in the habit of breaking my promises."

Why on earth couldn't I see who she was talking to? They must have positioned themselves just so behind that damn sculpture, but even so, the well-lit installation shouldn't have offered that good of a hiding place. I craned my neck, trying to peer into the shadows like Cee had told me—

The vision dissolved into the flickering lamplight and dusty elegance of my host's sitting room. Stomach reeling, I sank back into the chair. "What the hell was that?"

Cee shook her head. "I think that's enough." Gently, she pried my hands from the looking glass, and I snatched them back, folding them in my lap as she twitched the cloth back over the surface. "You look a bit green, dear. Wouldn't want you to lose your lunch, now, would we? This old carpet is the very devil to clean, you know."

"But I didn't see anything! I couldn't even hear—whoever it was she was talking to."

"It is as I said. You were not ready."

"That's bullshit! I *am* ready. This woman is corrupt, and she's going after people I love." I pushed back from the chair and stood, the brief wave of vertigo ebbing away. Now I was just angry. "Thanks for your hospitality, but I can't stay here. Do you think I could use that phone you mentioned?"

Cee grunted and rose, leaning heavily on her cane as she shuffled to the sideboard. Had she expended some of her own power to help me look for answers? What kind of power did she wield, anyway? The word "witch" kept coming to mind, but I didn't dare say it out loud in her presence, in case she took it as an insult.

"Here you are." The old woman thrust an object into my hands, a heavy, unwieldy rotary telephone with an antique horn-shaped mouthpiece. "You do know how to use one of these, I hope."

"Uh...Cee, this isn't connected to anything. Are you sure it works?" On the one hand, it seemed belatedly ludicrous to think she would have a telephone line, even if this wasn't some otherworldly dimension. On the other, a wireless-equipped antique novelty phone probably wouldn't get service here, either.

"There's nothing less free than the mind of a skeptic, daughter of Samael," she retorted. "You believe what you saw in my mirror, don't you? Technomancy isn't my specialty, but powerful folk find they owe me favors, now and again. It works."

"I guess I'll find out. What about 411?"

"You'll have to make do with the yellow pages." Cee herded me out of the mirror room, grumbling about young people shackled by empiricism who couldn't solve the simplest problems or understand basic sorcery. Despite her disapproval, however, the phone book she had Mara fetch from upstairs helpfully covered the San Francisco area code.

Talk about sorcery. I didn't even think they still published these, but it had last year's date on it. I paged through, looking for three numbers: the courthouse where I was due to appear the next day on Rae's case; Greg Grayson—Sebastian's attorney, who I hoped would stand in for me until I got back; and the local FBI field office.

It was time to stop running. Ready or not, I had to track down whoever was pulling North's strings.

To do that, I would have to give her what she wanted. I'd offer her a deal: keep me out of the silver cuffs, minimize the collateral damage, and I'd step willingly into her web.

I probably should have done that to begin with, but old habits died hard, and I always did like to run.

As it turned out, I didn't need extra time to travel back to the Bay Area. All Cee needed to do, as she put it, was open a door in any trackless forest, and as it happened, I knew just such a place.

With my plan in motion, I scheduled for first thing Monday morning the meeting that would probably mean the end of my freedom and agreed to spend one restless night under the roof of the gingerbread house.

"You're safe and sound," my hostess had reassured me. "As long as you don't go outside after nightfall, of course."

I closed the curtains tight, doing my best to sleep while nameless things snuffled around the outside of the walls. Of course, Cee's woods must be full of bears and other creatures. That was only natural. At least, that was what I told myself. I decided not to ask questions I didn't want to know the answers to.

In the bright light of the following morning, I said my farewells. Then I stepped through the black heart of a hollow tree into the fog-swathed redwood forest from whence I'd fled only twenty-four hours ago.

After about a half-mile hike downslope, I caught a glimpse of the abandoned cabin through the trees, as Cee had promised. All lay quiet, with no sign of any other person. I crossed the little clearing, headed for the road that lay beyond, and paused. For the first time since those visions in the glass, my resolve wavered.

Then a twig cracked somewhere behind me, and I leaped upward, wings out on instinct, turning in the air to face the sound.

North stepped out from around the corner of the cabin, gun in hand, aimed straight at my heart. "That's far enough, Ms. Knight," she said with a dry, triumphant smile.

This was it. All according to plan, but some part of me had started to hope I would make it home free. My heart sank so hard and fast that I dropped several feet in the air before my wings caught me. "I didn't come here just to put up a fight, Officer. I'll come peacefully."

"Put your hands up and get on the ground," she barked. "Don't think I won't shoot you."

"It never crossed my mind." It surprised me more that she hadn't tried it yet, after all the times she threatened it. I lifted my arms and palms toward her, drifting back to earth. Once my shoes touched the forest floor, I folded my wings and let them fade back into immateriality.

North kept me in her sights, still unappeased. "What's in the bag?"

"Clothes, a hat. I don't have any weapons, if that's what you're asking."

"Take it off and throw it over to me."

"All right." Careful not to make any sudden moves, I shrugged the backpack off and tossed it over. It landed in front of her, and she toed it closer as if it might explode.

"Don't move," she snapped.

I stood obediently, but my whole body tingled with sudden alertness, because it occurred to me that something had changed.

Unlike the other day, she had no backup.

"We should talk about this, North." I used my most gentle and reasonable tone despite the turmoil churning inside me, the tone I used to calm weepy witnesses and butter up opposing counsel. I didn't bother with a Presence, though. That wouldn't get past her protective silver. "Tell me, what are you really after? You know I didn't kill Helena Ritter or Jared Williams."

"I don't know anything of the sort." Strain crackled in her voice. "You had motive, opportunity, and a history of violence."

Aha. "In other words, you don't have anything on me." No wonder her supervisor had gotten antsy. "Where's your team, North? Do they even know you're out here this morning? Or is this a less official meeting than you led me to believe?"

"Shut up." Her gun had dropped a fraction. "If you didn't kill them, you know who did. It was one of you, wasn't it? Don't deny it. Demons of a feather stick together."

"Oh, please," I said, disgusted. "We don't all know each other. Not even close."

Her eyes had that fanatical gleam again, wild in her flushed face. "But you know *him.* Don't you?"

Him. That was my clue, the thread I could pull to summon whatever lurked in the shadows at the center of this web. "Him, who?"

"Don't play dumb with me, Ms. Knight. You're rash, but you're smart, and that makes you dangerous. He was right about you." Her voice dropped. "He was right about *everything.*"

Cold tendrils slithered up my spine. "I have no idea who you're talking about."

"I don't believe you." She refreshed her aim, but this time, the barrel shook perceptibly.

Competent, unemotional. North was *spooked.* More than spooked. She was afraid of whoever *he* was. I had to keep my own shiver out of my words. "Be more specific."

"Come on, Knight." She said it through gritted teeth, as if it cost her. "Our files refer to him as Subject D14. His age is indeterminate, but records suggest it might be on the scale of centuries, possibly millennia. Your association ended in the desert around October of last year."

The earth seemed to tilt beneath my feet, my wings stirring under my skin to re-balance me. Like that would do me any good. "No."

"No? Feel free to stop me when this starts to sound familiar. As far as we can tell, that association goes back years, to a little brownstone apartment in Manhattan's West Side. He's gone by multiple aliases over the decades we've tracked him, but you most likely remember him by what he calls his 'demon name'."

A numb sensation welled up within me and spread rapidly outward, like I was turning to stone from the inside out. "That can't be."

"Why not? Because you killed him, is that it?"

"Yes," I whispered. "I killed him."

I'd plunged the stake into his chest. I'd watched the amber light go out of his eyes and felt his energy flow back into me. With it, my strength of will had returned. His death released the hold on me he'd maintained all those years, the claim that had lulled me into trusting him even when he violated my boundaries.

"Surely you didn't think we'd let such an important specimen go to waste," North said. "Not after decades of work. To have him fall back into our hands after such a long time in the wild—we couldn't let that kind of opportunity blow away in the wind."

"You *saved* him?" I stared at her, open-mouthed. "But to do that, someone would have to—*oh.*" My shock turned to horror, killing the words on my lips.

I hadn't witnessed him crumble into dust. I'd given all I had to save Danny from death in turn, and when the military helicopters showed up to whisk us away, I didn't have enough left in me to resist. I certainly didn't think to ask what they'd done with the body.

Even if I had, I never would have asked if they'd brought him back. I never would have imagined my own government could be *that* clueless.

On second thought, that probably said more about me than it did them.

"We did what we had to do." Her mouth flattened into a thin, determined line.

"That's...wow." Someone would have had to volunteer to give him kether, skin to skin. Worse, pulling him back from the brink like that, from silver to the heart, would require more than a mere touch. Much more. "It was you, wasn't it? *You* did what you had to. You volunteered."

She shrugged. "What if I did?"

It was fucked up, that was what. He *had* died out there, and she had what, screwed him back to life?

A mirthless laugh bubbled up in my throat, dry as stones in a dead riverbed, bitter as the bile in my belly. "Holy hell. You really don't know anything about demons, do you?"

"What are you talking about?" Her gun had dipped, and a spark of fear flashed for a moment in her eyes.

"You gave him energy. You gave him *life.*" I shuddered, the full import of it sinking in as I spoke. "That means you forged a bond that goes deeper than touch, deeper than sex. That silver you wear can't stop it. You're part of him now, and he's part of you. He's in your head, in your heart."

"You're lying."

"I wish I were." Gods and monsters, how I wished it. "A forced bond on either side—if that's how it happened—that'll screw you up even worse. I'm surprised it didn't kill you outright."

"I'm *fine!*"

"No, you're not." The numb void in my gut churned with nausea, the dizzy tilt of an out-of-control roller coaster through the theme park of my worst nightmares. "You're obsessed with me and with him, but you're just a pawn in one of his sick games. He's manipulating you, and you can't even see it."

"He told me what you did." Her voice wavered, though, the cracks in her conviction widening. "You're a killer. You took everything from him. His life, his freedom, and then his daughter."

"Wait. This is all about *Eve*?" It made a horrible kind of sense. I had replaced him, and he couldn't abide that. "No. Those are his words in your mouth. Did you ever think who else might benefit from me getting framed for a murder? *He* killed those people. You must see that."

She went pale, a slow drain of the blood from her face, and the gun dropped further. "I—no, that's not possible."

"Oh, it very much is," I said, and in her moment of doubt, I sprang.

My wings exploded outward, launching me up and over her head, faster than she could react. She cursed, swinging the pistol wildly to the woods and road and the air overhead—too late.

Looping one arm around her throat in a choke hold, I grabbed her gun arm with the other. She struggled, cursing, with kicks aimed at my shins and her free elbow jamming into my ribs, but she didn't have the strength to break my grip.

I tightened my hold on her windpipe, squeezing hard enough to let her know I meant business. "Drop the gun. I don't want to hurt you."

"You'll regret this." But she let the weapon fall. It made a muffled thump on the soft ground. "Assaulting a federal officer is a felony."

"Put it on my tab." I pushed her forward and toed the gun to the side, out of reach. A swift pat-down turned up no additional weapons besides a government phone, its blank screen offering another piece of the puzzle. "You didn't come here in your official capacity, did you? You're off the rails, North."

Her throat worked under my arm, a convulsive gulp. "You don't know what you're talking about."

"Don't I? Your agency told you to drop this vendetta, but you agreed to meet me with nothing to offer, no backup, and your phone powered down." I gave her a little shake for emphasis, pocketing the phone in case it came in handy later. "You're smarter than that, so I figure you came here hoping to clean up your mess. Or did he put you up to this, too?"

She stiffened and started to protest, but at my final question, a tremor shook the corded muscle under my arm. "He...tricked me." All at once, the fight seemed to drain out of her, as if the acknowledgment dissolved her stubborn will. "I thought I had it under control, but he was so strong."

"Yeah, well, you wouldn't be the first." Damn it. I wouldn't sympathize with this woman who had violated my rights, put me in poison cuffs, and threatened to kill me multiple times. Still, I eased up my grip a little. Sometimes I didn't know my own strength. "Survival is one thing. Getting free is something else."

"That's because you're weak," she snarled and took the opening she'd engineered. Twisting in my grasp, she dove sideways, going for the weapon I'd kicked away.

She was desperate and cunning, but I was faster. One hard shove had her on the ground. "The problem with you government types is that you always underestimate us." I pinned her arms behind her with one gloved hand, knee planted at the small of her back. With the other hand, I collected her gun, pressing the muzzle against the nape of her neck. "It's best to let us handle our own, so you better tell me what you know. Where is Ariel now?"

"Funny you should ask." Behind me, the smooth, musical tenor brimmed with a veneer of light amusement over the cold malice beneath.

My entire body went cold at that voice, my lungs instantly too tight to hold even an ounce of breath. Under my knee, North exhaled, limp with relief or resignation.

Moving with the slow, sticky paralysis of a dream, I turned my head, the pistol a lead weight in my hands as I dragged it around to aim the barrel squarely at a dead demon's heart.

23

WHEN THE DEVIL DRIVES

Ariel stood before me in the flesh. Not a dream wrapped in shifting shadows, but a living nightmare, undeniable in daylight.

No wonder Cee's dark mirror wouldn't show me his face, the one I couldn't ever in a million years have prepared myself to see.

"As it happens, I couldn't agree more." A smirk curled his lips. "I can take this from here."

A little distance away, he stood in a perfect beam of sunlight. Like it had burned through the fog and angled between the limbs of the redwoods just for him, it gilded his blond curls and illuminated his beautiful features, chiseled enough to make Michelangelo weep.

He was *here*. He was North's backup. He had come for her. And standing in front of him—

"*Eve...*" The name formed soundlessly on my lips.

She stared at me, wide green eyes clouded with fear, shock, and distrust. He gripped her by both shoulders, as if holding her in position between us.

I lowered the weapon, my hand sweating and slippery in its glove, chest hollow and echoing like a drum. I didn't have a clear shot, not with Eve's body shielding his center of mass. Despite occasional, infrequent training sessions with Sebastian, I couldn't trust myself not to hit her with one of the silver bullets that North had doubtless loaded in her gun.

Wordless, Eve shook her head, one quick jerk of her chin. Then her father's hands flexed on her upper arms. She stilled and stepped backward, casting a sideways, wistful gaze up at him.

Of course she craved his attention, his good opinion, his love. I couldn't blame her for that. Any daughter would, no matter how good or bad of a person her parent was, no matter what terrible things she heard or imagined of him. He was still her father, after all, and back from the dead beyond all belief.

Was she here by choice? If nothing else, this week had taught me that the arrival of a prodigal father could bring on overwhelming, confusing emotions. Unlike Samael with me, Ariel would have taken full advantage of that vulnerable state to bend Eve to his ends, bombarding her with love and lies, building her castles in the air.

How long had she kept this secret from me? All those absences from school she hadn't wanted me to know about—maybe this explained it.

"Well, Lily fair?" His smirk widened as he drank in whatever reaction showed on my face. "Aren't you going to say hello? Surprised to see me, after what you did?"

"No." I finally found my voice. "I already saw you once this week. I thought I imagined you, but you were there. All along...I should have known."

"Probably. I must say, I didn't expect it would take you so long to catch on." Oh, how I hadn't missed that deliberate needling, always with a smile, at least until the mask slipped. "But then again, you had good reason to disbelieve. Resurrections like mine don't happen every day, in these times at least."

"I hear you have the government to thank for that." That must rankle him as much as dying did. Two could play with needles if no one cared about losing an eye. "What's your game here, Ariel? What do you want from me?"

"No games this time." His smile didn't waver. "You should be grateful. I've come to take a problem off your hands."

"What..." North gasped from the ground, where I still had her pinned. "I told you I'd take care of it! You weren't supposed to be here."

I'd almost forgotten she was there. "Shut up," I hissed at the same time as Ariel said, "Quiet," and she subsided.

"I'd appreciate it if you gave my friend some space to breathe," Ariel continued. "Her methods are questionable, but needs must when the Devil drives. She's my responsibility."

Unsettled, I rose, but I kept the gun trained on North. "I think you've mistaken the dynamic in this situation. I'm armed, and you're not." Or at least, I hoped not. He hadn't tried to kill me yet, hadn't made any aggressive moves at all. Somehow, that didn't comfort me.

"You wouldn't shoot a federal officer in cold blood just to spite me. And in front of Eve, too?" He shook his head, brow creased in a perfect facsimile of sorrowful concern. "Even I couldn't save you from that rap."

"Oh, so you're here to save me?" I nearly laughed. "That would be a first. Thanks to the two of you, I'm already a wanted woman."

"Then you're already in plenty of trouble. Come now, Lily. You're smart enough not to make it worse for yourself."

"Don't count on it," I said, teeth bared. "Needs must, like you said. Maybe I'm desperate. Isn't that what you wanted? Maybe I've got nothing to lose."

North stayed silent, but she twitched at that, head snapping back and forth between us as we negotiated her fate. She had training under fire, but I wouldn't want to change places with her. Not that my situation looked much better.

"Really?" He cocked his head. "I doubt that very much. The way I see it, you have plenty left to lose. What do you think, Eve?"

Eve jumped when he said her name, as if something had stung her. "Lily, please. She's not worth going to jail for."

"That's my girl," Ariel purred. "Listen to her, Lily. Let me rid you of this meddlesome Fed, and then we can go our separate ways in peace. I assure you, it's the best outcome for everyone involved."

Tempting, but I'd be the world's worst patsy to take him at his word. "So you can dump her somewhere for me to trip over later, like those last two bodies? Gotta say that sounds less than ideal."

Eve's sharp gasp punctuated my words. I bit back a sigh. "Wouldn't he? You know what he's capable of, Eve." She'd once confided in me that she thought he might have killed her adopted human parents, yet she still wanted to believe the best of him.

Well, he was her father, and I'd wanted to believe the same, before trauma had drilled that youthful optimism out of me. Too bad she couldn't learn from my mistakes.

North had begun to edge toward Ariel, but she stopped short as well. "What do you mean?"

"Didn't you listen to a damn thing I said? He killed those people. This is all a scheme to get me put away—or put down."

"How convenient, making me the big bad guy in all this." Ariel chuckled. "Same old Lily, clinging to your moral absolutism, like you're any better than me. You still haven't learned that not everything I do is about you."

I glared at him. "Isn't it?"

"It's your call, Meghan," he said softly, ignoring me now as his focus narrowed on the woman he held in thrall. "You can believe the self-professed desperate fugitive holding you at gunpoint or trust a friend who wanted to keep his daughter safe."

Damn him. He played both sides so well, even I had trouble telling which end was up. North looked from him to me, then back to him, and nodded.

"Better the demon you know, I guess." I shrugged, stepping back. "If that's what you want, it's your funeral."

North stumbled toward him, and Ariel wrapped an ungentle arm around her. She cried out in pained protest, but he paid her no mind. Dragging them both with him, he backed toward the road that waited beyond the screen of trees, Eve's small body still positioned strategically between himself and me.

"You bastard," I whispered. "You worthless fucker."

I didn't give a damn about North, but I wouldn't let Eve come to harm. He knew I wouldn't try to fire on them if she stood a chance of taking the bullet for him. My eyes burned with furious tears, blurring my vision.

When I dashed them away, the three of them had disappeared. *Damn demon speed.* The loud slam of a car door echoed through the silent forest, and I roused myself, sprinting the way they had gone.

A squared-off, shiny black four-wheel-drive SUV sat on the dirt road—American-made, which probably made it North's ride courtesy of the US government, whether sanctioned or otherwise. On the other side of the hulking vehicle, Ariel ducked down to speak quietly to Eve.

She nodded, rounding the front of the SUV with keys in hand, eyes huge as she climbed into the driver's seat and settled behind the wheel. Ariel shoved North between the two and took the passenger seat.

The rumble of the engine filled the forest, revving a little too high. I held my breath. Maybe Eve, a novice driver, would stall the damn thing, give me a chance in hell at getting her out of this.

No such luck. The gears ground with an ugly screech when she shifted, but she successfully threw the vehicle into reverse and gunned it backwards down the hill, tires squealing and spitting gravel as they went.

I took to the air. Wheeling and canting to avoid the trees in my path, I dived toward the road after it.

The gun weighed heavy in my hand, and I dropped to the ground in the road, mouth gritty with the dust raised by the wheels. I trusted my aim in motion even less than standing still. Planting my feet as Sebastian had taught me, I raised the weapon, trying to sight down it. Maybe if I shot low, I could safely hit a tire, slow them, stop them.

Who was I kidding? I couldn't clear the blur of tears and dust from my eyes, couldn't see anything except Eve's gaze fixed on me through the dirty windshield, her face white and set.

My hand dropped once more, the gun hanging useless by my side. Eve swung the wheel, coaxing the truck into a tight turn. I winced as the vehicle shook and pivoted in a cloud of flying gravel, spinning out. Whether by luck or instinct, though, she maintained control. The SUV stopped its spin facing downhill, leaped forward with another scream of gears, and vanished into the trees.

I launched into the sky, rising above the treetops and scouting the slope. The dirt track barely showed from this vantage point, only visible when the trees thinned here and there, a faint scar on the thickly forested hill. A wispy trail of dust and flashes of reflected light gleaming between the arrow tips of redwoods betrayed the SUV's position, moving fast downhill.

Eve always wanted to drive too fast. A dull, bruised sensation settled in my chest, and I flew lower, following at a distance and staying just above the canopy. Downslope, the wilderness began to give way to human civilization. Larger estates cropped up first, dotted at wide intervals among the trees. Smaller, more close-knit homes joined them lower down to form a small suburb nestled at the knees of Mount Tamalpais, the Sleeping Lady.

I gathered my shrouding Presence around myself. I had enough problems without setting off a wave of UFO or Mothman sightings to spark more law enforcement attention and a media circus.

The black SUV tore through the little town at breakneck speed, running at least three traffic lights on its way to the southbound freeway onramp. Maybe I should have spent more time helping Eve learn to drive. It seemed likely now that Ariel had stepped in where I feared to tread and taught her all the wrong lessons, yet again.

My safest path took me parallel to the highway along the wooded ridges that stretched south toward the peninsula, but I couldn't keep the SUV in sight without climbing higher and breaking out from the tree line. By the time I had eyes on the tunnel that led out to the headlands to the Golden Gate Bridge, I had lost them completely.

Fog still clung around the narrow peninsula this side of the bay, so I cautiously dropped lower into its covering mists and finally alighted to perch on top of the bridge's north-most tower. Hunching my wings around me to shield myself from the worst of the damp, I squinted, scanning the crowded lanes below for any sign of them.

A surprising number of Californians drove dark SUVs, it seemed. The fog made it harder to distinguish them, and from above, I couldn't see inside the cabs. No way to tell if one of them had an unlicensed teenage driver with a need for speed, a possibly kidnapped federal agent, or a beautiful, demonic asshole in the passenger seat.

Well, I couldn't sit here forever like a disgruntled hawk who'd failed to catch her prey. The fog would burn off before long, denying me even this small semblance of cover.

Besides, I had a court appearance on the docket, and I needed a change of clothes.

Swallowing a scream of frustration, I took to the air again, winging south toward the city. With any luck, North's bosses had gotten enough of a case of cold feet to reassign whatever surveillance detail she'd assigned on the condo.

In the meantime, Ariel would probably pack Eve on a plane to New York and be long gone by the time I picked up his trail again. I shuddered, my altitude dipping. I couldn't go back there, where I'd spent my least proud moments in his tutelage, learning his lessons, feeding his appetites, losing sight of myself.

Over open water now, I took North's pistol out of my belt and dropped it into the gray, misty sea far below. It sank beneath the waves without a trace.

Maybe I should let Eve go, too. If she had chosen him, who was I to argue with her decision? She had almost reached legal majority. She didn't want me telling her what to do anymore. In fact, she didn't really need me to tell her anymore.

Ariel was her father, after all, and I was just a hot mess of a functionally orphaned half-demon. I had no idea of what it really meant to belong to my own father's people.

Still, I'd done my best with her. I'd tried to teach her a different way, but I couldn't make her choices for her. Eventually, she would have to choose for herself.

It hurt that she hadn't chosen me, and it hurt even more that she'd chosen *him* instead. Ariel would say I deserved that hurt, and maybe I did.

Maybe I never should have gotten attached to her in the first place.

Either way, they were gone. Ariel had Eve. He had North. He had me where he wanted me, off balance, on the run. He'd caught me in a tangled web of his lies and my regrets, heart sinking fast with the weight of my guilt. He certainly had the upper hand.

And just as I had before, I'd let him get away with it.

24

BETWEEN SINNERS AND SAINTS

I crept into Sebastian's house like a thief in the night, or more accurately, like a bedraggled demon on a damp and dreary morning. I'd taken the first flight of my life from his bedroom balcony a year ago, and now its redwood deck became my last remaining refuge.

I'd circled for a while in the fog above Pacific Heights, in a holding pattern despite senses vibrating on raw alert for the beat of helicopter rotors. I didn't want to drag Sebastian into this more than I already had, but my condo didn't seem like a safe spot to go to ground, hardly mine at all. As for Danny, I couldn't face her yet, not given what Cee's dark mirror had revealed. Besides, I hadn't gotten a chance to peek in on Sebastian like I had on Eve or Danny.

With a soft thump, my sneakers touched down on the ruddy planks, the opened hearts of trees whose living forest I'd just fled from. My wings dissolved into the fog, and with the sudden return to human gravity, a wave of dizziness washed over me. Gut churning, I clung to the balcony's railing, sagging against it and waiting for the spinning sensation to end.

Did Sebastian even know I was alive? Everything had happened so fast, and I hadn't had time to call, not that I could with my phone dead somewhere on the bottom of the San Francisco Bay. He had no reason to believe I hadn't died with it. He deserved better than that, more than the role of resting place of last resort.

I pushed myself upright on unsteady legs and cautiously approached the bedroom window. The filmy white curtains on the other side obscured the interior, even when I pressed my face up to the glass like a hungry ghost. Anyone inside would see my silhouette, at least if they wore a silver ring that made them immune to my cloaking glamours. I didn't drop those, just in case North had someone watching the house from the street.

Nothing stirred, and I couldn't feel his energy anywhere nearby. The downside of his silver ring, I reminded myself in a vain attempt to shake the spider-silken veil of unease settling over me. What if Ariel had gotten here before me? It would amuse my enemy, wouldn't it, to just keep taking them from me, one by one until I had no one left but him?

No more stalling. I didn't have time for it. If I had to, I could break in, pass my hand through the glass of the balcony door, or just step through the window like my nemesis once had, with his flair for a dramatic entrance.

I didn't need the theatrics, thankfully, since that trick called for a level of self-possession I doubted I could muster in my current state of shock. The handle yielded, and the door swung open, unlocked. It shouldn't bother me as much as it did—who could get up here, besides a demon like me, unstoppable by locks in any event? Unlocked doors hadn't boded well for me lately, though, and Sebastian loved his security. He'd built his fortune on it, his company, the one that for my sake he'd let slip through his fingers.

The bed lay empty, neatly made even this early in the morning, or maybe just unslept in. Sebastian wasn't here, though a whiff of his aftershave lingered, familiar notes of dark wood and bright citrus. I took a shuddering breath, memories of better days crowding in with the scent. I'd leaned into happiness here and found my power in his touch. Learning how to let him love me hadn't come easily, not for someone—something—like me, but Sebastian's patient lessons had taught me everything I knew.

How would he react when he found out I'd learned enough from him to let a new love in?

In the unlit stillness of the room, I ran wind-roughened fingers over the gray silk and eiderdown of the comforter. The urge rose in me to wrap myself in it and disappear, sleep for a year and a day until I woke up as someone new, a woman who belonged here.

Then I heard it. Sound filtered upward from the house's lower floor, a faint stream of melody from soft-struck strings—Sebastian's baby grand piano, notes flowing out in the gentle minor key of a requiem.

Ariel didn't play the piano, at least not as long as I'd known him. The practice it required wouldn't have interested him, not even in his thousand years or more of troubling this world. I abandoned the temptations of Sebastian's expensive duvet, smoothed back my wind-knotted hair to little avail, and ventured down the stairs.

As I descended, the tune shifted from a classical sonata into a more modern arrangement, an instrumental that went with lyrics I half-remembered—about the waiting game of a spectator among sinners and saints, left behind in the clash of greater forces.

It takes and it takes...

The piano faced away from the room's entrance, and he didn't hear my footsteps behind him, lost in his music. I had more than enough time to stand adrift in the doorway, taking in the taut lines of his back and shoulders, the messy state of his normally neat dark hair, and the way he'd rolled the sleeves of his creased shirt up past his elbows.

When I finally spoke his name, his slender fingers jerked on the keys, the melody trailing off in a discordant, jagged phrase. He spun to face me, pale as if I really were a ghost, blue eyes burning from the shadow of more than one sleepless night.

"Lily. You're all right." The crack in his voice shook me to my core. "I thought... Thank God."

I had a lot of entities to thank for my continued existence, but none of them were gods, not exactly. "Have a little faith," I said. "I'm not so easy to get rid of—hi."

The stool nearly toppled, but he'd ignored it in his haste to get to me. With the desperate grasp of a drowning man, he crushed me against him, spun me around, and buried his face in my hair, whispering words too quick and broken to catch.

I hugged him back, startled. It wasn't like him to lose composure this way, and I hadn't even started to tell him my worst news. "Sebastian?"

"It's not you. They said—" His slim back heaved with a caught breath under my hands, almost a sob. "Where have you been?"

"It's a long story. You go first. They said what?" Who were they? The Feds, probably. North, most likely.

"It's Helena," he said, flat-toned. "She's gone."

Oh, no. He must have seen the news reports about my fugitive status, but how much did he know about why? If he thought she'd just left town, I didn't know if I had it in me to break that news to him. "What does that mean?"

"They said it was a broken neck." He pulled away from me, but he wouldn't meet my gaze. "They wouldn't say anything else. They kept asking about you."

They said you were a murderer. Was that what he had almost blurted out? "Oh, Sebastian. I'm so sorry."

"She could have had an accident," he said. "Maybe a fall. She wouldn't have done something to hurt herself. That wasn't the kind of person she was."

"That's not—" I cut myself off. It sounded as though no one had told him where she'd died—or who had found her. Why would North cover that up? I cleared my throat, but my next words still came out hoarse with nerves. "Um. There's something you should know."

Now his eyes snapped back to mine, but I couldn't read them. He held my gaze for a breath, and then he said, "I'm not so sure I want to know."

"No," I answered softly. "You probably don't. But you need to. It might help you make some sense of this."

"How?" The single, raw syllable snapped out like a whip, and I flinched. "You ran from federal custody, Lily. You leaped from a bridge. I saw it on the eleven o'clock news. The same night my ex-wife— No. Nothing about this makes any sense at all."

He'd never admit it, but he thought I'd done this. The realization burned like silver through my heart. "Maybe not." I couldn't sugar-coat what came next, just spit it out heavy and bitter as lead. "Here's the thing, though. Ariel's back."

The words rocked him back, half a step, half a stumble. "I thought he was dead."

"Me too, until this morning when I saw him in the flesh."

"I don't understand." He passed a hand over his bloodless face. When Ariel came calling, trauma left his mark on everyone, and Sebastian had watched his lover die because of him. "Dead people don't come back."

"Dead demons do, it seems." I should have killed him harder. I should have stayed and watched him crumble into dust. "When we went to see Helena, that beach house stank of incubus. He was using her." Then, when she wasn't useful anymore, he discarded her on my back porch.

Sebastian's mouth tightened. "He was using her to get to me."

"No," I said. "He used her to set me up." It fit Ariel's profile. Helena, North... Who else had he gotten his claws into? He moved them all like pawns across a chessboard, sacrificing them when it suited his purposes.

"I knew something wasn't right." He dropped his head into his palms. "She was acting so strangely. I should have known. I should have said something. Maybe I could have stopped this."

"Don't do that, Seb. Don't blame yourself." I tugged at his wrists, peeling his fingers away from his face so I could force him to look at me, even as I bit back my own self-excoriation. "You once told me that I couldn't fault myself for what he did to me. If that's true, then it's even more true for you and Helena."

"I swore an oath to her." He raised his gaze, washed clear and colorless, to meet mine. "*Til death do us part...* She deserved better than this."

"We all do." *Especially you.* I smoothed the hair back that had fallen over his forehead.

He twitched under my hand like a nervous cat. "If Ariel's back, I should call in a tip to the Feds. A new lead might get them off your back for a while."

"No! It's not that simple. He has his hooks in one of them, too."

"You're serious." Sebastian ran his hands through his hair, leaving it messier than before. "There has to be something we can do."

"Yeah. I could kill him. Again." At his wince, I plastered on a smile. "Kidding. Mostly."

"No, you're not," he said without a trace of answering humor. "Please, Lily. I don't like the idea of you fighting this on your own."

"Who said I'd be on my own? I still have a trick or two up my sleeve. I have friends in high places—and low ones, which might be more useful." I had a goddess in a jail cell, where my client awaited her trial later today. If North decided to arrest me at the courthouse, things could get awkward fast, which was where calling in my other favors would have to come in.

"I get the idea you're still not telling me everything." Even in his current state of grief and exhaustion, he noticed too much.

"Hm," I said. "Well, my dad's in town. I met him right before everything went to hell."

He frowned, but interest sparked in his expression like sunlight on ice. "I thought you and your dad didn't talk."

"Not that one. The other one. He's..." What was Samael? Nice? Strange? Interesting? Frustratingly vague about all the questions I wanted answered? I settled for what he'd said about me. "Unexpected."

"That's one way to put it." Sebastian's eyebrow arched. "So, he's like you."

"A demon, yes, but in fact, he reminds me of you. Not in a weird way," I hastened to add as the eyebrow lifted higher. "It's just—I didn't want to like him, but I think I do."

"Somehow, I feel you just damned us both with faint praise." Sebastian's expression softened. "I'd like to meet him sometime. If that's okay with you."

In the current circumstances, it seemed almost ludicrous to consider my boyfriend meeting my father. An image rose in my mind of the two of them shaking hands over a glass of bourbon, in black and white like a father and prospective son-in-law in a classic film. I didn't have any real-life context from which to pull.

"Sure," I said. "If you want."

Funny enough, Danny had said she wanted to meet Samael too. My imagination added her to the bourbon drinking scene, toasting me and saying something wry but affectionate that made the rest of us laugh as she drained her glass, her short pink hair a repudiation of the grayscale 1950s aesthetic I'd conjured for them.

I liked that image better, this strange family that didn't fit any mold I'd been handed. *Is that what I wanted from them?*

"There's something else," Sebastian said. "I saw it just now in your face. Come on, Lily. I'm a big boy. I can take it, whatever it is."

Steeling myself, I swallowed hard. *No more lies.* "I slept with Danny."

Surprise bloomed across his handsome features. Whatever he'd expected me to say, that wasn't it. "You certainly work fast, but like I said, I don't have a problem with it."

"I didn't plan on this," I said quickly. "It just sort of happened. I needed a source, and she offered to help."

His expression stilled, as if I'd turned him into stone. "You took energy from her."

"It was an emergency. I was on the run, and then we got lost in the woods. Don't look at me like that."

"I'm not looking at you any particular way," he said, but his eyes had frozen over. "It's well within our agreed upon terms."

"Then why—"

"I haven't slept these last few days." He turned to fuss with the piano, folded the sheet music and set it aside, then wiped down the keys with a silk cloth. "I'm tired, that's all. So are you. We can talk more later, but I think now is...not a good time." The lid closed over the keys with a sharp, final clunk that vibrated the strings within, a whispered memory of music.

"Sebastian, I..." What else could I say? The whole point of our non-exclusivity was to allow me to get my energy needs met elsewhere. Yet I had obviously hurt him by doing so with Danny, and he didn't feel ready to tell me why. "I have to go."

"Do what you have to do." Sebastian had finished at the piano, but he didn't turn. "Don't worry about me."

He was right. Now wasn't the time, and maybe it never would be. Things didn't work out like that for me even at my best. Ariel's return had stolen my chance to salvage something good in the wake of all my mistakes.

Besides, I had to call a man about a warrant. Then I had to defend a goddess in open court against charges of murder she had definitely committed.

I couldn't beat Ariel alone, but as I'd told Sebastian, I had a few more tricks in my back pocket, one of them literally. It dug into my hip with the weight and awkward shape of an oversized government-issue smartphone.

With it I carried the faint hope that one person in a position of power might believe in my innocence and do something about it. If I could get Ira Delaney on the line, maybe I could let someone else handle this for a change while I got back to figuring out all the regular complications of my normal-ish life.

I glanced over my shoulder. Sebastian stood still at the closed piano, long back rigid and his dark head bowed.

It was definitely time to call in the big guns.

25

ON MY OWN

At first, the Feds claimed not to know an Ira Delaney, but when I informed them that their own officer had been compromised by an informant and failed to report the full circumstances of said informant's escape from custody, the façade of certainty betrayed a slight crack. When I mentioned the word "incubus," they started to sound downright nervous.

Eventually, they gave up and put me through to another line. I paced Sebastian's front porch while it rang in an odd double pattern for a full minute. By the time it finally clicked over, I was cursing fluently into the receiver, on the verge of giving up.

"Lily Knight," said a familiar deep voice on the other end, breaking into my stream of expletives. "You must have pulled some major strings to get through to this line. This better be an emergency."

"Oh, it's an emergency all right." I shuddered and gripped the phone tighter, clenching my teeth to keep myself from falling apart. Ira needed facts, not my feelings of terror and relief at hearing the voice of an authority who just might believe my wild story. "My old friend Ariel is alive and he's here in San Francisco. I'm pretty sure he killed two people—two *humans*—and tried to pin it on me."

The rest of the story spilled out onto the staticky line in a rush of words—the bodies I'd found, North's rush to charge me, her breaches of protocol, my wild flight, and the confrontation in the woods.

"I see," Ira said after a longish pause. Delay on the line, perhaps, or maybe he didn't have a good response to the panic I couldn't keep from my voice. "Do you have proof that he killed them?"

"No. Not proof. But I smelled incubus on one of them." Telling Ira about the other incubus skulking around town would only muddy the waters. "It's just like him to play games like this. And Officer North—she knew he was alive all along. She saved his life for some sicko government plan to weaponize his powers."

Another pause lengthened on the line. "Coercing a hostile member of your kind would be considered an extremely sensitive operation."

"It's a monumentally reckless one. He used their bond to manipulate her. Did you know about any of this?"

"My division has explored the possibility of conscripting one of your kind by force," Ira said finally. "We judged it untenable for multiple reasons."

"Untenable is right. That's not a real answer, and you know it."

"Don't overestimate my clearance, Knight. If some higher-up approved that plan, I wasn't made aware of it." He coughed, voice dropping to a wry undertone. "Some would say even one demon, properly harnessed and controlled, could serve as a powerful military asset."

The words *harnessed and controlled* sent a chill through me. "Well, someone in authority definitely decided this was a bright idea."

"As I told you, I'm in no position to second-guess the chain of command." Ira's voice sounded faint and far away now, almost disinterested.

"Aren't you listening to me?" It took all my self-control not to scream it at him. "He's a known killer, capable of almost anything. He's a monster."

"That may be true," he said, infuriatingly calm. "However, you may wish to remember that there are some who would say similar things about you."

"Excuse me?" I drew the phone away from my ear and stared at it, biting my tongue on a number of choice expletives. "Ariel believes humans are rightfully subservient to our kind. Just last year, he tried to recruit me for his demon supremacy campaign! Why don't you sound more worried about this?"

"What would you like me to do?" Ira's tone sharpened to a cold point.

"Make them take me off the wanted list, for one thing! Get North off my back. Help me find Ariel before he hurts anyone else. I know you have the resources. We've worked together before—"

"You seem to have mistaken our limited-term contract for an ongoing professional association," he said, chillier than ever. "Believe it or not, your personal history with this individual does not place him at the top of my list when it comes to imminent threats to human life. Not now and not ever."

"And I'm telling you, that's a big mistake. This guy is seriously bad news, and not just for me. More people could die." The line crackled, interference whispering in my ear. "Where the hell are you, anyway? You sound like you're on a satellite phone at the bottom of a well."

"That's none of your business and way above your clearance." His sigh transmitted loud and clear despite the static. "Given the irregularities you described, I can likely persuade the agency to drop the charges. You're on your own for the rest."

"I don't mean to sound ungrateful, but—that's it?"

"It's quite a lot, all things considered. Besides, Knight, you're the kind of person I call to handle things like this. So, handle it. Stop running. Use that magic sword I left you."

"I'm no swordswoman, Ira." The only person I knew who could handle a sword was currently in jail awaiting a trial due to start in a little over an hour, and her lawyer would have to wing it. My prep time had taken a hit with the whole going on the run thing. "Thanks for the help, I guess." I couldn't keep the sarcasm out of my tone.

"I do what I can," he said gravely, without a hint of return irony, and the phone beeped to let me know he'd hung up.

"*Fuck.*" I clutched the phone harder than I meant to, and the metal crumpled like aluminum foil. The glass of the touchscreen shattered, driving shards into my palm. "Fuck!"

If Ira refused to help, I was truly on my own against a threat I never thought I'd have to face again. He didn't seem to care that his government had set this in motion when it enabled North's hubris and tried to tame a sociopathic demon for their own nefarious ends. They couldn't leave well enough alone, couldn't let the dead stay dead, couldn't let him crumble to dust in the desert where he belonged.

And now I had to clean up their mess.

Dr. Harlow said it took time, that I couldn't expect my trauma symptoms to stop just because the trauma had come to an end. Now, though, I had run out of time. The trauma had literally come back to life and had me in its sights, like a high-speed train screaming toward me from the dark tunnels of San Francisco's underground. I could fight or I could flee, but deep inside something in me stood frozen in its headlights, like a small, doomed creature hypnotized by its oncoming fate.

I pulled slivers of glass from my flesh one by one and wiped the blood away on my jeans, the wounds healing over as if they never existed.

If only the power flowing through me could heal the scars Ariel had written on my heart.

"I want to put you on the witness stand," I told Rae McGuire.

The prosecution had wrapped up their opening arguments before the court adjourned for the evening. They seemed to skate over the testimony of their star witness, one Meghan North, who had apparently dropped off the map and thrown the whole team off balance. In truth, however, they didn't need her to make their case. While I had managed to select a not-unsympathetic jury, their sympathy for a wronged woman couldn't overcome her signed admission of guilt.

Rae frowned. "I thought you said that wasn't a good idea."

"I changed my mind. I think it might be our best chance."

"That doesn't sound good." Her sharp gaze skewered me, her aura blooming with storm clouds. "Be real with me. What does my best chance look like?"

Even if I had good evidence she'd confessed under duress, the chances fell somewhere worse than four to one, but she didn't need to know the odds. "The confession does make things difficult."

"How does putting me on the stand fix that?"

I met her eyes squarely. My plan might work better if she didn't know, but it didn't feel right to spring it on her without warning. "The best way to counter a confession is by introducing a confession from someone else."

Understanding bloomed bright around her, followed by a shadow of doubt as she sat back in her chair. "You don't want to call me. You want to call *her*."

"Yes. She's at the center of this whole mess. The prosecution can't win if they can't prove you intended to kill, that you acted of your own accord. *Mens rea, actus rea*. It wasn't you who murdered those men, Rae."

Her energy twisted, coiling like fighting snakes. She still didn't like the idea, but she didn't care for the prospect of twelve life sentences, either. "Can we do that?"

"You're the defendant. You always have a right to testify."

"But if you're saying she's *not* me..."

"It's a catch-22." I had to boast a little to the one person I could actually talk to about this. "The prosecution would have to agree you are two separate people in order to object to the testimony."

"Oh, then it's easy," she deadpanned. "All you have to do is convince that jury I have a goddess sharing my skin with me."

"I won't give them a choice," I said softly, ignoring her sarcasm. "They'll believe their eyes. She isn't very like you, not really."

"No, but she's terrifying. People don't react kindly to that."

"We don't need them to be kind. We need them to understand." I leaned forward. "I won't do it unless you agree. It is your body, not hers. Your choice."

"If you think it's my best chance, I'll do it. I told you, though, she doesn't speak to me these days. She hates that I confessed, called it a surrender... Anyway. If you really want her to come out, you'd need—"

"I'd need to use her sword." As I said it, I lifted the long, slender case from its spot against the back wall of the meeting room and placed it on the table before her. I'd retrieved it from the locked closet in my office when I stopped by to change into the extra suit I kept there and pick up her case files.

Her face changed, lips parting in surprise. In the depths of her eyes, a flame ignited. "How did you get that in here? It's a deadly weapon!"

"Technically, it's Defense Exhibit 1," I said. "Would you like to see it?"

"No." The light in her eyes flickered, a banked bonfire of wild hunger, and her aura hummed with electricity. But there was something else there, too, the cold, sharp fall of fear. "Not until it's time."

"You think she'll answer, though."

"Oh yes." Her nostrils flared, jaw going tight. "She'll answer all right."

"Rae, is something wrong?"

"You should put that away," my client said. "Keep it out of my reach. Please. It's not safe, having it here with me."

Hastily, I set the case back on the floor, out of sight. "What's going on?"

Rae panted, small shallow breaths through her mouth. When she spoke, the words took on an eerie quality, harsh and hollow, the echo of a voice that didn't belong to her.

"She's waking up," the Morrigan's vessel said.

26

HOME TO ROOST

The condo's interior sat quiet and dark, but the faint scent of frankincense lingered in the entryway like a stubborn ghost. My spine prickled. It would be exactly like Ariel to lie in wait for me to come home and ambush me just when I let my guard down. That's what he'd done when he resurfaced last year, sitting in my darkened apartment as if he owned the place.

Except in this case, he did own it.

Cold adrenaline sliced through me, and I sharpened my night vision. Outside on the patio, crime scene tape flapped in the evening breeze. The condo's front room showed the signs of a ruthless search, cushions overturned, cupboards emptied onto the counters. Had the Feds done this as part of their investigation, or had someone else rifled through my life while I went into hiding?

Belatedly, it occurred to me that the shambles of the living room also noticeably lacked its normal layer of teen detritus. No coats thrown across the back of the couch, no shoes strewn across the floor. Even Lucifer the snake was gone. The bathroom sink that normally bristled with skin care and makeup bottles that multiplied like barnacles now lay bare, only a multicolored stain left behind to mark my charge's passing.

Backing out of the bathroom, I pushed open the next door to Eve's room. It, too, sat empty, with a sense of having been hastily swept bare, like a tornado had passed through and vacuumed up every trace of its occupant. A few stray pages of notepaper littered the carpet as though ripped from her school binder.

I bent to pick them up, hoping for some kind of clue, that she'd left me a message or some hint of where she'd gone. But the pages held nothing of note beyond the normal arcane inscriptions of adolescence. Tiny hearts circled names of classmates. Doodles of flowers intertwined with stylized letters in the margins of a half-written set of notes on the five parts of a persuasive essay.

How silly of me, groping for an easier way when I already knew what I needed to do. Find Ariel and I'd find Eve. Whether she'd leave his side again was another problem entirely and one I couldn't solve with documentary evidence.

"You miss her, don't you?"

The deep, silky voice curled around my heart and held it fast, like a vise. I spun, still in a half-crouch, holding the sheaf of loose-leaf pages and their innocent scribblings against my chest as if it could shield me from him, keep both Eve and me safe. A fantasy. "Where is she?"

Ariel loomed in the doorway. He took up the frame, stole the air from the room. "Eve is fine." He held something cradled in his arms, a small soft bundle of fur that wriggled against his grip.

Delilah. I froze. "What are you—put her down. *Now*, Ariel."

"I don't see why I should." He snuggled the gray cat closer. She pushed against him, paws to his chest, and he looped a hand around her neck—loosely, but deliberately, his eyes on me. "Hush, little one. I need to have a little talk with your friend here."

"Don't you hurt her." I stood, slowly, gaze fixed on his hands. Delilah seemed to understand the threat, or maybe even she sensed some hint of his power. She stopped struggling, her wide, dark, panicked pupils shining in the half-light. "Don't you fucking dare hurt my cat or I will end you in a way you can't come back from this time."

"Now, now. No need to be rude about it." His lips stretched over bared teeth, a semblance of a smile. "She really is just a tiny thing, isn't she? All fluff, no substance. Mortal creatures are just so fragile."

"I mean it. Leave her out of this."

"I'm afraid I can't do that," he said. "There's a good chance you'll try to end me either way. I won't underestimate your violent tendencies this time. That's why I like to have an insurance policy close to hand."

It shocked me, to hear him admit it like that. "You're a monster."

"Name calling, too? That's low, even for you." He sighed. "As I said, even I make mistakes on occasion. It would be so easy to squeeze a little too hard."

"A mistake," I said flatly. "Is that what happened with Helena?"

"Her? Of course not." He dismissed her with a slight lift of one shoulder. "Between you and me, she was in our way. Whoever took care of her did us both a favor."

"And Jared Williams? Was he a favor, too?"

"Who, that pathetic loser on the pier?" Ariel scoffed. "He would have killed you if you didn't kill him first. Don't pretend you didn't go out there prepared to get your hands dirty."

"So you did kill him."

"I never said that. All I'm saying is, when the chips are down, we're the same kind of monster, Lily. We both do whatever it takes to survive."

A storm raged within me, a fire that seared and froze. In its still eye, I dropped cold words like shards of ice. "What do you want, Ariel?"

"I just want to talk," he said, sweetly, innocently, holding my cat's head lightly in his raw-boned, merciless hands. "I thought perhaps we could come to some sort of agreement."

"You came here to *negotiate*?" I almost laughed out loud. Blood roared in my ears. "Why? You already got everything you want."

"Ah, Lily," he said, shaking his head, his expression mournful. "If only it were that simple. But we both know it's not."

"Seems simple enough to me. You have Eve. You beat me. Did you just come here to gloat?" A flash of adrenaline quickened my pulse. He couldn't face me without a hostage, wouldn't dare come near without a hold over me. First Eve, now Delilah, threatening the ones I cared for, shielding himself with their lives.

This wasn't like last time. He was afraid of me. Maybe I could use that somehow.

"It's Eve," he said, after a long pause. "She doesn't want to leave California."

Now I did laugh. I couldn't help it. "And you think I can do something about that?"

"I fail to see why that's so funny."

"You want *me* to convince Eve to change her mind about staying. You've got to be kidding me. It's like you don't know your own daughter." I wiped tears from my eyes with the back of the hand that still clutched her note pages, even though he was right. It wasn't that funny.

"Need I remind you what's at stake, Lilith?" Glowering, he flexed his fingers and Delilah mewed. It sounded more like irritation than pain, but it sobered me, nonetheless.

"No reminder needed." I swallowed my objection to the name he'd given me. "If you really came here to negotiate, put up or shut up. What's your ask, asshole?"

A muscle leaped in his jaw, his flat amber eyes flaring with sudden heat. It hurt him, whatever he came here to ask of me, and I'd be lying if I said no part of me enjoyed that.

"She chose me," he said through gritted teeth. "She wants to stay with me. But she says she won't agree unless she gets to see you, too."

"You want to *co-parent* with me?" I stared at him, open-mouthed. "That's not—you're a goddamned murderer!"

He shrugged, his face giving me nothing. He might care what Eve thought, but he didn't give a damn about any of the other people he'd hurt, including me. "She's my daughter. Whatever you think of me, know this: I'd do anything for her."

"So what, you're taking her on the run with you? You want me to cover your tracks for her sake, is that it? *God.*" This wasn't so different from last time after all. He wanted my complicity. He wanted to drag me down to his level. "You haven't changed one bit, coming back from the dead."

"It's not for me," he said. "It's for her. She needs a family, Lilith. It's all I ever wanted for her, from the beginning. If I could just make you understand—"

"You can't make a family out of threats and devil's bargains, Ariel." I took a step, eyes locked on his. "Let Delilah go. Leave me and mine alone. Then maybe, for Eve's sake, I'll think about it. For now, give me my cat and *get the hell out*."

His eyes blazed golden, and for a moment my heart stopped. Then he broke. Delilah dropped to the floor with a yowl, streaking past me into Eve's abandoned room with fur on end, and Ariel moved faster than I could track him. The patio door slammed and then silence descended, still rich with the incense stench of him.

The adrenaline drained out of me all at once, and in the sudden, brutal comedown, I gagged, then retched. Racing to the bathroom, I fell to my knees on the tile, emptying my stomach of its scant contents. I hadn't eaten since Cee served me breakfast in another world, an age ago, just this morning.

After a while I rose, cleaned up, and rinsed my mouth, though the chilly water from the tap couldn't touch the raw and bitter scald inside me. I opened all the windows to drive out the overpowering scent of incubus with the damp breath of the San Francisco night. Then I dragged the lock box that held my gun and its precious box of silver bullets out from under the bed.

Whatever else the next few days held, I wouldn't let Ariel catch me unarmed and unaware ever again.

I had time to experience several heart attacks in the time it took Danny to answer her door.

"What took you so long?" I demanded when it finally swung open. "I thought you might be—oh."

"Sleeping?" She squinted at me, her acid tone a flimsy cover for the bleakness beneath. "I was, thank you." Her short hair stuck out every which way and her mis-buttoned flannel shirt skimmed the top of her bare thighs.

I'd draped that same flannel over her, the one she'd brought to the hotel, to keep her warm as she slept in the little mountain cabin where we'd loved each other. "I— Crap." I didn't know where to look. "It's not even nine p.m. Did you spend all day in bed?"

"No. Who does that?" Danny wiped her cheeks with a hasty, impatient movement, her eyes red and puffy. "What are *you* doing here, anyway? You promised you'd leave."

"Sorry to disappoint." The words stung, catching me off guard. A cottony anesthesia of shock had taken hold of me since my confrontation with Ariel. Now it yielded to a harsh ache abrupt enough to bleed into my tone.

"That's not what I meant, and you know it." Concern sharpened her voice and stirred in her aura. "You were supposed to keep moving, lay low. What if North—"

I shook my head, the weight of it all crashing over me and washing the words I needed away. "North is the least of my problems right now."

She looked at me, really looked at me this time, and whatever she saw in my face made her swear softly under her breath. Grabbing my arm, she dragged me into the house. "Something happened. Tell me what."

"Not just something. The worst thing." I was stalling. I didn't want to say it out loud, not to her, the one person who truly knew what it meant, but she needed to know. She deserved to know. "He's back."

"Oh, lord. Not this again." She cast her gaze to the ceiling. "Please don't do that unnecessarily cryptic thing you do, Sugarbean. Not when your face looks like *that*. He, who? Is it your dad?"

"Not my dad." I swallowed hard. The name rose thick in my throat, where it swelled and stuck there, stealing my breath. "It's Ariel," I croaked finally. "He's here, in town. He came to the house."

The blood gradually drained out of Danny's face, leaving it ashen under her tan. "*Dios mio.* You're not kidding."

"Dead serious. I wouldn't kid about this. He threatened to strangle my cat."

"Holy crap. Are you okay?"

No, I wasn't okay. I was so far from okay that I couldn't even see okay from here. "I'm fine."

"You're the worst compulsive liar in the history of liars," Danny said. "Are you sure it's him? I mean, we saw him die. It looked pretty permanent."

"Apparently it didn't stick, and that's not all." I bowed my head, heavy with failure. "He's got Eve with him. I think he wants a—demon joint custody agreement. It's so screwed up."

"Yeah, he's a real contender for father of the year." Danny's forehead creased as she took in my agitation. "Well, she is his kid, after all, and she'll be eighteen soon. She's probably safe enough with him, right?"

I opened my mouth to reassure her that he only wanted to hurt me, but I couldn't do it. "I wouldn't count on it." *No more lying.* Ariel wouldn't hesitate to hurt an innocent bystander if it furthered his ends, and he could get to me by hurting those around me. "You didn't see him in the woods. He literally put her body between him and a silver bullet. What kind of a parent does that?"

"The heinous kind. Ariel's kind." She grimaced, leaning her shoulder against the door as if to keep me from running away again. "Am I harboring a fugitive here, or what? I'd like a little warning if Agent North is going to burst through my wall like the Kool-Aid man."

"Ariel got to North, too." I rubbed my temples. "I think he got her in trouble with the chain of command. Anyway, I was in court all day today. She didn't show and nobody tried to arrest me. I guess Ira managed to call off the dogs after all."

"Hell of an assumption," Danny said. "I love you, Sugarbean, but coming back was a big risk. You should have followed the plan."

I looked up quickly, but she didn't meet my eyes. "Oh, well." We had said we loved each other plenty of times before this, so why did I expect this to mean something different? "Too late now."

"Yeah." Danny fixed her gaze on the floor. "Too late for a lot of things, these days."

"Danny, I—" But what could I say? I didn't want to say I was sorry about what we did, because I wasn't, not really. *No lying.* I couldn't promise to make it better, either. All I could do was be here for her now.

"Berry left." Her gaze didn't leave the floor.

"I figured." It didn't seem like the best time to own up to magically spying on her personal life, even if I hadn't meant to see that particular moment of it. "Is it...?"

"It might not be over for good. But I can't blame her if it is." She gave a little half-shake of her head. "It hasn't been... It was only a matter of time, I think."

"No way. You two were good together."

"Maybe. She was good to me. I couldn't..." With a gust of exhaled air, she raised her head, skewering me with a glance that left me breathless. "It was me. I broke things off. It happened right after game night."

"You did?"

"I told her I had to know. Whatever it was, with you. That it wasn't fair to her."

"You never said anything!"

"We didn't exactly have time while we were running from the Feds. And then it felt too—well, complicated."

"All we did that night was hold hands."

"It was more than that," Danny said. "It always has been. And you know it."

"Yeah," I said softly. "I know." Under the circumstances, reaching out to pull her closer wouldn't do either of us any favors. I closed my gloved fingers in a fist by my side. "What did you tell her?"

In the light of day, now that we weren't running anymore, what we'd done looked a lot like cheating, even if she'd given me an out on a technicality. Did it make my part in it less shitty if their relationship had already started to founder? Or did it make it extra shitty, since I had been the one to clasp her hand and drag us over the rocks?

"The truth," Danny said. The set of her jaw belied the grief echoing through her aura. "Don't worry about me, Sugarbean. I'll take my lumps. Honesty is the only way forward. It's what we both deserve, you know?"

"You're right." I tried to smile, but the expression twisted on my lips, as though her pain burrowed inside me too. "You usually are."

Except for the moment she decided to throw it all away on me. That had probably been a mistake.

"Hey." Now Danny reached out to me, squeezing my fingers tightly in hers before releasing them just as quickly, her gesture a safety line in my personal sea of self-loathing. "This is between her and me. It's not your fault."

"I wouldn't be so sure of that," I mumbled.

"My choice, my consequences. I'm sure." She grinned, a fragile flash of defiance like a beam of light cracking through clouds. "I'm always right, remember?"

"I didn't say always." I mustered a real smile for her, but it quickly faded as reality set in.

I had my own choices and consequences to reckon with. Danny made honesty look brave, but my attempts at coming clean hadn't gone well for me so far. I still hadn't heard from Sebastian since this morning. Ira had taken some of the heat off me, but clearly the cavalry wouldn't ride out to save me this time.

"We interrupt this broadcast for your regularly scheduled brood," Danny said. "Was it something I said?"

"I know what I need to do," I mumbled. "I just don't want to do it."

"Listen to me." Danny's energy flared up in a fierce penumbra around us. "We'll get her back, Lily. You're not going to give him what he wants. You're going to fight him."

"Oh, we'll give him a fight. Don't worry." I took a deep, shuddering breath. "Dan, go get dressed. I have to make a quick stop at my office, and I'm not letting you out of my sight."

She frowned at me. "I know you're a recovering workaholic, but it's almost ten. How exactly are you going to lawyer yourself out of this one?"

"I'm not," I said. "I can't do this on my own, so I'm going to call in all my favors. I already tried Ira. That leaves me with my deadbeat daddy dearest."

"Wow," Danny said. "You're asking for help. I think that's character growth."

"Don't give me too much credit. Like I said, he owes me one." Samael hadn't been there to protect me when I needed it most, but maybe he could protect me and mine now. If anyone could take on another incubus, it would be him.

"Okay," she said, "but don't sell yourself short. If you ask me, he owes you a lot more than that."

The glow of her loyalty loosened the cold grip of fear on my heart.

I wouldn't sacrifice my principles for Ariel's twisted purposes, not yet—but if that's what it took to ensure my loved ones stayed safe, I wouldn't stop at sacrificing my pride.

27

LEAP OF FAITH

Neither Danny nor I heard the outer door of the office suite open or Samael's footsteps in the hallway. He simply materialized on the threshold, as silently and suddenly as if I'd summoned him from the ether to darken my door in the middle of the night.

"You are working very late," he said by way of greeting. "Or, perhaps, very early."

At the deep, sepulchral tones, Danny started up from where she'd drowsed in my desk chair. "What the—oh. It's you. Hi. You're really tall."

"Hello." Samael sounded bemused. In fact, I had summoned him by way of a brief and very awkward telephone conversation, though he had said nothing to confirm or deny his location in the ether.

"Sorry for the late hour," I said. "It couldn't wait."

"I was not asleep, so you need not apologize. I'm relieved you are well. After you left, and they came searching for you, I feared..." He cleared his throat. "No matter."

"Thanks for covering for me." Sternly, I reminded myself to keep my guard up. I couldn't trust him, no matter what favors he did me. He might be my father, but he was still no angel. Probably.

"It was no trouble. The officers asked many questions, which I declined to answer. After some time, they gave up and went away." His gaze shifted back to Danny. "I don't believe we have been introduced."

"Oh, right. This is my—" I ducked her raised eyebrow and Samael's speculative expression. "This is Danny." What was she now, to me? What were we to each other? We should probably talk about that at some point, when everyone's lives weren't endangered by the embodiment of my rampaging past trauma.

"It's an honor to meet you, sir." Danny's energy sparked with nervous energy.

"You may call me Samael." He gave her one of his funny little half-bows, as if he did it by habit before he forgot people didn't bow these days anymore. Then he turned back to me. "I did not expect to hear from you again so soon. The contact I gave you—did she not—?"

"No, no. She was great. Weird and creepy, but kind. She sent me back because I asked her to." I rose, pacing to the window, where the lights of the city burned like will-o-the-wisps in the fog. "The rogue demon who you warned me about—he taught me what it meant to be one of us. His name is Ariel, and he's bad news."

"*Ariel.*" Samael stiffened, leaning forward. "You learned our ways from him?"

"Among other things. He took me under his wing, as it were. You know him?"

"I did, yes. A long time ago." His expression darkened. "That explains a great deal, if he was your teacher."

"Yeah. Apparently he did a shit job of it, too." Now that I'd opened that particular wound, I might as well poke it just to see if anything nasty came out. "Who was he to you?"

"He is one of the eldest. We were brethren." With measured steps, he came to stand beside me, staring out at the shrouded night. "I didn't know that he was in this part of the world. I certainly didn't think that he might have found his way to you. If I had…"

"What? Done something different?"

The look he gave me blended anguish and aggravation. "There is much I would change if I could. But even the most powerful of our kind cannot turn back the flow of time. If we could..." His chin sank on his chest, a brooding shadow crossing his face. "Never mind. What was it you wished to ask of me?"

"Ariel took Eve and North, and now he's stalking me. I don't know where he's hiding out or where he'll strike next." The words stuck in my throat, but I pressed on, determined. "I need a plan. I have to find him and stop him before he hurts my people—my *family*. Will you help me...Father?"

Admitting my weakness rankled, especially now, especially to this man—this incubus—this absent parent who had never given me a chance to ask favors of him before. I clung tight to this last shred of defiance, my refusal to call him "Dad."

In a city full of bridges, that was a bridge too far.

"Anything further, Ms. Knight?" The judge aimed a pointed look my way. Clearly, he still believed I was wasting his time and everyone else's to boot.

The trial's second day had dragged on longer than anyone cared for, but I wouldn't have another chance to make my play. I rose. "I have one more witness, Your Honor."

"Objection," the DA said immediately. He knew as well as I did that I'd called everyone on the witness list. "The People haven't received any notice of an additional witnesses."

"Ms. Knight, is this true?"

I lifted my chin, daring them to try and stop me. "Not in this instance, Your Honor. The defendant has informed me that she would like to exercise her right to testify before the court."

The judge's eyebrows shot up, but he nodded. "Objection overruled. Proceed, Ms. Knight."

"Thank you, Your Honor." I dropped a hand on Rae's shoulder, giving it a brief squeeze through her suit jacket. The fine wool weave under my fingers sent a pang through me. Eve had helped me pick out Rae's court outfits before everything went wrong, doing an excellent job striking the right balance between respectability and relatability. "If it please the court, the defense now calls Regan McGuire to the stand."

A rustle of whispers spread through the court like wind through grass as Rae rose from her chair at the front of the courtroom. She cut a tall, imposing figure despite the stiff set of her shoulders and the shadows under her eyes.

"Go ahead, Ms. McGuire," the judge said, frowning at both of us.

"Please stand and raise your right hand." The clerk, unruffled by this turn of events in the way of courtroom clerks everywhere, smoothly took up the affirmation. "Do you promise under penalty of perjury that your testimony in this court shall be the whole truth and nothing but the truth?"

White-faced, Rae faced the jury. "I do."

"Please state your full name for the record."

"Regan Danae McGuire."

"You may be seated."

"Your witness, Ms. Knight." The judge probably thought I had lost my marbles. Maybe I had. I didn't know what would happen when I summoned the goddess to the surface.

From the way Rae had reacted when I explained my plan, and the tremor in her voice as she spelled her name for the record, she didn't know either.

My questions now set the stage for her story: the trauma she'd survived at the university, her abandoned degree, and her new life advocating for fellow survivors. She gave short, subdued, almost mechanical answers, her flat affect betraying a minor dissociative state. None of this came easily for her.

I pressed forward toward the real purpose of this exercise. "Let's jump forward in time a little, to about two years ago. Did you take a trip around that time?"

"Objection," the DA put in. "Relevance."

The judge held up a hand. "This better be leading somewhere, Ms. Knight."

"It's relevant, Your Honor."

"You may answer," the judge said to Rae, his tone bored.

"Yes," Rae said. "I took a trip to Ireland two years ago."

"What was the reason for that trip?"

"I wanted to visit the cave of the Morrigan."

"Ms. Knight," the judge said, warning me.

"Please, Your Honor. I promise this pertains to the case." I turned back to Rae. "Who is the Morrigan?"

Rae flushed. "She's—well, she's a pre-Christian goddess, very ancient. In Irish myth, she's a queen of the otherworld, a protector of the weak, and a warrior spirit."

"And why did you want to visit her shrine?"

"I felt called to do so. I..." She swallowed. "I had a vision."

"What kind of vision?"

"It was like a dream, but real. She wanted me to find something for her, a relic of her power. When I woke up, I knew the name of the place and that I had to go there myself."

"What did she want you to find?"

Rae sat up a little straighter. "She wanted me to find the Sword of Light."

I nodded to the bailiff, who handed the case over. He looked as nervous as I felt.

"Your Honor, this object was never entered into evidence." The prosecutor sounded worried, too, though probably for the reasons he should have been.

"Ms. Knight, you're on thin ice here. Better let him see it."

"What is all this about, Knight?" My opponent's irritated energy congealed into dismay when I wordlessly set the case on his table, unzipped the case, and opened the lid halfway, "Holy... Is that what I think it is?"

Behind me, Rae's sharp gasp electrified me.

"Yes, Counsel. It's a sword."

"Your Honor, I think the murder weapon." He shot a look of appeal at the judge. "She can't do this. It's been outside the chain of custody."

Nothing less free than the mind of a skeptic. Cee's words echoed hollow in my mind. I could win this case, but only if I could make the jurors my believers, and for that, I needed the judge to believe too. Just a little, just enough to give me the opportunity to see this through. I didn't feel proud of myself for it, but I leaned on my Presence for a moment.

"I'd like to see where you're going with this." The judge cast a glance at the clock, which was creeping past three o'clock. "But make it quick."

"Thank you, Your Honor." I let the lid of the case fall closed and turned back to face my client. She sat still as stone, but her aura writhed with power. The scent of ozone and petrichor tingled in my sinuses.

I was the only one who could smell the goddess coming. No one else in the courtroom reacted. The judge, in the grip of my Presence, leaned forward, bemused, and DA Jimenez scowled at me. The jury looked confused. They couldn't see the stormy vortex forming around Rae like a rapidly spinning supercell shot through with traceries of lightning, a core of darkness eclipsing her natural light.

"Ms. McGuire, is this the relic you went overseas to find?"

A long moment passed before she shook herself, as if settling back into her skin. Her gaze focused on the sword case with some difficulty. Her pupils had expanded almost to the edge of her irises. Only a thin rim of their natural gray remained.

Good. Now that I had her attention, I lifted the lid and drew the sword from inside.

"Yes," Rae rasped. Then she cried out, a harsh wild sound, a bird's cry against a storm.

I spoke quickly. "I call to the stand Morrigan, the Queen of Phantoms. Come forth and be bound by the oaths of your vessel."

Panic rattled the district attorney's aura. "Your Honor, this is—"

Rae's head dropped to her chest, her body shuddering. Behind me, the gallery muttered, and the jury stirred in alarm. Now they felt her power too.

"Too late," I said, and Rae raised her head. Only it wasn't her anymore.

The goddess looked out of glittering, flat black eyes, her head cocked to the side, her sharp avian gaze fixed upon the weapon in my hands. Red hair swirled around her face, stirred by an otherworldly wind and crackling with static.

This was a leap of faith. I had to trust the ancient being under Rae's skin to protect her best interests, or at least recognize that she couldn't fulfill her goals from a prison cell.

I also had something she wanted.

The sword jerked in my hand, as if wrenched by an unseen force. It sizzled like a live wire, but my demon strength matched it, held it. As Rae had promised, wielding it would give me some control. At the summit of Mount Diablo, the goddess had sprung at me with the speed and strength of any demon. Now she sank back, glaring from the witness box with the fury of a cornered feral creature.

"You *dare*?" Her voice rasped, a raven's croak, but she made no move to challenge me.

"Yes, I dare," I said. "Your law requires that my challenge be heard. I challenge you to speak the truth. Swear it."

"My word is my power and my bond." She spat it like a curse, her face a mask of rage.

"Let the record show the oath," I said.

The clerk frowned. The court reporter, in the midst of typing, paused.

"Ms. Knight," the judge said. "Explain yourself."

"Rae McGuire didn't commit murder. She lacked the requisite intent." I gestured to the witness box. "A third party controlled her body at the time of the murders. That third party is now present in the courtroom, ready to testify. Permission to treat her as a hostile witness."

"Another witness?" Jimenez was on his feet. "Your Honor, we never received notice of *this*."

"This is highly irregular," the judge said, but his normally pompous manner had ebbed away. His eyes darted sideways to the occupant of the witness box. "The identity of the witness, whether she and the defendant are one and the same, is a matter of fact to be determined by the jury. You may proceed, Ms. Knight. But...carefully, please. And must you brandish that sword?"

"Thank you, Your Honor. I'm afraid I must. We might all regret it if I didn't."

"I see." His tone was that of a man who didn't see or understand, nor want to. "Then she's your witness, Ms. Knight."

I nodded, adrenaline pulsing through me. If I pulled this off, I might just win this case. I would certainly gain *some* kind of reputation.

"State your name for the record, please," I said to the goddess.

"I have many names," she said, an echo of the words she'd said to me at our first meeting. *I am many things to many people.* "Your people often call me the Morrigan, though you don't know what it means. My vessel used the old name, Morrighu. Either will do for now."

Of course she would give an overly elaborate answer. All that work I'd done to prepare Rae as a witness, and none of it mattered. "Tell me how you came to know Rae McGuire."

"She called on me." The black eyes glinted, cunning and inhuman. She hadn't changed her shape, but everything else about her had shifted. Her voice rang out deep and harsh, and where Rae had hunched her shoulders, she sat tall, with the regal, dangerous poise of a predator ready to pounce. "I answered the need she offered."

I wished she didn't make it sound so much like my experience of energy exchange. "And what need was that?"

"Justice," said the Phantom Queen, and smiled her terrible smile.

28

HOSTILE WITNESS

I faced the goddess on the witness stand, a rush of nerves coursing through me. By calling forth the supernatural creature who shared Rae's body, I had broken rule one of trial practice. Most attorneys would hesitate to ask a question of a witness without already knowing the answer.

Most attorneys couldn't be me. The sword in my hand hummed with her power, crackling with faint electricity that snaked along its blade. It drew her eyes like a magnet as I pressed my direct examination.

"When Rae McGuire asked you to bring the men who had hurt her to justice, did she tell you what justice looked like to her?" I held the sword before me like a knight in an old painting, pointed straight down with blade resting on the carpeted floor, my gloved hands folded around the pommel.

"No." The goddess's hungry gaze stayed fixed on the sword. "She was full of rage, but she had nowhere to place that anger. She brought it to me as one would bring an offering, in my holy place under the hills, and I knew she would do."

"You knew she would do for what?"

"I had a purpose of my own," the goddess said, with a hint of wariness now.

"What purpose? Remember your oath."

Rae's body shuddered, but the goddess didn't recede in her eyes or her aura. "I was bound to that place, with no form, no flesh beyond it. I had a mind to return to the world."

"Objection," DA Jimenez burst out. "Your Honor, surely you don't believe this."

"Overruled. An unbelievable story is no grounds to strike the question. You'll have your chance to examine the witness. Continue, counsel."

With a dip of my head, I turned back to the witness box. "Enlighten us, please. How did Rae fit into your plan to return to the world?"

"I needed a strong and willing hand," she said. "One who could wield my sword and carry out the necessary sacrifices."

Internally, I winced at the choice of words. "Why was that necessary?"

She narrowed her eyes at me, black as an offended cat's. "The return to this world in full required the guilty blood of thirteen mortal lives. They did not deserve to keep them."

"When she came to you for help, did Rae McGuire know what you would ask of her?"

"She did not know of the blood price." The goddess spoke haughtily, a great queen making the witness box her throne. "She did not need to know."

I itched to challenge the unconscionable contract terms she'd concealed from a vulnerable human who had come to her in pain and desperation. Talk about cases of first impression—that would be one for the history books, assuming I survived it. "What happened then?"

"I offered the justice she sought. In trade, she gave me free use of her form."

"She allowed you to possess her." I let a tone of surprise seep into my tone, stoking the stir of whispers in the jury box.

The goddess inclined her head. "Once, my people would have considered it an honor to carry my aspect for a while."

"Maybe it was common in your time, but it's not anymore. You'll have to explain it to me like I'm five, I'm afraid." Someone in the gallery let out a nervous giggle, which they abruptly suppressed into a cough. I appreciated them following my sense of humor, but I didn't let it show. "Did she really have no control over her body?"

"That was the deal we struck. She would fall into a strange, dark dream when I took hold of her. Like a dream, it faded when I returned her to herself."

I leaned forward over the hilt of the sword and sharpened my Presence, urging the jury to *pay attention.* "Could she do anything to stop you if she disagreed with what you did?"

"No. She rode as an observer only. She could not act, and she forgot quickly."

"How horrible that must have been for her."

"Speculation," Jimenez muttered. "Counsel assumes...well, *things* not in evidence."

"Withdrawn." I didn't need her answer.

"There is a reason I let her forget," the goddess offered slyly. Perhaps she did intend to help me after all.

"Strike that," the judge said, stern. "The witness will allow the defense to ask their question before answering. Ms. Knight, proceed."

"Thank you, your honor." I had to tread with care as I pushed judge and jury to the edge of a world for which they had no framework and likely limited patience. With a deep breath, I moved to bring us home. "My question is this, and again, I'll remind you of your oath. Morrigan, did you kill the twelve men for whose murders Rae McGuire stands accused today?"

A murmur like a rising wind swelled in the courtroom. If they all thought I'd lost my mind before, now I'd convinced them of it.

"No one could have stopped me," the witness said. "They were mine by right to take."

A single silent moment passed, and then the courtroom erupted. DA Jimenez leaped to his feet, his objection unheard in the sudden outcry from the gallery. The jury sat wide-eyed and stunned. The court reporter removed her hands from her keyboard, blank-faced, as the judge slammed his gavel on the bench, shouting for order.

Finally, the chaotic noise ebbed away, though the energy in the room churned with suspicion, fear, and horror. In that uneasy silence, I hefted the sword in my hand.

"No further questions, Your Honor." Head held high, I strode toward the defense table.

"Well, then, Mr. Jimenez." The judge sounded shell-shocked. "It... She's the People's witness."

I laid the sword on the table and sank into my seat, still grasping the hilt. I didn't trust it not to fly across the room into the goddess's waiting hand.

The DA's voice shook a little. "If I may propose a recess until tomorrow morning, Your Honor? If this witness is *not* Rae McGuire, and she has now confessed to the charges..."

"Your Honor," I interrupted, dulcet toned. "Please consider the risk to the public, let alone the physical toll exacted on my client, if I'm required to call her for a second day."

The judge cast a look at the clock, then fixed the prosecution with a severe stare. His aura carried a sickly sheen as he clung for dear life to the comfort of civil procedure. "Are you prepared to stipulate that the witness is in fact another party?"

"No, sir. Er, I mean, no, Your Honor." Jimenez wiped his brow, the mistake a sign of just how much we'd rattled him.

"I thought not." The judge sighed. "We'll take a ten-minute recess, then proceed with cross examination. Get it done today if you can, counsel."

"Yes, Your Honor." The DA's furious energy dropped to a dull roar as he resigned himself. With a significant glance at his second chair, he grabbed his valise and beat a hasty retreat out the side door. The bailiff shepherded the jury from the box as the judge stepped down from his high seat and vanished into his chambers.

I didn't stir. I had a goddess on a leash, and the leash was the sword under my hand. Now she stared directly at me, her eyes eclipse-black and glittering.

I met her gaze with all the will I had to muster. Could she read an aura the way I did? On the off chance the sword opened some channel of connection, I aimed a mental warning her way.

Don't fuck this up for us.

Her head cocked to the side in that sharp, twitchy, birdlike manner of hers. Invisible feathers ruffled in the shadowy energy that enveloped her, a crow's challenge, before her chin dropped a few millimeters.

In that modicum of accord, we waited to rejoin the battle.

The prosecution returned for cross, pushing the goddess to recant. She met his leading questions with a queen's disdain when he implied that Rae had dissociative identity disorder or a hell of a talent for acting. Then bringing out the hit list from Rae's old room, he demanded to know if the goddess had crossed out each of the twelve faces in garish red with a sharpie marker.

"Whose hands held the pen?" Jimenez demanded. "Yours, or Rae McGuire's?"

"I told you they were mine." Her gaze bore down on him like double barrels, and I winced. My admitted maneater of a client would probably have intimidated the best in the biz.

"Convenient, isn't it, that she also blamed these men for ruining her life?"

"I promised her justice. All the better if her justice and my sacrifice could be carried out together." The goddess laughed, a terrible sound, full of sharp echoes in the tense and silent room. "You English have a brutal idiom. *Kill two birds with one stone.*"

"It wasn't a coincidence." He was back on his game. "She chose the targets, didn't she?"

"There are no coincidences. I needed well-deserved destruction, and she had their names in her mind. It seemed fitting to me. Does it not to you?"

"No, I—" He stopped himself. "Murder is still a crime, Ms., um. Ma'am."

"And what of their crimes?" Gasps rose from the gallery as the goddess half-rose in her seat. "Did they ever face your judgment?"

The judge, white-faced, rapped with his gavel again. "The witness will be seated."

"You turned your faces from her," the goddess cried, ignoring him. "No wonder she turned to me, when your halls and heroes held no justice for her. You stand guilty of that."

With that, Rae's body crumpled. Her eyes rolled up, whites showing eerily as she sagged in the chair like a broken puppet. The charged atmosphere in the room dissipated. A restless energy had traced the sword with faint light as it twisted and pulled in response to her fierce words, but it faded all at once and the weapon lay quiet under my hand.

The bailiff leaped toward Rae, but I stepped between him and my client's limp body, stopping him in his tracks with a raised hand and the pulse of my Presence. "Your Honor, if you would—Ms. McGuire is not well."

"Recess now called," he said, his relief palpable. "We'll reconvene at nine tomorrow morning." With that, he fled as if all the demons of hell were chasing after him.

I placed the sword into its case and closed the lid, slinging it over my shoulder before I bent over Rae. "Hey," I said softly. "Hey, are you all right in there?"

Her eyelids fluttered, a pained whimper keening from her throat. "It hurts," she muttered.

"Can you get up?"

"I don't know." The words came raw and hoarse, as if the goddess had bent her vocal cords to a shape not made for them. "She takes everything. I'd forgotten that part."

"She's a nasty piece of work." I threaded my arm under hers, helping her sit up.

"She's a *goddess*," Rae said, her ravaged voice reproving. "Neither good or bad. A force of nature."

Rae was in no shape for an argument, so instead of answering, I pulled her to her feet. She leaned heavily on me, steps dragging and stumbling. The bailiff brought a wheelchair over, but he wouldn't look her in the eye as they escorted her back to her cell.

They all feared her now. It sparked a respect the officers hadn't shown her before, when they'd only seen her as a woman who'd fought back against her abusers—and won.

Your halls and your heroes held no justice for her.

The goddess had a point. All I had was the scant hope the jury would prove her wrong.

29

COLLATERAL DAMAGE

A mélange of spices hung heavy in the air as I stepped into my apartment. Notes of frankincense, yes, the scent that Ariel and my father shared, not that I wanted to consider that creepy fact too heavily, but also chiles, garlic, cilantro, and onions.

"What's going on in here?" I demanded.

Danny waved at me from the kitchen, while Samael stood at the sink with his back to me, a towel over his shoulder, washing dishes with demonic speed. "What does it look like?" she said. "We're cooking dinner."

"You know how to cook?" I directed this at Samael. Danny's home cooking abilities were never in question.

He set aside the last dish, wiping his hands. "It is not my strong suit. But I can follow directions. I have been recruited to serve as a sous chef."

"I figured you would need some comfort food," Danny chimed in.

Danny's enchiladas definitely qualified as comfort. I laid the sword case carefully against the wall beside the couch. "Any news from you-know-who?"

Her forehead creased, and she shook her head. "Nothing. No calls, no unannounced visits."

"We checked the beach house as you suggested," Samael put in. "At least one cubine has been in the house recently, but how long ago, we couldn't tell."

"What about Sebastian? Did you check on him?"

"I did," Danny said, grinning. "Don't look so horrified. We had a nice long talk about you. It's not the first time we've compared notes, and it certainly won't be the last."

I didn't know what to feel about that, so I settled somewhere between encouraged—maybe there was hope for the hopeless, i.e. me—and outright terrified. "But he's safe. You warned him that Ariel's still lurking around?"

"He said he'd load the silver bullets, but I did you one better. I made him promise to come over for dinner tonight. He's late, but he said he'd bring guacamole and reposado. The expensive stuff."

"Wait, what?" When I had pictured Danny, Sebastian, and my dad all hanging out together, I hadn't imagined it would happen so soon, and certainly not under these weird circumstances. I wasn't ready for these new dynamics, let alone prepared to pressure test them.

"Safety in numbers, right?" Danny pointed her spoon at me. "These are war room enchiladas, baby."

"How did it go today in court?" Samael inquired.

I thought about that, about the fierce, flat black eyes of the goddess and the hopelessness in Rae's. "Interesting," I said finally. "I took a big risk, but I won't know if it worked until tomorrow."

"Sounds like a thrilling courtroom drama," Danny said.

"Well, it would be the first time in history a woman got acquitted because she was possessed by a supernatural entity, instead of getting burned at the stake." Putting it that way made me gloomy, as did the radio silence from Ariel. I couldn't fight him if I couldn't find him, and it left me in a helpless state of hypervigilance, waiting for the other shoe to drop.

Maybe that was his goal all along, to destroy my sense of safety, to demonstrate his control once and for all. Maybe it was never about Eve at all.

"Here. I think you need this."

I looked up to find Danny standing over me with a glass half-full of amber liquid. "You broke into my liquor cabinet?"

"Cabinet my ass. It was out on your counter." She pushed the glass on me. "Drink it. You'll feel better."

"You know I can't get drunk." It wasn't strictly true. I'd learned recently that if I drank while in enough of a drained state, I could in fact experience tipsiness.

At the moment, I had enough kether still in reserves that my body would easily flush out any toxins, including alcohol. That was thanks to Danny, who kept sneaking in touches when she thought I wasn't paying attention. Even now, her fingers lingered over my wrist, the narrow strip of skin where my sleeve and glove didn't quite meet.

Instead of pulling it away, I folded my other hand over hers for a moment. Then I took the glass of neat whiskey from her, holding it under my nose and breathing in the potent fumes. "Thanks," I said softly.

"Of course, Sugarbean. I know how you like it." She met my sharp look with an unrepentant grin before resuming her dinner preparations, clearly pleased with herself and her double entendre.

I stayed quiet and drank my whiskey as the doctor ordered. The amber liquid swirled as I turned the glass in restless fingers. When it caught the light, it reminded me of Ariel's eyes.

With a grimace, I took another sip. The burn helped even if the buzz didn't deliver, but it couldn't dispel my lingering dread. I'd missed something. "It's not like Sebastian to run late. He hasn't called?"

"No..." Danny frowned. "Here, take my phone. His number's already in there."

I snatched the phone out of her hand and dialed. On the fourth ring, it went to voice mail. Sebastian's deep tones washed over me, familiar, a little impersonal, and not comforting in the slightest under the circumstances.

"He's not answering." I dialed again. This time it didn't even ring before the voice mail message played. "Now his phone's turned off."

"All right. Whoa, whoa." Danny plucked the device from my trembling fingers. "Maybe he got caught in traffic. Let's not jump to the worst-case scenario yet."

"Are you kidding me? My whole life is a worst-case scenario!"

"I think you're being a little bit melodramatic—"

"No, I'm not! Don't you get it? Ariel is back. My shitty, evil ex was *dead*, and now he's back. I'm not being dramatic, I'm being realistic."

"Honey, I'm not minimizing that." She put out her hand as if to pat my shoulder, then pulled back. Her energy clouded over with a swirl of mixed emotions. "I'm just saying, sometimes people don't answer their phones for perfectly normal reasons. It doesn't automatically mean catastrophe."

"This isn't normal." Seized by the restless need to pace, I rose. Then, at the shrill ring of the phone on the kitchen wall, I almost dropped my glass.

Danny jumped too, cursing. "What the hell? Why do you have that thing?"

"It's there so visitors can get buzzed in to the elevators. No one else should have that number. Except..." Ariel would have it. Eve would have it.

The phone shrilled again. "Well?" Danny demanded. "Are you going to answer it?"

"It's probably Sebastian. Maybe he forgot the elevator code." Had Sebastian ever forgotten the code? I couldn't remember it happening even once. Even if he had, it wouldn't make sense that he'd turned off his phone when I called and then rang from downstairs.

Time seemed to slow down as I grasped the cool, slippery plastic of the handset and raised it to my ear.

"Hello, Lillian," said a voice that wasn't Sebastian's at all. "I'm so glad I caught you at home."

I clenched my jaw, but still, my voice shook. "We've been looking all over for you, Ariel. Where have you been hiding?"

"Surely you have a better opinion of my intelligence than that, my dear." He sounded genuinely surprised. "I have no reason to give up my advantage. Not when you still haven't given me my answer."

"I told you. I need some time to think."

"Ah, yes. Time." His tone turned meditative. "I gave you time. Now it's time to have a little talk."

"We have nothing to talk about."

"I beg to differ. Have you considered my offer?"

"You mean your threats and demands? You have nothing to offer that I could possibly want."

"That's where you're wrong." The musical, lilting chuckle on the other end of the line made my spine crawl. "Unless I'm mistaken, I have something here of yours that you will very much want back."

Fear scuttled along my spine and laid its long, cold, spidery fingers on my heart. "What are you saying?"

"Tsk, tsk. All unawares, and here I'd thought it a calculated risk. Careless of you, unless things have changed since you last stabbed me in the heart."

"You better tell me *exactly* what you mean."

"Just that it pays to have insurance. You're so very prone to making rash decisions, so I must protect my interests. Besides, it's more fun if I raise the stakes, isn't it?"

"Stop playing games," I said through gritted teeth, "and get to the goddamn point."

"Oh, dear me, no. This isn't a game at all." The artificial warmth drained out of his voice, leaving it cold and cutting as the wind above the city. "The gift of silver will always betray you, Lillian. You left your weak point unprotected and unclaimed. You broke your bond when you gave him that ring, and now you've lost him, too."

"Sebastian," I whispered. "What have you done?"

"Wrong question," Ariel said. "The question is what will *I* do—or rather, what *won't* I do. And the answer, my dear, depends on you. Try any clever tricks, he dies. Call the police or your government friends, he dies. Make the wrong choice, he dies. And if you come for me with silver in hand—"

"Enough! I get the idea." Nausea roiled in my stomach, because Ariel was right. I should never have left Sebastian alone, no matter how things stood between us right now. "Does Eve know your plan to win her loyalty involves threatening the lives of people she cares about?"

He laughed again, a genuinely happy sound. "Oh, Lillian. My daughter has so much more mettle than you ever will. Yes, she knows about my plan. In fact, she's agreed to help me with it."

"No. She wouldn't."

"Oh, but she would. She's a very cunning girl when she puts her mind to it. She takes after her father, if I do say so myself. Without your influence, she has the makings of a true menace to mortal society."

"You're wrong," I said. "She's nothing like you. She loves you because you're her father, of course, but she doesn't trust you any more than I do."

"She trusts me," Ariel said, but he didn't sound quite as sure. "Or she will again soon. You've done your best to poison her against me, but she can't deny the power of her birthright. No one can. Not even you, Lilith Fair."

"I never asked her to." I gripped the phone hard enough that the plastic handset creaked against my ear, which would have made it the third phone I'd destroyed in the last few days. "Is she there? Put her on. I want to talk to her."

"I'm sorry, but no. If you want to play mother, you must accept my terms. It's what Eve wants, and isn't that the most important thing?"

In custody cases, the child's well-being came first. With an effort, I eased up and schooled my tone into some semblance of capitulation. "Don't hurt Sebastian. Tell me your damn terms."

"Oh, I don't know." His amusement shivered through the line. "I find I'm enjoying this, and you needed time to think. So do take your time, Lilith. Think about it, but don't think too long. In the meantime, your *boyfriend* and I might have a little heart to heart."

"Fuck you."

"Manners, my dear," he said with a click of his tongue. "I'll be in touch."

The line went abruptly dead. I replaced the handset on the wall carefully, so as not to break it. The soft click echoed through the silent kitchen with the finality of a bullet, cutting across the bubbling sound of the saucepan on the stove.

A gentle hand caressed my back, and I started, then raised my head to see Danny standing close beside me. For the space of an inhalation, I let myself lean into her, the sweetness and spice of her aura surrounding me in a warmth I could get used to if I wasn't careful.

"It's going to be okay." She stroked my hair, her fingertips barely brushing my scalp, just enough to let a hint of kether spark through me. "We'll figure this out. We beat him once before, remember? We can do it again."

She sounded so sure, but I couldn't stop thinking that we hadn't beaten Ariel before, not really. I'd won myself a reprieve, that was all. Now all my choices had come back to haunt me, just like they had before.

"No. *We're* not doing anything." I still had my half-full glass clutched in my hand, forgotten until this moment. Now I tossed back the rest of its contents. "You're staying here, and I...I have to go."

"You don't have to do this alone," Samael said, frowning.

"The way I see it, I don't have much choice." With deliberate steps, I crossed to the counter where she'd left the bottle sitting out and poured myself another glassful of whiskey. I had no reason to be stingy on the pour at this point.

Danny scowled. "That can't be true."

There's always a choice. I'd said that once. I'd said that to Ariel, right before I'd killed him.

"It is what it is, Dan." The whiskey scalded the back of my throat, and I welcomed the harsh burn of it. Anything to ward off the cold inside.

"No, it's not." Danny faced me in the small kitchen, hands on her hips, jaw jutted forward as if daring me to argue with her. "I don't want to hear any of that self-sacrificing bullshit. You are not going to run off alone tonight and indulge your white knight complex."

"I don't have a white knight complex!"

"Sugarbean, you don't just have a complex, it's your whole damn name."

The fierce light in her eyes made me love her more than ever, and I looked away, down at the glass in my hand. "Fine. But if I tell you to leave, don't wait. You come right back here."

"Lily..."

"I mean it," I said. "There are places I might have to go where I can't let you follow. Promise me."

She sighed. "I promise."

"Then let's go. Maybe it's not too late." The words rang hollow in my ears. Ariel would have never tipped his hand if I had a chance of stopping him. For all I knew, Sebastian was already dead.

Behind the icy flood of adrenaline, a grim sense of calm settled over me. I hadn't felt shock at hearing Ariel's voice on the phone. I'd almost expected it.

Deep in my bones, in their marrow, I had always known it would come to this.

30

BLOOD ON THE KEYS

"You're brooding again," Danny said, from the passenger seat of Blue Betty. "Wanna talk about it?"

"I'm not sure what there is to talk about. I don't see any way out of this. Not without someone getting hurt."

"Yeah, so we'll make sure the *someone* is that asshole."

"It's a lot harder when the asshole is the one who doesn't care about collateral damage." Approaching the entrance to Sebastian's driveway, I slowed. No lights shone in the windows, and my stomach twisted.

Danny noticed the direction of my anxious gaze. "Looks like no one's home."

"Yeah. I don't like it." I steered Betty up the drive, grateful for the gun loaded with silver weighing down my coat pocket. The closer I got to the house, the more it seemed likely that he'd used Sebastian to bait me into a trap.

The worst-case scenario haunted me, one in which we found him standing over Sebastian's broken and bleeding body, already gloating at what he'd taken from me. *The question is what will I do—or rather, what won't I do.*

I already knew the answers, because he'd once shot Danny to prove he would stop at nothing to control me. Damn it, I shouldn't have brought her here, no matter how fiercely she glared at me.

On the other hand, it never hurt to have a forensics expert along while you investigated a potential crime scene.

I shuddered. Every stop on my train of thought got more horrific than the last. I couldn't deny the reality of Ariel's superhuman strength and speed. Even armed, Sebastian would have a slim chance against him if it came to a fight.

The garage opened to my code, and Betty's headlights illuminated Sebastian's only remaining vehicle parked by the stairs to the house. Another bad sign, telling me that Sebastian should be at home despite the darkened windows.

Parking the roadster next to Sebastian's car, I sat for a moment, gathering my courage. I slipped my hand into my pocket and closed it around the grip of the pistol, careful to keep my trigger finger parallel with the barrel.

The first thing Sebastian had ever taught me about gun safety involved trigger discipline, and even though I couldn't resist making it into a sex joke at the time, I hadn't forgotten the lesson. Nor had I forgotten the way he touched me then, both of us full of wild desire and uselessly trying to hide it.

Being desperately horny for teacher really left an indelible mark on your memory. That had been the morning of the day that had ended with us in bed together, my wings spreading from my shoulders for the first time in my life, with a nighttime flight into the desert to save Danny's life.

It had ended with me stabbing Ariel through the heart.

"Do you want me to stay in the car?" Danny prompted me gently. "Or should I come with you?"

"No, I'm not leaving you here by yourself." I'd asked Samael to stay at the condo in case Ariel decided to show. Now I regretted erring on the side of caution. With deep, shaky breath, I switched off the car. "He could be anywhere. You know he can walk through walls, right?"

Danny glanced around the garage, now lit with smart light bars installed in the ceiling. "So you've said."

"Stay close," I told her and touched the lock pad.

Inside, the house sat as dark as it had looked on the outside. I flipped on the light, stretching out my awareness for some hint of Sebastian's essence. Then I remembered his silver ring. I wouldn't be able to feel him either way.

The gift of silver will always betray you, Lillian.

Rings could be removed, and so could fingers. The thought struck me like a fist to the sternum.

You left your weak point unprotected and unclaimed.

What if Ariel...what if *Eve*...

Despite my fears, no bodies or murderous incubi awaited me in the kitchen. I cleared each room with gun in hand at the low ready position. If my heart didn't insist on beating a wild tattoo in my throat like it did and my stomach didn't churn like I was about to throw up, I might feel like a badass. Instead, I just felt sick and empty-hearted, waiting for the next terrible thing.

"Lily," Danny said behind me as we stepped into the piano room, and her tone said that we had found the terrible thing before I saw it.

A struggle had gone down here. The piano bench lay on its side, the floor lamp beside it shattered. And on the cream-colored carpet beneath the instrument...

I drew a choking breath. The carpet wasn't cream colored anymore, but splotched and marred with rusty stains. Someone had bled here and bled a lot. They had reached for the lamp and left bloody smudges on its graceful, curving neck.

Danny moved past me to squat near the stains, examining them closely without touching them. "These aren't yet dry. Whatever happened here, it happened recently."

"I should have been here," I whispered. "I could have protected him."

She shot me a severe look. "You can't be everywhere at once. If it hadn't been Sebastian, it would have been me. Or the cat. Or Eve. You know it's true."

"It's a lot of blood," I said. "Do you think he's..."

"No," Danny said quickly. "I don't. Look." She jerked her chin at the right-hand corner of the piano beneath the instrument's open lid, where a spatter of dark drops now marred the ivory keys of the high notes. "Someone hit their head, right here. There's even a little—no, you probably shouldn't look. But head wounds bleed a lot, even if they're superficial."

"He's obviously injured. He could have a concussion. He might be bleeding out."

"Lily, we don't even know that this is his."

"It has to be." I forced myself to step closer. "Cubine blood doesn't stay tacky, not like this. It starts to flake and turns all dusty, like the rest of us." I knew from experience that even mine did this. It made dry cleaning my own clothes a lot easier when they got bloodstained, but it reminded me just how little I knew about my own body and how my human and cubine genes interacted.

"It could be from that rogue FBI agent. Isn't she working with him? Maybe Ariel sent her. He doesn't like to get his hands dirty."

"Maybe." Unconvinced, I started to pace, but Danny grabbed my arm.

"Stop. Don't disturb the scene. We should call SFPD, have them bring in a full forensics team."

"I can't get the police involved in this," I said. "The Feds dropped the last charges, but that doesn't mean they think I'm innocent. I already called in my favors there."

"All right. Then what?"

I shook my head. "I don't know." The fact that we hadn't found Sebastian's body gave me some kind of hope. "All I know is, this isn't over. The next shoe is going to drop. It's just a matter of when."

Danny caught me in a tight hug, enveloping me in warmth and safety that I didn't deserve. It took all my effort not to fall completely apart, and as soon as I could, I drew back, putting space between us.

I turned my face away, though my demon senses meant I still felt the pain splintering her aura just the same. That was the whole problem, wasn't it? Whatever I did, I couldn't escape the knowledge of how much I could hurt them.

Sebastian and Danny both suffered for loving me. I made their lives harder and more dangerous, and I couldn't protect either of them from my enemies or my own emotional baggage.

It was then, in the silence that stretched between Danny and I in the wake of her rebuffed touch, that her phone shrilled from her jacket pocket.

We both jumped and froze, staring at each other.

Danny bit her lip as she pulled out the insistently ringing device. "Shit. Uh, Lily?"

"What? Who is it?"

She turned the screen toward me wordlessly, showing Sebastian's name on the screen.

Foolish hope mingled with the dread that curled around my ribs, clawing for my heart. I took the phone from her, fingers too numb to register the moment they brushed hers. It took me a couple tries before I managed to accept the call.

"Seb? Are you there?"

Ariel's low chuckle rolled across the line. "I'm afraid not."

"Where the hell is he, you bastard?"

"Oh, don't you worry, love. He's safe...for the moment."

"Stop this." My voice got away from me, sharp and strained, and I cursed myself for letting him hear my distress. "I'll do whatever you want. Just let him go. You name the time and place." Sickness wrenched at my gut as I spoke the words, but I had already decided.

I'd offered myself to Ariel in exchange for someone I loved before. That time, I'd managed to outplay him. Somehow, I doubted it would work a second time.

"That's my girl. Much more like it." His delight shimmered over the slight crackle on the line. "Very well. If you want to talk, come out to the festival tomorrow night. I'll find you."

"The festival..." Hadn't Eve mentioned some street festival last week? That seemed so long ago now. "Why not tonight?" I couldn't stop the tremor in the words.

"You'll understand when you see it," he purred. "It's as if it was made for us. So many people, so many humans pressed skin to skin, so much power for the taking right out in the open. This city really knows how to party."

"Insurance," I whispered. "Of course."

"Now you're catching on. I do hope you won't plan anything stupid. It could go very badly for so many of those mortals you seem to love so much."

"You're a monster."

"And you tried to murder me. I believe that makes us even. Until then, Lily." Ariel sounded obscenely pleased with himself. "Be there, or you can say goodbye to your human pet. Forever."

"Wait!" I cried, as the line beeped mockingly at me. He'd hung up. I fumbled with the phone, trying to call the number back, but it just went to voicemail. I hadn't even gotten proof of life. He'd given me nothing.

I bowed my head. He had me trapped again. If I refused to join his horrible mockery of a nuclear family, he wouldn't hesitate to kill Sebastian. If I did join him—I shuddered, remembering the way he had co-opted my consent, how he'd exerted control over me with mind games, coercion, and worse.

He'd want me as a source again, in his bed, in his thrall. He'd always wanted that. Before I killed him last time, he'd confessed he hated depending on human energy, considering them weak and inferior to our kind. He preferred to launder their kether through a cambion like me, one who could generate kether of her own, if a limited amount.

Now I understood why, but I hadn't then, not with only his dubious tutelage to guide me. He could avoid the inevitable energetic bond with a human that way, for our claim bound us to them as much as them to us. And he wouldn't stop at keeping me drained and weak to serve his purposes.

Ariel would do everything he could to drag me back into the role he'd always planned for me. Sebastian's welfare was the stick, and Eve's welfare was the carrot. And I had no good options left.

"So that's it," Danny said, face ashen, and the bitter charcoal rasp of her aura left my throat dry and aching. "You're just giving up. You're not going to fight him at all."

I shook my head. "If I fight, he'll kill Sebastian. I can't let that happen."

"Okay, so you let him think you're giving up. Wait until Sebastian's safe. Then you kill him, just like last time."

By then, it would be too late. He'd have me in his thrall again. Or he'd just kill me first. If I were him, I wouldn't let me get close again after I'd kissed him and stabbed him, even under thrall.

"Sure, Dan. Like last time." I mustered a smile, but I could tell she wasn't buying it from the way her scowl deepened.

"Don't humor me," she snapped. "You think I can't see what's happening here? Lily, this is your trauma talking. What did your therapist call it again?"

"Learned helplessness," I said automatically. "The instinct to freeze."

"Right. *Helplessness*," Danny said. "He taught you the lesson that you can't fight back. You're buying into his narrative. But it's not true. It never was." She stepped forward and took my face between her hands, forcing me to meet her gaze with all its hope and faith and love, all of that for me. "You're strong, Sugarbean. You always resisted him. You resisted when you moved out here and started a brand-new life. You resisted when he tried to make you like him. You resisted when you made him pay for it."

I was like him. That was the whole problem. "I didn't make him pay enough."

"Fine. Now's your chance to collect."

"It's not that easy, Dan." People like Ariel always found a way to shift the burden. He'd exact a greater price from me than I could ever wring from myself, unless I forfeited Sebastian's life—and Eve's future—to stay free.

Tears sprang into my eyes, and I furiously blinked them back. This wouldn't end any other way. I'd bear the cost. It didn't matter what I did, only what, and who, and how much I had to lose.

Gently, I took her wrists and pulled her hands away. I didn't deserve the flow of her kether from her palms. I didn't deserve the belief she always had in me.

"Come on," I muttered. "Let's get out of here."

I moved toward the door, then paused, the toppled bench drawing my gaze. The last time I'd spent in this room, I'd made intimate acquaintance with its leather cushioning, with Sebastian whispering in my ear as he buried himself inside me. This piano meant something to him, too, a new direction and a new life—with me.

Of course Ariel had used it to hurt us. He had a knack for that, even if there was no way he could have known. It was what he did, tainting the things I loved. It was all he ever did.

I *had* resisted Ariel after his ambush in the forest, and again when he threatened me at home. I had sent him fleeing, and for a moment I had believed I could win. I had taken some small comfort in the realization that he feared me.

Now all I had to show for that moment of hope was the blood of someone who loved me.

31

VIGILS

"The question is," Danny said, plunking a plate down in front of me, "how do you find a demon who doesn't want to be found?"

I normally wouldn't say no to her enchiladas, but now I pushed the dish away. "You don't."

"Unfortunately, Lily's right," Samael said. "Fully fledged on kether, our kind can fly both fast and far. The conceivable search radius would span hundreds of miles."

"But if they were carrying someone—"

I shook my head. "It doesn't matter. He took you to Nevada, remember?"

"I wasn't exactly conscious at the time, so no, I don't." Danny refilled our wine glasses, then sank into the chair beside mine. "You should try to get some food in you, Lily. Keep your strength up."

For what? "Oh, sure." No matter how good the enchiladas, they couldn't give me the kind of strength I needed to face Ariel, and I couldn't ask Danny for that kind of nourishment now. "Eat, drink, and be merry, for tomorrow...you know."

"Don't say that." She appealed to Samael. "There must be something we can do."

Samael shot me an apologetic glance. "If you still had an extant bond with your Sebastian, you might have a way to track him. But with his life energy muted by silver…"

"Wait," Danny said. "Lily didn't tell me that was part of the deal."

"It's news to me." I forced down a bite of food, just to show Danny I'd tried. "Bottom line is, I'm fucked because I tried to do the right thing." The enchiladas had gotten somewhat charred around the edges before Samael pulled them out of the oven, then cooled and congealed by the time Danny and I returned from Sebastian's. They still would have tasted amazing, though, if only I could swallow down the bitter ash of regret that choked my throat.

"We have ways of protecting our own if the bond is strong enough," Samael said. "Don't blame yourself. No one ever taught you these things."

"I just don't think they would go too far." After a brief bout of visible consternation, Danny let the implications of my newly revealed GPS slide, returning stubbornly to the matter at hand. "You must have some idea of where he would hole up."

"We've searched all the obvious places." I'd taken Danny on a whirlwind tour of my local traumas after we left Sebastian's house: the Black Cat Club, the warehouses behind the San Francisco Museum of Modern Art, the spot in Golden Gate Park where I'd spied on North and her unseen co-conspirator.

"I have a few preparations to attend to." Samael finished his wine and rose. "This meal was sublime, Daniela. Thank you for having me."

"It was all right," Danny said, cheeks pink. "Not my best… Thank you for coming."

With a little bow towards her, he glanced quickly in my direction, as if about to say something else. Then, seeming to think better of it, he slipped out the back door into the night.

"He's very mysterious," Danny observed, trailing me as I abandoned the table in favor of my wine glass and the couch. "Do you still hate him?"

I wedged myself into the cushions, pulling my knees up into a self-protective ball. "I don't know if hate is the right word. I don't *know* him."

"He seems to care about you, at least." She flopped down next to me, not so close that our bodies touched, but close enough that I would only need to reach for her.

"Hm." Noncommittal, I cast a sideways glance at her. "He's trying, I'll give him that."

"That's not nothing." Danny poked me in the arm. "I can see the resemblance, you know."

I rolled my eyes. "Is that supposed to be a compliment?"

"It's a compliment to him," she said, and when I twisted around to look at her full on, her desiderata sparked with genuine heat and affection, fragrant with the cinnamon flavor of her wanting me.

"Danny," I said, and couldn't go on.

I needed her right now, more than ever—or did I just need what she could give me? Every moment like this one, drawing out endlessly between us, seemed like a betrayal of the partner I'd failed this night to protect. Even though he'd given his blessing, I still didn't like where we'd left it, and now we might never have a chance to figure it out.

"You don't have to torture yourself, you know," she said. "It doesn't help anything."

"Yeah, well." I curled into myself further, my shoulders hunching to my ears as if I could somehow escape how well she knew me, how clearly she saw me. "Feel free to tell me what would."

"I can think of a few things." Her voice dropped, sparking heat at the base of my spine.

"No, Dan. I can't. Not tonight."

"I know," she said instantly. "Shit. I'm sorry. I didn't mean... You don't have to look so stricken, Sugarbean."

"Is this what you want?" The question dropped from my lips before I could think better of it, an impulse I couldn't turn aside. "What I can offer...it might not be enough."

"What? Non-monogamy?" She sipped her wine, feigning nonchalance, but the dizzy swirl of her energy betrayed her. "This may come as a shock, but I've given it some thought lately."

"And?"

"Not out of the question, but like you always say, it's complicated." Smiling slightly, she swirled the dregs in her glass. "That's not necessarily a bad thing."

I thought of how Sebastian gave me freedom easily, as though it took nothing away from him, until... "Things are always complicated when there are feelings involved."

"Who said anything about feelings?" Her tone was casual, but her look was anything but.

"I literally just did," I said, and then I hesitated. "Danny, I told Sebastian what happened. With us."

"Oh...*Oh*." Her face fell. "He isn't OK with this. Shit. Now I look like a real jerk."

"Pretty sure the biggest jerk here is me." I sighed. "I don't know, honestly. He said he was fine with it, but I'm not so sure. He may just need some time to get used to the idea."

"Got it," she said. "Ixnay on the uckingfay. And probably the issingkay. Any word on the uddlescay?"

"I have absolutely no idea what you just said."

"Cuddles, you uncultured ass. Can we have those?"

"Under the circumstances..." I shut my eyes for a moment, her desire a siren call, a promise, an offering I craved. "What the hell. Why not."

I could think of plenty of reasons, as her aura blazed up like a fire in the half-light. And yet...if it came to a fight, if I wanted any chance of winning, I would need my strength, like she'd said.

"Well, thank fuck for that," she said, "because there's no earthly way I'm letting you sleep alone tonight of all nights."

She threw her arm around me, pulling me close, and this time I curled into her instead of pulling away into myself. With a sigh, I pillowed my head on her shoulder and let her aura wrap itself around me.

"Tonight of all nights," I repeated, sleep swiftly stealing over me.

Danny's chin rested on the top of my head, and I pillowed my cheek against her chest, her heart beating steadily in my ear, her breath warm as it stirred my hair. For one more night, we could have this together.

For tomorrow...

Well. Whatever happened tomorrow, I refused to regret this moment now.

Untold hours later, I awoke to a rush of frankincense-infused air and a tall shadow looming over us. Danny made a sleepy noise of protest as I jerked upright.

"It is only me," a deep voice said, and I slumped back, exhaling.

"Samael. You scared the crap out of me."

"I am sorry. Would you like me to make myself scarce? I had no intention of interrupting anything."

It wasn't quite a laugh, that sudden hitch in my chest. Here I was, thirty-two years old and for the first time in my life, I'd been caught by my father while cozying up to a girl. The demon apologized, but the man who had raised me would have condemned me for that, and I still didn't know whether it made me more grateful or angry at Samael.

"We were just sleeping." At my side, Danny sighed and snuggled deeper into the couch. Cold blue dawn seeped through the French doors, and I sat up. "Hell. I have court again today. I can't miss it. You'll keep watch on the house until I come back?"

In an ideal week, I would have spent the previous evening refining my closing arguments for the trial. But today, at the end of a week from hell, I'd have to wing it.

"About that," he said in his voice like a mountain's stony roots.

I turned, blinking the grit of sleep out of my eyes so I could really look at him this time. He stood in the shadows of the hall with Rae's sword in his hand.

A flickering glow ran down its blade, so faint I might have imagined it, faint enough to be a trick of the light.

"Hey! Put that down." Heart in my throat, I advanced upon him. "That sword is dangerous."

He stepped back, holding the sword upright in a practiced movement, something like a salute. "Indeed." It shimmered and flashed as he drew it back, its blue flame colder than the dawn's leaching light. "This is a powerful relic."

"You know it?"

"Have no fear, daughter. It was forged for those like us."

"Maybe so, but now it belongs to a goddess, and she's not the forgiving kind."

"They rarely are." With solemn reverence, he laid the weapon back into its case. "I would like to keep custody of this for now, and at the bacchanal tonight. With your permission."

Permission wasn't really mine to give, but I nodded. "Be careful. That thing can pack a serious punch."

"I hope that punch may turn the tide in our favor," he said. "There are few objects in this world that can overpower our kind, still fewer that can destroy us permanently. This is one."

"Are you sure about that?" I had taken its blade through my chest, and I lived. "It's not even silver."

"Silver is a different power altogether." Samael leaned the case up against the wall with assiduous care. "It breaks the bonds between our essence and our flesh. It cannot bind us or banish us from this world."

I frowned. "Wait. Even if we fall to dust…"

"We are not made of dust, child. We are merely tied to it. What is it that your scientists say? Energy can neither be created nor destroyed."

"I don't understand. Silver drains our energy, and when it's gone, we're gone."

"It is not so simple," my father said. "We are not mortal in the same way humans are."

"We were angels once," I murmured. "That's what Ariel told me. Is it true? Did we—did you—*fall*?"

Samael's expression changed. He almost looked embarrassed. "I don't know."

"You told me you're one of the eldest generation." My depth of disappointment startled me, as if answers to the secrets of the universe would make up for all my fatherless years. "How can you not know?"

"As with humans, time steals our past from us, and we have forgotten more than we remember."

"I didn't realize demons got dementia." He didn't seem that addled, but even the looks of a Golden Age movie star could be deceiving.

"Very funny," he said austerely. "Humans have bones and science from which to reconstruct their origins. We, on the other hand, have nothing but dust and legends."

"What legends?"

"Where our people came from, why we dwell in fleshly forms, from whence flow our powers—there are many theories and no certainties." Samael sighed, a soft, exasperated sound. "As he implied to you, Ariel and many of our elders believe we were severed from some greater divine source, forced to make our way on Earth alone as punishment for a sin we can't recall."

"You don't believe that, though."

"It is possible. I have no way of knowing the truth of it."

"Ariel told me he didn't believe in any gods. Except maybe himself."

"Perhaps he does not believe in such things any longer." Samael's tone dropped, meditative now. "He was always dissatisfied with our lot in this world, from the beginning of memory. It infuriated him to know that our strength depended on those he saw as inferior."

"Well, that definitely checks out. Same old asshole. Same old Ariel." I wrapped my arms around myself, goosebumps rising on my bare arms. "You really think the sword will help us beat him?"

"As you said, he does not change," Samael said. "In his deepest core, he is a coward. He will not challenge me, not while I wield this weapon. I will watch the house today, and we will take the fight to him tonight."

"But when will you sleep?"

"I do not need sleep." He settled into the armchair across from me. Immediately, Delilah appeared as if from nowhere, leaped into his lap, and curled up as if he belonged to her. He stroked her, expression bemused.

"I think she likes you better than she likes me." It didn't mean anything, of course. "Her judgment isn't great. She liked Ariel, too."

"Animals always take to our kind," Samael said, matter-of-factly. "Cats in particular."

"Because they're demons too?" I asked, half-joking.

"That is a cruel word." His tone carried a slight tinge of reproof. "They are not demons, no more than us, but they are sensitive to energy in similar ways."

"Huh." I looked at Delilah with new eyes. She yawned and curled tighter, purring loud enough to wake the dead. "You're sure you're okay with this?"

"It is not a bad use of my time," Samael said. "Go and make your justice, daughter."

"I'll do my best," I muttered, and fled the pride in his eyes. He still hadn't earned the right to look at me with pride like that.

More than that, I still didn't know what to do with it.

32

SMALL MERCIES

Rae didn't glance up when I slid into the seat beside her at the defendant's table. I touched her shoulder and she stirred, blinking as if waking from a trance. "You're feeling like yourself this morning?"

Her aura betrayed no hint of lightning or ozone, but the presence I'd awakened inside her had left her energy muted, her shadowed gray eyes unfocused. "I'm here," she said in a soft, toneless voice. "What about you?"

"I'm fine. We should talk about—"

"I've been watching you this week." She ignored my attempt to head her off, and the quiet undertone took on a trace of the relentless focus that made her a good advocate in her own right, when she was free. "You're jumping at shadows. You twitch every time the courtroom door opens."

"I didn't think it was that obvious."

"Not to everyone. But if you know, you know."

I thought about that, which turned out to be a mistake. Trial mode meant shoving everything else aside, like the enormity of everything that had happened to me this week. Now it overflowed and swamped me, a flood of emotion that belonged to me and me alone for once, the part of me that knew Rae's story all too well.

Tonight, I would betray that part of me and walk back into the trap I'd escaped a year ago. Tonight, I would make a sacrifice not unlike Rae's and give myself away. After I traded my life for Sebastian's, my soul would once again belong to the man who had groomed me, undermined me, and lied to me until I didn't know the first true thing about myself.

This morning, Samael had implied he believed he could pull off some miracle with that damn sword, but I didn't put much faith in demons, or in miracles, if it came to that.

"Don't worry about me," I said. "Right now, I'm here for you." I'd think about choices and consequences later, when I didn't have a miracle of my own to pull off with a jury that didn't believe in me either.

"Please rise," the bailiff commanded, and the courtroom rustled as if swept by a strong wind while the judge climbed up to his high seat.

He wasted little time on preliminaries. All too soon, he hunched his shoulders in his black robes like the plumage of a crow on a cold morning and glared down at me. "Your closing statement, please, Ms. Knight."

"Thank you, Your Honor." I rose to face the jury and took a beat, head bowed before their judgment, using my energetic sense to gauge their reactions instead of trying to read the looks on their faces.

"The truth, as it's often said, can appear stranger than fiction." No matter how I read the room, it radiated skepticism. I had no choice but to speak to it. "Yes, what happened in this courtroom yesterday afternoon probably seemed strange, maybe even impossible. The details of the story you heard may well have sounded fantastic. If that's what you're thinking right now, I can't blame you."

"Here's what I'll say instead." I hadn't planned to say any of this in my closing statement. I hadn't planned anything at all. I was improvising. "There's an underlying truth that needs telling today, and this one isn't a tale of magic and mystery. It's a story that you all might find a little more familiar."

The force of the words gathered momentum, and I went along for the ride, finding a rhythm that had resonance in this hostile room. "This is a story of justice denied, and who among us hasn't felt that fury? This world tells us every day that life's not fair. Every day we witness the reality that some lucky people seem to live above the law, while others bear disproportionate consequences." I spared a glance up at the judge, who shifted in his seat, lips pursed as if he tasted something sour.

"I think it's fair to say that most of us feel powerless to change that reality." I had a few of my real audience paying attention, at least. "What hope is there, when someone whose power or wealth outmatches our own does us wrong? Who among us hasn't prayed for a person like that to get their just desserts? I know I have."

I didn't pray, but calling Ira had amounted to the same thing, with similar frustration levels. "When we feel powerless, all we can really do is pray for relief. We can petition someone or something who has the power we lack to do something about it. We've all done it in one way or another, in a court of law, in a church or a temple, on the steps of City Hall."

I'd done more than that, though. "We cry out to anyone or anything who will listen. Sometimes, we fall to our knees in a dark place, at our lowest point, or in a country far from home, without faith or hope that we'll get an answer." I'd driven silver home in Ariel's chest, and it still hadn't proved enough.

"The only real difference in Rae McGuire's story is that when she prayed for justice in her darkest hour, she happened to bend the ear of a power that answered her." I steeled myself against Rae's reaction to my words, even as I pulled at the dark thread of her desolation, spooling the weight of her desperate ache out to the twelve mortals sitting in judgment. "She got the justice she couldn't hope for, but at a terrible price."

If they had no empathy of their own, they could borrow mine. "Ms. McGuire knew that justice would never come for the men who hurt her. Instead, she fought to change the outcome for others like her. Along the way, she lost herself, and something terrifying found her." My client stirred at the table behind me, ready to defend her own personal demon, but I pressed on.

"This story is a tragedy. Ms. McGuire had survived the abuse of fortunate men who used her body as an object of their control and satisfaction." I wasn't just speaking to the jury anymore, but to someone else in the room, a goddess I suspected of listening. "To get her justice, she offered all she had to a force more powerful than herself—one that used her all over again to gain yet more power and sate a thirst for the blood of the guilty."

Take that, you unconscionable witch. "It was a terrible bargain, no doubt. It exacted a terrible cost. Ms. McGuire didn't know the full price she'd have to pay until it came due. By then, it was already too late. But then again, we've all made bad bargains, haven't we?" The jury's energy rippled at that, unsettled but not quite following.

"We often submit our will to those who can do more." I softened my tone, drawing them back to me, bringing them home. "We have little choice in the matter. We put our trust in a justice system, a government, a business, any power that promises to make things better or make things right. We do it in the hope of becoming part of something greater than ourselves. Instead, all too often, we're called to do what they can't, and pay the price our betters incur."

Turning, I gestured to the defense table, where Rae sat pale and rigid. "Regan McGuire is a woman who believed in justice. She was willing to sacrifice everything she had to see it done. Now one question remains: will justice believe in her? Or will she pay the price for the rest of her life?"

A faint whiff of petrichor tickled my nostrils. Time to wrap this up, or there'd be hell to pay. "I won't tell you what to believe. It's your job to make up your minds." I deliberately put my back to the vessel of the furious goddess, making my final appeal. "You are the ones with a choice today. It's a solemn duty, but it's more than that. When you sit in that box, you have a chance to define justice on your terms."

The sudden shift in energy from the jury box surprised me. For a moment, I let it sink in. Then I matched my own energy with theirs and amplified it, shining it like a spotlight over them. "You have the power to make things right. At least in this case, no one can take that away from you." I nodded to them and stepped back, leaving them to it. "Your Honor, the defense rests."

I could have done more to save her. I could have leaned on them harder. But when the moment came, I couldn't bring myself to manipulate their feelings to my ends. That was too close to what Ariel would have done, had done, would do again, too much like a goddess imposing her will on mortal flesh. In my last hours of freedom, I wouldn't walk that road, not even with the best of good intentions.

Instead of co-opting the jury, I had empowered them.

Now all I could do was trust them to make the right choice.

It was golden hour in San Francisco, and the downtown streets had filled with revelers who swayed in a joyous and uninhibited rhythm. Dance music pulsed from three competing stages, and rainbow flags flapped in the evening breeze. The soft light glowed like a caress over bodies of all shapes, sizes, ages, and genders. It gleamed off leather, steel, shiny PVC, and sweaty skin.

After six hours, Rae's jury hadn't finished deliberating, but I couldn't wait for judgment any longer. I didn't have time for faith. I had a date with my own personal devil.

Officially, the event ended at sundown, but the crowd seemed inclined to keep the party going, no matter how much I willed them away. *Get out of here. It's not safe!*

All my warning Presence did was make the human sea break around me and shy away, leaving me standing in a small empty space amid the chaos, alone. I didn't mind the isolation—a small mercy, since the crush of bodies against mine would fill my senses with the lure and demand of human desire.

The crowd around us hushed as though a shadow had passed over them all at once. The throb of electronic dance music from the main stage cut off mid-measure, and a second later, the competing beats from the other stages faded away as well.

Chills crawled up my neck. In that uneasy silence, feedback whined from a single microphone, and then a voice floated over the crowd, melodious and mesmerizing like the voice of an angel, but mocking and malevolent, the voice of a demon.

It was Ariel's voice, calling my name.

I turned toward the stage. The wash of adrenaline surging through me made time seem to slip and snag, as if I moved in slow motion, hypnotized or in a dream. Or maybe that was his power reaching me, the same thrall that held the human crowd around me in check.

He commanded the center of the main stage like a circus ringmaster, the microphone held in a practiced hand. His Presence amplified his beauty and his threat as he stalked the boards, and his hair and eyes glowed matching shades of gold. He wore a shirt the color of old blood and one of the long black trench coats he'd always favored, the kind that flared dramatically around him when he moved.

"Lily Knight," he called again. His imperious gaze swept across the sea of human bodies, a hunter's gaze, a restless searchlight. "Show yourself. I know you're here."

I stood at least a hundred feet from the stage, but somehow Ariel seemed to pick me out anyway. His attention pressed down upon me with a tangible weight.

"There she is," he said. "Make way, you lot."

Before me, the sea parted, and a surge of bodies pushed me forward like a wave toward the stage where Ariel held court. I shook them off and strode the last few feet on my own power, while the humans behind me fell back, leaving an open space between them and the stage.

"Wise of you not to make a fuss." He smiled at my half-willing approach, clearly enjoying this.

"It's not like I have a choice."

"Indeed. But very like you to fight the inevitable."

"Where's Sebastian? And where's Eve?"

"Don't worry. They're nearby. Safe—as long as you keep them that way. Join me, won't you?" He came to the top of the steps leading down from the stage, extending a hand as if to help me up.

"This isn't necessary. I already told you I'll do whatever it takes."

"On the contrary, it's essential. That little shelter you've cozied up to gives good advice, doesn't it? One should always meet a violent ex-partner in public, and if I recall correctly, you did do your best to murder me."

The sheer audacity of his words over the loudspeaker hit me like a slap. "That's what you're going with? After everything you did? You're unbelievable."

"Am I?" He directed that question not to me, but to the audience at large. The gasps and sullen muttering that had arisen at his statement rose into a hostile snarl. They believed him all right.

Their condemnation flared at the base of my spine, between my shoulder blades, a spark that threatened to blaze up into violence. He had them eating out of his hand already, ready to turn on me.

The realization chilled me to my core. I knew what he wanted from me: my reaction, my rage, my fight. When I did, he would use it as evidence against me, show the world all how terrible I could be. He wanted that triumph, the validation and power he would find in the moment I had nowhere else to turn, no one on my side, no one willing to defend me.

He might not even have to kill me himself. Alone and with no source of kether at hand, I didn't like my chances against an angry mob.

"This is between you and me, Ariel." I ignored the hand he offered me, but scaled the stairs until I faced him, putting space between myself and the simmering threat of the crowd. "Let's keep these people out of it."

"I'm afraid I can't do that." He blocked my path for a moment, then fell back a step with one of his magnanimous gestures. "Besides, look at them. I think they're enjoying the show."

"You're even more twisted than I remember you. They came here to celebrate love in all its forms, and you just want to make them a tool of your hate."

"Hate? Or justice?" His smile widened, a shark's gleeful grin. "I do hope this can remain peaceful. After all, you can't know which of these belong to me. You left me plenty of time to stake some claims of my own today."

I gritted my teeth. "I'll come quietly."

"My dear, you never did come quietly."

"You wouldn't know," I said, leaning closer so the microphone in his hand would pick up the words. "You never did make me come."

Well, crap. That wasn't the de-escalation and surrender I'd planned. Ariel's face contorted, his eyes flashed with rage, and quicker than I could react, he shot out an arm and grabbed my throat with his bare hand, lifting me nearly off my feet. "You little hellion," he snarled.

A rapt "oooh" rose from our audience. No one stirred to intervene, caught in his smothering trance. I closed both hands around his wrist, but he struck them away with a blow that shuddered in my bones, grabbed them with his other hand, and held them fast. I struggled for breath against the crushing pressure on my throat. At the same time, the relentless pull of his kether draw dragged at me like an undertow.

The strength of it surprised me. Our ability to pull energy depended on the emotional bond between us and our partner. But for all I thought I hated him, it seemed the old connection between us still rang true. Maybe love and hate weren't so different after all, just two sides of the same coin. My vision blurred, my head swimming.

I kicked out at him, and he sidestepped me with adroit grace, lifting me further. My toes left the boards of the stage and beat against empty air. I drew on my energy reserves, needing my wings, but he'd already taken too much from me. Darkness swirled at the edges of my vision.

And then something fell upon us like a stooping falcon on great gray wings, a figure that held a flaming sword upraised as it dived.

33

BOLT FROM HEAVEN

Ariel pressed his face close to mine, his expression alight with triumph. His hot breath washed over me, sickly sweet with his incense—and then his face changed. Alarm flared in his amber eyes.

"Release her." Samael's words echoed like the roots of the earth given voice, like the clang of a huge, deep bell, and the air trembled.

Ariel's grip on my throat loosened a fraction, but not quickly enough. Spots swam in front of my eyes, and Samael struck.

He hit Ariel bodily with the full momentum of his dive, a bolt from heaven that shook us both. Ariel dropped me, and I fell to the stage, gasping for air through a bruised and battered windpipe. Wind swirled around me, a small personal cyclone that whipped hair into my mouth and obscured my vision.

Rolling onto my back, I squinted through the writhing gray fog of oxygen deprivation. Two winged shapes grappled above me, dark silhouettes against the fading sky as they rose higher.

They darted and clashed with the speed of striking snakes. I propped myself up on my elbows, and the view from the stage came into focus. Below me, a close-packed sea of humans below roiled uneasily, their faces tipped up with scattered cries of wonder and fear.

They were angry, confused, and panicking, the taste of it acrid in the back of my throat like bile. I rolled over and stood on unsteady feet.

The rage of a mob was one thing, but a mass panic would be much, much worse. Their anger only had one target—me. That, I could handle. That, I might even deserve. Either way, I had the strength to face it. On the other hand, a sudden stampede might wind up killing innocent people.

I had enough blood on my hands already, and they had come here for the sake of joy, love, dancing. I wouldn't let Ariel taint their euphoria like he had so much of mine and turn it into a memory of pain.

At the edge of the crowd, an eddy of shouts and jeers swelled as a knot of black-clad men shoved their way toward the stage.

Were they cops, FBI, or more of Ariel's civilian minions, disgruntled men who felt injured by my work like Jared had? From here, I couldn't tell the difference, and it might not matter. Either way, they probably had a role to play in his insurance plan.

A troop of burly guys in leather vests pushed back at them, and then one of the interlopers threw a punch. All at once, the unsettled energy in the street boiled over into a brawl.

The microphone had rolled downstage. I scrambled to grab it, and the whine of feedback cut through the shouts and screams, the thump of fists on flesh. Worried faces turned toward me, a note of hope added to the chord of their confusion, desperate for direction, for guidance.

These poor souls had never asked for a front-row seat on my personal drama, and I needed them out of my way before I made my next play. The responsibility weighed heavy on my shoulders as I dug deep for a Presence that would calm them, even as I couldn't soothe my own fears.

Do not be afraid. The age-old phrase sat on the tip of my tongue, the traditional greeting of angels revealing themselves to human eyes.

Angels. *Ha.* If one of my father's brethren had come up with that, if they were really angels of a sort, they must not have understood humans at all. Was there ever a less effective greeting, or one that denied its listeners the dignity of their entirely valid emotion? No one in distress wanted to hear some asshole tell them to calm down.

Lucky for them, then, I was no angel, and all I had to tell them was the truth.

"Hi, beautiful people," I said into the microphone. My voice echoed out of the PA system, momentarily startling me with its resonant, husky tone. "I know you're probably pretty scared right now. I'm sorry you had to see all of that."

Their energy smoothed out as I spoke, their gazes fixed on me. It seemed Ariel's threats of having them under his thrall had been more of his lies. I should have known.

From somewhere above us, a sharp report rang out. The brief moment of peace dissolved like dust in the wind. Screams broke out again as they stampeded for safety, pushing and shoving, trampling anyone unlucky enough to fall.

Gunfire? I tipped my head back, scanning the sky for the source of the shot. The distant dark figures of the two incubi grappled hundreds of feet up, northwest above the city now, flitting and tumbling like a pair of fighting hawks.

The last red light of the sun caught the edge of the blade that Samael carried. The third gunshot shattered the hush in the air like the crack of a bull whip, and the winged figure wielding the blade stalled in midair.

"No..." The wind whipping at my face ripped the plea from my lips, a prayer to nothing and no one, a prayer that no power could answer.

For a split second, Samael seemed to hang suspended there, wings still and folded around him in a protective shield.

Then he dropped like a stone. His wings came apart around him, shredding into shadow and dust from the tips of his pinions inward. The sword slipped from his hand. It flashed as it fell like lightning from a clear sky. After him dived Ariel, his faint laughter rippling down to me on a stray gust of the Peninsula's evening breeze.

I charged through the canyon of skyscrapers, eyeballing an intercept course, but it didn't matter. Earthbound, I couldn't stop Ariel, catch Samael, or retrieve the sword before it fell into the wrong hands. Without my wings, without a source, I didn't have the power.

The breeze above the city carried the sharp wild scent of the sea, overlaid with petrichor and copper. Alien energy prickled at the edge of my awareness.

In the street at the base of the Pyramid stood a woman, seemingly oblivious to the honks and shouts of angry drivers. Dark hair whipping around her, she raised her arm to the heavens, crying out in a low, ringing voice. I didn't understand the harsh, musical language she spoke, but I recognized it.

The verdict must have come down after all. "Rae?"

The sword dropped into her up-flung hand as if drawn by a magnet, and blue-white lightning darted along the blade. It wasn't Rae, of course, not anymore.

Her eyes glittered black at me, a crow's eyes above a fierce and terrible smile. Then she wasn't a woman at all, but a great dark bird arrowing upward toward the diving black arrow that was Ariel.

She cried out again, now with a crow's harsh voice, and from the small stand of redwood trees at the tower's base, something inhuman howled in answer. The wild sound lifted the hairs on the back of my neck, and I froze. Dark shadows swirled under the trees, impenetrable even to my enhanced vision.

In that moment, Samael's body struck the pavement with a sound like a thunderclap.

His wings had dissolved entirely away. The air sparkled with a cloud of motes that caught the last of the fading light, ethereal drifts of down and shredded feathers.

Throat tight, the sound of his fall still resonating in my bones, I ran to him. The street had cracked as though from a meteor strike, and fractures ran in spiderweb patterns from a shallow crater. His body didn't look broken, but he lay unmoving, eyes closed, graven features frozen in an agonized rictus. Dark blood seeped from his shoulder, from his nose and mouth.

"Father," I whispered and folded to my knees beside him, taking his wrist in one tentative hand.

I couldn't find it, but he had to have a pulse. We did have blood in us, after all, and every other human organ. It was what held us together that made us different, the binding of spirit and flesh, the link that silver broke.

In the street around me, night fell in a single blow. The swelling darkness exploded out of the trees. It flowed toward us, splitting neatly around us like black water meeting stone. The city's noise faded away, as if I knelt trapped in the eye of a storm.

The storm had a wild voice all its own. Snarls, shrieks, howls, and pounding hooves echoed in the rush of shadow, woven through with the clear, high call of a horn. In my periphery, red pinpoints of eyeshine glowed, and something huge and horned snorted above them.

The hellish procession passed us by, streaming down the street in the direction from which I'd flown, but I only had eyes for the angel who lay on the pavement before me.

He stirred at my touch, his eyelids fluttering open. The hunters," he whispered. "They came."

"This is your doing?"

"Not mine. They're Cee's people. I simply...asked for a favor."

"I wondered where you went last night." Black wolves and horned monsters made for a hell of a favor. I shivered. "That's two we owe her, then."

"Not enough," he said. "I...failed. I'm sorry."

"It's all right." I pressed his cold hand between mine. "I wish—"

He made an abortive motion, a half-shake of his head that brought another wince of pain. "Don't. Only you can stop him now."

"I don't know if I can."

"You must. He has them...there." His fingers twitched, pointing up at the tower that loomed above us, jutting out of the unnatural dark occluding the street. "The sniper guards them. Eve and a human man."

"Sebastian." He was here, and I could guess at who that shooter was. "Alive?"

"I think so. He moved. I could not...sense him."

That must have meant he still wore my ring, and that was something. "I have to get to him." Standing, I let Samael's hand slip from mine. "I'm sorry."

"Do not...be sorry." Sharp gasps broke his words, his breath labored. "Go now. Before your adversary recovers his advantage."

"I don't think he ever lost it. That tower is hundreds of feet high, and I'm..." Weak. Grounded. *Human.* "Gonna have to take the stairs."

There was no way I'd get there in time. The knowledge weighed my steps, heavier than gravity. Somewhere high above, a crow screamed in pain or fury, and then something hit me from behind like a cannonball.

"You *jerk.*" Danny's embrace nearly bowled me over and knocked the hard-won air out of my lungs. "I thought he'd killed you up there. Is your dad okay?"

"You shouldn't be here." I kept my eyes fixed on the point of the pyramid. It glittered, the last stray light of the setting sun catching a flash of movement at its pinnacle, where a dark square gaped in the mirrored glass. *"Get down!"*

We hit the pavement, my body shielding hers as another sharp report echoed around the high rises. "What the hell?" Danny shrieked, indignant.

"I told you not to come." Tearing my gaze from that ominous missing pane and the light glinting off the muzzle of something high-powered and deadly, I checked her over. No dark stain bloomed on her shirt, and I breathed again. "It's not—"

"I don't care about *safe.*" She softened under me, but her jaw held its stubborn, fierce set. "I care about you."

"I was going to say *over.*" I held her gently by the shoulders and waited until her eyes met mine, dark and shining as her aura. "This is worse than last time, and that was bad enough."

"I know. I was there, remember?"

I remembered all too well how her life's blood had sluiced over my hands. The bullet from the gun he'd seized from me had lodged beneath her ribs, a seed of poison that almost killed us both. "He's got way too much leverage already. I can't lose you."

"You're right," she said, far too calmly. "You need me. That's why I'm here."

"What—" The words faded as she laced her fingers around my neck and drew my forehead down to hers.

She didn't kiss me. She didn't have to. This closeness, her touch, her warm brown gaze locked into mine, had everything I needed, like she'd said. Power flowed strong and soft and sure between us, more than I ever thought possible, a lifeline, a promise, a bond I couldn't deny.

"There." Her eyelids fluttered closed, voice breathy and faint as she fought the torpor of the energy draw. "Now go get your boyfriend back."

The life force she'd given pulsed through me, my shoulders flexing with the stir of wings. I had to leave her here with Samael, helpless, drained, and undefended. "Promise me you'll go home." My voice shook, and I gripped her shoulders. "Please."

"You're not the boss of me." She pushed at me, ineffectually, until I released her. Rolling over, she crawled to Samael's side. "Go on. Do your hero thing. I'll take care of your old man."

"You can't—he's not—" With my claim on her, she couldn't give him what he truly needed to live. He looked bad, face tight and ashen, eyes closed.

"I'm a *doctor*, Lily. I've got this." With visible effort, she levered herself upright, kneeling by the injured demon, and turned to glare at me.

I gave up. "Thank you." I squeezed her forearm when she reached for my hand, unwilling to take more. Then I leaned to brush my lips over Samael's cheek. "I'm glad I met you, Father."

His brow knit, his voice barely a whisper. "What...will you do?"

"What I have to." I straightened, but I wouldn't lie to either of them. Not anymore. "I'm going to end this," I said, and took off running.

My pinions erupted as I ran, lofting me into the air. I hurtled upward at a sharp-angled trajectory, not looking down to watch the two small figures receding fast below me.

34

Fury Rising

The crow had harried Ariel away from the tower, forcing him to dodge and circle, darting down to peck at him and then dancing away when he tried to strike back. She had given me my chance.

I rose toward the glinting top of the tower, spiraling around the other side from the broken sniper's window. Even with all my Presence, I couldn't count on the advantage of surprise, but I still had my superhuman speed. The tower blurred in my vision, wind whistling past my ears, until I shot over it and hovered for a moment above its peak.

Beneath the textured glass of its roof, three figures occupied the small space. One paced the circular room, golden hair gleaming in the last light of the sun. *Eve.* Another sat against the wall, knees drawn up, dark head bowed, and my heart clenched at the way he curled into himself. It didn't seem right to see Sebastian that way, diminished and afraid and hurt because of me.

The last person stood at the window with a rifle poised, waiting, tracking the flight of incubus and crow far out across the cityscape. The military posture and high ponytail pulled through the back of her dark blue baseball-style service cap didn't shock me. Of course North would still do Ariel's dirty work. I'd tried to warn her, back in the forest, and hoped I got through, but I couldn't counter his thrall. She was too far gone.

I didn't hesitate another breath. Folding my wings, I dropped and kicked downward with all the force in my body. My booted feet met the glass, and with a splintering crash, the ceiling gave way.

North jerked the rifle up too late. I landed heavily atop her, and we both hit the floor. She didn't let go of the rifle, though. She was only human, but she was trained to fight.

"Lily?" Eve's voice, shaky with disbelief, came from behind me.

"Little busy here." I ducked North's attempt to rifle-whip me and pinned her to the ground. Kneeling on her upper arms, I wrested the weapon out of her hands. She cursed me furiously, her face twisted with rage and hatred.

I held her there and chanced a look over my shoulder, just in case Eve was ready to come to the disgraced agent's defense. But Ariel's daughter had her hands to her mouth, eyes wide. Sebastian remained huddled against the far wall, eyes closed, head lolling sideways, unmoving. Dried blood caked his left temple where a nasty purple bruise spread over his eye. Fear sliced through my heart. Did he even know I'd come for him? What if I hadn't made it in time?

"Lily, you can't." Eve didn't look defiant. She looked afraid. "He'll be so angry. He'll kill you. Please..."

"Is that what he told you?" I sat back as North bucked, trying to dislodge me, bearing down on her chest to hold her still. Something cracked, and she let out a strangled scream. Belatedly, I eased up. Fighter though she was, she was still human, and fragile. I wasn't here to kill her unless she forced me to.

"He just wants us all to be together. He said he wouldn't hurt you if I went with him. He promised me."

"Yeah, well, his promise and a nickel won't buy you a goddamn thing. Not in this economy. Will you *stop*?" I hissed at North, who was still kicking up a fuss beneath me despite her gasps of pain.

"Let me up," North panted. "I think you broke my rib."

"And you shot my father. I'll break more than that if you make me." I scowled down at Ariel's handmaiden, trying to calculate the force it would take to knock her out with the butt of the rifle without caving her skull in. "Sebastian! Talk to me. You good?"

When he didn't answer, Eve's breath hitched, a stifled sob. "Lily, he hit his head. It's bad. I staunched the bleeding, but... Please, you have to believe me. I tried to stop Father, but he wouldn't listen."

I didn't have to believe her, but I found that I did. I hauled North upright and dragged her with me, ignoring her grunt of paint as I shoved her against the wall a few feet from Sebastian. "Sit down. If you move, I'll blow your head off." It turned out her skull integrity didn't matter to me as much as I thought.

She slid to the floor, eyes fixed on the weapon I trained on her chest, and I dropped to one knee beside Sebastian. His cheekbones stood out stark under his closed, shadowed eyes, his skin waxy and pale. A shallow, slow breath stirred his shoulders.

Relief choked my throat like tears. I brushed back the hair that had flopped over his forehead, lank and damp with the sweat beading on his too-warm skin. "Hey. It's me."

His eyes cracked open, wincing. With that head wound, he probably had a concussion. "Lily. You came."

"Don't sound so surprised." I traced fingers along the crease in his brow, watched him shiver. "You're burning up."

"You should have stayed away," he said, but he turned his head into my stroking hand. "He planned it like this. I'm just..."

"Bait. Of course." I gritted my teeth against a hot and bitter rush of fury. "I don't care. I'll kill him. Again."

He lifted his head. It took a visible second for his gray eyes to focus on my face. "You'll have to," he slurred. "He's worse than I thought. He hates you. He'll do anything."

"Believe me, I know." I'd been through this dance before. The only difference was this time I had even more to lose.

"Lily." Eve's voice cracked on my name. "*Look out.*"

I straightened, rifle in hand, and turned in time to see Ariel hurtling toward me, wings beating in silhouette against an orange and violet sky. Another, smaller creature harried him, diving and pecking at his head and shoulders until a sweep of pinions sent her spinning, out of control and out of sight.

Still he came on. I swung the rifle up. He made an easy target. I could end this now.

The sudden heavy strike across the back of my head *burned*. It wrenched a scream from my throat. I went down hard, my one shot echoing through the enclosed space like thunder and shattering another pane of glass. A heavy weight pinned my arms, scalding the exposed flesh of my wrists and stealing the strength from my limbs.

"Got you, demon," North hissed in my ear, pressing her silver bracers into my skin with ruthless force. I'd forgotten about those.

Just like that, it was all over. The poison of the silver took my power, took my wings, took all the sweet hope Danny had granted me minutes ago. It drained out of my skin like the light from the sky, and the nauseous inevitability of my failure sank into my bones.

"Well, well, well," drawled a voice above me. That voice had haunted my nightmares for a year, and now it crawled along my skin, a caress I cringed away from. "How the tables do turn. Are you done fighting me yet, Lily fair?"

I tried to lift my head, tried to find the strength I needed to stare Ariel in that beautiful face of his, to spit in it. But I couldn't raise myself up enough before North pushed me back down. I could only stare at his boots, the scuffed steel of their toes. My vision blurred and ran, splintered by pain as the silver pressed against my skin chewed into my flesh.

"Enough," I rasped. "I'm done. You win."

"Ah," he breathed, and as if at some signal, North let up the pressure of her bracer on my arms.

I didn't move. If I did, I might vomit. The skin of my wrists had already split and blistered, the burns oozing around their suppurating edges. I didn't want to know what the back of my head looked like where she had hit me. My hair would probably fall out in chunks.

Not that it mattered anymore. Not when Ariel had me dead to rights. Or more accurately, just plain dead.

His boots stepped closer, filling my field of view. I cringed, waiting for the kick.

What came instead was worse than any blow. His touch caressed my clammy forehead, and I felt the pulse of an energy gift. Not much, but enough that I sucked in a breath of relief and hated myself for it.

He wanted me to. He wanted my dependence, my gratitude, my self-loathing acquiescence as much as he wanted my suffering. It was sicker than silver, a gesture so familiar it felt like coming home.

No. Maybe I had lost, but I wouldn't lose myself. I couldn't let him take that from me. "Don't touch me," I muttered, though my tongue stumbled, thick and unwilling.

"As you wish." He used his old, light mocking tone, confidential and teasing, the one that said, *We both know you don't want what's good for you.*

"What I wanted never mattered to you." I had just enough strength to call out his bullshit, if it was the last thing I did. It might be. "You have what you want from me, for all that's worth."

"My family. Yes. My girls, together at last." His voice took on a mournful tone, and I heard the warning in it. "It's all I ever wanted. Why did you always have to fight me so hard?"

"What about our deal?" Dread rose in my throat, choking me. "You said you'd let Sebastian go. Do it, and I won't fight you anymore. Please."

Ariel laughed, a soft and terrible sound. "Get her up," he said, and all the false sorrow and softness vanished in an instant. "I want her to see this."

North grabbed a handful of my hair and yanked me upright onto my knees. My burned scalp tore, and I swallowed another grunt of pain. Something hard jabbed me in the small of my back—the rifle's muzzle, a silent and inevitable threat.

"See what?" I whispered. "Ariel. You promised." *In this economy? That and a nickel won't buy you a goddamn thing.*

Ariel paced in front of me, his yellow eyes blazing out of his back-lit silhouette. "You're right. We had a deal. But you broke it, just like last time."

"I'm here, aren't I?" I squinted at the broken windows behind him, searching for the flutter of a crow's wings, my last remaining ally. The empty sky glowed, colors fading fast from deep rose to shadowed lavender, sun lost below the bank of fog that loomed like a cresting wave above the city's jagged horizon.

Had he killed the goddess when he struck her? Could an eldritch being fall so easily? Or perhaps she had simply abandoned me, considering her debt now paid in the time she had bought me, the time I'd already squandered until it ran out.

"I warned you," Ariel said. "You knew the cost of your choice. You called your *daddy* to fight your battle for you like the silly child you always were."

"You knew." My breath caught on the words and snagged, painful as a hangnail.

"Samael always did think he was so much better than me," he mused. "Imagine my surprise when I found out he had sired a half-human spawn. Even the most perfect angel has his weaknesses, it seems."

"Oh. You *always* knew." It hit like a fist to my sternum and took my breath away. "Why didn't you tell me?"

"It was never mine to tell." He shook his head, clicking his tongue in disapproval. "He didn't want you to know. If he had, he wouldn't have left you for me to find and foster."

"You're wrong." But doubt shadowed my words. "You hid him from me."

"He never looked for you. His loss, my gain, though you always did make enough trouble that I wondered whether he made the right choice, after all."

"You're a monster."

"Manners, Lily dear. It takes one to know one." He pivoted, grinning without mirth. "Never mind. That's all in the past, and we were talking about our bargain."

I clenched my jaw until it ached, searing as my impotent rage. "Our bargain. You have me. So let him go."

"Tsch. No. You breached the covenant you made with me, and your paramour must pay the price. Eve, bring him here."

Goddamn him. "Eve. Don't do this."

A rustle of movement and Sebastian's sharp, bitten-off groan behind me told me she wasn't listening to me anymore. At least she handled him gently enough, his arm slung over her shoulder as they passed me while I swayed on my knees. His eyes sought mine, a silent plea plain on his face, though his ring still hid his aura from me.

"Good girl," Ariel said, in that awful, caressing way I knew so well. His smile transformed his face, glowing with pride, as if the brilliance draining out of the sky had come to live in him. "Over here, to the edge."

"Father, please." Eve faced him, her spine straight, but her voice trembled. "He's a good man. He's always been kind to me. He doesn't deserve—"

Ariel slapped her, hard, across the face. The sound echoed through the small space on top of the tower, the crack of flesh meeting bone. It shocked everyone into silence for a moment.

Eve stood still, shoulders shaking, her hand raised to her cheek. Ariel turned away, brooding out at the twilit cityscape. North took a sharp breath behind me, and the pressure of the rifle muzzle eased slightly from the small of my back. Maybe she was having second thoughts.

As for Sebastian—he had drawn himself up, pulling Eve closer instead of leaning on her. She buried her face in his shoulder, stifling a sob, and my throat ached for them, the way he offered her the care her blood father should have given her. Sebastian had his other hand behind his back, his fingers fiddling with something. My silver-fogged brain couldn't fathom what.

The moment of silence passed, and Ariel spun around again. He wrenched Sebastian away from Eve, dragging him toward the shattered window. Eve flinched back, collapsing into herself.

"Come here," Ariel snarled. "I want you to see this."

At his words, North seemed to remember who she served, and she renewed the jab of the rifle in my back. "Get up," she snapped.

I rose, stumbling forward, and several things happened at once.

A small item dropped from Sebastian's fingers, glinting as it fell. It hit the tile with a resonant ping like a very small bell, bounced once, and rolled to land at my feet. My heart stuttered in my chest.

It was the ring I'd given him. His aura struck me like a wave, fear and anger and sorrow, and under it all, a depth of devotion I couldn't fathom, except...*is that for me?*

The window exploded inward in a shower of glass and a rush of storm-scented air, and with it dove a crow—not a crow, because it transformed in flight. A familiar figure hit the floor with the force of a lightning strike. A halo of blood-red hair floated around her head, a sword crackled with power in her hand, and she scanned the room with sclera-less black eyes.

Behind me, the rifle clattered to the floor. I chanced a look over my shoulder and found North backing up, her eyes blank with horror. Not even her silver bracers or Ariel's thrall could shield her now. The dread of the goddess fell upon her.

Sebastian, too, had gone limp in Ariel's grasp, the light of his aura quenched to dark embers of animal fear, ebbing and flickering as he slipped in and out of consciousness.

The goddess in Rae's body held the sword pointed at Ariel's chest, but her wild, dark gaze sought mine. "This one is yours to judge. I shall honor your verdict."

"Not another step, either of you," Ariel said. "Call off your bird witch, Lillian. Or I'll drop him."

Sebastian slumped in his grasp, hanging over empty air, his bare feet bloody where Ariel had dragged him over the broken glass from the window.

"Hold." My voice shook, and I stepped forward, putting myself between the sword and Ariel.

Sebastian had taken his ring off on purpose. He'd made himself vulnerable. He'd offered me a chance to take my power back. But now his eyes were blank and dull with fear, his mouth slack. He'd done all he could, more than I could have asked.

I looked Ariel in the face and said, "Give him back first. Then we'll see."

And Ariel, that bastard, grinned at me. He must have used a little Presence, because his beauty blazed forth again, cruel and terrible, merciless as the light burning in his golden eyes.

"No," he said. He opened his hands, and let Sebastian fall.

I didn't think. I didn't even hesitate. Behind me, someone shrieked with fury. Was that Eve screaming? A crack like thunder shuddered through my ears, through my whole body.

Silver burns forgotten, I launched myself after Sebastian, and though I had no wings, a demon's momentum drove me faster than the pull of gravity. I wrapped my arms around him and we tumbled together through a glass-and-concrete gorge toward the streets of the city far below.

35

SACRAMENTS

The wind howled past my ears. Sebastian stirred against me. His lips found mine and we were kissing, still in free-fall, and the sweet, rich force of him flowed into my mouth and my veins like wine, like a sacrament. The ground rushed up to meet us.

Then my wings snapped out and caught the air, and we weren't falling anymore, but soaring. Sebastian gasped into my mouth, a dead weight now in my arms. He had given me everything, and in his injured state, it hadn't taken much to drain him. But it was enough.

Something else plummeted past us, another body, wingless. I turned in the air, following its fall. It had golden hair and blank, startled, staring eyes. A wound in the center of the chest marked where a high-powered round had torn through it, soaking the red shirt with darker blood.

Ariel hit the pavement far below us with a wet, echoing thump and lay still, a crumpled, broken shape, no longer larger than life.

With slow, careful wingbeats, holding Sebastian's limp body tight against my chest, I lifted upward and away, back toward the tower room. I didn't have much energy to spare, but I had enough.

The goddess had North backed up to the wall with a sword at her throat, but I paid her no mind. Eve stood in the center of the room. She held North's rifle in her hands, staring down at it as if the hands weren't hers at all.

When I said her name, she lifted her head, and tears streamed down her face. "Is it over, Lily?" she whispered. "Did I do it? Is he gone?"

"Yes." In my arms, Sebastian slept with the untouchable abandonment of the demon-kissed. The wound on his temple looked bad, and he was still too pale, but his lips quirked at the corners, the ghost of a smile.

"And Sebastian? Is he...?"

"Just drained." I could give him back what I'd taken when we all had safely made it to solid ground. I shifted his weight onto my shoulder and reached out to Eve, who dropped the rifle, darting into my embrace. "I'm sorry you had to do that," I said into her hair rich with its succubus scent of sandalwood.

"I'm not sorry," she said in a fierce, choked voice. "Not for that. I'm sorry for letting him in, though. He made so many promises..."

"I know what he's like." I probably knew better than anyone else. "You don't have to explain. Not right now." I did want to hear it from her, how long she'd known he was alive, what he'd told her to lure her to him, what plan he had for them or us if he succeeded, but all that could wait. I closed my eyes, holding Eve tight.

My family was safe. Ariel hadn't won. I had.

The air sharpened around us with the crackling tension of a rising storm, redolent with ozone and the overwhelming, coppery scent of blood. At a cut-off, choking sound from behind us, I raised my head.

The ancient sword in Rae's hand had already sliced North's throat open. Her body sank to the ground and the blood kept coming, not pooling on the ground but writhing and spiraling upward to wreath the blade in a gravity-defying ribbon of scarlet. The weapon pulsed in the hand that held it with a terrifying light, not a light at all but its absence, unlight, blacklight, so darkly brilliant it hurt my eyes and mind to look at straight on.

"What have you done?" The words scraped at my own throat, the electric charge in the room thickening the air until I could hardly breathe.

The sword's bearer did not turn, but she shuddered. Rae's red hair stood out around her head in a static-electric halo bright as the liquid flowing into the sword.

Her shoulders dropped, her chin tipped back, and her sepulchral voice held no trace of the mortal woman I knew at all. The sky darkened over us with fast-moving clouds, traceries of lightning gathering at the edges of the sky. Thunder rolled, far off, getting closer. "She was guilty."

"She was just a pawn!" Ariel had captured her in his thrall just as he had captured me once. I had no love lost for North, but while she'd made terrible choices, she hadn't chosen this. He'd chosen her.

The entity inhabiting Rae's body didn't answer me. Something was happening, a play of power between the woman's body, the sword, and the sky. Her back arched, a spasm that held her rigid, and the crackle of energy in the sword leaped upward as lightning flashed again. The flow of blood slowed to a trickle. North's body crumpled to the ground, skin ashy pale and tight over the bones of her face, a corpse's face.

A growl of thunder shook the tower, and understanding struck me. *The blood of the guilty.* The goddess in Rae had needed the lifeblood of thirteen guilty souls to come back into the world. In her previous rampage, she'd claimed twelve. I had denied her the last when I gave my own blood, and almost my own life, to stop her on the mountain. I thought, I'd hoped, that had been the end of it.

I'd been wrong.

"It is...finished." The cry tore from the chest of the figure before me, the ribbons of blood turning to ultraviolet non-light that swirled around her, rising like a whirlwind, blurring her in my vision.

She no longer held a woman's shape. Another form superimposed itself over the mortal body that had contained her: dark and winged, it towered over us, tendrils of its blacklight power reaching and twining through the tower room, into the sky. Thunder rolled again, and in its wake came a strange clamor of voices: the harsh cry of birds or the baying of hounds, and among them words I didn't understand, a language I didn't know falling from the lowering clouds like rain.

Whatever had come into the world at her call, that darkness that had flowed outward from beneath the grove of redwoods beneath us, now answered her call again. It circled upward around the tower with the howling force of a hurricane.

"What's happening?" Eve clung to me, her voice cracking. "Is...is that Rae?"

"Not anymore," I said. "Not right now." And then I ducked, covering her body with mine, just in time.

With a crack as loud as a gunshot, lightning split the tower and grounded itself in the upraised sword. For a moment Rae's body hung in the air, rimmed in electricity, convulsing, seizing, bent backwards in an impossible arc.

Then, abruptly, the howling chorus ceased. My ears rang in the sudden stillness. I blinked, my vision blurred and burned with afterimages that faded with the alacrity of dreams.

Eve moved first, extricating herself from me, calling Rae's name. I rubbed my eyes, squinting, as my sight returned little by little.

Rae lay crumpled by North's bloodless body. The sword had fallen beside her, not flaming now with any charge of power but mere metal, inert. Eve knelt by Rae, eyes wide as she looked back at me.

I rose to my feet, my steps unsteady as I went toward them. Over our heads, the clouds had swallowed the last trace of the dark lightning that had danced through the tower room. Thunder grumbled again, but farther off this time, moving quickly away. I picked up the sword, turning it over, examining the blade for some sign of blood or magic. It hummed gently in my hands as if still resonating from its last strike, but no lightning dripped along its edge.

"Is she dead?" Eve asked.

Kneeling by Rae's body, I picked up her hand and turned it over, pressing my fingers into her wrist. Her pulse beat beneath them, faint and slow. And with it, I felt something else, the sluggish pull of her life energy inaccessible to me in her unconscious state but present, human, intact. Unclaimed.

"No." I dropped her wrist, sat back on my heels. "She's free."

"What *was* that?"

I considered this. It was a problem, certainly. We'd killed a demon and unleashed a force of war and vengeance, once bound to the sword and Rae's mortal body, into the world.

"I think it was the end of something," I told Eve. "Or maybe the beginning. Something new."

Either way, I decided, it was a problem for another time, another place. Future Lily could deal with the fallout.

I hefted the sword in my hands. The juddering beat of a helicopter's rotors echoed through the fading twilight, and somewhere below us, sirens wailed. The fallout was already on its way, it seemed.

A hand intertwined with mine, and I looked up into Eve's green eyes as she pulled me to my feet.

"Come on, Lily," she said. "Let's go home now."

Home. What did that even mean, anymore? I didn't want to go back to Ariel's condo, no matter how dead he'd looked on the ground. I didn't want any of that. I didn't know what I wanted. I wanted something that belonged to me from the start.

I gathered Sebastian up, and Eve followed my lead, picking up Rae's unconscious body. I thought of Danny, waiting below with my father, if he lived.

This little family belonged to me, at least. It wasn't new, not exactly, but it felt complete in a way it never had before.

With our burdens held light to our chests, we took to the air together.

Ariel's body hadn't yet crumbled to dust. It lay crumpled, smaller than he'd loomed in life, on the uneven pavement of the empty street.

Gently, I laid Sebastian's unconscious but breathing body down on the sidewalk. Then I strode toward the still, broken form of my enemy, dragging the sword behind me as I went. The metal shrieked against the concrete, sparking. It left a long scratch behind it like the mark of a giant claw.

With one booted toe, I rolled him over. I needed to see the face that had haunted too many of my dreams before he returned to torment me in waking life again. I had to make sure this would be the last time, and I had to do it now, before the sirens screaming down on us brought questions from authorities who wouldn't like any of the answers.

Waxen now, the mobile mouth slack and devoid of any smirk, the bright predator's eyes closed, he didn't look like the monster I remembered. The high-powered round had torn a brutal wound in his chest where his heart would have been. All that blood and ruined flesh made him look almost human.

"Do it." The deep voice from behind me caught on a pained breath, labored but no longer fading.

I glanced over my shoulder. With Danny supporting him on his right and Eve on his left, Samael made his halting way along the street toward me.

"You're alive." Caught between the shattered remnants of the past I'd lived through and the bleeding reminder of the one I never got to have, I swallowed hard.

"You must know we are not so easy to kill." He nodded toward the body in front of me, then winced at even that small movement. "All the more reason for you to ensure a clean and final strike."

"High powered rifle," Danny said, mouth tight. "The bullet went clean through Sam's shoulder. Rae will live too, just passed out. Is Sebastian...?"

"He'll be all right. I hope." With Danny's help and an energy push, I could probably heal the physical damage, but trauma wasn't so easily repaired, and I didn't know all of what he'd suffered at Ariel's hands. "That head wound doesn't look good, but he's breathing."

"Go on, Aunt Danny. I've got this." Eve's gaze swept from me to the sword to her fallen father, bright with agony and hunger.

"Be right back." Danny extricated herself from under Samael's arm and jogged toward Sebastian, already swinging her bag off her shoulder. She had come prepared, it seemed, as attested by Samael's splinted arm and neatly bandaged side.

"Eve, maybe you should step away." I turned back to the body at my feet. "It won't be easy. There's no coming back for him this time."

"I shot him, didn't I?" A stubborn note crept into Eve's voice.

"Yes, and that was extremely brave." I lifted the sword from its resting point. "But it doesn't mean you have to witness this. It's my responsibility."

The sword hummed in my hand, faintly, not flaming. Maybe my human blood didn't activate its full powers. Would it still do the job I needed it for?

"You know what must be done, Daughter." Samael sounded puzzled, maybe disappointed in me. "Yet still you hesitate."

"Hey," Eve said. "Grandpa. It's complicated, all right? Don't be a dick."

The sudden silence behind me spoke volumes about the bracing experience of getting adopted as Eve's elder.

"It's true, though," she continued. "My father...he wasn't what I thought. He's hurt so many people, Lily. He hurt me."

"I know," I said and raised the sword. "I'm sorry."

With one clean, quick strike, I brought the blade down with all my remaining strength. It sang as it fell, a soft keening whistle in the cool night air.

Severed from his body, Ariel's head spun away from the force of my strike. For a moment, nothing else happened except the ragged catch of Eve's shuddering breath.

All at once, the lines of his body blurred. As if his cells had lost their hold on each other, his edges fell apart like sand into a sinkhole. Now a shimmering cloud hung in the air around where he lay, partially obscuring his form, his head. His shape remained, but insubstantial, losing its coherence grain by grain.

For a moment, it lingered close to the pavement, pale as mist in the city lights. Then a gust of wind sharp and cold with the salt-scent of the bay swept in and blew the rest of him away.

36

Cinnamon and Maple

"Hey, sleepyhead." I leaned over the bed in Sebastian's room, speaking softly in his ear, lips not quite close enough to touch. "You alive in there?"

He stirred at my voice. "Am I?" He blinked up at me, hair tousled from sleep in a way that made him look younger, almost boyish, and my chest tightened with protective affection. "Something smells amazing. Is that bacon?"

"Bacon, eggs, French toast. And coffee." I looked him up and down. The wound on his head looked better in the morning light after disinfecting and rest, along with an experimental trial of therapeutic three-way energy transfer.

That made it sound a lot more adventurous than what had actually happened, mostly cautious skin contact and holding hands. Still, embodying the point of the energetic V between two people who loved me definitely qualified as a novel experience.

"You made breakfast?" His tone hovered between disbelief and concern, but amusement flickered through his aura. It felt strange, feeling him again after so long. It felt like coming home.

"Don't sound so worried," I said dourly. "I'll put your fears to rest. *Danny* made breakfast. I'm just the serving succubus."

He raised an eyebrow at that, but his smile quickly faded as his energy dropped into shadow. "Lily, we should talk."

"I know." Heart heavy, I set aside the tray of food. "I messed up. I'm sorry. I love you. But I love her too. I don't—"

"Stop."

My mouth snapped shut at his tone. Even lying in bed, recovering from injury and energy drain, he had that effect on me, it seemed. I sank to the bed, dropping my head in my hands. Now came the price, the cost I hadn't paid yet. I'd gotten all of them back without making good on my deal with the devil, my bargain with Ariel. Even Samael had pulled through after Danny called his source—identity protected, she insisted, by patient confidentiality—and sent him off to recover in private.

It stood to reason I had to lose something. I deserved to lose this.

Sebastian was still speaking, and it took a moment for the words to filter through. "I always knew I shared you with her— Lily, look at me."

His fingers encircled my wrist, and his essence pulsed through me at the touch as he drew my hands away from my face. With a gentle, inexorable grip, he took my chin and turned it so I had to meet his clear blue gaze.

"What are you saying?" I asked finally, struggling to comprehend what I felt from him now, because it matched none of my expectations.

"I'm saying my only regret is that you felt afraid to tell me what you wanted."

"I didn't know," I said. "Not...not entirely. I didn't dare to want it." I didn't believe I deserved one man's love, but the love of two people, my favorite humans? I hadn't earned such a gift.

"When I told you I didn't need exclusivity from you, I meant it," Sebastian said.

"You aren't jealous?"

"Oh, I was." He laughed, his short, rich, startled chuckle that I loved so much. "But not because of that. I was mostly hurt that you fed from her but wouldn't feed from me."

"I don't understand." I had his ring in a box in my pocket. I'd planned to offer it back to him now that we weren't in danger, if he'd accept it.

"What's not to understand?" he said. "I'm here for all of it, Lily. I liked being connected to you that way. I started to wonder what was wrong with *me*."

"I was trying to protect you at first." Or I'd convinced myself of that, at least until recently. I'd tried to protect Danny the same way for too many years, and when the dam broke, I couldn't hold back anymore. "The truth is, I was scared. Of what it meant, of what it could mean. Of taking too much from you, or anyone."

"I knew that here." He tapped his temple below the wound that Danny had carefully cleaned and dressed, wincing a bit as he realized his mistake. "But not here." He put his hand over his heart.

I thought about this. Holding that boundary had its upsides. His energy was a heady liquor, one I craved, but I also liked the mystery I'd discovered in him when he wore the ring, the way it shifted the power between us. Maybe we'd find some middle ground to play with there. "So, what now?"

"Breakfast, I hope," he said. "I'm starving."

Eve had told me that despite her best efforts, Ariel was capricious and inattentive to the needs of his human prisoner. If it had gone much past a day—I shivered at the thought. It had ended well, but every time I looked at him I remembered what I could have lost.

"Right." I retrieved the tray for him, arranging the pillows to prop him up. "And after that?" I ventured when he had settled in.

His mouth already full, he looked up and swallowed hastily. "We'll figure it out. All three of us."

"Danny likes you," I said, "but I don't think you're her type. Last night notwithstanding."

He flushed. "That's not what I meant."

"It would never work, anyway." I grinned at him, enjoying this now. I didn't get to fluster him often. "You're both tops."

That got a double eyebrow lift. "I've never been less shocked." An answering smile played around his mouth, belying his dry tone with a flicker of interest for what it would mean to join forces against me.

And just like that, I was the one being flustered.

I left him to his smile and his breakfast, heading downstairs on bare feet to the kitchen where Danny and Eve sat at the bar-style counter, demolishing a prodigious amount of French toast between them. I snagged a piece for myself and took the seat next to Danny. Both of them turned to look at me.

"Well?" Danny said after a long silence in which I chewed, stalling.

"She's happy," Eve said helpfully.

"So you talked to him?" Danny's tone was stern. "About everything?"

I swallowed, put down my fork. "I talked to him," I said. "It's… I think we're going to be okay."

Fear moved through her aura, chased by hope. "We? What about *us*?"

She wasn't making sense, but I understood. I turned in my chair to face her, my friend, my love, my anchor in every storm, her brown eyes warm and open and sweet as the maple syrup on my tongue.

"Us too," I said simply and leaned forward, kissing her softly until Eve's whoop of triumph made me pull away. I leaned around Danny to make a face at my foster daughter, and she beamed back at me, unrepentant.

Danny didn't let me get away so easily but caught my fingers under the bar, entwining hers with them in a quick squeeze.

Her joy was sweeter than the maple and the cinnamon together. It filled me, fed and watered me, and for the moment, I had everything I needed in the world.

EPILOGUE

I leaned my elbows on the railing of the wooden deck and took a deep breath of evening air. Across the valley, the bay lay half-obscured by fog, bridge lights twinkling across the water in graceful curves. If I leaned far out, I could just glimpse the city glittering beyond it, a bright mirage on the horizon. It looked different from up here on this ridge north of the Golden Gate. It felt different, too, seeing it from a house of my own, the home I shared with the people I loved.

The door behind me slid open, and soft steps across the redwood planks brought Sebastian's aura with them, a still, deep well that shone with pride and contentment. He slipped an arm around me and brushed his lips up the side of my neck, the sensation of his touch and energy drawing a pleasant shiver from me as I leaned back against him.

"Our guests will be here soon," he murmured and pressed a cold glass half-full of amber liquid into my hand.

"What is this?" I turned the drink in the twilight, held it to my nose. Garnished with thin, curled shavings that looked almost black in the half-light, its scent offered a complicated, potent sweetness with a hint of something fragrant and dark. "Is that chocolate?"

"It's a chocolate old fashioned. I made it just for you."

I sipped it, eyes locked with his, watching him watching me, thrilling at the stir of desire beneath his calm surface. "It tastes like you." I'd confided my synesthetic impression of his energy to him recently, hesitantly, unsure it would make sense when put to words. Apparently, he'd taken it as inspiration.

"That's the idea." He laughed softly, leaned on the railing beside me. "Enjoying the view?"

"I can't get enough." Moving out of the city and the delicate negotiations of blending my life with those of three other people, on top of helping Eve navigate her GED exams, had taken all my attention in the last weeks. "I should probably come in and help you in the kitchen instead of dreaming out here."

"No need. Danny and I have it handled. Eve is an excellent sous chef."

"I see how it is. You just don't want me messing anything up."

"We all have our talents," he said, judiciously diplomatic. "You can do the washing up, how's that?"

"Deal." I took another meditative sip of my cocktail, savoring it. "You two make a good team. I'm glad."

"With you as our fulcrum," he said, "it's only natural. We have a fair bit in common, it turns out."

I wouldn't have thought about it that way, but it made sense. In their own ways, Danny and Sebastian each anchored me, kept me—not grounded, because Sebastian had insisted on a house in a high place from which I could easily take flight, but balanced, guided, as a bird navigates in the dark by the pull of two magnetic poles.

The door slid open again, and we both turned. "Hey," Danny said. "If you're done canoodling out here—"

"We're not canoodling," I said. "We're talking."

"About you," Sebastian added.

"Maybe canoodling a little," I amended in the interests of honesty and went forward to steal a quick kiss from her.

"Uh huh, knew it," she said but she twined an arm around me and kissed me back. "Thought you might want to know that your dad's here, Lily. He brought us some stunningly expensive champagne. And he brought a date."

"What?" A tiny sliver of trepidation chilled the warmth that their combined presence and affection sparked in me. "Who is it?"

Danny shrugged expressively. A chime sounded from the front of the house. "I'll get it," she said and left the sliding door pointedly ajar.

I followed Sebastian inside. Voices from the entrance heralded the arrival of Rae and someone else whose tones I didn't recognize at first, until a child's sweet, high laughter pealed out. Naia and Keira had made it after all. I hadn't felt sure they would come, or even that they received my invitation, since the US Post Office didn't deliver to undersea addresses. But Rae, as always, had her connections.

We found Samael examining the baby grand piano in the living room, running one thumb over the chipped key in the high registers with a thoughtful expression, and no date in evidence. My father had disappeared for weeks after his injury and fall during his fight with Ariel, but had reappeared recently, apparently none the worse for wear. He and Sebastian shook hands as I hung back a bit, still unsure how to address him. *Father* had sounded right when I thought one of us might die before I had another chance to say it. With plenty of chances now, I didn't know what to think, except that *Dad* didn't sound right at all.

"This is a lovely instrument," Samael was saying to Sebastian. "You are a musician?"

"Trying to be." Sebastian laughed, flushing, his tone far too modest. He had started doing some recording work in the little studio under the garage, and sometimes I would sneak down and listen after I got back from a day's work of lawyering in the city. Whatever happened with this project of his, it filled my heart to know he had a dream to follow, rather than faithfully walking in his father's footsteps as he had before.

Samael sought my eyes, looking like he was about to say something else, but before he could the others came around the corner from the hall. Eve, in the lead, was luminous in her "graduation" dress, its material a softly iridescent gold with a hem that swirled around her knees. She and her friend Cormac, one of Rae's followers, had their arms slung around each other's shoulders like old friends. The two of them had gotten closer recently, and I thanked my lucky stars I didn't have to worry about a succubus teen getting pregnant. I did worry about

Cormac being a devotee of a rage goddess I had recently released, but he seemed equally devoted to and respectful of Eve. Plus, no one had heard anything more from the goddess.

"Grandfather! You're here!" Eve greeted Samael with none of my own hesitation, throwing her arms around him. As far as we knew, they weren't related beyond the kinship that bound all demons. That didn't bother Eve, though. She didn't call me mother—it made both of us uncomfortable—but the title drew Samael's rare smile when she first dared to try it on him, and it had therefore stuck.

Naia came to me and gave me a quick, shy hug as Keira looked around wide-eyed at the house and the people now filling it, hiding behind Naia's legs. "Thank you for having me," the selkie woman said softly. "It's a nice way to come back from the sea."

"You look good. Happy." I met her ocean-deep gaze, the salt tang of her aura sparkling in the back of my mind. "Thank you for coming."

"I wasn't sure I could, but Rae offered to drive me and Keira."

"It wasn't any trouble," Rae put in. "Plus, we talked on the way up, and Naia has some good ideas for Safe Haven. Ways to widen our outreach to help more people like her."

People like her? Were there other selkies in situations like the one I had helped Naia escape? Rae's aura had a sheen of creative inspiration and a spark of her advocate's fire in it. Her energy had changed since the goddess left her. No longer eclipsed and bloody, it still held a tinge of darkness, the scars of the pain that had brought her to the goddess in the first place. But she had a green bloom to her that had been missing before, like the first mist of regrowth over earth blackened by a wildfire.

"We think you can help, Lily," Naia said eagerly. "The laws are so unclear on our rights. We need someone who understands that our people are people first of all."

She wasn't the first to say so. Since Rae's trial, I had received an influx of calls from potential clients who had, or who believed they had, some connection with the supernatural. Most of the questions involved family rights and criminal defense, and they all made my heart ache.

"I'll help however I can," I promised Naia, and her eyes lit up.

The chime of a struck glass interrupted us, and I turned to find Samael raising a champagne flute as Eve fluttered around dispensing glasses. I waved mine away, gesturing to the cocktail Sebastian had made for me.

"A toast," Samael said in his deep resonant voice. "To family found and family made, new homes and new hearts. And to Eve, whose hard work has earned her high exam scores and the dreams to match. Congratulations, Granddaughter."

Eve beamed. We all raised our glasses.

"Lily?" A quiet voice behind me froze me with my drink at my lips. I knew that voice, but I hadn't heard it in a long, long time.

She stood in the hall, between the front door and the bathroom, as if she'd ducked in there when she came in, a slight, dark-haired woman with a lined face and faded eyes, in a wine-colored dress a few decades out of style.

"Mom." The word escaped my lips like a sob or a curse, and her smile pleaded with me. I couldn't answer it. I spun to glare at Samael. "*She's* your date? What the hell is this?"

"I thought you would be pleased," he said.

Tears rose in my throat, a tide, a storm, and I gulped the rest of my drink to wash them back down. The chocolate flavor hung bitter on my tongue. "You *thought*. You could have asked me."

"I can go," my mother whispered. She glanced between me and Samael, her aura fragmented and nervous, full of heartbreak and guilt.

"I—no," I said. "I just—I need a moment." Turning, I stalked away out onto the empty deck, taking the steps two at a time down to the lower level, into the darkness of the street. Up here on the ridge, there weren't too many streetlights, and the trees arched their branches thick over the winding, narrow road. I liked it that way and even more right now.

My steps took me out of the yard and a few yards down the hill before my mind registered the figure I'd passed, his face nearly hidden in the shadows of the leaves.

"Ira?" I focused my night vision, found him gazing after me with a curious frown.

He strode forward to meet me, hands deep in his pockets. "Ghosting your own party, Knight?"

"I don't remember inviting you." A bitter laugh spilled from my lips. "Though it seems that doesn't mean much tonight. What are you doing here?"

"Looking for you, of course."

I sighed, giving up my escape for the moment. If Ira had taken the trouble to come all the way out here to ruin my party, he was a few minutes too late. "Well, you've found me. This better be good."

"I'm not sure good is the word I'd use." Ira drew something from his pocket that I eyed with suspicion, but it turned out to be a pack of cigarettes that he slapped into his other palm with the practice of a deliberate ritual.

"You smoke?"

"I quit." A lighter flared in the darkness, illuminating his face for the space of his inhalation, leaving the glow of the cigarette behind. "It didn't take."

Had I imagined how his hand seemed to tremble, holding that slim cylinder of poison to his lips?

"Something's wrong." A chill crept along my spine. "If this is about North…"

"It isn't. As far as the Bureau's concerned, whatever happened to their agent in that tower, it left them one less mess to clean up. No one wants to own how badly Meghan botched that demon soldier project of hers. But what got released, now that's another matter."

"Rae's goddess, you mean. It wasn't her fault, Ira."

"I'm not here to arrest her," he said. "I would like to know what she knows, though. She's part of this, and so are you, Lily."

"Don't speak in riddles, Ira. Part of what?"

"Something coming," he said. "Something changing. Something ending, perhaps."

More riddles, and with every word I liked them less. "What ending?"

"Could be the world." Smoke puffed out with every word. "Could just be life as we know it."

I turned back toward the house, eyes seeking the warm golden light of the main room on the house's second story, the silhouettes gathered there. A liquid stream of notes from the piano flowed suddenly down from above, Sebastian taking a cue like a pro and distracting them all from the little drama I'd just played out for them. No one had followed me, for once, and I blessed them for it.

Strange as it was, as fraught and broken as some of that little gathering might be, I knew in that moment I would do anything to protect them and hold them safe. I wouldn't let whatever was coming take this peace of mine from me, not when it had been so hard won.

I wouldn't run away. Not this time. I set my jaw and faced Ira, meeting his patient gaze. He already knew, didn't he? He knew before he came, what I would say.

"Tell me what I need to do," I said.

FIN

Acknowledgements

To my editor, Heather McCorkle – thank you for your patience and support in this process. This was my first book conceived, drafted, and revised on a timeline that affected others besides me. It ended up needing far more time than I thought at every stage. I truly appreciate your flexibility and kindness, especially when my day job responsibilities ate into my writing time.

Sending so much gratitude and love to the Discordant Nest. I'm incredibly lucky to have found a group of indie authors who support each other through all the ups and downs of this creative life. I don't think I would have made it this far without you. You are some of the most talented, generous, determined, and hilarious writers I know. You all deserve the freedom and license to pursue your creative dreams.

I'm forever indebted to the Chaos Bakers, Emericans, Cool Kids, G-squad, and every creative community that nurtured me over the years. Online connections may shift and change shape, life's swirling currents may pull us in different directions, but these found families will always have a special place in my heart. It fills me with joy and pride to see so many of you spread your wings and take flight to find the success you've earned, as I whisper (or scream), *that's my friend!*

And of course, it all comes back to you, Jake, Best Bear, my home and my heart. I couldn't write a love story sweeter than our friends to lovers' journey, never dreamed of a partnership that would empower me like you have, and it keeps on getting better every day. Thank you for letting me take these chances and standing by me no matter how the dice may roll.

Erin Fulmer is a legal aid attorney by day, author of urban fantasy and science fiction by night. She lives in California's Central Valley with her husband and two spoiled cats named after famous dragons. When she's not writing or working, she enjoys soaking in nature, taking pictures of the sky, playing nerdy games, and napping like it's an Olympic sport.

Read more from Erin at her website where she occasionally blogs about writing, publishing, and mental health. She can also be found on Instagram, Threads, Tumblr, Facebook, or TikTok.